Sword o

Steven A. McKay was born in Scotland in 1977. He is the author of two previous series of historical fiction, following Robin Hood and the warrior-druid Bellicus in post-Roman Britain. He plays the guitar, is the co-host of historical adventure podcast *Rock, Paper, Swords!* along with author Matthew Harffy, and lives just outside Glasgow with his wife and children.

Also by Steven A. McKay

Alfred the Great

The Heathen Horde
Sword of the Saxons

STEVEN A. McKAY

SWORD OF THE SAXONS

CANELO

First published in the United Kingdom in 2024 by

Canelo
Unit 9, 5th Floor
Cargo Works, 1–2 Hatfields
London SE1 9PG
United Kingdom

Copyright © Steven A. McKay 2024

The moral right of Steven A. McKay to be identified as the creator of this work has been asserted in accordance with the Copyright, Designs and Patents Act, 1988.

All rights reserved. No part of this publication may be reproduced or transmitted in any form or by any means, electronic or mechanical, including photocopy, recording, or any information storage and retrieval system, without permission in writing from the publisher.

A CIP catalogue record for this book is available from the British Library.

Print ISBN 978 1 80436 612 7
Ebook ISBN 978 1 80436 618 9

This book is a work of fiction. Names, characters, businesses, organizations, places and events are either the product of the author's imagination or are used fictitiously. Any resemblance to actual persons, living or dead, events or locales is entirely coincidental.

Cover design by Jet Purdie

Look for more great books at www.canelo.co

Printed and bound in Great Britain by Clays Ltd, Elcograf S.p.A.

To Matthew Harffy

for being a good friend and colleague,

but mostly because

he dedicated one to me.

PART ONE

CHAPTER ONE

AD 878, Wessex

February

Alfred stood with his back pressed against the trunk of an ash tree, which remained bereft of foliage after what had been a hard winter. A winter that was not yet over, for it had snowed lightly that very morning. Around the young king were more leafless trees of ash and elm, and twenty or so *hearthweru* – his loyal hearth-warriors – all standing grim and silent in the gloom. It was only midday, but heavy grey clouds obscured both warmth and light from the sun, making the atmosphere heavy and oppressive. Or perhaps that was just how Alfred felt, knowing what was about to happen.

His shoulder length brown hair was tied back beneath his helmet, and his spear was gripped in his right hand, shield in his left. The linden boards were painted a deep red, with the golden dragon of Wessex emblazoned around the iron boss in the centre. Alfred's life had been saved a number of times by this shield, but he kept it hidden for now, knowing its colourful imagery would stand out starkly against the browns and greys all around them. He peered along the trail which weaved through the trees, seeing nothing, not even his captain, Ealdorman Wulfric.

Alfred knew Wulfric was concealed within the bushes about fifty yards distant, along with another twenty warriors, yet he could barely make out any of them.

To his right there came a splattering sound and he turned, seeing one of his men emptying his bladder, the steaming liquid landing on the sodden, brown leaves that carpeted the entire area. For a moment Alfred thought about upbraiding the soldier but he held his tongue. These men had remained loyal to him despite the fact the enemy king, Guthrum, had effectively seized control of Wessex and driven Alfred and his family into hiding here in the marshes and woods around Athelney.

A hearth-warrior taking a piss was nothing to get angry about in the grand scheme of things.

Someone grunted a wordless warning, and Alfred's eyes snapped back to the trail. Striding along, chattering noisily as if they hadn't a care in the world, came a party of Danes. Alfred's people called all the raiders 'Danes', 'Northmen', or even 'sea-wolves' as simple catch-all terms – but many of them were Swedish, or Norse like Guthrum himself, and some hailed from even more eastern lands such as Estonia or Finland.

Although Alfred's West Saxons shared some similarities with the invaders – in language, dress, and their love for drunken nights spent in the mead hall, for example – there were many clear differences that separated them from one another. The king looked at the men hiding with him, eyes travelling across each of them, making sure they were ready for the work to come. They were all Christian, while their enemies worshipped heathen gods such as Þórr and Óðinn. The struggle between the two peoples was a Holy War as much as a clash between rival kingdoms – a battle for spiritual supremacy as much as a battle for land, wealth, and glory.

The Danes came closer. The one at the front seemed to be the loudest, the brashest, and Alfred guessed he was a hersir – a minor nobleman who commanded small warbands like this one. Most of the others listened to the loud banter, laughing dutifully when required, while the ones on the periphery of the party were quieter and more alert to their surroundings.

Even so, none of them noticed the warriors of Wessex hidden within the woods flanking the trail ahead.

Alfred knew what these men were doing: they were a scouting party, sent out by Guthrum to find Alfred's hiding place, and to forage for food and supplies. While 'forage' usually meant searching for berries or hunting for game, to the Danes it also meant stealing from the West Saxon settlements they passed. If the locals tried to stand up to them, the raiders would kill, rape, or enslave them. Alfred wondered just how much the population of the Northmen's homelands had swelled during the past dozen or so years with people carted off in longships to exist as mere thralls.

He gritted his teeth, enraged by his thoughts and by the arrogant manner of the men striding towards him. These were Alfred's lands by birthright, yet Guthrum had managed to take control of them, almost killing Alfred and his family during a raid on his estate in Cippanhamme. That had been in January and, ever since, the West Saxon king had been forced to hide away like a fieldmouse moving through rushes, hoping the sparrowhawk that hovered overhead would not strike.

Today, Alfred would no longer play the part of the mouse.

As he watched, Ealdorman Wulfric suddenly appeared, stepping out from behind a tree on the trail behind the enemy foraging party. At well over six feet tall, Alfred's captain was an imposing, impressive figure. A born warrior, with a lean build and a scar on his face, Wulfric held a throwing spear in his right hand, and he drew it back with a snarl before sending it arcing through the air with terrific power.

There was a thump and a cry of pain as the spear hammered into the back of a Dane and then the woods exploded in shouts of alarm and the commands of the enemy hersir to form up in a line, shields raised. His orders did not come quickly enough though, as the other Saxon spearmen arrayed alongside Wulfric released their missiles too, and more Danes died before they knew what was happening.

'Charge!' the hersir screamed, but Alfred repeated the same command and now he burst from his hiding place, hearth-warriors close behind, sprinting towards the enemy.

Caught between two lines of West Saxons, the raiders lost any semblance of discipline. Rather than following their hersir's panicked commands to form up into a line of their own, his men acted upon their own impulses. Some continued running forward, to engage Wulfric's group, while others turned and came back the way to face Alfred, while the rest simply ran off into the trees in hopes of saving their own skin.

One of the braver raiders, a big man clad in a heavy wolf pelt and wielding an axe, strode directly towards Alfred. He had no shield, for his axe required two hands to wield it, but he did let go of the weapon for just a moment with one hand, to lift the hammer amulet he wore on a thong around his neck and kiss it. Then he broke into a run and swung his mighty axe at the king of Wessex.

Alfred stopped running and dodged desperately, narrowly avoiding the iron axe-head as it whispered through the air a hair's breadth from his ribs. Snarling, he lunged, hoping to thrust the point of his spear through his opponent's unprotected neck. The momentum from the Dane's swing carried him out of reach of the spear, however, and he raised his axe before chopping it down, screaming the name of Þórr. The iron blade smashed into Alfred's shield, the tremendous blow sending splinters flying, and almost breaking the young king's left arm. When the axeman tried to draw back his weapon for another blow he realised it was embedded in the shield but, before he could let it go and draw out the seax sheathed at his waist, Alfred threw down the shield and plunged his spear into the Dane's chest, the leaf-shaped tip tearing through the wolf pelt, on through the mail brynja beneath, and finally into flesh and bone.

Abandoning the spear in the dying Dane's body, Alfred drew his sword and hacked down into the arm of another enemy, practically severing the limb at the elbow. Warm blood sprayed across Alfred's chest and face.

Screaming, 'Godemite! For God Almighty!' the king moved on, parrying the sword thrust of a young Dane who was sobbing in terror even as he attacked. At that moment Alfred had no mercy within him, and he kicked the lad in the knee, knocking him off balance, and then brought the edge of his blade down as hard as he could on his enemy's head. Even if the crying youth had been wearing an iron helmet rather than a cloth cap, it wouldn't have saved him. He fell silent as his skull shattered beneath Alfred's vengeful sword.

Breathing heavily, the king looked around, eyes blazing, searching for another Dane to slaughter. It took him a moment to realise the fight was over already.

'Are you injured, my lord?' Wulfric was striding towards him, barely out of breath at all, yet spattered with enemy blood and gore.

'No,' Alfred gasped, trying to collect his thoughts as the battle-lust started to fade. 'I don't think so. Some of the bastards ran off, though. Have our men hunt them down.'

Wulfric did not need to repeat the order for there were warriors just waiting for this command, and they eagerly sprinted into the trees to track the fleeing enemies.

Alfred removed his helmet, shaking out his hair which was slick with sweat despite the cold that made his breath steam as he sucked in deep, calming breaths. He was not frightened now that the battle was over, but, as always when his anger and need to kill wore off, he was left feeling drained and shaky. He looked down at the young Dane he'd just killed and stared dully at the lifeless body. 'Such a waste,' he murmured sadly. 'May his gods grant him peace in their afterlife.'

'He can burn in hell,' Wulfric growled, lip curling. 'All these thieving sea-wolves can.'

Some of their men voiced agreement, but Alfred felt only sorrow at that moment. It was his duty to defeat the raiders, and take back his kingdom from Guthrum, and he would do it no matter how many of the enemy he had to slaughter. He did not think it glorious, though, to dispatch a sobbing, beardless lad who probably wished he'd never sailed here in hopes of winning wealth and renown beside his pagan kinsmen.

Already his hearth-warriors were stripping the dead of their valuables – gold and silver arm rings and other jewellery, mail vests, swords and seaxes, purses filled with silver coins bearing Alfred's own image, and whatever else could be carried off.

'What will we do with the bodies, my lord?'

Alfred looked at Wulfric, then he shrugged. 'I've no desire to waste time burying them or building a pyre for them. Let them rot where they are. The animals and birds will be glad of the food. We'll carry our own to the camp and Oswald can give them the proper burial rites.'

'Are you sure you're not injured, lord?' Wulfric asked quietly, gazing at him with a worried expression.

'No, I'm not,' Alfred replied, shaking his head. The war-sweat was drying now, making him feel even colder than before the battle. 'I'm just exhausted. Exhausted by everything that's happened over the past few weeks, my friend, and tired of hiding in a damn marsh from these raiders.' He grinned then, and clapped Wulfric on the arm. 'Come on, let's head back to the camp and get a drink. I think we've earned it!'

CHAPTER TWO

Alfred had been crowned King of Wessex seven years before, when his older brother Aethelred died from a wound taken during a battle with the Danes. The crown had passed down to Alfred immediately, with little ceremony or fanfare for the invaders continued to ravage the settlements of the West Saxons. At last, after many battles, the raiders were defeated when their king, Guthrum, led an enormous invasion of the southern coast of Wessex. One hundred and twenty enemy ships, on their way to join Guthrum's siege of Exanceaster, had been caught in a titanic storm with the loss of thousands of warriors. As a Christian, Alfred could only view that astonishing event as a miracle. So many heathen raiders would have easily overcome his smaller army had they survived, so how else could the West Saxon king interpret the storm which had proved to be his saviour?

There had been peace, then, and Alfred travelled between his various estates in Wessex with his growing family – residing in great halls built from sturdy timber, with blazing firepits, plentiful meat and ale, and enjoying the finest of all things, including a library of rare and valuable books. These, he treasured above almost anything else, despite needing his priest, Oswald, to read to him the ones written in Latin.

And then Guthrum had struck again. Riding unimpeded through lands belonging to Alfred's own supposedly loyal ealdormen, the Danes had attacked Cippanhamme just after Christmas, as the West Saxon king celebrated Twelfth Night. The town was not prepared for such an assault and Alfred only just managed to escape with his family, his children's nursemaids, and a few loyal hearth-warriors, including Wulfric.

Now, mere weeks after that terrifying night, Alfred no longer sheltered from the sleet and snow within the walls of a great hall while supping fine ale and eating delicious roast meats. Instead, the king and his retinue lived within drably coloured tents, eating and drinking whatever they could forage or scrounge in the settlements nearest to their camp in Athelney. Alfred sat in his tent now, downing stale ale, and feeling like he'd failed not only the people of Wessex, but his family too. It tore at his heart to see his beloved wife, Ealhswith, huddled in an old blanket, trying to keep warm by the light of candles made from pungent-smelling pig fat. Their four children, Aethelflaed, Edward, Aethelgifu, and baby Aelfthryth seemed to view the flight from Cippanhamme and subsequent hiding out in the marshes as something of an adventure at first, but they, like Alfred, had grown quickly tired of it. Aethelflaed, the oldest at seven summers, was a precocious little girl who liked to run and climb and play-fight with anyone who would take her on. Recently she'd asked her father to show her how to properly wield a sword and even begged to go with the warband when they'd marched out that morning to ambush the Danes.

Life as a fugitive was not only hard, but also boring. Oh, there was always something to do, for they all had to pitch in, but washing or mending clothes, preparing and cooking meals, maintaining weapons, and foraging for food, had quickly lost their appeal. Especially when the only thing separating them from the wind and snow and pounding rain were the thin layers of canvas that formed the walls and roofs of their tents.

Alfred took another swallow of ale. At least they had that and the warmth it imparted, even if it was an illusory, passing warmth.

'You look sad,' Ealhswith said to him softly. The children were asleep beside them, and she'd been reading a book of prayers – or trying to – by the meagre candlelight, but now she set it down and took her husband's hand in hers.

Alfred turned to her, seeing new lines around her eyes. She was still as pretty as ever to him, but, although they were both just approaching thirty summers, the king felt at least ten years older than he was after everything that had happened since they'd wed in Mercia a decade before. He forced a smile. 'I do sometimes feel sadness,' he admitted. 'But it would be much worse if you and the children weren't with me. I give thanks to God every day that He's allowed us all to remain together, even if we are forced to live in squalor.'

Ealhswith chuckled and brushed a lock of brown hair away from her face. 'It's not quite squalor, my love,' she said. 'We might not have the comforts we enjoyed in Ceodre, or Wichamtun, but what use would golden trinkets be to us out here in the wilderness? Besides, there are many poor people in Wessex who'd love to have a cosy tent like ours, and the food and drink, simple as it is.'

Alfred sighed, feeling the dark clouds of depression closing around him once more. He did not need to be reminded about the plight of his subjects. The West Saxons had looked to him to deliver them from the brutality of the Danes, and he had failed.

'Cheer up,' Ealhswith said, pressing her head against his and squeezing his hand. 'Have faith in God. He'll see us safely out of this but, in the meantime, we have heat, and light, and sustenance, and each other.' She grinned. 'Not to mention Oswald to read to us, and Wulfric and his guards to protect us. Think of St Cuthbert, who lived as a hermit in Northumbria, going out at night to stand in the sea up to his neck and pray. Now *that* is a hard life, even if otters did come to dry him with their fur and warm him with their breath!'

As always, his wife's bright smile and optimism raised Alfred's spirits, and he leaned across to kiss her. 'I may not have tame otters to call upon, but I *am* blessed,' he declared. 'To have you and Oswald and Wulfric by my side. I don't know what I'd do without you all.'

'You also still have the loyalty of many of your nobles,' Ealhswith noted. 'Like Ealdorman Aethelnoth. He's been good to us since we've been forced to hide out here in his lands.'

Alfred had to agree with her. Aethelnoth, Ealdorman of Sumorsaete, had made sure supplies were sent to the fugitives and even offered to take them in. Alfred had refused though, knowing Guthrum would come for them, throwing everything he had into their destruction. They would hide for now, until the time was right to come out into the open once more.

They remained leaning against one another for a time, the crackling of the few small campfires that Wulfric allowed the men to keep burning through the night and, once, the eldritch screech of a barn owl the only things to disturb the silence. At last, the king turned, pressed his face into Ealhswith's hair, and kissed her again before standing.

'Is it your turn?' she asked.

'Aye, it must be by now,' he said. Even a king had to stand watch when there were enemies all around, and no walls to keep them at bay. 'Read for a little longer, but get some sleep, all right?'

She nodded and took up her book again, waving as Alfred put on his sword belt, threw on his thick cloak and went out into the night.

He put his fur-lined hood up, surprised by how cold it was outside. The tents were warmed by boulders which were heated in the campfires, then carried inside wrapped in blankets. The heat they emitted was not much but, within the confines of a tent crowded with four of five other people, it was enough to keep the worst of the chill at bay.

'My lord.' Wulfric was sitting beside one of the fires enjoying the heat, although he had his back to it, so the light would not spoil his night vision more than was necessary. If some Danish would-be murderer sneaked into the camp, Wulfric would be ready for them.

'All quiet?' Alfred asked his captain who stood up respectfully as the king approached.

'Aye, lord. The men guarding the perimeter have just changed. Nothing to report other than that bloody owl, shrieking like a witch.'

Alfred shivered and reached up to touch the cross he wore around his neck, feeling its reassuring bulk beneath his clothes. 'Don't mention such things,' he said. 'It's bad enough fearing the sea-wolves, without worrying about witches and ghouls as well.'

'With all the praying you do, my lord,' Wulfric replied sardonically, 'I don't think we need worry about any evil spirits coming into the camp.'

Alfred gave him a withering look. Wulfric was a Christian, like all the West Saxons, but he was not as devout as the king. 'Perhaps if you prayed more often, my friend, we might not be in this predicament.'

Wulfric did not reply to that, but he smiled, eyes sparkling in the reflected light from another nearby campfire.

'It was a good victory today,' Alfred said, holding his hands out to the flickering flames, enjoying the dry heat for his fingers had already started to become numb as frost settled across the camp.

'The men needed it,' Wulfric agreed. 'We've been running for too long. It was good to finally stand and fight, even if there were only a few Danes to kill.'

'Only a few for now,' Alfred said, turning away from the fire and gazing out pensively into the darkness. 'But that was just the beginning. Now that we're comfortable hiding out here in the marshes, and know our way about, we can really start to strike back at Guthrum's forces. Draw loyal men to us, and, eventually, retake Wessex.'

Such an outcome seemed ridiculous at that moment, for they were few and the Danes were many. But Alfred, no matter how depressed he became, always had faith that God was on his side. That kind of faith was inspiring, and infectious, even to someone who did not believe quite as strongly in divine assistance, like Wulfric.

'If you say so,' the captain replied lightly.

'I do say so!' Alfred replied, his voice ringing out in the night as he glanced apologetically at the tent housing his family. 'Come,' he said. 'Let's walk the perimeter.'

They went out, between the tents, nodding to the few warriors who were tending to the fires and keeping watch over their comrades catching some sleep within the canvas dwellings. There was no moon that night but there was enough light to see where they were going. The camp was positioned low down, to hide the light from their fires, but there was a small hillock on the northern side, and it was up this that the pair walked.

'You know, when we were betrayed by our own noblemen, I feared Wessex was lost forever.' Alfred stared up the slope, glad to see one of their sentries silhouetted against the stars, watching them alertly. 'I genuinely thought I should find a ship and take my family away to Francia, or Rome. To live a life of peace, safely away from Guthrum and his damned Northmen.'

'We could still do that,' Wulfric said, but it was a half-hearted suggestion. His ultimate goal was to keep the king alive, but running from the Danes was not in his nature.

Nor was it in Alfred's. 'Since we've been here in Athelney it's become clear that many people in Wessex still support me,' he said as they reached the crest of the hill and murmured a greeting to the pair of sentries there. They looked out on the lands shrouded in darkness, and Alfred nodded to himself. 'The likes of Ealdormen Wulfhere, and my so-called friend, Diuma, might have forsaken me, and thrown their lot in with Guthrum's raiders, but I believe the majority of the people remain loyal to me.'

The sentries nodded enthusiastically. 'It's true, lord,' one of them said. 'I've been in the towns nearby to get supplies and I've heard the talk there. The folk still believe in you, as does Ealdorman Aethelnoth.'

Alfred grinned at Wulfric. 'You see? We might be stuck here in the marshes for now, with no way to muster the fyrd, but we'll bide our time and soon enough there will be a chance.'

'What'll we do until then, lord?' the second sentry asked.

'The same as we did today, Aedan,' Alfred replied, recognising the man as one of his best hearth-warriors, a man of Irish descent with a red beard and hair that was shaved in close at the sides. 'We remain hidden, spreading the word around Wessex that I'm alive and waiting to retake my throne. And, while we wait, we strike at any Danish warbands foolish enough to come to Athelney.'

'We don't have the numbers to attack some of those larger groups,' Wulfric cautioned, but that merely made Alfred's grin even wider.

'Maybe not,' the king replied slyly. 'But that doesn't mean we can't cause some mischief, right, lads?'

The two sentries laughed, nodding. They vowed to do as much damage to Guthrum's raiders as God would allow.

'Stay alert then, men,' Alfred said, patting the sentries on their arms and leading Wulfric back down the slope towards their tents and the welcoming orange glow of the little campfires.

'This is all very well,' Wulfric said when they were out of the sentries' earshot. 'But there's still some of the nobles who do *not* support you, as you said yourself, like Bishop Deorlaf, and Diuma, and his father Ealdorman Wealdmar of Brycgstow. Not only do we have Guthrum's sea-wolves to deal with, but we also have to contend with our own mutinous folk. What are we going to do about the likes of them?'

Alfred turned to his captain in surprise. 'What are we going to do?' he demanded. 'What do you think we'll do? What would *you* do about Diuma and the rest of those traitorous bastards?'

Wulfric shrugged. 'Kill them.'

'Exactly,' Alfred growled, and his earlier good humour evaporated in that moment, replaced by a fierce determination. 'Those men pledged loyalty to me, and then renounced their oaths when Guthrum offered them a few pounds of silver. I believed Diuma was my friend, but he proved himself the worst of enemies and, for that, he'll pay. Christ taught us to forgive those who do us harm, Wulfric, but even I can't follow that teaching in this instance. Once I'm in control of Wessex again, all who betrayed me will get what they deserve. By God's Holy Blood, I swear it!'

CHAPTER THREE

Guthrum gazed out at the green fields surrounding Cippanhamme and breathed in the clean, fresh air with a deep feeling of satisfaction. Overhead, a red kite hovered, its wings carrying it gracefully, almost languidly around the sky as a pair of angry carrion crows tried to attack it without success. Guthrum felt like the red kite, powerful and deadly, while the exiled Alfred was a crow desperately trying to strike at him with little success.

True, word had come in that morning of a foraging party being wiped out by Alfred's men but that was nothing to worry about. Losing a handful of men was a drop in the whale road considering the numbers and, more importantly, Guthrum had a tactical advantage thanks to the lands he'd seized in Wessex, and the alliances he'd made with certain Saxon noblemen.

He waved to a group of Danes who were fishing in the River Avon, and they responded cheerily, suggesting they'd had some success at their task. Of course, it mattered little if they caught much for Cippanhamme had been well stocked with food when Guthrum's raiders took control and, since they'd slaughtered many of the inhabitants during the fighting, there were less mouths to feed. It had been a comfortable winter for the Northmen as a result. Still, no fisherman liked to spend his time without catching something he could boast about once he returned to the mead hall later that day and, as Guthrum watched, one of the group shouted, his line tugging. After a mighty struggle, the fisherman pulled a huge, wriggling carp from the water. He cheered in triumph as the thing flailed desperately. And then, as it flopped on the grass, the fisherman took a short wooden club and ended its suffering.

Guthrum looked up, seeing that the red kite had moved much higher in the sky, hovering on the wind currents. The carrion crows had given up trying to catch it and flew off to the south, screeching irritably.

'What are you smiling about?'

Guthrum turned in his saddle and looked at the jarl riding by his side. 'I'm happy, Ubba,' he replied. 'The gods have been good to us. To me! I have fifty mighty warriors to ride with me this day, and just look! Look at these green lands, bursting with life and wealth of all kinds, which is now ours. Óðinn be praised, Alfred gave us a good fight, but we defeated him, and his Christ, in the end.'

Ubba looked sourly around him, lip curling at the excited fisherman and his companions who were crowded around his catch, measuring it and chattering gleefully. 'Fish?' he muttered. 'Birds?'

Guthrum laughed. 'Come now, my friend. Is your hangover paining you? Go and find some mead, then, and come back to me when you're in a better mood. If a man can't find joy on a wonderful day like this, he needs to fill his belly with mead, or some willing lass with his seed!'

Ubba stared at him. 'Is that from the *Havamal*?' he asked, referencing the old collection of sayings the Northmen often looked to for wisdom. Ubba's dead brother, Halfdan, had been a great lover of the *Havamal*'s teachings, often reciting them in conversation. Guthrum had adopted the idea on occasion, thinking it made him seem more intelligent.

'No,' the king grinned. 'Not from the *Havamal*. From in here.' He tapped his temple. 'My own store of knowledge. Advice to live by, don't you think?'

Shrugging, Ubba murmured agreement. 'Drinking and fucking,' he said. 'Two of life's greatest pleasures.'

'Then go and do one or the other,' Guthrum said to him, waving back towards Cippanhamme. 'Do both! But, for the love of Óðinn, cheer up!'

Ubba turned his horse and rode away, heading for the town, his hersirs – six of them – following at a canter.

'He's a dour-faced pain in the arse,' one of Guthrum's companions, a stout hersir called Floki, said. 'He always was, but he's been even worse since we heard of Halfdan's slaying.'

Guthrum heaved a long sigh. 'Halfdan used to tell him off for drinking too much, or not combing his beard. Without his brother to keep him in check he's become... wild.'

'More like feral,' said Floki, whose own brown hair and beard were always immaculately combed. 'You should find something for him to do, other than humping slaves and downing mead until he wants to fight with everyone around him.'

The king nodded, thinking it would indeed be a good idea for Ubba to leave the main army for a time. He was decent enough company, and Guthrum had a lot of respect for his family since Ubba was one of the famous Ragnar Lodbrok's sons. The only surviving son actually, now that Halfdan and Ivar the Detestable had both been killed in separate fights in Ireland.

'Perhaps you're right, Floki,' said the king. 'Ubba comes from a line of great warriors. Maybe we should let him loose, to cause as much mischief as possible for those who remain loyal to Alfred.'

'If it gets the mouthy bastard away from us,' Floki laughed. 'I'm all for it. With any luck, he won't come back!'

The spirits in the group rose again, just as another of the nearby fishermen pulled a second flopping fish from the Avon and this time Guthrum joined in with the jubilant cheering. 'Come on,' he called to his men who were all mounted on horseback and clad in full war-gear. 'Let's ride. We have settlements to visit, to make sure they do not offer the hiding Saxon king any assistance, and to offer us tribute for very kindly not destroying their homes. Yet!'

Laughing and shouting obscenities about Alfred and his beaten West Saxon people, the Danes thundered westwards, scattering a flock of sheep being driven along by a shepherd boy.

Westwards they would go, until they found themselves at last in the town of Brycgstow. There, Guthrum knew he would find food, and ale, and comfortable beds for the night, for, like some other powerful Saxons, Wealdmar, Ealdorman of Brycgstow, had renounced his oath to King Alfred, and thrown his lot in with the Danish invaders.

—

'I can almost – almost! – understand Ealdorman Wealdmar giving in to the Danes without a fight,' Wulfric said to Alfred as they rode towards the little coastal village of Bryn on the outskirts of the Somerset marshes. 'But his son, Diuma? Refusing to let us into the town when he knew the Danes were hunting us? Gods, I was starting to like the man, and I believed he was a fiercely loyal thane to you, my lord.'

Alfred cleared his throat and spat into the bushes on the side of the road, disgust twisting his features at the memory of the night Wulfric was referring to. 'So did I,' he growled. 'But it seems Diuma was only ever loyal to himself.' He shook his head and made a cutting motion with his hand. 'I might possibly be able to forgive some of the men who've betrayed me, like Ealdorman Wulfhere. Perhaps they felt like they had no other choice. But Diuma? I treated him like a friend. And Brycgstow? That was far enough away from any of Guthrum's forces to be a target for them! No, Diuma has no excuse for what he's done. I hope the sea-wolves bleed him and his father dry, and then, eventually, I'll come face to face with them and hear their excuses before…' He trailed off, jaw clenched, knuckles white as he gripped his horse's reins.

There were only two other men with them that morning, for they were merely riding to collect a few supplies but, more importantly, to make sure the good people of Bryn knew that Alfred was still very much alive and hadn't abandoned his kingdom despite Guthrum's invasion. The king believed it did the people good to see him in person, rather than his hearth-warriors simply carrying word of his survival to the towns and villages located around Athelney's marshes. He was a man, after all, not a myth.

'When are we going to send out word to gather the fyrd, lord?' The question came from one of the other riders who'd accompanied them, a small but sturdily built warrior called Dunstan. He'd been thane of a village in the north of Wessex which had been utterly destroyed six years earlier, by a party of Northmen led by Jarl Ubba. After that, Dunstan pledged himself to Alfred and now served as one of his fiercest hearth-warriors.

The fourth man in the small group was the sentry from the previous night, Aedan, and he too looked with interest at Alfred, wondering what his reply would be to Dunstan's question.

The king shook his head slowly. 'In truth, I don't know,' he admitted. 'I'd like to make sure we have the support of as many people as possible in these nearby settlements. We need to know that we can call upon a decent sized fyrd from the lands around Athelney before we look at enlisting people in towns further away.' He noticed Dunstan and Aedan sharing uncertain glances. 'I know you two are desperate to take the fight to Guthrum, but we can't afford to act rashly. First, we build our foundation here in Sumorsaete, and then we move on from there.'

Even Wulfric appeared displeased by Alfred's answer. But the king ignored the looks of his companions. He was the king, and he would not act rashly. He had too much respect for Guthrum. Perhaps if he'd respected, even feared, the Dane before, none of this would have happened. There had been more than one chance to simply kill Guthrum in the previous year and Alfred, being the merciful Christian, had refused to take them.

They reached Bryn before midday and found it a busy place despite only being inhabited by around a hundred or so people. Alfred's library, of course, contained detailed records on population numbers within the settlements of Wessex, but those had been lost along with the rest of his kingdom.

Bryn was a typical small village, where the cooking fires gave off mouth-watering smells, while dogs, cows, and sheep made their own sounds and smells of welcome or otherwise as Alfred's party passed through the rickety old gates. Their presence was noted immediately, for four well-dressed, armed and armoured noblemen did not often come to Bryn. None recognised them, but Alfred noticed some of the tougher looking villagers – both men and women – had collected weapons, just in case the small group of riders would be followed by yet more warriors. It was not only raiders from across the sea who caused trouble for simple folk at times.

A child dressed in filthy rags ran in front of them, looked at Wulfric, plainly decided the huge ealdorman was not a man to annoy, so instead went to Alfred and, gazing up at him from large, hazel eyes, stuck out a palm. It seemed like the entire village held its breath, expecting the nobleman to kick the boy out of the way and ride on, but instead Alfred smiled sadly.

The child took that as encouragement.

'How old are you?' Alfred asked.

'Seven,' replied the boy.

Alfred felt a pang of guilt for the child was so small, so malnourished, that the king had taken him for no more than four or five. 'Where's your father?' he asked.

'Dead. Went to fight the Danes and never came home.'

'Your mother?'

'At home, working.'

'Where do you live?'

The boy hesitated, then turned to look along a dirt trail that led northwards to half a dozen small houses with thatched roofs. The wattle and daub buildings had all seen better days and almost made Alfred's tent seem like a royal palace.

Just then, a tall, middle-aged man came hurrying towards them from the centre of the village, accompanied by eight men carrying spears and shields. None appeared frightened – if anything they looked up for a fight.

'Beorhtric,' murmured Wulfric, nodding towards the leader. 'He's the reeve.'

'Who are you men?' Beorhtric asked levelly, stopping a few paces in front of them as his men formed a line beside him. They did not level their spears at the riders, but they stared at them unflinchingly.

'I'm going to talk with the reeve,' Alfred said to the boy who was still standing with his hand outstretched. The king smiled, admiring his tenacity and courage, although he did wonder if the boy was merely stupid. 'Come and find me in a little while – and bring your mother with you. All right?'

The child hesitated but when he'd fully digested the words he nodded and ran off, along the trail in the direction of the ramshackle houses.

'My lords?' The reeve called to them again, a little more respectfully now as he took in the quality of the riders' war-gear and bearing. 'Who are you? What brings you to Bryn?'

Alfred dismounted, nodding to his three companions to follow suit.

'Do you not recognise me, reeve?' Alfred asked.

'Or me?' Wulfric demanded, spreading his arms and moving to stand directly in front of the reeve, who, although tall, had to look up to meet Wulfric's eyes. 'Eh, Beorhtric?'

Now realisation dawned on the reeve and a smile lit up his face, quickly followed by him bowing to the ealdorman, and then literally falling to one knee in the road as he finally understood who had come to his village beside the Severn Sea. The spearmen behind him looked confused for a moment, but word of Alfred's presence in Athelney had spread all around the neighbouring settlements and soon enough they too were kneeling, and so were the other villagers looking on.

'Lord King,' Beorhtric said, eyes firmly on the ground. Gulls cried out overhead, as he apologised for not recognising Alfred sooner.

'You may stand,' Alfred said, smiling at the men who got up, and around at the locals who now seemed awestruck. Most of them had never seen a king in their village before, and even those who'd served in the fyrd had not been close to the commanders.

Apart from Beorhtric, who had met Wulfric before. They clasped arms, and Wulfric nodded approvingly at the spearmen who now looked somewhat sheepish at their chilly welcome.

'You men did good,' the big ealdorman reassured them. 'There's Danes abroad, and it's always sensible to meet them with shield and iron. Especially with Bryn being beside the Severn Sea. As it is, you never know when the bastards' longships might appear.'

'It's good to see you, Wulfric,' Beorhtric said. 'And your companions. We've heard about Guthrum's cowardly attack on Cippanhamme at Twelfth Night, and your lucky escape, Lord King. God goes with you it seems. But what brings you here, my lord?'

'I've heard the fishermen of Bryn catch the best fish in Wessex,' Alfred replied. 'So we came to buy some, and find out for ourselves if that reputation is deserved.'

'Oh, it is, lord,' the reeve replied enthusiastically. 'Come to the hall and I'll serve you some myself!'

They spent an hour or so drinking ale and eating fish, which was indeed superb, in the modestly sized but cosy hall in Bryn. Beorhtric was a fine host, and it was a good afternoon. When Alfred stood to make ready for the journey back to his camp the reeve promised him the men of the village would be ready to come when he called them to war.

They went outside, Aedan and Dunstan complaining about having to go so soon for they'd been thoroughly enjoying the food and drink and sitting inside a proper hall rather than a tent for a change, and some of the local ladies had been giving them attention too. Alfred ignored their muttering – he hated staying in one place for too long for there was always a chance some enemy would turn up and attack them.

It was a terrible thing, he thought, not to feel safe within one's own kingdom.

As they came out from the hall, the sea air hit them. Alfred took a long, deep breath, greatly appreciating the smell. It reminded him of the time when he and Wulfric had defeated seven longships full of Northmen on a beach; a truly happy memory for him. He had even walked among the unsuspecting enemy sailors as they drank and played dice on the sand, before his fyrd had struck like—

'My lord?'

The king looked down in surprise. It was the dirty little boy, staring up at him from those wide, transparent eyes.

Beorhtric shooed the child away angrily, but Alfred held the man's arm and assured him it was fine, for he wanted to speak to the boy. 'You may go about your usual business now, reeve,' he said. 'Thank you again for your welcome, and the fish, and your loyalty. It'll not be forgotten when I'm back where I belong.' His words were an obvious dismissal and Beorhtric bowed, gave the child one last angry look, and then went away, leaving Alfred with his three companions.

The boy was not alone now, a woman was coming up behind him. She was cleaner than the child and looked like she'd hastily run a comb through her hair, but there was no fat on her bones. She was as malnourished as the youngster.

'This is your mother?' Alfred asked.

'I am, lord,' the woman replied, and she too was giving the lad an angry look, as if wondering what mischief he'd been up to, and what punishment she was going to receive in return.

'Come into the hall, please,' the king said to her, gesturing for Wulfric and the others to remain outside. 'You can wait here too, lad.'

The boy nodded, still wide-eyed, and gaped up at Wulfric, admiring the ealdorman's seax.

Alfred went into the hall and examined the woman discreetly. She was about twenty-five, gaunt, and visibly exhausted. The world had not been kind to her, judging by her looks.

'What's your name, lady?' he asked kindly.

'Merewyn, my lord,' she replied.

'Your husband went away with the fyrd and never returned?' he asked her.

'Aye, my lord,' she replied. Her tone was not disrespectful, but she sounded like a prisoner taken after being defeated in battle. Like she had nothing left to give and knew her lot in life was to be a bad one.

'How many children do you have?'

'Just the one,' she said. 'Draca. The others died.'

'I know that pain,' Alfred replied sympathetically, then he smiled. '"Draca"? The Dragon. He has a fiery temper?'

Now her dull eyes brightened, and she met Alfred's gaze. 'Oh no, lord, he's a very quiet, clever boy.' The love in her voice was unmistakeable, and the king felt glad that the pair at least had each other.

'How have you supported yourself, Merwyn, since your husband...?' He trailed off, unsure how to finish the sentence.

'I bake.' It was a bald statement, but there was just a hint of pride in it.

Alfred thought about that. He'd seen the houses she came from. They were barely adequate as dwellings, never mind as a bakery. He suspected the villagers paid her more than the going rate for whatever she made, and it was just enough to keep her and the boy alive. Her eyes were on the rushes on the hall floor, and he stared at her. A sudden feeling of guilt came over him as he imagined her with more meat on her bones, her hair thicker, cleaner, and little Draca full of life and fun, instead of being hollow-cheeked and dull.

'I...' He started to speak but had to stop and draw in a breath to steady himself. 'Your husband gave his life to fight for Wessex, and his king. Me. You should not have to suffer so much in his absence.' Awkwardly, he reached into the purse hanging on his belt and took out some silver coins. 'This should make things easier for you,' he told her, taking her hand and pressing the money into it. 'Please take care of Draca. He's a good boy; I knew it from the moment I saw him.'

Confusion warred with hope in Merewyn's eyes as she opened her fist and stared at the coins Alfred had given her. She took a while to count it, for she did so three times, as if unable to believe what was happening. 'This is—'

'Enough to buy you a few good meals,' the king finished for her. 'I'll have a word with the reeve as well, and make sure you're taken care of in the future. It's the least I can do.'

Tears were rolling down the young woman's cheeks, leaving clean marks on the grubby skin, and a sob burst from her mouth as she slumped against the wall, almost collapsing. Alfred grabbed her and she clutched at his arm, squeezing herself against it as she tried to gather herself. After a few moments she moved back, apologising for touching him and thanking him profusely for his kindness. Still, there was a wary look on her face, as if she half expected him to demand something in return for his silver.

'Come,' he said, not wishing to cause her any fear or discomfort. 'It's time I returned to my wife and family. They'll be worried the Danes have found us.'

Merewyn's mouth formed an 'O' but she remained silent as they turned towards the door. As Alfred reached out to lift the latch there was a sudden cry – one of the most feared sounds in any village.

'Fire!'

They rushed out into the dull day and Alfred saw Wulfric gazing towards the north. A plume of grey smoke was rising above a group of houses.

'That's *my* house!' Merewyn cried, pushing past the ealdorman and Dunstan and sprinting along the dirt trail towards the fire. Local men were already running in that direction, some carrying buckets they'd filled in the Severn Sea, and Alfred led his companions after the woman. There was no sign of little Draca.

'This is all she needs,' the king growled as he jogged along, although part of him wondered if those pitiful hovels being destroyed might be a good thing, as long as no one was hurt in the process. He regretted his thoughts though, realising Merewyn's house might not be the grandest, but it contained memories of her husband, and raising little Draca. It was important to her; it was her world as much as Cippanhamme, Ceodre, Wintanceaster, and Wichamtun had been his.

The plume of smoke did not seem to be widening much and, as they reached the house that Merewyn had disappeared inside it was clear the fire had been discovered before it had a chance to spread to the adjacent buildings, or even do much damage from the looks of the walls and the thatch on the roof which remained intact.

'This is your fault.' Draca suddenly burst out of the house as the last of the dark smoke dissipated over the house. The boy was looking at Alfred accusingly, and, naturally, every eye turned to the king, wondering what had happened, and how it might be blamed on him.

Before he could demand an explanation from the lad, Merewyn came outside, carrying something black in her hand. 'That's enough, Draca,' she scolded. 'That's the king you're talking to, child. Show some respect!'

Alfred walked forward, frowning as he tried to see what the young woman held in her hand. He reached out and she handed it to him, but there was relief on her face, and he understood then what had happened as he took the object in his hand.

It was a small, circular cake of ground cereal grain which had been cooked within the embers of Merewyn's fire. Alfred was very familiar with these, for they were a staple part of most people's diet in Wessex. This particular hearth-cake had caught fire however and was blackened almost beyond recognition. Certainly, it was quite inedible.

'You kept my ma away from her baking,' Draca said, glaring at Alfred. 'And all her cakes have burned. We've nothing to sell now. How will we buy more flour? Or cakes for ourselves to eat today?'

There was genuine fear in the boy's voice, and again, Alfred felt a stab of guilt. To be so dependent on your next meal was a terrible thing. Draca had obviously missed many meals in the months since his father had gone off to war, and the thought of missing another was proving too upsetting to contemplate.

'Don't worry,' the king said, crouching down so he could look the child in the eye. 'You won't be hungry tonight, I'll make sure of it, all right? You'll not be hungry from this day on, and neither will your mother. Here.' He fished inside his pouch and found another silver coin which he handed to the boy.

Draca took it, examining it with astonishment. Then his eyes narrowed, and he looked from the coin to Alfred, then back again. 'That picture on it doesn't look anything like you,' he said.

Wulfric burst out laughing, as did Alfred. 'Maybe it's not the best likeness,' he admitted. 'Perhaps I should have a word with the people at the mint, and tell them to do a better job, eh?'

The villagers who'd come to fight the fire, or merely to gape at the excitement, went back about their own business and Merewyn took Draca into their house to clean up the mess the burned hearth-cakes had made.

'Come,' Alfred said to Wulfric and the others. 'Let's get our horses and ride back to camp. I have a sudden desire to see my wife and children.'

Before they left Bryn, the king spoke again with Beorhtric and told him to make sure Merewyn and her son were well looked after from now on, even commanding him to set aside a small part of the village's taxes to feed and clothe them. 'The next time I come back here,' he said to the reeve. 'I want to see more flesh on their bones.'

Beorhtric promised he would see to it, and then he showed them the sacks of supplies he'd had packed for them.

'Some of our famous fish, for you and your lady wife to enjoy tonight, Lord King,' the reeve said, grinning as he patted one of the sacks. 'Along with some bread, and beef, and other things.' He grasped the king's outstretched wrist and nodded. 'And don't forget, we're just waiting for the call to fight for you, lord. This is a small place, but Bryn remains loyal.'

They finished their farewells and then Alfred, Wulfric, Dunstan and Aedan rode out of the village, picking up speed once they were outside the gates, for they all wanted to reach camp as soon as possible. There might not be a sturdy palisade wall around their camp in the marshes, but it was, for now, home.

'That was an interesting day,' Wulfric noted as they slowed to pass a fallen tree that had blocked the road.

'You just know that little lad is going to tell everyone that the king burnt his ma's cakes,' Dunstan chuckled.

'You might be right,' Alfred nodded ruefully. 'But our visit to Bryn has shown me one thing: we must get rid of Guthrum and his Danes as soon as possible. So many families have lost their men because of these raiders, and even now Wessex is on edge, and divided by the enemy presence.'

'What's the plan now then?' Wulfric asked.

'We move forward faster than I suggested we would on the road to the village this morning.' Alfred said. 'We strike at the Danes mercilessly, slaughtering their foraging parties, and causing as much damage to their supply lines as we can. At the same time, we send out more messengers, find out who remains loyal to me, and, once we know... We muster the fyrd, and finish Guthrum for good.'

'Yes!' all three of his companions cheered, fists clenched.

'And not just Guthrum,' Alfred continued fiercely. 'For there'll always be another sea-wolf waiting to sail from their homeland to come and plunder Wessex. Well, let them try! Let them come in their longships and, like those cakes in Bryn, their vessels will burn!'

They all grinned, excited by the thoughts of retaking Wessex from the invaders. It was big talk from Alfred, and there was no real reason for him to be so confident, but it did not matter at that moment as they cantered towards their camp with sacks full of fish and other useful supplies.

They had faith in God, and they had faith in Alfred.

Wessex would be theirs again one day. They simply had to reach out and take it back.

CHAPTER FOUR

It was almost pitch black as the group of men made their way through the countryside, hoping they wouldn't fall down an unseen hole or disturb some demon napping on the grass. They wore dark clothes and their faces, as well as the blades of their weapons, had been blackened with soot or mud just in case some glint of light shone upon them. That seemed unlikely at this moment for the night sky was cloudy, hiding the moon, and the men could barely see their own hands in front of them. They prayed their leader knew where he was going, although it felt like they'd been walking for ever. Some of the group were starting to think they'd stumbled into another world where it was night all the time.

Wulfric had an astonishing sense of direction, however, and, as he trudged across the damp grass, he did not fear they were lost. He'd scouted these lands two days before and felt certain they were almost at their destination. Besides, they hadn't been on foot all that long – they'd ridden there on horseback, and only left their mounts tethered in some woods a mile or so back.

'Not long now, lads,' he growled, voice quickly swallowed in the cloying blackness that enveloped them. 'We're almost there.' He knew his companions were nervous, he could sense their unease, but he also knew they would not question him even if he led them off the side of a cliff. He'd earned their trust over the years, and even those who'd only recently joined Alfred's camp in the marshes had quickly learned to respect the big ealdorman.

'How can you tell?' one of the men behind him asked. 'It's like walking in a cave twenty fathoms underground without a candle! Guthrum and his entire army could be standing right beside us, and I'd never be able to tell.'

'You'd smell them!' someone muttered humourlessly. 'They all stink like fish from being on the sea so much. And dog shit.'

There were murmurs of agreement. It was a supposedly well-known fact how bad the Danes smelt, although Wulfric – who'd been in the company of the likes of Guthrum – knew the enemy warriors were at least as hygienic and well-groomed as any West Saxon. Probably more so, for the Danes never went anywhere without their combs and even little utensils shaped like tiny spoons to clean the wax from their ears.

'You're right,' the ealdorman said, though. It was always wise to dehumanise one's enemies. 'Guthrum himself smells like he's been rolling in pig turds for a week. And that's just his breath.'

'Ubba is the worst, I've heard,' someone declared. 'He smells vile because the sweat from all the women he's raped clings to him.'

Wulfric believed that one might actually be true. Although many of the Danes were cultured and honourable, at least to their own heathen standards, Ubba was well known for being cruel. It was quite possible he carried the sweat of defiled maidens on him. Wulfric truly hoped to meet the final surviving son of Ragnar Lodbrok in battle one day. He would enjoy repaying the whoreson for all the horrors he'd perpetrated on the people of Wessex.

And who knew? Tonight, Alfred's men might get the chance to do just that.

For the past three weeks, ever since Alfred had visited the village of Bryn, the exiled king and his hearth-warriors had ramped up their efforts to disrupt the Northmen who were occupying the lands around Athelney. As word of his commitment to resisting Guthrum's raiders spread throughout the kingdom, support found its way to his camp. Food, weapons, clothing, and hard men looking to kill as many Danes as possible in service to their king all arrived in Athelney. And Alfred used those resources to their fullest.

Of course, having more men in his warband meant that Alfred could attack larger foraging parties of Danes, picking his ground and ambushing the unsuspecting enemy troops without much danger to his own warriors.

Traps were laid using ropes, spears, sharpened stakes, even boulders – and dozens of Guthrum's raiders were slaughtered, their bodies stripped of valuables before the West Saxon attackers disappeared back into the marshes like barrow-wraiths.

Wulfric suspected he might look back rather fondly on these days and nights hiding out in Sumorsaete, for there was a real sense of camaraderie and purpose amongst the men and women in Alfred's camp. Even the royal children had grown accustomed to their strange new life as fugitives in their own lands, with the precocious, and often very funny Aethelflaed brightening the gloomiest of days. And there were many gloomy days as winter still had not been completely banished, although the temperature had been creeping up with every passing week.

Mercifully, it was not frosty on this night, for Alfred had given Wulfric a new and extremely dangerous mission to carry out. One that would truly send a message to Guthrum and the people of Wessex when they heard about it.

'There,' the ealdorman said in satisfaction and with just a hint of relief. His fabled sense of direction had not led them astray as the impenetrable blackness continued to stretch out, around them for mile after mile. The oppressive night quickened Wulfric's heart now, though, as directly ahead on the horizon, a radiance appeared, growing in brightness as the hushed men moved towards it.

Clearly, it was a camp, for the glow in the sky split into individual points of light – fires – which seemed to beckon Wulfric and his men closer. This was not Alfred's camp hidden in the marshes of Athelney, however. The warriors in the tents up ahead were Danes, and there were dozens of them; far more than Wulfric commanded.

The wonderful scent of roasting pork wafted through the air to the men of Wessex, setting mouths to watering and bellies to rumbling and Wulfric called a halt, eyes scanning the horizon for signs of sentries or patrols. Against the backdrop of orange light, silhouetted spearmen could be seen staring out into the night, watching for enemies, although Wulfric suspected they would not truly expect an attack from Alfred's followers. The Danes were too many in this camp, and clearly enjoying themselves.

'Bastards,' the man next to Wulfric grunted. 'Listen to them singing, as if they hadn't a care in the world.'

'And feasting on roast meat,' another added, sniffing the air jealously. 'Probably with bellies full of good Wessex ale too.'

'No doubt,' Wulfric said softly, although he wasn't paying much attention to the conversation as his mind was forming a plan for how they should proceed.

The enemy camp held a couple of hundred warriors, or so he'd gauged during his scouting mission two days past. In contrast, Wulfric had brought with him just eleven men. It was a shocking state for the kingdom to be in, overrun by invaders, but the ealdorman had no choice but to get on with things as he always did.

'You know what we're here for, lads,' he murmured, looking at his companions' faces which he could now just about make out in the dim light from the enemy campfires. 'To make as much of a nuisance of ourselves as we can, right? To make those bastards nervous about being here in our lands. To put the fear of God into them and let them know they're never safe in Wessex, no matter how many of them there are. But most of all, to do some damage!'

The men were naturally anxious about the coming work – the odds were hardly in their favour after all, and if they were to be discovered, things would go very badly for them. Wulfric knew he could count on them. Their grim smiles convinced him he that he had chosen them well, and he prayed that every one of them would make it safely back to Alfred's camp by the time the sun came up the next morning.

'We'll split into three groups, as agreed,' Wulfric said, nodding to the three men he'd designated to follow himself. 'We go in quietly, try to avoid detection, kill anyone who tries to raise the alarm. If your group is discovered, make as much noise as you can and lead the Danes away to the northeast, allowing the other two groups to move in the opposite direction to safety.'

There were silent nods of assent. It was clear that discovery meant certain death, but such was the lot of a soldier.

'May God protect us,' Wulfric said, meeting the gaze of every one of his men. They knew he would die for them – and it gave them heart, if any needed it.

'God protect us,' the men intoned, some looking to the cloudy sky, others down at the ground. Had Alfred been there they might well have said a prayer together, but Wulfric was not as devout as his king, and they were all eager to be about their business. The coming hours might be dangerous, even deadly, but they would also be satisfying and even, in some grim fashion, enjoyable.

With murmurs of encouragement the three groups moved towards the enemy encampment. They spread out as they went, two parties heading for the far ends of the location while Wulfric's made for the middle. All three aimed for darker areas, less well lit by fires which would naturally mark the places where most of the Danes would be gathered. On a chilly night like this the warriors would seek out the warmth and light offered by a well-tended, blazing fire, while there would be no reason for wagons and tents containing supplies to be afforded the same luxury.

As they approached, it became obvious that the Northmen did not fear any kind of attack. There were hardly any sentries, as far as Wulfric could tell, and most of the men within the camp were in tents, likely asleep, or drinking, singing, and gaming. It was a noisy, raucous camp, much like any other gathering of soldiers in the field and Wulfric might have felt an affinity with the Danes had he not hated them so much.

He raised a hand, and the three men with him paused as he crept silently ahead. With his face and weapons blackened he was little more than another shadow in the night and the sentry did not sense any danger until Wulfric's seax hammered into his back. By then it was too late, and he could not even cry out for a massive, stifling hand was firmly clamped over his mouth. When the bloodstained blade came around and sliced through his windpipe, the way into the camp was clear.

Quickly, Wulfric grabbed the dead man by the armpits and dragged him further away from the dim light, dropping him where the shadows were deepest. The corpse was not invisible, but it would not be stumbled upon by accident, at least not for a while, the ealdorman hoped. Wulfric stared at the Dane's face, hoping that it might — by some miracle — be the despised Jarl Ubba he'd killed. But instead, it was an older, smaller man.

There was no change in the ambiance of the camp as the singing, chattering, and even shouting as if a couple of men were having a heated argument, all continued, and Wulfric gestured into the darkness. Moments later he was joined by his three companions, and they moved up against the back of a poorly maintained tent. The thing was squint, suggesting the framework was damaged, and there were un-mended holes in the canvas walls here and there. This was not used as a dwelling, it was a store, probably for food or weapons. Wulfric motioned the other men onwards, to find their own targets, while he used his seax to slash an opening in the tent big enough for him to slip through.

He sniffed, but could not detect the musky odour of a person, or any sound of breathing. It was almost pitch black within the tent, so he shuffled forward, hands before him, until he felt something piled up. He knew immediately what he'd found – the thick wooden shafts led up to iron, leaf-shaped tips: spears. Grinning to himself, he moved around the large pile of staves which seemed to be contained within a wooden frame and his smile widened, for there were other, more valuable things within this tent.

Wooden handled swords in leather scabbards, helmets with soft canvas caps, shields of linden wood, even light vests of mail were gathered together. Wulfric used his hands to feel these items, carefully, for he did not want to injure himself. Many seemed in good condition, although some were slightly damaged, as if waiting to be repaired. Either way, there was a small fortune in war-gear stored inside this tent.

He waited, eyes closed, feeling strangely calm, as if he were alone in the middle of a summer meadow rather than in the midst of an enemy camp. At last, he drew in a deep breath, mouthed a quick prayer to God, and then drew out his flint and steel. He had some dried stinging nettle stalks in a pouch, and he took these out now, setting them on the floor of the tent like a little bird's nest. Then he struck sparks into them, and it was only a matter of moments before one began to glow orange within his kindling.

He looked around, noting with satisfaction that his guesses about the tent's contents had been accurate. Weapons were piled up all around, and some were obviously valuable, with jewels and silver and gold glinting from their handles and blades. Those were stacked separately and looked in good condition, looted from dead enemies no doubt, just like everything else in the tent.

As his small fire began to spread, he lifted an armful of the most exquisite weapons and tied them with a belt, so they'd be easier to carry. Then he made his way out through the slit he'd cut into the tent's wall. Already his three companions were waiting for him, eyes shining with the heart-pounding excitement of the night's events.

Like Wulfric, they were laden with stolen goods – although said goods were in sacks so the ealdorman couldn't tell what they might be. Food, clothing, or even coins? Whatever they'd gathered, now was not the time to discuss it, for the smell of burning was growing steadily stronger, along with the crackle and glow of flames.

Wulfric led the way back towards the darkness, relieved that none of the Northmen seemed yet to have noticed the new fires within their encampment. By the time shouts of alarm reached them the four men were half a mile distant and jogging comfortably despite their stolen bundles.

Looking back over his shoulder the ealdorman laughed, noting the fires they'd set had taken hold with a ferocity even he hadn't expected. The dry timber frames of the tents, along with whatever was stored within them, proved to be perfect fuel and now flames were billowing into the air, sparks and embers soaring and fluttering hither and thither, as Danes roared for water, and scrambled to stop the blaze spreading even wider.

'Ha, look at the bastards running about. Like wasps when their nest's been kicked!'

Wulfric and his men slowed to a halt, catching their breath, and watching the entertainment. They'd reached the agreed meeting point and waited for the other two groups of saboteurs to rejoin them. More fires could be seen now, although they were not spreading with the same ferocity as the ones Wulfric's group had started.

A short time later the sound of running footsteps could be heard and then four figures were silhouetted against the burning camp.

'Praise God,' Wulfric said, nodding in satisfaction as he recognised Alfred's hearth-warriors, soot-blackened, but very much alive.

'My lord,' the foremost of the jogging newcomers said, spotting Wulfric and flashing white teeth in his grubby face. 'Good to see you!'

'And you, Dunstan,' the ealdorman replied. 'How did you get on?'

Dunstan looked at his three comrades. One of them shrugged apologetically and admitted he'd been unable to either steal anything of value, or get his kindling to take flame. The other two nodded however, laughing softly like naughty children for they'd both managed to get enemy tents blazing, and those had contained sleeping Danes.

'Ha,' someone grunted. 'With any luck they never made it out before the whole fiery mess collapsed on top of 'em!'

They waited then for the final four members of their small, but effective, resistance party to return. 'No sign of anyone hunting for us,' Dunstan noted with a grim, satisfied smile. 'The idiots must think the fires started by accident.'

'A burning ember falling on the roof of a tent,' another man agreed. 'Easy done.'

Wulfric felt a rising sense of apprehension, however. A tent catching fire when the weather was as damp and cold as it had been for weeks was not really 'easy done.' It was quite uncommon, in truth. The fact that the Danes hadn't sent out warriors to search for escaped pyromaniacs might have another, less amusing, explanation…

'I think we should head back to camp,' the ealdorman said, eyes still fixed on the panicked enemies rushing to and fro half a mile distant.

'Eh?' Dunstan turned and fixed him with a shocked glare. 'But our mates aren't back yet. We can't just abandon them, lord.'

A sudden, terrible scream filled the ember-strewn sky, and Wulfric met his subordinate's gaze. 'They've been captured,' he said levelly. 'At least one of them has just been killed, and it's probably for the best, for we all know what kind of tortures the Danes can inflict upon their enemies.' Images of the horrific blood eagle filled his mind, but he pushed them away with a shudder. 'We move, right now, and pray for our men's bodies and souls as we go.'

He turned and began walking, slowly at first, then picking up speed as he heard his men following him. He never looked to see if Dunstan was coming – if the man wanted to attempt an ill-advised and frankly insane rescue attempt, Wulfric would not try to stop him. There was a very good chance that at least one of the four missing men would tell their captors about the rest of the Saxons out here in the night. Even if they were to drop their looted goods, Wulfric and the remaining seven men could not outrun mounted hunters.

They had to put as much distance between themselves and the burning camp as quickly as possible. Losing four good men was a terrible blow to Alfred's small warband; losing all twelve, including Wulfric, the king's experienced captain, would be catastrophic.

Another tortured cry tore through the air, and then the unmistakeable rumble of hooves could be felt as well as heard.

'They're coming for us,' a man said, breathing heavily for their pace had quickened now that every one of them understood the terrible reality of their situation.

'Stay calm,' Wulfric grunted. 'It's pitch black, and they have no idea which direction we're going.'

The sudden barking and yowling of at least three dogs made him rethink his confident assertion and they all ran on even faster.

'Maybe we should dump this shit,' said one man who was carrying a sack.

'What's in there?' Dunstan asked him. 'I'll take a turn with it. Give you a rest.'

'Silver,' the man replied, gratefully handing it over to Dunstan without breaking stride.

'We're not dumping it then,' Wulfric said firmly. 'Unless we have to.'

'Give me those,' another, less laden warrior said to the ealdorman.

Wulfric gladly gave his armful of valuable swords to him. 'We'll rotate the loads between ourselves,' he said. 'Unless the

Danes are getting too close, and then we'll see about hiding it all. Come back for it another time.'

There were shouts accompanying the barking now, and it was obvious they were getting louder. Closer. Wulfric swore, wishing he'd stolen spears now – they might not be worth as much as the exquisite swords, but they'd be a hell of a lot more useful in facing down the horses that were steadily catching up to them.

The dogs had got their scent, unsurprisingly, for they must all be stinking of sweat. It was now only a matter of time before they were spotted.

The ealdorman saw something twinkling ahead and he pointed. 'There's the stream. Keep going, lads! We're almost back at the horses!'

'We're not going to make it,' Dunstan argued. 'They're right behind us.'

Wulfric knew their horses were about half a mile away from the stream. The clouds had dissipated somewhat, and the moon was up so it would make finding the animals a little easier. Yet he could hear the panting of the dogs quite clearly now and he had to accept the truth of Dunstan's words. The Danes would be upon them in moments.

'There,' he called, pointing into the gloom. A little way to their left stood a handful of spindly shadows he knew must be leafless trees. Around them were more dark shapes which he took to be bushes. 'Head there. And be ready to defend yourselves!'

The splashing of paws and hooves came to them, as terrifying as any sound they'd heard that night, even their dying comrade's scream. Wulfric had seen the dogs the Danes kept – they were big, ferocious, and probably half-starved. If they got one of the Saxons on the ground their flesh would not remain attached to their bones for long.

The trees they were running towards did not seem to be coming any closer, but they could hear their pursuers shouting insults now. Demanding the fleeing Saxons stand and face them like men. Calling on their gods Óðinn and Þórr to assist them. Threatening terrible, painful deaths to the arsonists who'd attacked their camp.

At last, Wulfric reached the first of the trees and had to duck to avoid a branch which would have surely sent him sprawling, dazed or even unconscious, had he struck it at full tilt. Gasping in relief, he grabbed the trunk and pulled himself around it while dropping his looted items and drawing his sword, praying his men would do the same.

He barely had time to take a breath before a snarling maw was coming towards his face. He desperately brought up his blade, hoping to skewer the dog mid-jump, but the beast was moving too fast, apparently unhindered by the darkness. The pommel of Wulfric's sword caught the beast a glancing blow on the jaw, and it fell hard on the ground but instantly came up and at him again. Its teeth clamped on his forearm, and he screamed in pain, trying without success to dislodge the slavering animal.

The pain suddenly disappeared, and Wulfric saw Dunstan's blade drawing back, out of the dog's chest. There was no time to thank the man, however, for the Danes were upon them.

The first of the enemy riders was focused on the dog attached by a long leash to his hand and failed to notice the branch that Wulfric had ducked beneath. It caught the Dane, throwing him backwards out of his saddle and onto the grass. From the agonized sounds that accompanied his unintentional dismount, Wulfric knew the man would not be a threat for a while.

Dunstan roared, 'For Wessex!' and spun around the tree, hammering the edge of his blade into the leg of another horseman. The enemy rider shrieked and fell off the side of the horse, thudding onto the grass where he lay cradling his injured leg, mewling and crying.

The other dogs were not so eager to fight as the one Dunstan had killed, and they ran back the way they'd come, no longer barking. In the darkness someone brought their blade down on the crying Dane's skull and Wulfric squinted, trying to see the rest of their pursuers.

How many had there been? Six? Ten? He could hear at least two horses galloping away – riderless or not, he had no idea. After that the only sounds were heavy breathing, and he hissed, 'Lads! Are we all alive?'

'Aye', someone replied, then another, and a third muttered, 'Here, lord.'

Dunstan was on his knees stripping the man whose leg he'd almost severed. Even in the dim light he was able to quickly divest the corpse of its valuables.

Wulfric counted his men, stepping carefully over three more dead Danes and the body of a horse that had fallen and broken its neck. 'Shit,' the ealdorman cursed loudly when his count of survivors only reached six, including himself. 'We've lost another two men.'

Dunstan murmured a prayer but then he came and stood next to Wulfric. 'We'd better get moving again, my lord,' he suggested. 'Or we'll lose more. Listen.'

Another pack of dogs was coming, and more riders, and the sun would begin its ascent soon, leaving the West Saxons completely exposed if they did not make it back to their horses in time.

Wulfric thought about carrying the bodies of their two fallen comrades with them, to afford them a decent burial. But that would slow them down terribly, and lead to them all being slaughtered by the vengeful Northmen who would surely want to make an example of them after their fiery night's work.

No, the dead men could not help the war effort. But the looted swords and sacks of goods might. 'Come on,' he commanded. 'Take the things we stole from the camp, and let's go. We'll return here for our fallen if we get a chance.'

They knew that wouldn't happen, but it allowed them to leave without feeling too guilty, and so they ran on again.

Although all were exhausted, it did not take them long to cover the remaining distance to their horses and Wulfric found the animals easily for the animals sensed the men approaching and whickered softly within the trees.

They hastily loaded the sacks onto the horses, making sure they were secure, and Wulfric held his collection of swords on his lap as they rode off towards Alfred's camp in Athelney.

It had been a productive night. The fires they'd set had quite clearly caused a tremendous amount of distress and damage within the Danes' camp, and the effect on enemy morale would be considerable. They had thought themselves safe, untouchable, thanks to their numbers. That a group of Saxons had managed to infiltrate their camp and cause so much trouble would embarrass and perhaps even frighten the sea-wolves. They would certainly not sleep so soundly from now on.

'Well done, lads,' the ealdorman said as they came at last to the marshes which protected their king from Guthrum's patrols. 'You've done well this night. Word will spread of our attack, and it'll give the people of Wessex heart to know Alfred and his hearth-warriors haven't abandoned them.'

Dunstan grunted. The others remained silent, and it was a gloomy party that rode towards the tents they'd called home for the past three months, slowly picking their way across the treacherous, sodden ground.

Wulfric felt their sadness, and shared it. Ultimately, though, they had set out that night on what they all knew might be a suicide mission so the fact half of them had returned alive could only be viewed as a positive outcome. It was a soldier's job to fight and die after all.

The ealdorman told himself all of that, trying to convince himself of the truth of it, but he could not shake the feeling that he'd failed the men he'd left behind. Alfred would be deeply upset too for every man there had been loyal and true and a valued member of his 'court' there in the marshes.

'The sooner the Danes are all dead the better,' Dunstan said as he dismounted from his horse and rested his forehead against the saddle, exhausted. 'I'm sick and tired of this fucking war.'

Wulfric could only agree.

CHAPTER FIVE

AD 878, March

Defenascir

Ubba inhaled deeply, revelling in the salt spray. He released it with a grin, gazing out at the glittering waves. The Whale Road the Danes called it, and, to Ubba, there was no more glorious sight. When Guthrum had suggested he leave the main body of the army and take his men off in their longships around the far western edge of Britain he'd been greatly insulted. How dare this upstart command him, a son of Ragnar, to leave the army? Ubba had been tormenting Saxons for years with his brothers, only for Guthrum to come along and take control.

However, Ragnar's youngest son was not stupid, despite the rumours that circulated about him, even amongst his own people. He knew he was not particularly well liked by Guthrum's other jarls or hersirs. The rank-and-file troops had more time for him because he acted like one of them with his drinking, whoring and generally undisciplined behaviour. While Halfdan and Ivar had been by his side he was allowed more leeway to act as he pleased, for his powerful brothers would ignore criticism of him. The sons of Ragnar Lodbrok were fiercely loyal to one another, no matter what.

Ubba greatly missed his siblings, and his father. But when he thought rationally about Guthrum's suggestion that he lead a warband of his own, it made sense. If he remained with Guthrum he would forever be in his shadow, and if – Óðinn forbid – something happened to the king, Ubba would be well down the pecking order to step into his place.

So why should Ubba not sail westwards, taking his family's fabled raven banner, and those men who wanted to follow him? He could prove himself to be a mighty leader in his own right, finally come out from the shadow of others, and write his own name in the saga tales.

A blast of sea spray hit him in the face as the longship plunged down into a trough, but he did not flinch. He stood looking out at the coastline that was approaching, running his tongue over the grooves filed into his teeth, with thoughts of death and glory rattling around in his mind.

'It's been a productive few weeks,' his second in command, the hersir, Orvar, said, stepping across to stand beside Ubba. 'I have a good feeling about things, lord. These are the final days for Alfred, and the beginning of a new Wessex. One that we will control.'

They looked at the craggy coastline along the Severn Sea, a major inlet which would take Ubba and his twenty-three ships directly into the heart of Defenascir.

'Agreed, my friend,' Ubba laughed. 'Our time in Dyfed,' his gaze turned to the lands on the northern side of the channel, 'was good. We slaughtered many Wealas, plundered much wealth, and wrote our names into the skalds' songs. But now the real work begins.'

Dyfed was where Ubba had sailed to when he left Guthrum's command, for no reason other than they'd stopped there to repair damage to their ships after a minor storm and found the lands of the Wealas to be an easy target since the king, Rhodri Mawr, had died recently. The natives called the invaders Black Heathen and Ubba had certainly tried to live up to the sinister term. With over one thousand men at his command, they had faced little opposition, and routed any who stood against them.

Ubba had thought about pushing further north but he knew he would face stiffer resistance there, so Orvar suggested they send word, requesting even more Northmen sail to join them. But then they'd heard about Guthrum's continuing troubles with Alfred in Sumorsaete, and his inability to kill the West Saxon king. The Danes were not popular in those lands and Ubba knew the people would eventually rise up in support of their exiled monarch.

Unless Alfred was crushed once and for all.

So, Ubba made the decision to leave Dyfed, cross the Severn Sea to Defenascir and, from there, push east, back towards Guthrum's army. Alfred would be caught in the middle and, when he was dead and his resistance smashed, Ubba would be seen as a hero by all the Northmen.

At last, he would be recognised as a warrior and a leader as mighty as the rest of his family, and it was about time. Had he not killed as many enemy warriors as any now serving in Guthrum's army? More!

Again, he breathed deeply of the sea air, chest puffed out, grinning like a *vikingr* with a purse full of coins in a brothel.

'You think we'll face much resistance in Defenascir?' Orvar wondered. He was slightly taller than Ubba, with blond hair and beard, and a missing tooth that had been knocked out in battle, leaving a scar on his lip. He smiled often, despite that gap in his teeth, and was popular amongst Ubba's men.

'Perhaps,' the jarl replied thoughtfully. 'The ealdorman there is called Odda. Guthrum sent messengers to him before we overran Cippanhamme, just as he did with other Saxon leaders. Odda, if I remember right, seemed reluctant to take sides, but Guthrum thought it was because the Saxon dog wanted a bigger bribe to renounce Alfred. So...' He shrugged. 'Maybe Odda and Guthrum have come to some agreement since we've been in Dyfed. We'll find out soon enough.'

Orvar turned, squinting as the sun peered out from behind a cloud making the waves shine like fire. They were almost at their destination, and, despite the large number of ships Ubba commanded, it looked like there were no Saxon warriors waiting to meet them on the beach. They had been spotted, naturally, and horsemen had followed them as they progressed further along the Severn Sea, but, if Odda had been given word of their presence there were no signs that he'd mustered his fyrd to stand against them.

Ubba took that as a good omen. Odda, like the people of Dyfed, was probably terrified by the thought of a thousand rampaging Danes suddenly arriving on his shores.

'The ealdorman is most likely on his knees in some draughty old church, begging the White Christ to make our longships go away,' he said with a grim laugh.

'Like Alfred,' Orvar agreed. 'Always on their knees, praying, these Saxon fools.'

Ubba's smile faded somewhat. 'Maybe not quite like Alfred,' he muttered. 'That one has done well to keep us at bay over the years. Far better than the likes of Edmund in East Anglia, or Burgred in Mercia. By Óðinn's balls, Alfred even killed Bagsecg in battle, and that was no mean feat!'

'True,' Orvar conceded. 'King Bagsecg was a monster. I honestly thought he'd lead us to an easy victory over the Saxons. But Alfred is different – most of his kind, like the other two you mentioned, are cowards and weaklings. This Odda would have already had a shieldwall lined up waiting for us if he wanted a fight. Yet,' he gestured towards the empty coastline. 'We are about to set foot on his lands completely unimpeded.'

'Remember,' Ubba said, checking his weapons and armour were all securely fastened in place as their vessel cruised gracefully through the water towards the beach. 'We're here to subdue Defenascir. We are not here to ravage these lands unless just yet. If Odda will agree to renounce Alfred, or if he already has, we will move onwards to Sumorsaete.'

The longships came up onto the beach, hitting the ground, and the men jumped down. They were well drilled and did not need their hersirs to command them into a defensive formation, for they were already doing it.

'What about the ships?' Orvar asked.

Ubba grinned. 'They can wait here for a couple of days, just in case we need to escape. After that, their captains can sail away to wherever they like.'

'Should we send scouts on ahead?'

Ubba shook his head. 'What's the point? We need to march east no matter what. Let's just get moving – I want to meet with the Saxons as soon as possible, and there'll be towns on the way that we can plunder!' He raised his voice as he spoke, and the men nearest heard and cheered. Ubba laughed. 'Anyone would think they hadn't just spent weeks ravaging the lands – and women – of Dyfed!'

Orvar also laughed. 'There's always time for more ravaging, lord, you know that.'

Ubba's smile faded and he gripped his sword hilt, looking at the Defenascir hills. 'I do,' he growled. 'So, let's get to it.'

He strode ahead, past his men, many of whom were still on board the ships, for it took a long time for an army to disembark. There was a palpable sense of excitement and confidence amongst the Danes since they'd found Dyfed to be relatively easy pickings and they expected much the same here. Ubba's martial prowess might not be as respected as his brothers', but it hardly mattered when there were a thousand well-armed, well-trained men following him.

The Jarl strode ahead, leaving the shingle beach behind and clambering upwards onto the grass. This area was more hilly than other parts of Wessex and the Northmen had to make their way parallel to the beach, hoping the terrain would level out soon. It might not be the fjords and towering, snow-capped mountains of home for Ubba's followers, but marching through this part of Defenascir was going to prove more strenuous than they'd hoped.

'Lord.'

Ubba turned to Orvar, noting the slight touch of concern he heard in the hersir's voice.

'What is it?'

'Look.'

On the crest of the hill ahead Ubba noticed small figures moving. As he watched, he realised there were a lot of them, and it was clear they were carrying spears. A surge of battle-lust made his blood surge, and he flashed a predatory grin at Orvar. 'It seems Ealdorman Odda has decided not to ignore us after all.'

'What should we do? We can't get into a fight here, there's no room for us to make our numbers count.'

Orvar assumed they had more men than the Saxons, and Ubba thought it was probably true. Even if Odda could muster a fyrd big enough to match the raiders, it would take time, and Ubba's force had only just landed in Defenascir.

'For a start, Orvar, we won't panic,' the jarl growled. 'We'll send scouts on ahead to see what awaits us up ahead.' He turned and looked for his riders. There were not many for horses did not like travelling in longships, and they took up a lot of space. But they were valuable in situations like this, when speed counted, so Ubba had brought a dozen or so animals along with them, stolen from Dyfed. He waved to their riders now, gesturing them forward.

'Half of you, ride on ahead and see what the Saxons are doing. You see them up there?' He pointed to the hillside, and the horsemen nodded. 'I want to know how many of them there are, and what they're doing. All right?'

Six of the riders cantered along the path that ran beside the beach and soon came to a split in the terrain. Their leader turned back and gestured to Ubba. There was a road heading upwards there, and that's where the scouts went, disappearing from view as the rest of the soldiers marched along behind them.

Now the army was able to spread out more, forming a long line four or five ranks deep, spears and shields held ready for whatever the Saxon ealdorman was planning, if anything.

Ubba walked forward himself, looking left and right, trying to get some idea of the topography but it was impossible for the hills and trees obscured his view. The gap his riders had gone through proved to be a road right enough, and it stretched seemingly all the way ahead and probably up to the top of the huge hill to the north. He looked at that hill, and envied Ealdorman Odda. The sun was shining on the green grass, and there were even some small houses on the hillside, practically glowing in the sun. It was an idyllic, lush setting for a nobleman to rule. Lands like this one were the reason why so many Northmen came here. They wanted to settle, build a farm and a home tended by slaves, while enjoying richer soil and a climate that was more temperate than that of their homelands.

Odda was a lucky man to live here in Defenascir. Whether his luck would hold out in the coming hours and days would depend on how the Saxon dealt with Ubba, of course...

The jarl's thoughts were interrupted by the thundering of hooves. 'That was quick,' he muttered as his scouts came into view, galloping down the slope towards him. He frowned at their pace, wondering if someone was chasing them. Surely not – the Saxons would know the outriders were merely the vanguard of a much, much bigger force. As he looked on, however, the last of the horsemen was catapulted off the side of his mount and then the sound of howling and jeering drew Ubba's eyes up.

There were many trees on that section of the hill, but the top was clear, and there the jarl saw dozens of figures, arms raised aloft. Some held spears and shields, but others had bows. As he scanned the terrain he saw more archers halfway down the hill, hidden amongst the bushes and trees, and it had been one of these who'd managed to hit the rider with an arrow. The rest of the horsemen thundered down the trail, scowling in righteous indignation.

Ubba waited for them to come to a halt before him. He could see no signs of pursuit and the Saxon warriors on the hillside remained where they were, as if challenging the Danes to come and get them.

'What happened?' he asked the scouts' leader. 'Did you speak with Odda?'

'No, lord,' the man replied. Like most of the Northmen he was bearded and broad-shouldered. 'We never reached the top of the hill. The Saxons had blocked the path and, when we stopped, they shouted at us to get back in our ships and go home. Then they shot one of our men and we retreated.'

Ubba counted them. There were only four. 'Their archers hit another one of you when you were riding back down here,' he said, eyes roving across the hillside once again. 'All right – it seems the horses won't be much use in this terrain. Take them back to the ships, then rejoin your units.'

He turned and walked back to his waiting men. Orvar's face was stony as he asked, 'What now?'

'It seems Ealdorman Odda, or whoever's in charge of those farmers up there, wants a fight. Well, fighting is what we do best, right, lads?'

Those in the front ranks who were close enough to hear him roared agreement and others, guessing what was happening, joined in.

'Shields up,' Ubba shouted. 'Let's show these dogs what happens to those who defy the Raven banner!' He turned and walked towards the path that would take them up the hill. As they moved, the warriors struck their spear shafts against their shields, a terrifying sound given how many of them there were. The thumping filled the valley, echoing off the slopes around them and on they went, along the main trail and up through the trees. Ubba could imagine what Odda must be thinking as the Danes approached. It would look like a tidal wave had come to the shores of Defenascir – a tidal wave of iron and steel, and leather and linden wood, and death.

'The Norns have spun their web, Orvar,' smiled Ubba, noting that the Saxon archers who'd been hiding in the trees were scrambling up towards the top of the hill, not so brave now that their enemies were facing them. 'Odda had the chance to throw his lot in with us, but like so many of his mongrel kind, he is a fool, and now… We will be his doom.'

CHAPTER SIX

Ealdorman Odda looked on as the Danes climbed the hill. 'God has brought the heathen horde to our shores,' he murmured, feeling panic threaten to overwhelm him and reminding himself of his duty to the fyrd. He was their leader, and he must keep himself together, for if he was to give in to the fear that threatened to make him vomit his men would lose heart and likely run away. As he would dearly love to do.

'What do they want here in Lintun?' one of his thanes asked, eyes wide as he tried to count the numbers facing them.

'"Want", Cynesige?' Odda replied. 'What do they always want? Silver, goods, weapons, women, slaves. Many Danes have even taken lands in Northumbria and Mercia and settled there!' He turned away and looked at his fyrd, which numbered only around eight hundred warriors. 'In short,' he said. 'The sea-wolves want everything that's ours, and the only way to stop them is to kill them.'

'Or pay them off,' another thane suggested hopefully. He was an older man, beard fully grey, his bald head shining in the sun. 'Alfred did that with some success...'

'And look where Alfred is now!' Odda retorted. 'Hiding in Sumorsaete.' He shook his head sadly. 'No, Glaedwine, I wouldn't try to pay them off even if we had enough wealth to tempt them. Do you not recognise that white banner, with its dark raven?'

The thane looked and could easily see what Odda spoke of, for the enemy standard bearer was striding along the main trail. The white banner was shaped like the lower right quadrant of a circle, and was displayed on the top of a pole even longer than a spear. 'The raven symbolises Óðinn,' Glaedwine said, fingers tapping restlessly on the handle of his sword.

'It does,' Odda agreed. 'But that particular banner belongs to a son of Ragnar Lodbrok.'

'Ubba!'

'Aye, Glaedwine. Ubba. Come, we should retreat to the old fort before the Danes are upon us.'

The thanes followed their commander as he strode along the top of the hill. There was an even more palpable sense of urgency about them now for they'd all heard tales of Ubba and his exploits – not only as part of his brothers' armies, but also his recent savagery in Dyfed. The thought of such a man leading so many Northmen into Defenascir was terrifying, and Odda could hear his followers murmuring prayers as they headed for the ruined fort he'd chosen as the best place to make a stand.

The fort was known locally as Cynwit and had once been a mighty stronghold for the natives of these lands. That had been many generations ago, however, and nothing was left of the original structure save some earthworks. Of course, its location on top of the hill meant Odda's fyrd had a distinct advantage over the enemy warriors climbing up to meet them now. Added to that, Odda had set his men to strengthening the old earthworks, raising them higher and adding ditches.

The ealdorman had not wasted his time when he first heard news of the Danes' raids in Dyfed. Considering the Southern Sea was the only thing that separated the lands of the Wealas from Defenascir, there was always a chance the invaders would use their longships to sail here and attack Odda's lands. So Odda had mustered his fyrd, although he knew it would be a horrendous waste of money and resources should the raiders never come to Defenascir. That was a risk he was willing to take, for the alternative was unthinkable.

Now, the ealdorman was relieved to have summoned his men, but still felt a terrible unease at the sight of that raven banner. The West Saxons were outnumbered, and Odda's men were mostly farmers or fishermen rather than professional, skilled warriors like the Danes. Utilising the ancient hillfort seemed a much better course of action than meeting Ubba in open battle. Unfortunately, since there had been no way to know in advance where the raiders would land if they did come to Defenascir, Odda had not commanded Cynwit fort to be strengthened until that morning.

So, the ealdorman had been prepared, but not as thoroughly as he'd have wished.

It would have to be enough.

'Keep digging, lads,' he called to the men who continued to labour outside the earthen ramparts. 'The bigger you can make those ditches, the better chance we all have of surviving this.' He mentally kicked himself for not coming up with a more inspiring motivational speech, but he still felt like he might puke at any moment and began to actually look forward to Ubba and his sea-wolves appearing, so that they could get this over with.

Waiting for a battle was almost as bad as fighting in one.

There were guards posted on the outer perimeter of the fort and a couple of them came running back towards Odda now, followed by the rest.

'They're almost here!' the lead guard was calling, holding onto his battered old helmet, undoubtedly a family heirloom, as he ran.

'Everyone behind the ramparts!' Odda bellowed, his pulse quickening and the feeling of nausea mercifully lifting, replaced by a strange excitement. He suddenly realised he was smiling. 'Get safely behind the walls, lads,' he reiterated. 'And ready your spears, bows, whatever you have!' He turned to the thane, Cynesige. 'Make sure my hearth-warriors are in the centre, where the "entrance" is.'

The nobleman nodded silently, lips pressed in a tight, bloodless line, and turned to make sure the formation was secure, shieldwall properly formed up. As he went, he turned and looked back at Odda. 'Er, my lord?' he said.

The ealdorman glanced back distractedly. 'What?'

'I think you should come back behind the rampart yourself. You're a bit exposed there.'

It took a moment for Odda to understand what he was being told, but then he laughed and immediately hurried after Cynesige. 'I'm too eager to fight these bastards,' he said, moving through the ranks of his soldiers and climbing up the earthen slope that his men had built against the inside part of the rampart. From here he could look out on the entire valley and the Severn Sea far below and would be able to gauge the true size of Ubba's forces once they came into view.

The feared raven banner was the first thing he saw appearing, the stylised bird flapping noisily for it was quite windy where they were on the summit. And then the enemy army steadily grew in size and number, until it seemed the entire western side of the hill was filled with them.

'God help us,' Odda whispered, his desire to join in battle with these vicious looking warriors draining from him like the contents of a torn aleskin. He glanced at his own poorly armed levies, some of whom carried nothing more than long, pointed staves and had only their cloaks for protection. How could such men – farmers! – defeat the savage Danes?

The men of Defenascir would need a miracle.

Odda's eyes went to his priest, Waltheof and noticed the tonsured, middle-aged man was looking back at him. The priest showed no trace of fear as he recited a stream of prayers, blessing the fyrd and this ancient place of refuge. Odda felt shame at his own terror and clenched his jaw, turning back to look at the enemy jarl as he strode across the grass towards them.

The stories told about the sons of Ragnar all mentioned how tall and broad the three were, but Ubba did not look that large. He had the air of superiority about him that many, or most, noblemen had, though – an expectation that people would be drawn to him, as if his mere presence was enough to silence any gathering. In this case, he was right.

Striding boldly up to the earthen rampart, the jarl's eyes scanned the defenders arrayed along it, and those who formed the shieldwall in the opening where, ideally, strong gates should have been.

'What do you want, pagan?' Odda shouted, making his voice loud for fear that it might break. It did not, instead coming out calm and clear, and the ealdorman took heart from that.

Immediately, Ubba's eyes sought him out, and, when the Dane smiled it sent a chill through the West Saxon commander. Grooves had been filed into Ubba's teeth, making straight lines across them which were accentuated by some kind of red dye so that, even at this distance, the effect was striking. Shocking, even.

'I want you, and your men, to swear fealty to me, Christian,' the Dane shouted, gaze travelling from Odda, to his men, and back again. 'Why you commanded your archers to attack my scouts I do not know, as all we wanted was to pass peacefully through your lands and on to Sumorsaete.'

'"Peacefully"?' Odda shouted in disbelief. 'We all know you Danes never do anything peacefully. You've been rampaging through Dyfed,' he waved angrily across the glittering waters below, towards the distant coastline. 'And now that you've bled the place dry you've sailed here to do the same to Defenascir. Well, I'm not about to let you, Ubba Ragnarsson, by God's bones!'

Ubba let him finish and then laughed with genuine humour. 'Ah, you're right,' he said, turning to gaze wistfully at the distant land of Dyfed. 'We've had some good times over there recently. But you're also mistaken.' His humour faded. 'We came here merely to travel on to Sumorsaete, where your deposed king is hiding. We had no quarrel with you until you killed two of my men.'

The Danes behind him were strangely, almost eerily, silent. They'd ceased hammering their spear shafts against their shields some time ago and now stood without fidgeting behind their jarl, arrayed out in a huge column that extended right back down the hillside.

Odda swallowed and cleared his throat. 'No quarrel? You admit you seek to attack, to kill, Alfred, the rightful king of these lands? *My* king? I'm sorry, Ubba, but that naturally sets us against one another!'

The Dane walked slowly along the front of the Saxon rampart, looking at the men defending it. Gauging them, and their weapons. He did not appear worried at all, and showed this by curling his lip in disdain as he turned and moved back to his earlier position in front of Odda. 'You talk as if you lead a great army,' he called, voice carried by the wind, so that it reached everyone within the ancient fort. 'Yet you cower behind these feeble walls. If your God is with you, as you believe, why do you not come out of there and face us like true warriors? *Are* you warriors? Or are you, every single one of you, craven fools who know Þórr will sweep away your White Christ, like the sea washes away a fortress made from sand on the beach? Like our armies have swept away your King Alfred?'

His voice had risen in volume and pitch as he spoke, until he was screeching by the time he stopped, eyes bulging, spittle flying from his mouth.

'The time for Saxons to rule here has passed, Odda' the jarl continued in an even wilder tone, if that was possible. 'The Danes have come, and I, Ubba, last son of Ragnar, shall see you and your Alfred dead, while a new Wessex rises from the ashes of his funeral pyre!'

Odda knew this was the real Ubba they were seeing now – a man with a wild, violent temper, who allowed his base emotions and desires to rule him. The thought of Defenascir falling to such a man horrified Odda.

And yet, Ubba spoke the truth. Odda was too scared to lead his men out from Cynwit and meet the Northmen in battle there on the hilltop. Even if he had as many men as Ubba commanded, it would not be close to an even fight. Not with the training and war-gear the enemy had.

If he was being truthful, Odda did not even think he was up to this fight himself.

At thirty-two winters, he was younger than many ealdormen in Wessex, and hadn't long been in the position. His father had died of a wasting illness a few years before, leaving Odda to inherit his lands and title in Defenascir. The young man had been involved in skirmishes with unruly Wealas as well as major battles with Danes, but always as a subordinate to his father, or the king, or some other, more experienced, commander. This was his first time leading the fyrd against a sizeable enemy force, and Odda had no real idea how to approach it.

For now, the most sensible thing to do was remain within the fort. The newly strengthened walls would hopefully offer enough shelter against an attack by Ubba's men.

Maybe the Danes would do as Ubba said they had originally planned, and just piss off east, to Sumorsaete. Such thoughts made Odda feel guilty, for he was essentially hoping the enemy would leave him alone and go after Alfred, but he comforted himself with the knowledge that Alfred was in hiding. Many stories and rumours of the deposed king's efforts to strike out at the occupying Danes from his hidden camp within the marshes of Athelney had reached Defenascir, giving the people heart, and hope that one day their lands would belong to them again.

'Well?' Ubba demanded. 'Are you going to come out and fight like men, Saxon? Or hide in there like frightened sheep, cowering from the wolves stalking your pen?'

There were grumbles from some of the men who were eager to show their mettle, but most of Odda's fyrd were quite content to remain safely behind the earthen ramparts. Making it back to their farms and their families in one piece was more important than winning battle glory.

'I see no reason to waste the lives of my men,' Odda called down. 'If you wish to march east, as you claim, then carry on. We won't stop you.'

Ubba shook his head, a sneer curling his lip, red-stained teeth appearing again. 'Can't do that now,' he said, spreading his arms wide. Despite the sturdy timber his shield was crafted from, and its heavy iron boss, Ubba held the thing as if it was as light as a feather. 'You killed my men in an unprovoked attack, Saxon, and we will avenge their deaths, as all good Northmen should do. Come out and fight, or die behind your walls; it's up to you.'

With that, the jarl turned and strode away, back to his own men. For a long time, they remained there on the hilltop, watching the West Saxons who, in turn, gazed back. At last, the sun began to dip beneath the horizon and Odda's advisors came to join him on the rampart.

'Do you think they'll attack us during the night?' Glaedwine asked, wiping a sheen of sweat from his bald scalp.

'Not a chance,' the priest, Waltheof replied firmly. 'The heathen scum hate to lose men needlessly. They'll be content to sit outside until we come to them.'

'Or starve,' Cynesige agreed. 'Or die of thirst.'

Odda nodded. They had noted enemy scouts moving around the perimeter of the old fort throughout the day. Ubba would guess there was no water supply up here, and no way to find food. He'd also be able to guess that there would be limited supplies within the walls, and that meant Odda's fyrd could only last a siege of a few days at most before they would have to come out. And, by that time, they would be physically weak and suffering while the Danes remained as fresh and well-fed as ever.

The ealdorman looked out at the enemy warriors and felt a momentary surge of hope. 'They're leaving,' he cried, a smile splitting his face.

'They must have decided they don't have time to waste on a siege,' Glaedwine suggested. 'Perhaps Guthrum is expecting them to arrive in Sumorsaete soon.'

Their happiness was quickly dampened by Waltheof. 'They'll simply be moving out of range of our archers,' the priest said. 'Once night falls, we could loose barrage after barrage out there,' he gestured at the forest of spearmen who were marching down the side of the hill and out of sight. 'With so many targets it would be a massacre. Ubba is no fool. He'll set up camp at the bottom of the hill, surround it so we can't escape, and simply wait us out.'

Odda looked at the priest in dismay, but never thought to question his assessment of the situation. Waltheof had been a warrior himself once, when he was a young man, and a very successful, well-respected one too. What he said made complete sense. Indeed, Odda had been hoping to use the very tactic described, commanding his bowmen to shoot arrows at the hillside once it was too dark for the enemy soldiers to see them coming and make any effort to use their shields as protection.

He should have guessed Ubba would expect that.

'What do we do then?' Cynesige wondered glumly, almost as if he didn't want or expect an answer.

'I don't know,' Odda admitted, rubbing his short beard thoughtfully. 'For now, we simply wait, and pray God sends us an answer to this problem.'

'Maybe the bastards will keep going when they reach the foot of the hill,' old Glaedwine said, attempting to make his voice jovial.

'Aye,' Odda grunted gloomily. 'Maybe.'

CHAPTER SEVEN

Alfred gritted his teeth and pushed against the weight overhead, muscles straining, praying it would not come down upon him. 'Is it there yet?' he grunted, sucking in a deep, steadying breath as he tried to set his feet even more firmly on the ground.

'Just about, lord.'

'Well, hurry up!' Alfred gasped. 'I can't hold this much longer.'

'Yes, lord. All right, that's it now.'

Sighing in relief, the king slowly let the tension out of his biceps, fearing the great wooden beam would fall and pin him to the damp grass – but it held firm, and he arched his back, smiling in satisfaction.

'Good work, my lord,' said the carpenter who was overseeing the construction of this section of the gatehouse. He thumped a couple of long iron nails into the wooden beam, securing it in place, then jumped down from the ladder. Together, he and Alfred and the other men in the crew admired their handiwork.

'It's coming together,' said the king. 'Although it's as hard as we expected, building on such soft ground.'

Wulfric nodded. 'Aye, this is the firmest, most suitable section of land for miles, but it's still not ideal.'

The site they'd chosen for this would-be fortress was a small hillock, about two acres in size, which had once been the site of a cottage belonging to a hermit. That building, although not that old, was a ruin by the time Alfred and his men came to it, but, once the remains were cleared, its foundations gave them a sturdy spot to build the new stronghold upon. The king was no expert in such matters, but the Ealdorman of Sumorsaete, Aethelnoth, had sent skilled craftsmen to Alfred, and they suggested this part of Athelney would be the ideal spot for his base.

Indeed, Alfred and Wulfric thought they were right. Without a huge workforce to dig long ditches and erect a massive palisade wall, or warriors to man such sprawling fortifications, they had to look to nature for protection. Athelney provided it in the form of impassable marshes. To reach the hillock upon which Alfred's new fortress was taking shape the workers had to cross the waters in punts. Bringing the materials across – wooden beams, iron nails, tools, ladders, and so on – required even larger, flat rafts.

There was no way an enemy force would be able to approach the site once it was completed without being seen and attacked by the defenders, safe behind their small, but robust walls. Fighting from within a punt would be impossible, especially while arrows and spears were raining down upon the prospective invaders.

To begin, they'd erected a hall – compact in size but with thick walls and a heavy door that would not be smashed open without some effort. Eventually it would be a home for the royal entourage, but, for now, it provided a weatherproof base for the workers, and a store for supplies. With that completed, they moved on to erecting a palisade around the hall and the hilltop, and that was what they were working on today.

'What next?' Alfred asked the carpenter who was, during the building work at least, his superior.

'Next?' asked the man, looking up at the sun which was barely visible through the grey clouds and light mist which seemed to cover the Athelney a lot at this time of year. 'Next it's time for a quick bite to eat and some ale, my lord!'

There was plenty of food to go around, for Ealdorman Aethelnoth and the local settlements were happy enough to provide such resources to the exiled king. Loyalty went a long way, of course, but Alfred had also promised to repay them all once he had his throne back. That day seemed a long, long way off as they sat on piles of wooden beams chewing salted beef and supping ale, but most of the thirty-odd men who comprised the workforce believed it would come eventually.

'Do you know who that cottage we're building on top of belonged to, lord?' the carpenter asked Alfred. He was a large, local man, broadly built, with heavily callused hands and weather-beaten features. A pleasant, friendly individual who the king had immediately liked when they'd first met and come here to discuss the viability of this project.

'No,' Alfred admitted, tearing off another chunk of meat and eyeing the ground which had once been the site of the ruined cottage. 'A hermit of some kind you told me.'

'Aye, a hermit,' the carpenter confirmed. 'Two hundred years ago, St Athelwine lived here, on this very spot.'

Alfred stopped chewing and, eyes shining, looked at Wulfric. The ealdorman shook his head, knowing what was coming.

'St Athelwine?' the king demanded.

'Aye,' the carpenter said. 'The very same.'

'Athelwine, son of King Cynegils? I should have realised it was his cottage. You may smirk, Wulfric,' he said, standing up and gazing at their burgeoning fortress. 'But this just proves to me that God is guiding us!'

'No doubt, lord,' said Wulfric dutifully, if not quite sincerely.

Alfred merely laughed at his captain's inability to see the divine in everyday, apparently mundane events. Wulfric might not believe, but the king most certainly did. 'It's a sign,' he said to everyone gathered there, and, as usual when talking about Godly matters, his voice was filled with strength and confidence and the knowledge that he was being led by a higher power. 'Athelwine was a great man, a prince of Wessex as I once was, and rightly venerated as a saint. To know that he lived here, that we are building our stronghold upon his cottage…' He trailed off, overcome by emotion, and looked up at the cloudy sky, mouthing a prayer of thanks.

No matter how strong each workers' faith, the men could not fail to be touched by their king's performance. It inspired them all. Even Wulfric.

'Come, lads,' Alfred laughed. 'Let's get this fortress finished. Once it's up we'll have a safe, warm place to spend our nights – better than the tents we've been living out of these past weeks, eh? And we won't have to live in fear of attacks by the Danes for, not only will we have our spears, these thick walls, and the marshes to protect us – we'll have St Athelwine and Almighty God watching over us! And then?' He'd been gesturing towards the half-built stronghold but now moved his hand away, pointing to the northeast, before forming a fist. 'Then we'll gather the fyrd, and march to take back Cippanhamme from Guthrum, and, on the way, a stop at Brycgstow to deal with those traitorous bastards, Ealdorman Wealdmar, and his whelp, Diuma!'

The men got back to work, suitably inspired by the rousing speech and the fervour with which it had been delivered. The walls were almost finished, the gatehouse too, and then they could begin living and working within the stronghold, using it as a base to go on and do all the things Alfred described.

'There must be an easier way to get here,' Wulfric said to the carpenter as they hammered another beam into place, ignoring the light drizzle that had now started. 'I mean, other than those little punts.'

The carpenter expertly thumped a nail home with his mallet and looked down at the reed-strewn marshes surrounding their lofty position. 'I suppose we could build a causeway,' he said. 'It would mean you could get horses here, and supplies would be easier to bring over.' He took out another nail and battered it home. 'Take a lot of work, though. And time.'

Alfred looked at the waters, trying to imagine what it would be like there with even a narrow causeway connecting their small island to the mainland. He knew engineers could construct such a platform, somehow making them sturdy enough that they wouldn't sink, but he also knew it would take a lot of effort and resources they did not really have to spare.

'One day,' he said grimly. 'One day I will build such a causeway.' He wandered forward, forgetting the beam he was supposed to be helping lift into place, seeing another world, another time, when Wessex's crown was on his head once more. 'There,' he pointed. 'Imagine it leading here, through the brackish water and the swaying reeds. At the far end, on the land, there, will be a gatehouse to guard access to the causeway. Then here,' his eyes travelled along the imaginary platform, and he indicated a spot on the island. 'Will be another gatehouse. And this,' he looked back at Wulfric and the carpenter and the frame they were erecting for his fortress. 'This will be a monastery. A monastery dedicated to St Athelwine.'

There was a lull in the work as everyone listened to the king and took in his vision, trying to picture it themselves.

'A noble dream, my lord,' said Wulfric.

'Not a dream,' Alfred interjected. 'A promise. It will be thus, you'll see.'

Wulfric nodded. 'I believe you,' he said. 'But until that time when monks can sing the praises of God, and of the king who built their new home…' He raised his eyebrows and nodded at the beam he was holding one end of. 'Will you give me a hand with this, my lord? The place isn't going to build itself, and, knowing our gaffer there, it'll soon be time for another break!'

They did not take a break for a long time as it turned out. The men fell into a steady rhythm and, before Alfred knew it, the sun was beginning to set. The carpenter called a halt to the day's work at that point, sharing smiles with the labourers and encouraging them all to fill their bellies before getting a good night's sleep.

The others made their way inside to the hall while the king wandered around examining the construction that was slowly but surely taking shape, impressed by just how sturdy it seemed already, and imagining how it might look once completed.

'You think it'll be enough?' he asked, realising Wulfric had remained outside with him, a silent presence, always ready to guard his lord.

The ealdorman peered at the framework they'd spent the day building, examining the joints and the thickness of the timbers. At last, he grunted. 'It's better than I'd have hoped for, considering our situation and the fact we're essentially on an island here.'

Alfred chuckled at his captain's dour expression. 'Were you always so grumpy, Wulfric?' he asked.

The older warrior thought about it for a moment then shrugged. 'Perhaps. My wife used to laugh about it, just like you do, lord.'

Wulfric did not mention his wife, Sunngifu, often. Alfred knew she'd died around seventeen years ago, leaving behind the ealdorman and their daughter, Deorwynn, who was an adult now and living as a nun in Ilminster.

'You still miss her terribly, don't you?' the king asked softly.

Wulfric did smile now, although it was a sad smile that struck at Alfred's heart for it could not mask the obvious pain his friend was feeling. 'I do,' he said. 'I've come to realise over the years that I'll never really get over the loss.'

Alfred wished Ealhswith was there to give the ealdorman a hug, for he looked like he could do with one. He did not think it would be appreciated if he was to do it himself, however, so he simply sat in silence, allowing Wulfric to speak more about Sunngifu if he wished.

'It's a hellish thing,' said the big warrior at last. 'To lose comrades in battle. Even worse to lose a child...' His voice cracked and he paused, trying to regain his composure.

'I know that pain,' Alfred said quietly, feeling the familiar sorrow rising within, just as it did every time he thought of the babes he and Ealhswith had lost in infancy.

'I know, lord, and it's a hard thing to bear,' Wulfric murmured. 'To see a child die before they even have a chance to live.'

Alfred's eyes brimmed with tears, and he looked away, watching the sun turn orange as it dipped beneath the trees on the western edge of Athelney.

'Death comes to us all, though,' Wulfric went on. 'As warriors we know this better than most. We face our doom every time we draw our sword or heft a spear. Still, losing my wife at such a young age was… I found it impossible to comprehend for a long time. We were very close, you see. Childhood friends.'

Alfred was shocked to see his friend's face was streaked with tears. Never, in all the time he'd known Wulfric, had he seen the man so openly show naked emotion. He felt strangely privileged.

'You expect men to fall in battle. It's inevitable, isn't it? And childbirth is almost as dangerous, so to lose a little one is also not such a shocking thing to happen, even if it is hard to accept. But to watch my Sunngifu, only twenty-three summers old and full of life and love, take ill and just… fade away before my eyes…' He did wipe his cheeks then, an angry gesture. 'It took many weeks to get over her death but even then, it changed me forever. Aye, I was dour before, but I also had a lot of joy within me. And hope for the future. That all died when Sunngifu did.'

They looked at one another, sharing this moment of grief and loss, and Alfred felt closer than ever to his captain.

'You still have joy within you, Wulfric,' the king said emphatically. 'Maybe you don't show it often, but I see it. D'you think I'd want to be around you every day if you really were nothing more than the grumpy, grizzled soldier you usually show to the world?' He did reach out now, patting his friend on the arm and offering him a smile. 'I might be your king, but it's not my place to tell you how to feel. You are supposed to be *my* advisor after all. Just remember, though, that I'm always here if you want someone to talk to. We've been through so much together and you've been my strong right arm when I needed you, so it's the least I can do to be there in return.' He smiled mischievously. 'There's also Oswald. You could talk to him about your grief. That's what priests are there for, and Oswald is a fine listener. I honestly think I'd go mad if I didn't have him to hear my troubles and offer advice.'

Wulfric's mouth twitched in amusement, and he gave a shallow nod. 'My thanks for the suggestion, lord, but I don't need a priest.' It seemed his momentary show of weakness was over, and he stood up, stretching his back and groaning as he rolled his head from side to side in an attempt to ease aching muscles. 'Come on, lord, we should head inside, or they'll start to think we've been killed by Danes.'

'A sound plan,' Alfred agreed happily. 'I'm bloody starving anyway, and thirsty. Let's go in and find something to eat and drink.'

They walked side by side, in silence now, but there was nothing awkward about the short journey to the new hall. If anything, the few moments spent in conversation had made their friendship even stronger, Alfred believed. He doubted Wulfric would ever ask to speak with him about Sunngifu again but that was fine and, if he did, Alfred would be there for him, just as his captain was always there for him, and for Wessex.

CHAPTER EIGHT

'The men are thirsty.'

'And hungry.'

Odda's face seemed to have been fixed in a permanent frown for the past two days, and the words of his thanes did nothing to improve his humour. He opened his mouth to tell them that he would also love to feast on succulent roast pork and drown himself in a barrel of freshly brewed ale, but he forced himself to remain calm. They were merely reporting on the mood in the camp, after all, as they were duty bound to do.

The Danes had not marched east, as Glaedwine had rather hopefully suggested they might. Instead, they'd simply made camp at the bottom of the hill and spent the next couple of days drinking and enjoying themselves. They had looted Lintun, set fire to most of the buildings, and sang songs while the West Saxon fyrd remained in Cynwit Fort, gloomily consuming their meagre supplies.

It was humiliating for Odda, as he knew the men expected more of him. What could he do, though, other than lead them into a fight that would see most of them die? Even if, by some miracle, they managed to defeat the Northmen, the majority of Odda's warriors would be slaughtered in the process. Was that a worthwhile victory? Or was it madness?

His belly rumbled, and he placed a hand on it absently. He imagined he could smell meat roasting, wafted upwards from the beach below. Was he going mad already? What would he be like when there was no food and drink left, and his body began to consume itself? It was a horrific thought, made even worse by the knowledge he would not die alone, but surrounded by an emaciated, starving fyrd who had loyally answered his call to arms.

So far, they'd stoically held their discipline, although the general demeanour around camp was one of sullen, growing resentment.

The thanes left to try and reassure the men that all was well, leaving only the priest, Waltheof, standing atop the earthen wall with Odda.

'Have you ever seen men starve?' the ealdorman asked him quietly, not meeting his eyes but staring out at the Severn Sea which appeared so peaceful that day.

'No, my lord,' Waltheof said. 'But I've heard it's a most unpleasant, even painful, way to die.'

Now Odda did turn to look the priest in the eyes. 'Will you pray with me again? I fear Ubba was right, and the Danes have come to destroy us all, as they've done to Alfred. I fear...' His voice dropped to an even lower whisper. 'I fear that God has abandoned us.'

Waltheof stared at him and Odda saw, just for a moment before it was masked, disapproval.

'Of course,' the priest said, still boring into his soul with his eyes, or so it seemed. 'Praying is always helpful in situations like this, lord. But you, and Ubba, are much too quick to think Alfred defeated. Furthermore, if you're hoping to pray for some great miracle, such as when God destroyed Guthrum's fleet of longships off the coast of Polle, well, I think...' He trailed off, as if unwilling to speak his true mind.

'Go on,' Odda demanded, chastened. 'Say what you will, Waltheof. Be honest.'

'God helps those who help themselves, my lord. Have faith, Odda, in God, in Alfred, and, most importantly, in yourself.'

They gazed at one another for a long moment, and then Odda sighed.

'Let us pray, then,' Waltheof murmured, bowing his head and beginning, 'Trinity in unity, preserve me. Unity in Trinity, have mercy on me.'

Odda joined in, and together they petitioned God, Christ, and the archangels Michael and Gabriel to protect and guide them. When they finished, the ealdorman thanked Waltheof and, realising the day had almost gone, asked to be left alone that he might reflect on their plight.

By the time the men had eaten their pitifully small ration of food in the evening, Odda knew God had provided him with the way out of their dire situation.

'Cynesige! Glaedwine!' He called on the thanes, and the rest of his commanders, who came to him with looks of surprise and trepidation on their faces for Odda was strangely happy, and all wondered if the lack of food was already affecting his mind. When next he spoke, it must surely have served to confirm their fears. 'We attack the Danes,' he said, emotion making every word seem to thrum with power. 'Tonight! Prepare your men.'

'Tonight, lord?' Glaedwine asked. Even in the past couple of days his jowly face had grown noticeably slimmer, if not exactly gaunt.

'Tonight, before dawn,' Odda replied, eyes shining in the fading light. 'When the heathen dogs have finished feasting and drinking themselves into a stupor, we'll strike them from the darkness, with swords and spears that burn with the blinding fires of God's wrath!'

Waltheof smiled at that and crossed himself, making Odda believe this is what the priest had wanted all along. It was strange how men of God were so often the ones most ready and willing to fight.

'Are you sure about this, my lord?' Glaedwine asked quietly.

'Aye, I'm sure,' the ealdorman snapped. 'Would you rather die like a warrior, with a spear in your hand, slaughtering as many of those bastards down there on our beach as possible? Or wasting away up here, until your own body eats itself and you die the honourless, agonizing death of a coward?' He glared at the thanes and felt a righteous fury building within him. 'I know which I would prefer. We attack tonight, gentlemen. Go, and make ready.'

The men filtered away with varying degrees of enthusiasm, until only Glaedwine remained.

'This is madness,' he said. 'There must be another way to escape from this hill, my lord. The Danes fight with a savagery we cannot match. They have better weapons and armour. And Ubba… The man is a maniac!'

Odda felt a rush of anger at the old thane's craven attitude, but, as he looked at the greybeard, his rage turned to pity. Glaedwine had managed to survive into his sixth decade and wanted to enjoy his dotage. He had children and grandchildren, and much wealth. Much to live for. He did not want to die trying to defeat an invading army in the meagre light of one final sunrise.

'You can remain in the rearguard,' Odda told him levelly. 'If you get a chance to slip away into the trees, I won't hold it against you.'

Glaedwine flinched as if he'd been struck, and outrage vied with relief for mastery of his face. 'I am no coward,' he muttered with tears in his eyes. 'I'll be at your side, my lord. No matter what God sends our way.'

'Then go,' Odda said, nodding and clasping arms with the bald thane. 'I want to get this over with before I change my mind.'

—

Odda had managed to find three local men who'd grown up beside Cynwit Fort, and spent their lives hunting in the hills around Lintun. All three claimed they knew this particular hill in minute detail, and Odda hoped they were right for he'd chosen to go with them to search for enemy guards. His original plan had been to simply lead the entire fyrd down the slope and smash into the unsuspecting Danes, but hundreds of men would make a fair bit of noise, no matter how hard they tried to be stealthy. If the attack was to have any chance of succeeding, they would need to catch their foe as unprepared as possible.

So, the fyrd had come out from the fort and moved to the top of the hill while Odda and his three local men headed down the slope, moving slowly, taking advantage of the trees and undergrowth to remain hidden, hopefully, from enemy watchers.

'How many guards do you think they'll have around their perimeter?' Cynesige had asked, and it had been Waltheof, who replied.

'Probably not many. They're arrogant, and they believe us too frightened to come out from the fort's protection. Especially in the dark.'

'Besides,' Odda said with a confidence he did not really feel. 'We don't need to clear the entire perimeter, just a space wide enough for our army to pass through without the alarm being raised.'

'It won't work,' Glaedwine had protested, although without much vigour for it was obvious his protestations were beginning to get on everyone's nerves. 'But I'll come with you, if you like, my lord. I spent time in these lands as a youngster too. I might be of some use.'

Odda had smiled at that but refused the offer. The thane was too old, and, as Cynesige had pointed out, prompting some laughter, the moon might reflect from his bald head and warn the Danes of his approach. Even Glaedwine joined in with the mirth, and Odda was glad, for it lifted the mood somewhat.

Then he'd headed down the hill, ordering Cynesige to look out for his signal.

Now, trying not to walk into a tree or trip over briars, Odda was beginning to regret insisting he came with the Lintun locals, for he felt like a blind man as he tried to keep up with them. Their claims to know this hill were proving truthful, and they moved quickly and quietly down the slope despite being forced to hang back sometimes to let the ealdorman catch up. His foot slipped just a fraction on a loose patch of scree, and he felt a hand against his chest, before a warm breath whispered in his ear, 'Wait here, lord.'

Odda squinted into the darkness, just able to make out the shadowy shape of his warrior receding into the trees ahead. And then there was a thump, and a gasp, and then more thumps before the sound of footsteps and heavy breathing approached the ealdorman again.

'One down,' the scout reported in a low, excited tone. 'Let's move on.'

Odda nodded, then realised no one could see the gesture but his three companions were already moving to the left and he went after them, treading as lightly as he could while still keeping pace with them.

The sound of a melancholy tune being hummed came to them as they moved. It was not a melody Odda was familiar with, and he knew it must be one of the Danes, for who else would it be here on the hillside in the night? Again, his warrior came to him and whispered for him to wait, and, for a moment, the ealdorman thought about asking the man to kill his victim quieter, for the noises as the last Dane was slaughtered seemed to reverberate all around the trees. Before he could open his mouth, however, the chance was gone, and the shadowy form was away, followed this time by another of the local men.

The humming stopped, but this time there was a muffled cry of distress or alarm, before the clear sounds of a struggle. Harsh breaths, frightened whimpers, desperate grunts, and then Odda was running to help his men, with the third and final local at his back. By the time they came to the fight, it was over, and two bodies lay on the ground, wreathed in darkness.

'Bastard heard us coming,' Odda's scout reported. 'Killed the lad who'd come with me before I could take care of him.'

Odda cursed. He knew good men, good Saxons, would die this night, but it hit hard to lose one so damn early, before the main assault on the Northmen had even begun. 'We'll give him a proper Christian burial on the morrow,' he muttered. 'For now, we move back to the right and clear out any more of the enemy we find there. And then… We cleanse our lands of Ubba and his heathen taint for good.'

CHAPTER NINE

Ubba was fast asleep, having enjoyed a fair few drinks with his men the previous night. He did not take a turn on watch, for he was a jarl and did not think he needed to perform such menial tasks. He'd done his fair share of those things in years past but now, as leader of a thousand men, there were enough underlings to make sure the vast camp on the beach remained safe.

He was enjoying a pleasant dream, where he was walking in the sunshine upon some green, windswept hill bursting with spring flowers and birdsong.

With a start, he suddenly awoke, choking and gasping for air. This was not a new thing for Ubba, it happened often if he drank mead and then fell asleep on his back, but it terrified him every time. He glanced at the tent flaps, noting a pale light coming through and realised it must be near dawn.

The fear from his sudden, rude awakening, faded as it always did, and the memory of the pleasant dream returned. Perhaps it was the hills just outside his tent he'd been walking upon in that sleepy Otherworld. He stood up and rinsed the sourness from his mouth with some water from the skin beside his bedroll, stretching and rolling his neck from side to side. The air felt quite warm, and a pleasant spring breeze was coming through a gap in the tent's entrance.

Another day beckoned – drinking, eating, and enjoying songs and games with his men as they waited for Odda's Saxons to grow weak from lack of food and drink and, inevitably, surrender. Ubba knew that day was not far off, and he looked forward to making an example of the Saxon ealdorman.

He grinned, and rubbed a wet fingertip across his filed teeth, making sure they were clean. How to kill Odda had been on his mind ever since the siege started. He and his brothers, Halfdan and Ivar, had ended the lives of many Saxon noblemen over the years, often in amusing and entertaining ways. Ubba had finally decided he would torture Odda for a time before, eventually, ending his suffering by throwing him off his own hill onto the rocks far below. Ubba imagined the enemy commander flying through the air, every limb broken, screaming in pure terror as his doom rushed up to meet him.

Ubba was buckling on his sword belt, but he paused now, as it seemed his happy daydream had come to life when there was a sudden shriek from outside in the camp.

Had some of his men continued drinking throughout the night and started brawling amongst themselves? Perhaps. His brothers would not have allowed such a thing, and neither would Guthrum, but Ubba cared little for such heavy-handed discipline. If his warriors wanted to sink mead all night that was their business – they were mostly younger men after all, and without women to entertain them, why should they go to bed early?

There was another shriek now, and then shouts of alarm, and Ubba shoved his tent flaps aside, heading out into the pre-dawn air. He didn't mind his men getting into the odd fistfight, or even a duel that resulted in the deaths of one of two of them, but it was unusual for such a thing to happen so early. Normally that kind of combat happened at night, at the very height of the drinking, not—

Ubba gaped, wondering if he was still asleep. The hill from his dream was there before him, towering into the sky and bursting with elm, oak, and ash, but charging out of those gloom shrouded trees came a sea of armed men.

'Shieldwall!' the Dane roared, finally coming completely awake and understanding what was happening. 'We're under attack! Shieldwall!'

He was not the only one calling for the men to be up and alert; dozens of voices were clamouring for weapons to be grabbed, shields to be joined in a defensive line. The trouble was, throwing spears had already been launched by the charging Saxons. There was no single, co-ordinated missile attack – the iron headed spears had been let fly as soon as their bearers were within range, and now they were thumping down into the sandy beach, and – far more alarmingly – into the densely packed bodies of Ubba's men.

Screams mingled with shouts of alarm, and now the Saxons were bellowing war cries, exhorting their nailed God to bring them victory and sweep the invaders back into the sea that had spat them out.

'My lord, we're under attack!' Orvar, Ubba's second-in-command came rushing towards him, and the jarl shook his head in disbelief.

'By Óðinn's hairy arse, I can see that,' he retorted. 'Get the men into formation.' Ubba had lifted his own massive spear from where he'd left it beside his tent, and he hefted his shield as well now. 'The Saxons must be half-starved, and exhausted from their charge down the hill. They won't keep up the attack for long.'

Orvar nodded hopefully but, as he turned, shouting at the nearest men to form up, a short spear lanced down from the sky, punching through the hersir's left foot and pinning it to the sand. He let out a terrible, high-pitched screech of purest agony and dropped to his knees, staring at the bloody wound. The sand was not dense enough to hold the weapon in place and Ubba strode across to Orvar, reached down and yanked the spear out of his foot. It came free easily, but tore an even bigger hole in the flesh. The hersir screamed again, sobbing as he grabbed his mangled foot in his hands.

Ubba shook his head and walked on, taking up a place beside his men who had now managed to form a line of interlocked shields. There was nothing else he could do for Orvar, the man would have to bandage his own foot and make the best of it until the Saxons were defeated.

'Ready, lads?' the jarl called, holding up his shield and spear. 'Brace!'

The enemy charge did not slow and Ubba was taken aback by their ferocity as they slammed into the line of Danes. It seemed being starved and deprived of fresh drinking water for days had engendered a savagery within Odda's men that had not previously been there. But Ubba could not take too long to ponder all this, for he was forced to defend himself, only narrowly dodging to the side as an axe came down where his shoulder had been.

The sun had not yet risen above the great hill the Saxons had poured down from, but it was light enough for Ubba to make out what was happening. He was amazed, and momentarily terrified, to notice that his men now seemed to be outnumbered by their foes. How could that be the case? Had the surprise attack been so successful? The jarl knocked an oncoming spear upwards, thrust his own into his opponent's chest. In the moment of respite before another Saxon took the dead one's place, Ubba stepped back a few paces, trying to look along his line and more accurately gauge the numbers left on both sides.

At the far, western end of his shieldwall, Odda's warriors were visible and Ubba gaped, knowing that meant the Saxons were close to encircling them. Yet what could he do about it? He did not have anyone in reserve to shore up the flanks for the surprise attack had left him with no time to prepare for such things. It was a simple clash of two shieldwalls, and, unfortunately for the Danes, their superior numbers had been catastrophically thinned out by the early missile storm.

As he stood trying to catch his breath, he noticed some of his own men running towards the sea, where their longboats remained drawn up on the beach.

'Get back here you cowards!' Ubba croaked. 'Come back, or I'll kill you myself!'

'Fuck you, Ubba!' one of the retreating warriors called over his shoulder. 'You've led us to defeat. Fight the Saxons yourself.'

'We should have known following you was a mistake,' another shouted as he sprinted off, although Ubba had the bleak satisfaction of seeing a stone from one of Odda's slingers cracking the man's skull open, sending him sprawling lifeless onto the sand.

The other flank was overrun now as well, and more of the Danes were moving back towards the longships, completely ignoring Ubba's commands to stay and fight. He watched impotently as a group of a dozen or so simply turned and ran, dropping their spears and shields that they might move faster. They never even slowed when they came to Orvar, the hersir being trampled, his weak shouts of protest quickly silenced as the rest of Ubba's line broke and ran, their feet pounding like smiths' hammers across the beach.

Cheers of triumph went up from the West Saxons and another shower of spears filled the sky before careening down into the backs of the unsuspecting Northmen. It was total carnage, but Odda was not finished. Ubba could see the ealdorman now, right in the centre of his shieldwall, ordering his fyrd to advance, and kill as many of the stricken enemy as possible.

Ubba was alone, standing by himself in the centre of the beach as yet another rain of spears, arrows, and slingshot came down on the heads and backs of his Danes. Bodies littered the ground, many of them not dead but horribly injured, their limbs broken, eyes put out, holes torn through their chests... Or mangled beyond recognition like Orvar had been by the thumping, grinding feet of his own comrades.

Somehow – miraculously – Ubba had not been struck by any of those deadly projectiles. In fact, he did not have a scratch on him as he stood there alone, Saxon warriors hurrying past him as if he wasn't even there in their desperation to cut down fleeing Danes.

He was not invisible however, and he had been noticed.

'Ubba! What was it you said to me before?'

The jarl turned to the man addressing him. It was Odda. His hearth-warriors had remained with him while the rest of his troops pursued the enemy to their vessels, and the group of around two dozen well-armed warriors came directly for Ubba now, eyes unblinking, spears bristling. He noticed with horror that his own fabled Raven banner, a legendary symbol of his family's ferocity and strength, had been captured and was being carried along the beach by triumphant West Saxon soldiers.

'"The Danes have come." That's what you said,' Odda cried out, imitating Ubba's accent. '"And I, Ubba, last son of Ragnar, shall see you and your Alfred dead, while a new Wessex rises from the ashes of his funeral pyre!"'

Ubba's breath caught in his throat, and he thought he might vomit, but the moment passed, and his mind spun as he wondered what he should do. His legs wanted to run, to follow his men, to feel the sway and roll of a longship beneath them as he sailed away, to safety, and another day alive in Midgard.

His head knew that was not possible now. He would never make it to the sea. Yet giving up his spear would not save his life, he was certain of that. Indeed, the Saxon ealdorman would likely do to Ubba as he had wanted to do to the Saxon: torture and kill him in some terrible fashion.

'Look around you,' Odda commanded, eyes glittering triumphantly. 'Alfred is not destroyed, Ubba, and neither is Wessex. But you, and Ragnar, and your brothers, and all your warriors, are! So much for the Danes.'

The Saxon and his *hearthweru* were almost upon Ubba now and he bared his teeth, showing the shocking red grooves to his enemies before he broke into a run directly towards them. 'For Óðinn!' he cried, stunned by the beauty of the sun finally cresting the hill behind his enemies, and he knew he would like to settle on that hill one day, to raise a family and drink mead as he looked out at the whale road and told his grandchildren of his exploits as a young *vikingr*, fighting beside his famous brothers Ivar and Halfdan.

He thrust his spear at Odda, but the tip became lodged in the ealdorman's shield, and then he felt his filed front teeth shattered by the rim of that shield as he stumbled forwards, Something pierced him in the side, breaking ribs and knocking the breath from him, and he collapsed onto one knee, blood spraying from his ruined mouth, seeing Odda glaring down at him in triumph.

And then he saw no more.

The Battle of Cynuit was over.

PART TWO

CHAPTER TEN

AD 878, Athelney

Easter

'As Christ rose on this day, so we consecrate this new stronghold within the marshes of Athelney. May our great and noble king, Alfred, rise from this place, to go out once more into the land of the living, as Christ did, to bring peace once more to the people of Wessex.'

Oswald, the priest who'd been part of Alfred's household since his days as a young aetheling, raised his hands to heaven, and the congregation within the newly completed fortress solemnly intoned, 'Amen.'

It was a strange Mass, being celebrated not within a dedicated church, but within the main hall of Alfred's new stronghold. There had not been time to construct extra buildings, just this hall and a storehouse for food and drink supplies. It would be enough. Besides, Oswald was used to saying Mass even outside, before or after battles – at least here they were indoors and able to keep dry, despite the rain which fell on the marshes.

'That was a fine service, brother,' Alfred said to the priest as the celebrants – his wife, children, hearth-warriors, and some of the builders – helped themselves to the meat and ale for the Easter feast. 'Inspirational.'

Oswald smiled, round face crinkling as he bowed his tonsured head. 'I do my best, lord,' he said. 'But my task is made easier by the fact that I completely believe in what I was saying. It's more than blind faith that makes me think you'll retake your throne from Guthrum.'

Alfred watched as Ealhswith, ever the dutiful hostess, made sure everyone there had enough to eat and drink before she sat down beside their children – Aethelflaed, Edward, Aethelgifu, and baby Aelfthryth – to enjoy her own portion. 'I hope you're right,' the king said to Oswald.

'I do too, but I'm sure you've learned a great deal since the great heathen army first came to our lands.'

'You mean I won't be as trusting as I was back then?' Alfred asked with a sardonic smile.

Oswald was not the type to hide even when his words might have been taken by a king as criticism. He shrugged. 'Were you too trusting, or simply inexperienced? Whichever it was, I knew you then, and I know you now, Alfred. You understand better how to deal with Guthrum and his Danes these days, while still remaining true to your Christian faith. I'm quite sure of it.'

Alfred nodded, glad he could count on Oswald's support and honest advice. In his own way the priest was as strong an ally and as good a friend as Wulfric. A man needed moral and spiritual as well as military guidance at times, after all. And the clergyman's appraisal was true; Alfred had indeed been somewhat too trusting, even until recent months. He had not really believed his own ealdormen would throw their lot in with the enemy, yet the likes of Wulfhere and Wealdmar had done just that, betraying Alfred, their sworn liege lord. The worst was Diuma – it still hurt the king to think of his friend's betrayal. And they *had* been friends, so, when the thane turned Alfred and Ealhswith and the rest of them away from the gates of Brycgstow the night they'd fled from Cippanhamme it had been utterly devastating.

Cups of ale were handed to them by the warriors on the next bench over and Alfred sipped his gratefully. It was still chilly, especially within the damp marshes, and anything – be that a blazing firepit, or a cup of ale – that might help stave off the chill was welcome.

'I will not make the same mistakes I made before,' he told the priest grimly. 'I will not allow Guthrum to swear false oaths or take prisoners who he'll simply murder as he did at Werham. When I defeat him this time, if he isn't killed in the fighting, I'll deal with him much more harshly. I will neuter him, and his army, so there's no repeat of their success at Cippanhamme.' He took another pull of ale and smiled at his wife who was listening to the carpenter explaining how they'd constructed such a sturdy fortress despite the sodden ground. 'I will also,' the king said, turning his attention back to Oswald, 'not be so trusting of my ealdormen's loyalty in future, as depressing as that statement may be. I really should have seen their betrayal coming, especially with the likes of Archbishop Ethelred's attempts to… defy me, over the years.'

Oswald pursed his lips, thinking of the letter Pope John VIII had sent to Alfred, admonishing the king for his 'fornication' and telling him off for impinging on Cantwareburh's dignity. That had been in response to a complaint Archbishop Ethelred had sent to the pope – such a complaint showed very well where the archbishop's loyalties lay, and made it quite clear he did not have much time for Alfred. It was possible, perhaps even likely, that the archbishop had supported Guthrum's takeover of Wessex, hoping a new, Christian puppet king would take Alfred's place and look more favourably on Cantwareburh.

'Well, in future you will have a better idea of who you can rely on, lord,' noted Oswald. 'Look to the likes of Ealdorman Aethelnoth, who's shown you loyalty and succour these past few weeks, while being more careful about others less eager to aid you…'

'Indeed,' Alfred nodded. 'Now, I must go for a piss. You enjoy the feast, my friend, I'll be back shortly.'

As he went outside, waving to the pair of guards who were stationed at the main door, Alfred was suddenly reminded of the terrible stomach complaint he'd suffered for years – since the day of his wedding to Ealhswith in fact, although he did not blame her in any way for it. Some days the king thought it was a punishment from God for his pursuit of carnal delights, on other days he believed it was simply a reaction to stress and guilt. The ailment usually disappeared when he was off on campaign, fighting the Danes; the focus on a deadly enemy, and lack of rich, abundant food and drink, seemed to agree with his body. His weeks in Athelney had mirrored life campaigning with the fyrd and he'd not felt this strong, this driven, for a while.

He came to the fenced off section of the small island which had been set aside as a cesspit for the fortress and undid the laces of his trousers. Easter was always a time he enjoyed, and now, even living this life in exile, Alfred could feel the closeness of God on the day His only son was reborn.

Alfred's feelings of pleasure evaporated faster than the steam from his urine however, as he noticed flames to the west. Squinting into the drizzle, he knew he was seeing one of his lookouts on top of Barrow Hill. The man waving the burning brand was clearly signalling to the new fortress.

Something important was happening – or had already happened.

Fastening his trousers, Alfred ran back to the hall, only slowing as he went through the doors, for he did not want to alarm Ealhswith or the children. His eyes sought out Wulfric, and two of his other hearth-warriors and he discreetly beckoned for all three to follow him outside.

'What's wrong, my lord?' Wulfric asked once they were all outside.

'Is that someone signalling?' another, softer voice asked, and Alfred turned to see Ealhswith standing beside them, gazing westwards.

'Yes,' the king replied.

'Is it trouble?'

'No, no. If it was, he'd have lit the main fire. It's probably just some interesting local news. I'll head over there with Wulfric and find out.'

'I want to come, too.'

Alfred looked round again, this time seeing his eldest child, Aethelflaed looking up at him coolly.

'Well, you did say there was no danger,' Ealhswith said, brows arched.

Alfred shook his head and gave a small smile. 'All right. Let's go then.' He reached out and drew his wife against him, kissing her gently on the lips. 'We'll be back soon.'

'Shall I get my seax?' Aethelflaed asked. 'Yes, I might need it. Wait for me, father.' She darted back into the hall, calling over her shoulder, 'Make sure he waits, Wulfric, or you'll be in trouble!'

The ealdorman grinned. 'We'll go ahead and get one of the punts ready,' he said, waving the pair of hearth-warriors after him as he made his way down to the water where some of the little rowboats were tethered.

Soon, all five of them, including the princess with her trusty, deadly sharp seax, were floating across the water. Reeds parted easily before them and Aethelflaed stared down into the waters.

'Don't look there for too long,' Alfred cautioned. 'Sometimes the faces of the dead appear in the water, making living folk like us go into a trance and fall in.'

None of the men were surprised when the girl grasped the handle of the seax and curled her lip disdainfully. 'They'll be sorry if they make me fall in,' she said, and even Wulfric laughed. Although Aethelflaed had only seen seven summers her take-no-prisoners attitude was well known on Athelney. 'I've heard that story before though,' she told them. 'It was about a silly boy who sees the faces and has nightmares about them. He takes his lady love to see them, and they both jump into the pool and drown.' The story seemed to unsettle the men in the boat much more than it did the scornful princess and the journey continued in silence.

It wasn't long before the punt rode up onto the Barrow Hill and everyone got out, perhaps a little disappointed that no faces had appeared to taunt them in the stagnant marsh.

'Maybe the rain affects their ability to appear,' Aethelflaed suggested, looking back at the rippling waters. 'It should be smooth for faces to form, don't you think, Wulfric?'

The ealdorman frowned. He did not let his imagination run free very often, and obviously found himself at a loss then. He shrugged and nodded, grunting, 'Aye, probably,' which seemed to satisfy the little girl and they trudged up the slope to meet the lookout who was coming down towards them.

'What's the word, Dunstan?' asked Alfred, recognising the stocky soldier. 'Why the lit brands? Please tell me it's good news!'

Dunstan nodded, and the huge smile on his face was encouraging. 'It is, lord,' he said. 'Best news we've had in a long time.'

'How did you hear it, all the way up here?' Wulfric asked, eyebrow raised.

Dunstan looked at him and his face reddened. 'Er, a traveller went by,' he said, but Alfred could tell the lookout was lying. It was undoubtedly a woman from one of the surrounding villages who'd visited. Not that the king could blame Dunstan, for it must be cold and lonely out here without company or anything to do but watch the horizon for signs of Danes. He'd be tempted to entertain a willing lass too.

'What did this 'traveller' tell you?' Alfred said, smiling sardonically and sharing a knowing look with Wulfric.

'She, er, he,' Dunstan replied, drawing a bark of laughter from Wulfric, and a further reddening of the poor lookout's features as he forged on. 'Told me that word has come of a great battle in Defenascir.'

The mirth evaporated like the morning mist as the sun came up and burned it away.

'Defenascir?' Alfred demanded. 'Ealdorman Odda? Who would attack him away out there in the west?' He was frowning thoughtfully, but then he remembered the reports from the Wealas, of Jarl Ubba's brutal exploits in Dyfed during recent weeks.

'Danes,' said Dunstan, confirming his thoughts. 'Led by Ragnar's son, Ubba.'

Alfred's heart sank for a moment, for Ubba, although not as wise, or as formidable as his father or brothers had been, was a dangerous opponent, and his army was not small. The rumours of what they'd been doing to the unfortunate Wealas had been mentioned often by the king and his hearth-warriors lately. Still, for all they felt sympathy for those folk, it was good to know Ubba and his *vikingar* were no longer in Wessex.

It seemed that had changed, and the hated jarl had returned to torment them once more.

'Well?' Wulfric growled. 'What happened, Dunstan? Get on with it, man!'

'Odda beat the bastards!' the lookout replied cheerily. 'Charged down at dawn from the old hillfort they'd been camped in and surprised the Danes. Stole the raven banner that Ubba always claimed had magic powers, and then Odda himself killed the whoreson.'

Alfred and the others gaped at him, digesting this incredible information, and then the king nodded. 'It's a sign,' he said. 'To come at Easter like this, it has to be.'

'You could be right, lord,' smiled Dunstan. 'For Ubba had been looking to march through Defenascir so he and Guthrum could attack us here in Athelney. Odda has removed that threat, from the west at least.'

Alfred laughed and reached out, embracing the astonished Dunstan. 'This is fantastic news,' he said. 'Miraculous! Almost as much of a miracle as God sinking Guthrum's fleet last year, and just as welcome.' He stepped back, eyes shining with the glory of his God and the possibilities for the coming months now that he knew the Northmen had suffered another terrible setback. 'This gives us a significantly better chance of retaking Wessex!'

Even Wulfric seemed struck by the symbolism of the heathen horde being devastated at this time, especially after Oswald had prayed for Alfred's rising just as Christ had done on this very day over eight hundred years before. 'We should strike the Danes, Alfred,' the ealdorman advised. 'Call more men to us. Use them to mount even more attacks on Guthrum's warbands searching Athelney.'

'Yes!' Alfred cried. 'Yes, Wulfric. Let's take the fight to them now. And make sure to send our thanks to Odda, with promises of a reward for killing that rat, Ubba. Come on, let's get back to the fortress and celebrate this properly.' He turned again to Dunstan, almost apologetically. 'You see out the rest of your watch, my friend, and join us as soon as you're done. I'll have an ale waiting for you.'

The lookout bowed happily, grinned at the others, then walked back up to the top of the hill to make sure no more Danes crept up on Alfred's stronghold within the marshes.

Wulfric was already leading the way to the punt that would take them back to the Easter feast. That celebration promised to become legendary now that the exiles of Athelney had something more to make merry about.

They got into the little boat and pushed off, two of the men dipping their paddles into the waters and guiding them back to the island that housed Alfred's little fortress.

'I want to fight Guthrum too.'

The men looked at Aethelflaed and smiled.

'Maybe one day, my lady,' said Wulfric. 'But war is no place for a young princess. A battlefield is for hardy warriors.'

'Like you?' the girl asked sweetly.

'Aye,' Wulfric nodded.

'Pfft,' Aethelflaed replied. 'You were terrified of falling into the water here and being taken by ghosts not half an hour ago.'

When the punt finally bumped once more against dry land the men's laughter still hadn't abated and Alfred, grinning, put his arm proudly around the little girl as they climbed the slope up to the brand-new stronghold and its protective walls.

If only all my people were as brave as Aethelflaed, thought the king. *The Danes would already have been defeated*. And then a powerful feeling of guilt struck him as they went through the heavy doors and into the smoky hall that housed Ealhswith and the rest of his hearth-warriors.

Alfred's people *were* brave. Braver than those in Northumbria, East Anglia, or Mercia, who had all capitulated to the Danes years ago. Only the West Saxons continued to resist and, come the summer, hopefully they would defeat Guthrum's sea-wolves in one final, legendary battle, placing Alfred back in his rightful place as King of Wessex.

CHAPTER ELEVEN

The mead hall was full in Cippanhamme that night, as it had been since Guthrum and his men seized control of the town. A skald had told a fine tale, not about one of the gods for a change, but a simpler story telling of the death of the world-tree, Yggdrasill. Guthrum found it depressing, no doubt in part because of the way things were going for him in Wessex. Ubba's defeat, and the loss of all those men... It was the talk of the countryside, and a disaster for the Danes.

Yes, they had easily taken Cippanhamme, secured the 'loyalty' of some powerful West Saxon ealdormen, and chased Alfred into the boggy marshes of Athelney, but things had not been progressing as well as expected in recent weeks.

'We should burn one of the nearby villages to the ground,' said the king's advisor, Floki. Despite the heat in the hall from the firepit and the closely packed men and women, Floki's rich blue cloak was as immaculate as ever, as were his hair and beard. His rough words belied his neat appearance, though. 'Kill everyone, apart from the good-looking women of course, and turn the whole place to ash and bone.'

'What for?' Guthrum asked, genuinely puzzled. He was, of course, used to the casual brutality of his warriors – that's what made them so good at their jobs after all – but the hersir's suggestion seemed quite senseless.

'Teach the Saxons a lesson,' Floki replied, staring at a pair of local musicians playing a jaunty tune on flute and lyre. Some of the Danes were making slave women dance to the music but it was not a particularly entertaining scene. Certainly not a happy one.

They'd been in Cippanhamme too long for most of the men.

'A lesson?' Guthrum sipped his mead, frowning. 'Wessex is ours now, Floki. Mine. I am as good as king here, now that Alfred has run off. Burning a village would only be weakening my own position.'

Floki glanced at him uncertainly. 'Tell the Saxons that,' he murmured. 'Not all of them have accepted us as their overlords. And they never will, until we break their spirit. Destroying a few villages will send out the right message and make them less likely to stand against us.'

It was all Alfred's fault, Guthrum thought sourly, not even tasting his mead much less enjoying its sweetness. If they'd managed to kill the Christian king during the attack on Cippanhamme everything would have worked out nicely. As it was, Alfred's survival meant the people of Wessex still saw him as a symbol of their resistance to the invaders. Alfred, the man who'd killed mighty Bagsecg – and many others – in single combat, still alive and thumbing his nose at the Danes.

Burning a village would merely make the Saxons hate Guthrum even more, and search for ways to support their exiled monarch.

'You know they've apparently built a fortress in the marshes?' Floki asked as the musicians moved on to another, even more dreary song. 'Had you heard that, lord?' The hersir laughed mockingly. 'A fortress. I can imagine it, a little flimsy hovel surrounded by stinking, stagnant waters, perpetually foggy and damp, while Alfred pretends to be Lord of the Bog.'

Guthrum did not share his subordinate's humour. '*Ja*, I've heard about his new stronghold. I do not think it funny, though. It's been hard enough trying to catch the bastards out there in the mist, running away and hiding whenever we send a warband after them. They've been able to strike at our patrols when they wanted to, and even attacked some of our camps. And now

Alfred has a fortress! If we do manage to find it, it will be as good as impregnable. Unless you want to try attacking it from the hull of a rowboat, Floki?'

The hersir did not reply, and that was reply enough. At last, scowling, he waved a hand towards the slaves dancing lethargically. 'Well, if Alfred is content to hide in his watery fortress, let him,' he said. 'While he's there, doing nothing to protect his people, we should do what we came to Wessex for in the first place: raid.'

Guthrum had thought about that for weeks. 'Perhaps you're right, Floki,' he conceded. 'I do not know, but I will think on it.' He emptied his mead horn then spat a disgusted oath. 'I do not want to turn the Saxons against us any more than they already are, but raiding would be more enjoyable than sitting here watching bored, beaten slave-women pretending to dance.' He stood up and bellowed at the musicians. 'Hey, you! Stop playing that slow, miserable shit! I want something fast, something to get my blood pumping. Something that'll make those women shake their big tits in my face!'

The warriors packing the hall laughed and cheered. The slaves did not. The musicians glanced at one another, fear plainly written on their faces – they wouldn't be the first entertainers to die in this mead hall because their talents weren't appreciated by the Danes.

'Think of something quickly,' Guthrum commanded, then turned to his skald. 'First, though – you can tell us a tale to stir the blood. Make it good!'

The skald blanched and sat motionless for a moment, thinking desperately for a story the king and his men would appreciate. At last, as Guthrum's patience was about to wear through, the skald jumped nimbly to his feet and spread his arms with a flourish. His unruly long hair and braided beard flew out as he twirled around, meeting the eyes of his audience.

'My lord,' he said in a rich baritone that easily cut through the smoky atmosphere in the mead hall. 'Proud warriors! Hearken to me, and I will tell you the tale of Hrapp the Black!'

Some of the men cheered, having heard this story or a variation of it in the past. Others, who were not familiar with the tale, nodded expectantly. Guthrum settled back into his chair and gestured irritably for a slave to bring him more mead.

'Hrapp the Black gained his name because of his vicious temper,' the skald began, making sure every other voice in the hall was silent before he went on. 'The man was a giant, and a brute, who lived for most of his life in a town in the far north. Eventually, a great many of the people there – victims of his violence – were demanding compensation and so, to avoid paying, Hrapp took his long-suffering wife and moved to a small village named Laxardale in the south, where he built a farm and continued his brutal ways.'

The men in the hall muttered darkly at this, for they were warriors, not mere farmers, and they, so they proclaimed to one another, would have quickly ended Hrapp's violence with an axe to the head. The skald nodded as if he believed the men's boasts, and went on with the story.

'Eventually, Hrapp the Black died of old age, and everyone in the village was happy. But he had given his wife instructions that he should be buried beside his farm, *standing up*, so that he could keep watch over the place even in death. So terrified was the poor woman that she did as Hrapp decreed, and he was buried upright.'

Such unusual funerary arrangements set the audience frowning and making signs against evil, for surely no good could come of it.

'Soon enough, several of the slaves on Hrapp's farm died mysteriously,' the skald said. 'And then villagers – hale and hearty young folk in some cases – dropped dead with no obvious cause. At last, the chieftain, Hoskuld, intervened and commanded Hrapp's body be dug up and reburied elsewhere, in the normal fashion. After that the strange deaths stopped.'

The skald paused and took a sip of ale from a cup beside him, swirling it around in his mouth and rolling his head as if his neck muscles ached. While this went on the men waited impatiently to hear the rest of his story, and Guthrum was just about to order the skald to get on with it when the skald put down his cup and began to speak again.

'Hrapp's son moved into the farm, but just weeks later the young man went mad and killed himself. No one from the village wanted to live in such an ill-favoured place after that, so a buyer was found from a nearby settlement, a man named Thorstein. This man packed his belongings into a boat along with his wife and two adult sons and they set out along the whale road to make the journey to Hrapp's farm. On the way there, however, a storm blew up and Thorstein's old wife was thrown overboard, drowning in the churning waters. This was no normal squall, though.' The skald paused, shaking his head, eyes wide in fear as he gazed around at the rapt listeners. 'Some vast, dark shape could be seen in the sea spray, guiding the wind to ever greater heights. On board the boat, Thorstein and his sons took out their spears and thrust them at the monster, but the thing could never be injured and, at last, both of Thorstein's sons were plunged into the water, and then the ship broke apart as if struck by some great, dark hand. Thorstein was carried to shore by the waves, where he managed to tell his story to the people there, before he, too, died.'

Talk of mysterious monsters made the warriors in the hall nervous, and more than a few, including Guthrum, cast anxious glances at the doors, as if Grendel himself might burst through and start tearing limbs from screaming men at any moment.

'Hrapp's ghost!' the skald barked, making Guthrum jump in momentary fright. He wasn't the only one, and the men laughed self-consciously at one another. 'Everyone in Laxardale knew it had been Hrapp's vindictive and vengeful ghost that had drowned Thorstein's family. After that, none would live in the cursed farm and it became derelict, lying empty for many years.'

The audience nodded, vowing that none of them would live in such an ill-omened place.

'Yet that farm had good land, with rich pastures, seal hunting, and salmon fishing nearby,' the skald continued. 'Over time, people began to think it a waste not to use such a place.' He smiled knowingly as his listeners reacted angrily to that. 'I agree,' he said to one man who was loudly decrying anyone who would take over a haunted place to live in. 'But some men do not fear ghosts. One such man was Olaf the Peacock. He needed a place for his family to live, and Hrapp's farm was lying unused, so Olaf took it over and lived there in peace for a time.'

The skald stopped to take another drink of mead, allowing the warriors around him to mutter amongst themselves about what misfortune might overcome unsuspecting Olaf the Peacock, who must indeed be as arrogant as his name suggested.

'Such peace could not last long at Hrappstead,' the storyteller went on soon enough, mouth and vocal cords suitably moistened. 'One day a cowherd came running to Olaf, saying to him, "The byre is haunted. Hrapp the Black's shade is in there, and I'm not doing another day's work for you until you deal with it!" Olaf was not afraid,' the skald recounted. 'He told the cowherd to calm down and stop acting like a baby. They would go together to the byre and see what was happening. At first the cowherd refused, but Olaf lifted his spear and told the terrified man that he would protect him from Hrapp's ghost.'

'You can't kill a ghost with a spear,' someone slurred from the centre of the hall.

'*Ja!*' Guthrum shouted. 'You cannot kill something that is already dead.'

The skald grinned. 'Maybe not, lord, but brave men will face anything when armed with a weapon.'

Guthrum took that in, wondering if he was being insulted, but then he shrugged and muttered agreement. Even he would face certain death stoically enough if he had his axe in hand.

'Olaf and the cowherd went to the byre, but the cowherd refused to go any further, even when Olaf commanded him.

Instead, the man was so frightened he ran off, leaving Olaf alone. When he went into the byre it was dark, and the door slammed shut behind him, making it even darker. And then…'

This pause was met by silence, as every eye in the hall was trained upon the skald. None of the warriors even raised a cup to their lips as they waited to hear what happened next.

'A giant man appeared in the byre, battle-scarred and heavy with the stench of the grave,' said the skald, eyes wide and gesturing expansively with his hands, as if he were beset by an invisible foe. 'The wraith of Hrapp the Black! It attacked Olaf, who tried to fend off the dead man's crushing blows, but it was a hard fight. Olaf thrust his spear at Hrapp but the ghost caught it and snapped the shaft in two while kicking out at Olaf with a massive, rotting foot. When Olaf came forwards once more with what remained of his spear, Hrapp's dark shade disappeared into the air like steam rising from a cauldron of stew.'

'Olaf won?' Guthrum demanded. 'He banished the ghost?'

The skald raised his hands, palms upwards, lips pursed. 'The next morning, Olaf went to the village chief, Hoskuld, and they journeyed together to the place where Hrapp the Black had been reburied. They dug up the body and found it as fresh as if it had only been put in the ground an hour before.'

His audience shuddered, fearing the dead far more than they did the living.

'Even more shocking,' the skald said, 'was the broken spearhead they found in the grave next to Hrapp's corpse. It was Olaf's spear – the one that had been broken during the fight in the barn the day before.'

The listeners murmured darkly at that and Guthrum glanced sidelong at Floki. They shared an anxious look, thoroughly invested in the tale which was not quite finished yet.

'Olaf and Hoskuld burned Hrapp's body on a massive blazing pyre. Then they took the ashes out to sea and tossed them overboard, into the water where Ran's daughters claimed them.' He leaned back, gazing into the smoky rafters high above, and let out a long sigh as though he'd been the one who'd gone through the tribulations Olaf had faced in the tale. 'After that,' he said, 'there were no more strange deaths in Laxardale, and Hrapp the Black was never seen again, dead or alive.'

The men, understanding the story was at an end, thumped their cups and mugs on the benches, showing their appreciation. Guthrum did not join in. It had been, in his opinion, an adequate tale, no more, but as he thought about Olaf and the man's courage in the face of his doom, Guthrum realised there was a message for him in the skald's story.

'What, lord?' Floki asked. 'Did you say something?'

'I was talking to myself,' Guthrum replied, and a grim smile was pulling at the edges of his mouth as he turned to address the hersir. 'The Norns have entwined Alfred's fate with mine, and, as the skald's tale shows, fortune favours those who strike even when common sense counsels against it.'

Floki peered at him drunkenly, clearly unable to fathom the meaning behind his king's words.

'We will do as Olaf did,' Guthrum said, clenching his fist. 'And strike at the ghost that haunts Athelney.'

Now Floki understood, and laughed. 'We will destroy him with our spears,' he vowed. 'And scatter his ashes, and the ashes of his family, and of his new fortress, all across the whale road.'

Guthrum was nodding, gazing into the firepit as if he could see it all playing out gloriously within the dancing flames. 'Ja,' he breathed. 'And then there will be no one to stand in my way, Floki, and finally... finally! Wessex will be ours.'

CHAPTER TWELVE

Alfred's hit-and-run tactics stepped up after Easter as he grew more secure in his new fortress, and more men pledged themselves to his cause with each passing day. Everyone in Wessex now knew that the king was still alive, had not deserted them, and was fighting for his throne. Of course, the presence of Guthrum's army around Cippanhamme still deterred many West Saxons from choosing a side, but Alfred and his followers on Athelney were pleased with how things were progressing.

Soon, Alfred promised, they would strike out from the marshes of Sumorsaete and show the heathen invaders the wrath of God.

Until that day came, Alfred's commanders, including Wulfric, continued to lead night-time raids on enemy patrols that were hunting for the exiled Saxon king. Striking hard and fast, with terrible brutality, before escaping into the darkness without taking any casualties was wearing down the Northmen. Alfred had heard it himself from the mouths of the sea-wolves as they trudged through the damp and misty woods around Athelney, trying desperately to locate him and put an end to the resistance once and for all.

The only thing ended on those occasions were the lives of the Danes, hacked apart in ambushes and left for animals to feast upon. No afterlife in Valhöll for those slaughtered search parties, Alfred prayed.

Spring blossomed, bringing birdsong, blooming flowers, and welcome warmth after a winter where the king and his companions sometimes felt like they might freeze to death. The marshes around the new fortress did not seem to abate at all, though, which Alfred had worried might be the case. Despite the heat and dryer weather the lands surrounding Athelney remained almost as hard to move around in as it had been in winter, and the punts used to ferry people and supplies to and from the little island saw as much use as ever.

'Where are we off to today, lord?'

Wulfric smiled and nodded at Dunstan. 'I'm glad to see your enthusiasm for killing Danes has not faded,' said the ealdorman appreciatively. 'That's the attitude we need if we're to win this war.'

'Agreed,' put in Alfred who'd just come out into the morning sunshine to greet his hearth-warriors before they went about their day's work. Their numbers had swelled since the fortress was completed, and around fifty men were on the island that morning. 'Thank you, Dunstan, and all of you, for your loyalty.'

It was not unusual for the king to praise his men in this way – he knew how important it was to show how much he valued them.

'It's not just loyalty, my lord,' Dunstan replied with a grim smile. 'We genuinely love slaughtering Northmen.'

That brought cheers and laughter and it was a happy group that Alfred looked upon; strange, perhaps, given their circumstances, but very welcome. If he'd been forced to spend winter with a group of sour-faced, subordinate soldiers, things would have been unbearable.

'Anyway,' the king said cheerfully. 'Loyalty, a simple thirst for enemy blood, or whatever drives you on, you should find plenty to enjoy this day, for our scouts brought word yesterday evening that another group of Danes is camped nearby.'

The hearth-warriors murmured amongst themselves.

'How many, lord?' Aedan asked, scratching his short beard. Although he appeared apprehensive, Alfred knew the wiry swordsman was a veteran of many battles and had even lost two of his fingers fighting the enemy at Readingum. Any fear he might have felt was for the king and his family, rather than his own skin.

'Thirty or so,' Alfred replied.

'Nothing we can't handle,' Wulfric put in firmly. 'We know where they're camped, but they don't know where we are. So we'll march out to find them this morning and, if possible, launch a surprise attack. If that's not an option, we'll leave it until night falls and do as we've done before – with fire arrows and throwing spears.'

Suddenly a small voice piped up from the side of the fortress, where the sun was rising. 'Barrow Hill is burning.'

Alfred spun to look where his daughter was pointing. Sure enough, the lookout position on the nearby hill was aflame. It was not a single man waving burning brands this time however, for the main signal fire had been lit.

'This isn't good,' Wulfric growled to Alfred.

'No, it's not,' the king agreed, gesturing at Aethelflaed to give up sunning herself and head into the fortress before turning his attention to the hearth-warriors. 'Get to the walls, men. Make sure you're armed and ready for the worst, all right?'

With words of assent and hasty salutes the warriors ran to take up their positions, marshalled by those of higher rank such as Dunstan.

Alfred and Wulfric hurried towards the gatehouse, calling up to the guards there, asking if they knew what was happening.

'No, lord,' a man stationed there shouted down. 'The signal fire was only just lit. But we can see the lookout coming here in his punt now. We'll get his report soon enough.'

Wulfric and Alfred lifted the great beam that held the gates shut themselves and went out from the fortress's welcome protection. Feeling exposed and pensive the king made his way down the slope towards the water. Sure enough, the man who'd been acting as lookout on Barrow Hill was paddling furiously towards them, his little boat scudding through the reeds with surprising haste.

'This really can't be good,' Wulfric said. 'For him to abandon his post, there must be danger nearby.'

Alfred did not reply, merely chewed his lip and felt the familiar, growing ache in his guts.

The sound of the paddle splashing in and out of the water grew louder and now the waiting king could see the fear on the lookout's face quite clearly.

'The Danes are here!' the man shouted. 'Dozens of them, my lords!'

Wulfric and Alfred looked at one another, and then back up the slope towards the hastily erected fortress and its palisade wall.

'It appears we're about to find out how effective our stronghold really is,' the ealdorman muttered, eyes already scanning the defensive structure for signs of some previously missed weakness.

'Aye,' Alfred agreed, waiting for the lookout to come onto land beside them. 'Come on then, we should take the punts in behind the walls so the Danes can't use them or damage them. Let's get ready, lads, this is going to be a long day.'

As they hurried up the slope, each dragging a punt, Alfred glanced back at Barrow Hill. The fire had burned itself out, but now the king could see figures there. At this distance it was impossible to make out details, but he knew they were looking back at him, and he knew it was only a matter of time before his family's new home was under siege.

'Bring in the rest of the punts, and then close the gates!' Wulfric commanded as the three of them came back within the safety of the walls. 'And string your bows, if you haven't already. It seems we won't need to go marching today – God has brought the Danes to us.'

'God be praised,' Alfred shouted, trying to make his voice sound jauntier than he actually felt. 'That saves us a journey.'

Some of the cheers his words engendered were half-hearted and filled with trepidation. But many were fierce enough that the king felt a sense of calm spreading through him as Wulfric made sure the walls were properly manned, and he strode off himself to see Ealhswith in the hall.

'Father! I want to fight them too.'

Alfred was not in the mood to coddle his daughter, yet, even so, it was not in him to be unkind to her. 'And you may get your chance,' he said, leaning down and grasping her gently by the arms. 'You must remain here with your brother and sisters, do you hear?' He saw four-year-old Edward, sitting wide-eyed beside Ealhswith. The boy did not look frightened for he was as brave as his big sister, although not as headstrong or eager to court danger. The king smiled reassuringly at Edward then said to Aethelflaed, 'You keep your seax at hand, all right? If the Danes breach the walls, you must protect everyone in here.'

He knew very well that, if the enemy did manage to get within the fortress, there would be no saving his family. Commanding his little daughter to act as a guard at least gave her something to take her mind off what was about to happen outside, he hoped, and stop her from coming out to help.

Ealhswith reached out as Alfred came close and they shared a hurried embrace. 'Stay here with the children,' he said, wishing now that he had sent his family away to live in one of the surrounding villages until Guthrum had been beaten. It was too late for that now, though, and Ealhswith nodded towards the door.

'Go, my love,' she said. 'Command your men, and come back to us once the Northmen are gone.'

There was fear in her eyes – he could see it quite plainly. But belief in his strength and his abilities was also in her expression, and Alfred drew from it, feeling righteous anger building within.

That the Danes had chased him from his hall in Cippanhamme was bad enough, but now they had come to torment him in his new home. It would not do. God's blood, he would not stand for it!

With a final sweet kiss of farewell, and a swift hug for each of his four children, Aethelflaed grimly promising to protect them all, Alfred left the hall and went out into the sunshine to await whatever fate would bring.

CHAPTER THIRTEEN

'They're coming from the south, and from the east,' Wulfric told the king, pointing as they stood on the walkway that ran the length of the palisade wall.

'We'll wait until they're in range, then hit them with our missiles,' Alfred replied in a cold, emotionless tone.

'There's a lot more of them than the lookout reported,' the ealdorman said bluntly.

Alfred glanced at him, frowning. 'More? How many more?'

'Well,' Wulfric pointed to the east, where men could be seen trying to make their way on foot through the water towards the fortress. 'There's about seventy there, I'd say?' It was a question, and he waited for Alfred's younger eyes to confirm his estimate before continuing. 'Well, there's around a hundred more coming from the south.'

The king took that information in, feeling a momentary thrill of fear at the knowledge they were so heavily outnumbered. It was quite possible there were even more Danes coming from other directions as well, and just hadn't been spotted yet. 'God protect us,' he murmured, then forced a smile. 'God, and the marsh, and these walls. They'll hold, won't they, Wulfric?'

His captain nodded emphatically. 'Oh aye, lord. The carpenter and his craftsmen knew what they were about. And we've walked the perimeter of the palisade ourselves – there's no real weak spots.'

'Then it'll be up to us – and our men – to make sure the Danes understand that trying to take this place is sheer folly.'

He leaned down and lifted a short spear, designed for throwing, and for causing as much damage to any enemy soldier unlucky enough to be struck by it. 'I don't know about you,' he said, raising his voice as the Northmen slowly came closer to their little island. 'But I'm ready to kill as many of those ugly, heathen whoresons as possible today. Who's with me?'

His statement was met with lusty cheers and thumping filled the air as the warriors slammed the butts of their weapons onto the walkway. Insults and threats were shouted towards the slowly encroaching enemy, who were discovering just how hard, and how dangerous, it was to traverse the marshes.

'Come on then, you stinking goat-fuckers!'

Alfred looked to his left and saw Dunstan shaking his spear at the cautiously moving Danes. More of the men took up his demand for the enemy to get on with it and bring the fight to them, but it was becoming increasingly obvious to the invaders that there was no way to simply march up to the island and lay siege to it.

Alfred watched with some amusement as messengers ran between both the enemy parties, taking a long time to do so and falling into the stagnant waters more than once, which, of course, brought hoots of laughter and more crude insults at the unfortunate, sodden Danes. It was growing quite warm now and the sun reflected off the armour, helmets, and weapons of their foes, as it did from the gently steaming waters. It was a strangely peaceful scene, in truth, once the shouts and catcalls faded away.

'Send half the men for something to eat,' Alfred commanded as the sun reached its zenith and it was clear no battle would be happening any time soon.

'Yes, lord,' said Wulfric. 'You want anything?'

Alfred nodded. 'I'll take some bread and ale, thank you. Send my family up to join me too, would you?'

Before long Ealhswith and the children were beside him on the walkway, staring out at the stranded enemy. The mood was as light as the afternoon, and it was a pleasant picnic they enjoyed as the Danes stood around impotently glaring up at the island and its apparently unreachable fortress. Some of the enemy warriors had scouted around as best they could, hunting for a causeway, or at least boats they might use to traverse the waters. When they had no luck, a few tried simply walking through the marsh directly to the stronghold, probing with spears for deeper sections.

As Alfred and his family watched, one of those scouts disappeared beneath the water with a cry that was quickly swallowed up. There were ripples as he flailed his arms, but his legs must have become entangled in reeds for he was unable to work his way free and his cries for help soon became choked gasps, and then silence as he disappeared under the surface, leaving only bubbles to show where he'd been.

Alfred's men laughed and hooted in delight, but he did not, and he was glad that his children did not glory in the man's suffering either.

'Will he go to Heaven?' Aethelflaed asked. Her face was pale for, although small, she and Edward were standing on top of stools so they could see over the wall.

'No,' Alfred replied levelly. 'He's a heathen. Who knows where they go when they die?'

'Hell,' said Oswald, walking along to stand with them. The priest had been going amongst the men, ensuring they were spiritually prepared for the coming fight, when he, too, had seen the scout die. 'It is right to feel compassion,' he said to the princess and her brother, who seemed more confused than anything else by the Dane's death. 'Christ taught love and forgiveness after all. But those men out there are here to hurt every one of us. So, do not feel sorrow for that man, just be glad that there's one less sea-wolf for your father and his soldiers to fight.'

'But...' Aethelflaed struggled visibly to put her thoughts and emotions into words and Alfred noticed her hand resting naturally on the pommel of her little seax. She was a born warrior, he thought.

'We can say a prayer for his soul if you like, my lady,' Oswald said to the princess kindly.

'I think we should,' she replied. 'He... He did not look that much older than me.'

'Then let his death be a lesson to you, and you, Edward,' replied the priest. 'He acted rashly, as youngsters are prone to doing. Look – his older, more experienced companions did not walk into the marsh. They were not so stupid.'

'Or maybe they're just cowards,' Aethelflaed said thoughtfully. 'And wanted someone braver than them to find an easy way over here.'

Alfred smiled and ruffled his daughter's hair, but he said to Ealhswith, 'Take the children back inside, my love. It looks like something is happening.'

The mood shifted at his words, and the queen consort quickly did as he asked, hurrying down the wooden steps and back into the great hall. Alfred watched as she carried Aelfthryth, too small to walk yet, while Edward and Aethelflaed helped Aethelgifu first traverse the stairs, and then hurry within the sturdy building. Oswald had gone with them and the sound of him placing the heavy beam across the doors reassured the king.

'What are the arseholes doing now?' Dunstan asked no one in particular, and Alfred returned his full attention to the enemy soldiers.

They were moving away, towards firmer ground, and the trees that grew there. The king looked over his shoulder at the southern end of the fortress. His men watching the Danes there showed no alarm, just the same curiosity he felt, and he assumed both enemy warbands were taking the same action.

What that action was became quite clear a few heartbeats later, as the harsh sound of living wood being hacked into reverberated across the marshes.

'They're cutting down trees,' said Wulfric.

'To make rafts,' Alfred agreed. There was no way to build a bridge or a causeway from dry land across to the island fortress, even for the mythically skilled woodworkers amongst the Northmen. The distance was simply too great, the ground too soft, to be built across at short notice, so the would-be besiegers had decided to make crude rafts instead.

'That'll take forever,' one of Alfred's hearth-warriors snorted disdainfully. 'They'll be exhausted by the time they're finished, and then they'll still have to make their way across here.'

'Let them come,' Dunstan shouted. He was the type of man who was always the loudest in a crowd, which could, occasionally, be irritating but, at times like this, was a boon. Such confident, loud individuals gave others with less courage heart. Or at least something to focus on other than possible impending doom. 'Let them come,' Dunstan repeated in an even more dismissive tone.

'Aye,' called Aedan from his post near the gatehouse. 'By the time they get here they'll be done in, and we'll have an even easier time killing them!'

Their banter did not completely convince many of the defenders though. They knew it wouldn't really take that long for the Danes to build rafts, and then the battle would not be postponed for much longer.

'What d'you think?' Alfred said to Wulfric as they stared at the trees on the other side of the water, seeing leaves shake as whole saplings were cut down. 'Say, eight to ten of them per raft? That'll give us plenty of big targets to aim for.'

'Surely they won't be so daft,' the ealdorman replied. 'They'll be sitting ducks for our missiles.'

Alfred shrugged. 'If Guthrum's commanded them to take Athelney, and kill us in the process, what other choice do they have? What would you do? They can't starve us out – they don't have enough men to patrol the entire marsh. All we'd have to do is put some men in punts and send them over to land under the cover of night to go and gather supplies. Besides, we've got plenty of food stored here. More than those bastards have brought with them.'

'And, although they number almost two hundred,' Wulfric said thoughtfully. 'That's not really enough to attack the nearby settlements. Ealdorman Aethelnoth would muster his fyrd to stand against them.'

'Right,' Alfred agreed. 'So, what would you do if you led those Danes?'

Wulfric pondered the question for a time, and then he snorted humourlessly. 'I'd bugger off and tell Guthrum to do it. It's not like these Northmen have any real ties of loyalty to one another. Whoever is leading the men here follows Guthrum today, but come the winter they might have moved on and be part of some other king's army, raiding Francia.'

'They're not leaving, though,' Alfred mused. 'Unless they're building rafts to sail to Francia in.'

They watched as more trees disappeared, leaving gaping holes in the tops of the woods like teeth smashed from a warrior's mouth in battle, and shouted conversations from the men around the fortress walls confirmed the same was happening on both sides of the marsh.

There was nothing to do but wait.

The sounds of chopping and hammering continued throughout the afternoon, making Alfred's men more on edge with every thump. The Danes were not visible now, working within the remaining trees, so what, exactly, they were up to, was left to West Saxon imaginations.

The warriors were not the only ones using their imaginations, for Alfred's children had been allowed out of the hall again, to enjoy the sunshine and fresh air. They did not seem overly anxious about the Danes, as the older two chased one another about while the others tried to do the same or found other, simpler ways to entertain themselves. Ealhswith watched them like a hawk the whole time, helped by little Aelfthryth's nursemaid who, like Oswald, had insisted on remaining with the royal family despite being given the chance to find somewhere safer to live when the fortress was under construction. She'd been with them since Aethelflaed was born, and would remain with the children as long as her services were needed.

Eventually, the sun began its inevitable descent, and the shadows lengthened until it was too dark for the children to play. The night was still clear, but, with the sun's light and heat gone, it grew cold and Ealhswith took her charges into the hall again, where a fire was laid and the doors locked once more.

The men remained on the walls, staring out into the eerily quiet night. The surviving trees could just be seen as the moon came up, branches reaching to the starry sky like demonic fingers. Or perhaps that was just Alfred's imagination, wishing those trees would come to life and strike down the Danes who'd used their leafy kin as material for rafts.

Only a few braziers had been lit around the place, so the men could move about without injuring themselves, but wouldn't lose their night vision unnecessarily. Every eye was turned outwards, every ear strained for the sound of their enemies approaching. An owl screeched somewhere, and a while later a fox screamed, but Alfred's men had the walls to shelter behind. They hoped the Danes would be feeling far more fear at the nocturnal ambience than they were.

Alfred dozed a little and then, during the very deepest part of the night, there was a sound, and the king came awake instantly. He could see the whites of his men's eyes turned in his direction, and everyone listened, hearing the noise again just a moment later. It was soon followed by more of the same.

Soft splashing.

'They're coming!' Alfred bellowed, unceremoniously dragging any others who might be dozing back to reality. 'Get ready!' He prayed that everything they'd done to prepare for an attack like this would be enough. If the Danes managed to pull down a section of wall, for example, or smashed through the gate, their greater numbers would be decisive. 'Remember what Ealdorman Odda did to Ubba Ragnarsson and his vermin!' the king cried, doing his best to inspire his men and himself. 'The Danes are not unbeatable, they die just like anyone else, and they have no way of getting over our walls, so use your spears and arrows wisely, lads. Make each one count. For Wessex!'

'For Wessex!'

Alfred's men had wrapped rags soaked in pitch around the heads of their arrows, and they used the braziers now to set fire to them. As the sounds of hasty paddling came closer across the gloomy marshes, the archers leaned up, over the walls, and let fly. The night was dark, and the flames ruined the king's night vision as he looked on. He could not see the enemy, so had no idea what their rafts were like until the fire arrows thudded home in the newly-constructed vessels.

'Oh, God!' Dunstan shouted in alarm. 'They've made shields for the fronts of the rafts!'

Alfred squinted, wishing the fires would grow so he could get a better look at the oncoming craft. The wood used to build the rafts was wet, and too thick for the flames to really take hold, so the marsh was a strange mixture of darkness and flashing light which reflected from the spear points, axe-heads, and sword blades of the approaching enemy sailors. 'Keep hitting them,' he commanded, hoping at least some of the arrows would kindle real, damaging fires on the rafts.

'It's no good, lord,' Dunstan called.

He continued to loose arrow after arrow, but Alfred could see the thane was right. The rafts would not burn, and the wooden shields at the fronts of the rafts stopped any of the missiles from injuring the Danes on board. In the flickering lights of the burning arrows arcing through the sky the king could see his estimate on the number of rafts had also been too low. There were more of them than he'd expected; more rafts, and more men on board them too. He could only assume it was the same story on the southern side, for those manning the walls there were shouting out in impotent rage as well.

Alfred could sense the despair rising within his hearth-warriors as their attacks proved fruitless and the noose of seemingly indestructible rafts that the Danes were tying around the fortress inexorably tightened. The Saxons' enthusiastic war-cries tapered off, as did the intensity of their missile barrage, and the king could see the defenders casting anxious glances towards him, desperate for some inspiration.

'We're wasting our arrows,' Dunstan shouted. 'My lord, this isn't working. We need to try something else, for they're almost at the island, and they've got ladders and ropes to scale the walls on those rafts!'

'Keep shooting,' Alfred repeated. 'Until I tell you to stop, just keep fucking shooting!' He watched arrow after arrow thud into the rafts without doing any damage at all, then he looked up at the sky and prayed that all of their preparations would be enough to stop the Danes from overrunning the little fortress.

CHAPTER FOURTEEN

Sigmundr Askelsson felt another arrow thump into the shield made from the trunks of saplings and grinned at the five other men on the raft with him. His plan was working!

When Guthrum had given him command of this mission Sigmundr had viewed it as a great honour. He was a young hersir, usually with only twenty men at his command, so to be placed at the head of a hundred of Guthrum's warriors was something to be proud of. And the mission, to capture or kill the exiled West Saxon King Alfred? If Sigmundr could pull it off, his name would ring through the ages! The *vikingr* who put an end to the resistance in Wessex, and brought the entire kingdom under the Northmen's heel! Skalds would sing his tale for eternity, and his place in Valhöll would surely be certain.

Then his column of men met up with the second warband Guthrum had sent to help him, and they'd realised just how difficult their task was going to be.

The marshes around the fortress covered a much bigger area than Sigmundr had expected, being all but impassable to so many warriors. Even if they could somehow find a path through the water, perhaps with the help of a local guide, it would leave them exposed to attack from the Saxon defenders atop the walls.

And those walls! Guthrum had played down the strength of Alfred's new stronghold, so it had been another unpleasant surprise when Sigmundr stood looking up at the island that morning and seen the place for himself. Certainly, the walls were not as high as many the hersir had seen in Wessex – but they looked strong enough and were situated at the top of a hill which was surrounded by water! Not only that, but there seemed to be many – perhaps forty or fifty – defenders atop those walls, all waiting eagerly for a chance to rain deadly missiles down on any Dane foolish enough to come too close. Of course, Sigmundr's warband had brought lengths of rope with them, but simply getting to the walls would be nigh on impossible, never mind actually climbing up and over.

Yet Guthrum had not chosen Sigmundr to lead this attack at random. The young hersir had proven himself to be not only brave and brutal in battle, but also cunning and patient. So there had been no question of the raiders simply giving up when they saw how hard it would be to take control of Athelney from the Saxons in the fortress.

Instead, Sigmundr came up with a plan. Once the foolhardy lad had drowned trying to find a path through the reed-filled, stagnant waters, it had become clear boats were the answer. And there were plenty of trees around, and enough hardy Northmen armed with axes to chop them down and fashion them into something functional, if not as beautiful as the longship that had brought Sigmundr along the whale road to these lands.

It was obvious those on the walls would attack them with whatever they had at hand as soon as the Danes started crossing the water. Arrows, spears, stones and more would form a deadly torrent when they were at their most vulnerable. So Sigmundr made the decision to mount the attack when it was dark, spoiling the defenders' aim, and to craft sturdy shields to defend each raft's crew while they paddled towards the island.

And it was working perfectly!

The hersir peered out through a gap in the planks that formed his shield and realised they were already halfway across the water. When he looked back, he saw that all of his men were close behind, paddling furiously. The Saxons' fire arrows were having no effect whatsoever, other than to add some light to the scene, and Sigmundr burst out laughing at how well his plan was going.

He'd even had the foresight to tell his men to make the rafts' shields detachable, so they could lift them off and carry them closer to the walls. Of course, there would come a time when the Danes would need to come out from their shelters and try to climb over the walls, but at least Sigmundr's plan would get them there without suffering many casualties.

And he knew they could afford casualties for, between his warband and the second one on the southern side of the fortress, they vastly outnumbered the defenders.

He peered through the gap in his raft's shield again and flinched back, yelping in fright as a fire arrow hammered into the wood just above his spyhole. His men laughed at his moment of terror, and so did he, for he had suffered no injury.

'You ready, lads?' he demanded. 'Remember, those of you with bows, use the shields as cover, and pin down the defenders. The rest of you follow me and get your ropes and ladders up as soon as possible. I want this place captured as soon as possible, all right? There's plunder and glory within those walls, and Alfred's pretty wife to do with as we please. For Óðinn!'

'For Óðinn!'

His men parroted the war-cry, and then the Dane at the rear of Sigmundr's raft screamed in pain and fell off into the water. Two of those nearest to him reached out and tried to grab him, but he was already gone.

It did not matter, thought the hersir. There were always casualties in battle, and a few men here and there would not be enough to stop his warband. Yet another fire arrow sailed overhead, lighting the scene for Sigmundr who watched as what appeared to be a spear came from the opposite direction – from the dry land which the Danes had just come from – and slammed into the back of another man crouching on the raft.

'Where did that come from?' someone cried out.

'From behind us!'

Sigmundr's mind whirled as he tried to understand what was happening. How had the spear managed to take his man in the back? Had it somehow changed direction in mid-air, perhaps blown by a rogue gust of wind?

That was, of course, ridiculous, and, as another arrow went past, the hersir's breath caught in his throat, for its orange glow lit up that distant bank his warriors had been standing on just a short time ago, launching their rafts.

His men were no longer standing there, for they were all on the rafts – yet Sigmundr could see many dark shapes there. Human shapes.

Another spear hammered into the back of the raft, not striking anyone this time, but making the whole thing shudder, and it was suddenly all too obvious what was happening.

'Paddle faster!' Sigmundr screamed at the top of his lungs. 'There's Saxons behind us, throwing spears! Get to the island as fast as you can!'

He could hear cries of pain and terror all around him and gritted his teeth, begging Óðinn to protect them until they reached the fortress and were safely out of range of the attackers to their rear.

'No wonder Guthrum didn't want the honour of taking this damn stronghold,' he muttered to himself as flaming arrows continued to light up their positions for the men on the bank to aim at. 'I should have known it wouldn't be easy.'

–

'Someone's out there, attacking the sea-wolves from behind!'

Alfred grinned at Dunstan's gleeful shout. He knew who the attackers were, and who led them: Wulfric. When it became clear the defenders of Athelney would struggle to hold off such large numbers of Danes, Alfred had asked Wulfric to take one of the punts and make his way quietly across the water, between what they hoped would be a gap between the two enemy forces. If he made it safely to land, he was to head southwest to the nearby town of Nortcory and enlist the fyrd there. It was a round trip of about eight miles, and would take probably two to three hours. Alfred had been worried that, even if Wulfric completed his mission, it would not be in time to help.

Praise be to God though, his captain had come through for them, as usual.

'Keep using those fire arrows, if you have any left!' the king ordered, lifting one of the pitch-soaked missiles himself and setting it alight before taking aim at one of the rafts and letting fly. There was a satisfying thump, and a shower of sparks which illuminated a rock as it hurtled through the air and crashed into the head of one of the Danes on the rocking craft. Alfred cheered in delight, but the battle was far from over, as some of the enemy rafts had made it to the island now, and the warriors were jumping off and hurrying up the slope towards the walls.

The king turned, looking at the other Saxon soldiers dotted around the walkway, and particularly those to the southern end of the fortress. They were throwing their spears now rather than fire arrows, or poking them downwards, and Alfred guessed the Danes were attempting to scale the walls there. He felt the palisade shudder beside him and risked a glance over, gasping as he saw a ladder right there, and a helmeted Northman climbing up towards him.

Wulfric and the fyrd from Nortcory had done their jobs, taking out – with any luck – maybe half of the attacking force, at least on this north-eastern side. Alfred had no way of knowing how the other sections of the fortress fared, but it didn't matter at that moment. He had a job to do.

'Look to the walls!' he roared, as the bearded face of the man on the ladder came into view, Alfred thrust his spear out. He used the butt end, not wanting to lose the spear if its iron point became lodged in his foe's skull. It was effective enough, and the Northman screamed as he flew backwards, off the ladder, to land with a clatter and roll down the slope, dazed or dead, towards the water.

An arrow whistled past Alfred's head and he ducked instinctively before leaning up and dropping his spear in favour of his sword. A hand appeared at the top of the wall and Alfred slammed the pommel into the fingers. There was a cry of outrage but, as the enemy tried to clamber up and over, onto the walkway, the king's sword came around in an arc, striking the Dane's unprotected neck. Wide-eyed and screaming, the man grasped his bleeding wound, but it was too deep to stem, and, as the strength ebbed quickly from his limbs, the man collapsed, sliding down the ladder onto the climber beneath him. Both men fell, and Alfred, seeing his chance, reached out and simply dragged the empty ladder up and dropped it on the other side of the walkway.

There were more ladders, and now ropes were being thrown up with beams of wood attached. These caught on the palisade and stuck fast as Danes put all their weight onto them and started to climb up. Alfred did not need to warn his men – they were rushing here and there, hacking and slashing at arms, fingers, heads, and ropes.

Suddenly a sea-wolf, more agile than his companions, jumped nimbly up onto the walkway right in front of the king. Eyes blazing with battle-fury, the Dane took out an axe and drew his arm back. Before he could throw it, however, an arrow from one of his own archers grazed the top of his head. It did not injure him, but it surprised him and threw him off balance, and Alfred took the chance to plunge his sword into the man's guts. The fire in his foe's eyes faded and the axe fell onto the walkway with a thump.

Alfred withdrew his sword and kicked the dying man away, off the walkway so his lifeless body wouldn't trip any of the defenders. Then the king bent down, lifted the fallen axe, and ran to the wall, peering out into the gloom and seeing yet another Dane desperately pulling himself up a rope. The king threw the axe, and it spun through the night air before the heavy blade struck the climbing man on the side of the face. He fell silently to land in a twisted heap on the ground.

Seizing the brief moment of respite, Alfred sucked in deep breaths and cautiously peered out over the walls. No more arrows were being shot at the defenders now; in fact, there was no one left standing on the ground outside. 'Where the hell are they all?' the king murmured, feeling a moment's joy as he guessed those of the enemy troops who hadn't been killed must have retreated. His happiness drained instantly away, however, when he noticed the rafts still lay where they'd been abandoned on the island. One of them had even, finally, caught on fire and the flames and smoke billowed into the dark sky, lighting the marshes and making it even clearer that the attackers had moved on.

There was a shocking thump from the southern side of the stronghold and Alfred even felt the walkway shudder. It didn't take him long to figure out what was happening, especially when the West Saxons defending the gatehouse were calling in fright for reinforcements at their position.

'Dunstan!' shouted the king. 'You remain here on the walls, make sure they don't come back and climb up here. The rest of you, spears and shields, follow me!'

He bolted down the steps and his men came after him, running towards the gates. The walls were still being scaled at this position and, while the defenders looked in no real danger of being overrun, they were heavily beset so could not come down to join Alfred as he called for a shieldwall to form up around him.

'Steady, men!' cried the king as the shields locked into position and spears poked out from between them.

They were just in time for with another massive thump the beam holding the gates shut gave way, wood splintering and flying apart in all directions. Time seemed to slow almost to a stop as Alfred watched the broken gates swing inwards, and then Danes were charging through the opening, roaring war-cries to Óðinn and Þórr and Týr.

Above them, the defenders on the walls who were not beset themselves rained down whatever missiles that were still at hand. Still the charging Northmen came though, knowing this was their final chance to take the fortress.

They ran into Alfred's shieldwall, their momentum pushing back the king's line. This was only for a few heartbeats however, for soon enough the charge was stopped, and the spears began their deadly work – thrusting into flesh and bone, ripping and tearing and rending, and the lusty war-cries gave way to screams of desperate fear and pain.

Some of the enemy warriors clattered up the steps, trying to take control of the walls, but they were far too few and, as their comrades gave up the ladders and ropes outside and hurried towards the open gate to join them, the Danes' attack faltered.

Alfred saw one man trying to rally the enemy soldiers, screaming at them to form a line and maintain their discipline but his words were having little effect in the chaos of the battle.

Drawing back his arm Alfred knew he should be exhausted by this stage of the fighting, but he felt as if God was filling him with righteous fury and power and, as if it weighed no more than an arrow, the king threw his spear.

In truth, the distance between himself and the enemy hersir was only a few paces, yet, even so, it took prodigious strength to launch the great ash weapon and Alfred watched as it tore through the air before thundering home in his opponent's chest.

With their leader's demise, the Danes completely lost any sense of direction and those who weren't quickly cut down decided to throw themselves on the Saxons' mercy. Shields, spears, axes, and swords – all were dropped, and the beaten enemy warriors stood gasping, eyes glittering with anxiety in the light from the braziers, knowing their lot would not be a good one, even if Alfred let them live. They had hope in their expressions, though, and Alfred knew they had heard of his reputation for forgiveness, and Christian mercy.

Quiet fell upon the place, exhausted men sucking in lungfuls of air as they waited for the king's orders. Behind them, in the hall, the sound of Alfred's children crying reached him even through the barred doors. The sound stirred something terrible within him, and, unbidden and desperately unwanted, images of what these Danes would have done to his family had they been victorious filled the king's mind. Forcing the disturbing thoughts aside, Alfred was left in no mood for mercy.

'Kill them,' he ordered, baring his teeth and raising his sword as he moved towards the terrified prisoners. 'Kill every last one of them.'

CHAPTER FIFTEEN

Guthrum's face was pale as he listened to the messenger deliver his news, and watched as a sack – with its dark red, dripping contents – was deposited on the hall floor.

'What's in th—'

His question was not needed as Sigmundr's head rolled out, skin peeling from the eyeless, lipless skull.

'They did not take Alfred's new fortress, then?'

'No, lord,' replied the messenger who had been despatched to Athelney for word on what had transpired and just returned that afternoon. 'None survived from the looks of it, and now their bodies are strewn around the marshes for the beasts to feast upon.'

Guthrum stared at the decapitated head at his feet. He had seen worse sights in his time; indeed, he had caused worse sights with his own blade. No, Sigmundr's blank stare did not make him squeamish at all, but the message it was delivering certainly worried the king.

Almost two hundred men he'd sent to take the fortress in Athelney. A place manned by, at most, a quarter of that number. It should have been a simple matter, but the fact that it hadn't been merely served to show Guthrum that he had badly underestimated Alfred. Two hundred men lost... It was a hammer-blow to the Danes in Wessex, who were already understrength thanks to the storm of the previous year that had drowned more than three thousand bold *vikingar*, and, on top of that, news of Ubba's defeat in Defenascir had come.

Guthrum might have control of Cippanhamme and still think of himself as King of Wessex, but how long would it be before his own men grew tired of their comrades being killed? Not to mention the West Saxon ealdormen who had betrayed Alfred and taken the Northmen's side; they would eventually renounce Guthrum and seek to find favour with their own, deposed, king.

'What do I do?' he muttered softly, so no one else could hear him. 'Óðinn help me, what do I do?'

'Lord?' the messenger asked. 'What would you have me do?'

Guthrum stared at him blankly. What did the man want from him? 'Do? Your task is already done,' he replied bleakly. 'Go and throw yourself in the river for all I care.'

The messenger scowled but did not reply, merely turned and strode from the hall. It was all very well being irritable with him, but Guthrum could see the rest of his men watching him from their places near his high table. Jarls, hersirs, these were his most powerful allies, commanders of their own sizeable warbands, and the men whose support he relied on. He wanted to reassure them that he was in control, that Wessex was fully in his hands, that Alfred was merely an annoyance. But how could he do that when the West Saxon king evaded death so consistently? The Christian and his followers were like ghosts, moving within the misty marshes at will, striking when they pleased, and never standing still for long enough to be killed. Guthrum almost smiled, for those tactics had been the very ones employed by his own people for years.

He knew now how Alfred had felt as the Danes used their longships to move up and down the Tamyse, striking at settlements, plundering them, then sailing onwards with a full load of slaves and booty before the West Saxon army could catch them.

Floki detached himself from the rest of the men who had, thankfully, returned to their feasting, giving Guthrum some time to gather his thoughts and decide on his next move.

The hersir expertly manoeuvred his sizeable midriff around the stools and tables between him and his king and finally sat down when Guthrum gave him a nod of assent.

'My lord,' Floki said. 'These are grim tidings.'

Guthrum could not be bothered snapping at the man for stating the obvious, managing only the sharp intake of breath the Norse used as a form of wordless agreement.

'Your warriors grow tired of chasing shadows,' Floki went on, clearly trying to keep his tone neutral and non-judgemental. 'If I could offer some advice?'

Guthrum nodded. 'I'm all ears.'

'Either muster all our forces and deal with Alfred once and for all, or forget about him and consolidate our positions in Wessex. Strengthen alliances, form new ones, and crush those who refuse to bend the knee.'

Guthrum felt his ire rising again but forced his voice to remain low. 'We can't just march away from here,' he said. 'If we do that, the Saxons still loyal to Alfred will take the town back. This is the problem with occupying a kingdom – our forces must be spread thin to keep the peace and deter revolts.'

'Then forget about their exiled king,' Floki advised. 'Let him rule over the bogs and quicksand in Athelney. Consolidate our position here, by taking control of the nearest towns. Or...' He trailed off, then shrugged. 'Take everything we can from Wessex and move on.'

Guthrum frowned. Move on. He'd thought of that many times over the past few weeks. Why hadn't he already done so? That was what Northmen did, after all. It was what he'd done himself all through his life. So why had he not done so now? He pictured the countryside around Cippanhamme, with its low hills, sparkling, well-stocked rivers, spring flowers, and warm summers, and realised he wanted to remain here in Wessex.

To rule this green and pleasant land until the end of his days.

The thought should have shocked him, but he knew it had been growing within him for many months. Perhaps ever since

Alfred had suggested he convert to Christianity and settle down, foregoing his life of raiding. The West Saxon king had planted that seed within Guthrum's imagination, and it had grown like the wood anemones, bluebells, and purple orchids flowering now in the surrounding meadows and fields.

Meadows and fields which belonged to Guthrum by right of conquest.

No, by Þórr, he would not simply move on. These were his lands now, and he would fight for them. That so many Norse and Danes had settled in other kingdoms in Britain and Ireland showed that it could be done, if there was enough of a desire. Hadn't the Saxons done the very same thing when they'd sailed here five, six hundred years ago and conquered, or assimilated with, the natives?

'Floki,' he said, smiling now, an expression which seemed to surprise the hersir since it was so unexpected. 'Have messengers take word to the Saxon settlements loyal to me. Tell them to gather their fyrds and prepare for battle.'

'We're going to Athelney?'

'Perhaps, eventually. To start with, we need more men to fully subjugate Wessex, so we will use those available to us. Wulfhere and the rest of the Saxons who betrayed their king must prove their value now, by helping us create a new Wessex, one populated by us, and them.'

'With us in charge,' Floki said, smiling uncertainly.

'Exactly so,' Guthrum agreed. 'By adding Saxons to our own army, it will make persuading all the other noblemen to come under our rule that much easier. Alfred thinks he can build his strength in the marshes, and then return to reclaim his throne, but I will not let that happen, by Óðinn. Wessex is mine, and so it shall stay! If Alfred wants it back, he'll have to come and take it.'

He was greatly pleased by this plan that had come to him in a sudden flash of inspiration, gifted to him by the Norns, undoubtedly. It would give his bored warriors something to keep them busy, and allow them to rape and plunder to their hearts' content. And it would solidify his alliance with the West Saxon nobles who'd chosen his side over Alfred's, for, once the fighting started and the likes of Ealdorman Wulfhere were battling their own people, well… There would be no going back for them after that. They would be beholden to Guthrum forever. Especially if Alfred came out from his hiding place and stood against them…

Nodding, Floki stood up and touched the hammer amulet he wore around his neck. 'I shall do as you command, lord,' he said, and left the hall, leaving Guthrum to dream about a Wessex ruled by Danes for many summers to come.

–

Alfred gazed out at the fine sunny day, watching the mist burn away as the heat grew and languid bees went about their business. He could see a deer off to the west, watching him, and he believed it to be an auspicious omen. 'You ever get the feeling a day will be a good one?' he said as Wulfric came to stand on the walkway beside him.

'Not really,' his captain replied.

'Ha, Wulfric, I sometimes wonder if it's all an act with you! Surely no one can be as unimaginative as you appear to be at times.'

'I'm a realist, lord,' Wulfric shrugged.

'And that's why we make a good team,' Alfred laughed. 'A realist, and a dreamer. One who looks to God for his inspiration, and one who is firmly rooted here on the earth. You believe fully in your own strength, Wulfric, your own abilities – while I do not have such boundless self-confidence. I often wish I did.' He looked back to the west, but the deer was gone now. 'What news, my friend?'

'Guthrum has changed his tactics after we destroyed his warbands here the other night. He's looking to bribe our people now, asking them swear fealty to him in return for silver.

Building a new army from the sound of it, undoubtedly to attack those who will not accept his rule.'

Alfred scowled. This was not good news at all.

'Oh, don't worry,' Wulfric said, reading the king's black expression. 'His emissaries aren't having much luck. The folk don't want to swear Christian oaths to serve a heathen king. It does show us that Guthrum has plans to remain here, however, and fully subjugate Wessex.'

'That bastard,' Alfred spat, slamming his hand against the palisade wall, his enjoyment of the day rather dampened. He lowered his voice, so none of the guards on the walls or freshly-mended gatehouse could hear him. 'You know, one of the hardest things about being forced to hide out here in the marshes is the shame of how I let Guthrum best me.'

'Shame?'

'Aye!' Alfred's eyes blazed as he met his captain's unflinching gaze. 'Shame. When my brother died, I swore to be a good king, to carry on the work he'd started. To defend Wessex against the threat of the Danes.' He shook his head, fury replaced by sadness as he looked out at the fens again, trying to catch another glimpse of the young deer that had captivated him before. 'Yet here I am, while he lives like a lord – a king! – in my own hall at Cippanhamme. I had more than one chance to defeat him, and I failed. I failed my people, I failed you, I failed my family, and I failed myself. It hurts, Wulfric. Very much.'

The big ealdorman listened in silence, as he always did, and then he said, 'But you're still here, Alfred. I am still here. You're not beaten yet, and Guthrum's position is far from secure. Look at what we – you – managed when we were besieged here.'

Alfred thought back to that night of violence and brutality – images of the men he'd slaughtered still fresh in his mind, as was that of the young Dane who'd been swallowed whole by the stagnant water surrounding the small fortress. When it became clear the enemy warbands were building rafts, and would attack under the cover of darkness, Alfred knew they could not win. Unless he came up with something the Danes would not expect. It had been a masterstroke, sending Wulfric into the night for aid from the nearest settlement, and only added to his growing legend as a master warrior and tactician.

'Guthrum may have won some battles,' Wulfric said. 'But the war is not over while you are still alive to lead us.'

'He's right, lord.'

Alfred turned to see Oswald walking towards them, rubbing his tonsured scalp.

'You have nothing to be ashamed about. Not when it comes to Guthrum at least.'

Alfred raised his eyebrows at the thinly-veiled rebuke, but Oswald didn't go into detail on why the king might have reason to feel shame. There was no need, they both knew of Alfred's vices, even if they had been forcibly halted while in exile.

'You've tried to behave towards the Danes with honour and compassion, as a good Christian should,' the priest went on. 'And you expected them to wage war with the same morals and respect for tradition as we do. Yet they continually break oaths, murder hostages, and attack us when we're celebrating our religious festivals.'

'I should have learned before now,' Alfred insisted.

'Perhaps,' Oswald admitted. 'But you have another chance to be the king you were born to be, my lord. The scales are finely balanced – a miracle in itself, given the circumstances that brought us here.'

'He's right,' Wulfric said. 'Your time has come, my lord. We should strike Guthrum now, while he's still reeling from the defeats he's suffered here, and in Defenascir.'

Alfred absorbed their words and felt somewhat better about himself and his right to lead the people of Wessex going forward, yet… He remained unconvinced that he had enough support to defeat the Danes. 'Guthrum still commands the loyalty of the likes of Ealdormen Wealdmar, and Wulfhere. Those are sizable fyrds.' He sighed and wandered along the walkway, staring out at the countryside and feeling as if he was stuck in a prison of his own making.

'We'll kill those traitorous bastards,' Wulfric replied, striding after him. 'Make an example of them.'

'Or maybe just strip them of their titles and lands,' Oswald put in. 'Killing our own people is not what Christ would want, Wulfric.'

'Not being ruthless enough is what's brought us to this point, priest!' Wulfric retorted. 'Alfred needs to rule with an iron fist from now on. And those who betrayed Alfred deserve to die for what they did.'

The king slowed, eyeing the land to the north. 'What Alfred needs,' he said, speaking to himself more than anyone else. 'Is a sign. Something to show me what God wills.'

Oswald stood beside him and said, 'Would you like to pray, my lord? Beg God for guidance?'

Wulfric rolled his eyes, not even attempting to hide his annoyance, but Alfred nodded enthusiastically.

'Aye, I would,' he agreed, again giving thanks that this priest, this friend, was always there by his side when he most needed him.

'Then let us pray,' murmured Oswald, and began reciting one of the king's favourite prayers as both men bowed their heads and stared at the walkway underfoot.

O God the Father,
origin of Divinity,
good beyond all that is good,
fair beyond all that is fair, in whom is calmness, peace, and concord,
do Thou make up the dissensions which divide us from each other,
and bring us back into the unity of love,
which may bear some likeness to Thy divine nature.
And as Thou art above all things,
make us one by the unanimity of a good mind,
that through the embrace of charity and the bonds of affection,

we may be spiritually one,
as well in ourselves as in each other,
through that peace of Thine which maketh all things peaceful,
and through the grace, mercy, and tenderness of Thy Son, Jesus
    Christ.
Amen.

'Er, my lord?'

Alfred glared at Wulfric, angry at him for disturbing Oswald's prayer and their moment of quiet reflection. 'Good God, man, be silent until we're done. It also wouldn't have hurt you to join in.'

'But, lord, I think your praying might have already had the desired effect.'

'Eh? What are you—' Alfred raised his head to peer out at the marshes where Wulfric was pointing. Three figures were making their way towards the fortress, moving with a speed that showed at least one of them was a local, with knowledge of the hidden pathways through the reed-infused waters; probably one of the guides Alfred himself had employed on occasion.

'Messengers?' Oswald wondered aloud. 'From Ealdorman Aethelnoth?'

'Maybe,' Wulfric said, but his eyes were scanning the countryside for signs of more men approaching, perhaps another army sent by Guthrum to finish the job his earlier warbands had failed to complete.

They waited for the travellers to come closer, and it became ever more obvious one man knew exactly where to step. He never put a foot wrong, while the two with him occasionally stepped in the water, cursing as they splashed back onto the pathway their guide had picked out. As they came to the section of marsh that surrounded Alfred's fortress the leader headed straight for a punt concealed by some bushes, and held it steady as the other two men climbed gingerly on board.

As the small vessel shoved off and began making its way across to the island, the mist that was rising up from the water in the sunshine parted, and Alfred gasped as he recognised one of the men in the punt.

'By the body and blood of Christ,' he said, making the sign of the cross. 'Look who's decided to leave his hiding place and come to us here in Athelney.'

It was Ealdorman Wealdmar's son, and Alfred's erstwhile friend.

Diuma.

CHAPTER SIXTEEN

Alfred was amazed to see Diuma, but even more so to see Wulfric showing his emotions so openly.

'You've got some nerve coming here, you little bastard,' the big ealdorman growled as the gates were thrown open and the three travellers came inside. 'Take their weapons from them.'

Diuma's face was pale, but he met Wulfric's malevolent gaze steadily enough, although without offering a reply as the guards divested him and his companion of their sword and seax. There was only a year or so between the thane and Alfred, but Diuma looked younger than his twenty-eight winters, with his straight, dark hair neatly combed and his short beard doing little to cover the shallow scar on his cheek which he'd earned fighting the Danes in the Battle of Ascesdune.

'He's right,' Alfred grated. 'You have no shame turning up here, Diuma. But whatever your business may be, you can tell us about it within the hall. I'm sure my wife, and my children, and all the hearth-warriors you turned away from Brycgstow in our hour of need would love to see you and hear what you have to say!' He nodded to the local guide who seemed quite petrified to have stumbled into this unexpectedly tense situation. 'Be welcome, and go refresh yourself, my friend,' Alfred said to the man. 'You can hear what this traitorous sack of horse dung has to say for himself too.'

'Who's this?' Wulfric demanded of the third newcomer.

'I'm Lord Diuma's captain, Tatberht,' replied the man who was tall but slim, and quite young, perhaps only twenty or so.

'We thought it safer to travel as a pair, given the heavy presence of Danes in this area, my lords.'

Wulfric laughed at that. '"Heavy presence of Danes",' he repeated sarcastically. 'The Danes are in these lands because of your thane conspiring to let the rats walk through his lands and attack the king in Cippanhamme!'

Tatberht did not flinch from the older man's ire, but he did not deny the charge either.

'Come,' said Alfred. 'We can hear all about it in the hall. Look, the door's already open for us. Word has spread of your arrival, Diuma.'

Ealhswith was standing in the open doorway, with little Aelfthryth in her arms and a thunderous look on her face darker than any storm that had beset Athelney during the previous winter. Alfred could see Diuma visibly blanch when he noticed her, and waver for the first time since entering the crude fortress. The thane quickly rallied, however, and walked towards the hall straight-backed and stoic, almost as if he expected to walk a gauntlet of blows and gobbets of spit.

None of Alfred's people struck him physically as he walked inside, although all glared murderously at him, and more than a few muttered threats and insults. Many of those living on Athelney with the king had been there that terrible night when they'd been chased from Cippanhamme only to be cruelly turned away from the locked gates of Brycgstow by Diuma and his aged father. Even those who did not think of the young thane as a friend were outraged by the way he'd behaved, putting all their lives in danger and breaking his sworn oath of loyalty.

The hall was warm, for the fire was lit – a cauldron of meaty-smelling broth bubbling away over the flames. Alfred saw beads of perspiration on Diuma's brow and he was pleased by his erstwhile comrade's discomfort. Let the turd sweat!

The king went to take his place at the high table, although it was not actually raised for the hastily built, simple hall had a flat, level floor. Alfred's place was at the far end of the building though, taking pride of place, and he led his family there now. Ealhswith and Oswald sat to his left, Wulfric the right, and, the children, wide-eyed, stood behind them. Aethelflaed glared at Diuma with the same cold fury in her expression as her mother, while Edward seemed more curious.

Everyone else took up their usual positions at the benches where they sat for meals, while Diuma stood beside the firepit with his captain, Tatberht, both trying to appear calm and unflustered – but their fidgeting hands and shared glances betrayed the anxiety they were feeling.

Alfred did not take pity on them. Rather than allowing Diuma to say his piece immediately, he commanded his people to furnish themselves with drinks of water or ale and, if they were of a mind, to help themselves to bowls of broth. Cups were filled for the king and his family too and, at last, Diuma, whose sleeve was stained with the sweat he'd wiped from his forehead, was addressed.

'Well, then, traitor,' demanded the king. 'Why are you here? Bringing word from your master, Guthrum? Demanding my surrender perhaps?'

'This should be good,' Ealhswith growled, and Alfred squeezed her hand. Although she was doing her best to mask it, he had never seen his wife so angry before, and that only made *him* angrier. There were laws to hospitality, ancient laws that protected travellers – *Xenia* the Greeks had called it – and Alfred had always honoured those ancient codes of conduct. Even so, he was not sure if he could let Diuma leave Athelney alive after he'd delivered his message...

'I have come here, my lord,' started the thane, but his voice was hoarse and he had to clear it before repeating himself. 'I have come, lord, and lady,' he looked at Ealhswith and gave her a sickly smile which was not returned as he forged on, 'to beg forgiveness for what happened on Twelfth Night.'

'Forgiveness!' Ealhswith breathed in a venomous tone, and Alfred barked a sardonic laugh that was echoed by most of the people there.

'Forgiveness, aye, my lord,' Diuma said, meeting Alfred's gaze and dropping to one knee before the king. 'I would beg your pardon, lord, for Brycgstow's heinous lack of hospitality that terrible night, and...' He paused, drawing in a deep breath as shouts and jeers of fury filled the hall, then he said in a louder, stronger voice, 'And I have come to tell you our fyrd is ready to join you, and march with you, my lord, to face the Danes.'

The jeering stopped then and Alfred stared at Diuma, wondering if he'd heard the man right.

'You wish to join us again?' he asked.

'I do, my lord,' Diuma replied earnestly, still on one knee. His captain had also dropped to one knee and was nodding hearty agreement with the thane's pledge.

'You want to reaffirm your allegiance to the king now,' Wulfric murmured. 'But did not feel the same on the night we came to you after Cippanhamme was attacked.'

'He's right,' Alfred agreed. 'Explain your actions that night, Diuma. You put my entire family in danger, yet come now seeking forgiveness? We could all have been killed thanks to you!'

Diuma was visibly distraught as he listened to the king's tirade. 'That...' Again, he broke off, took a deep breath, and continued, 'Was my father's doing. He had agreed a deal with Guthrum to refuse you aid.'

'You blame your wizened old father,' Ealhswith said in a hard voice. 'But I saw *you* on the walls of Brycgstow that night, Diuma. I heard *you* tell us you would not let us into the town, and I heard *you* tell us to go away and seek sanctuary elsewhere!'

Diuma was nodding and his cheeks were wet with tears now, something Alfred had never expected to see for the young thane was usually haughty and proud and, as a warrior, hated to show weakness, especially in front of so many people as were gathered in Athelney's new hall.

'I am sorry, my lady, truly sorry,' he said, head tilted to one side like a chastened puppy. 'But I could not go against my father's orders. He was still ealdorman. He still controlled our fyrd and the guards within the town, and...' He trailed off, staring at the floor as he shook his head. 'He's my father. It's my duty to obey his wishes.'

'It was your duty to obey your fucking king!' Wulfric roared, making everyone in the hall jump.

'I know that!' Diuma retorted, becoming angry himself now. 'And it killed me to turn you away. You are, or at least, were, my friend, Wulfric.' His eyes travelled from the ealdorman to Alfred, Ealhswith, the children, and then around the room to the other men he knew there. 'You all were. But what could I do? My father commanded the loyalty of our men, if I tried to countermand his orders I'd have been locked up and stripped of all my power. I *had* to do as I was commanded that night, as much as it pained me.'

Alfred gazed at him, wondering if his words were true. Unless Diuma was as good an actor as the ones the king had seen in biblical dramatizations during his childhood visits to Rome, he appeared to be speaking honestly, and to be genuinely hurt by what had happened.

'What's changed now, then?' Ealhswith asked, brow still furrowed as she eyed Diuma, although her tone was not quite as harsh. 'Has Ealdorman Wealdmar died, allowing you to assume command of Brycgstow?'

'I hope he has,' someone in the crowd muttered, and another added viciously, 'Aye, painfully!'

Diuma winced at the barb but did not address it. Instead, he spoke to Ealhswith, saying, 'No, lady, my father is still alive, but I – with the help of Tatberht – have spent the last few months sowing the seeds of discontent among the people of our town. Turning them against the Danes, and building support for you, Lord King.'

'How admirable,' Wulfric muttered.

Diuma ignored that. 'Last week, I decided I'd gained enough support amongst the warriors of the town, and we seized control of the place. My father did not offer much resistance, I have to say, for even he has grown tired of how things are going in Wessex since you were forced into exile.'

'And now you come to us in our hideaway here in the marshes,' Alfred sneered. 'Like the risen Christ. A saviour!' He was in no mood to forgive Diuma, but he felt Ealhswith's hand tightening on his and turned to her.

'I think he speaks the truth,' she murmured in a low voice. 'And we could use his fyrd, or we might be stuck in Athelney forever.'

'Christ does teach forgiveness, lord,' Oswald added.

'What if he's lying, though,' the king asked. 'And this is a ploy by Guthrum to bring us out into the open so they can attack us? It wouldn't be the first time Diuma and his father have betrayed us after all!'

'My lord,' Tatberht said, leaning forward almost desperately although he remained on one knee. 'This is no trick.'

'No one gave you leave to speak, boy,' Wulfric said, and the two captains stared at one another haughtily.

'Let him say his piece,' Alfred shrugged, waving a hand at the young warrior who nodded respectfully.

'At first the people of Brycgstow were content to go along with Ealdorman Wealdmar's wishes but, as the weeks passed and rumours spread about what was happening to the other people of Wessex, well, unrest began to set in.'

'The older folk, soldiers included,' Diuma elaborated, 'took longer to realise my father might not be leading us in the right direction. But, with Tatberht's help, I convinced the younger people that the Danes should be stood up to, and you, our rightful king, should have been supported all along.' He spread his hands, nodding. 'Eventually, even the elders were questioning how things were going. When the call came from Guthrum a few days ago, demanding we raise our fyrd and march to join the Northmen's army, that was enough for me to make my move.'

Alfred shared a look with Wulfric. Guthrum was building his army again? For what purpose? Nothing good, that much was obvious.

'Your father?' Ealhswith was asking Diuma, and Alfred forced his attention back to the thane.

'He is well, lady,' Diuma replied, ignoring the disappointed groans of those packing the hall. 'But, when even his own closest advisors chose to side with me, he realised it was time to hand over power to someone else.'

'Why come here yourself with this wonderful news?' Wulfric asked. 'You must have known there was a chance one of us would kill you before you even got within our walls.'

'That was a possibility,' the thane admitted. 'But I thought you would believe me more readily than some messenger. You can look in my eyes, my lords and ladies, and judge whether I speak truly or not.'

Alfred stood up then, staring at Diuma and probing a tooth with his tongue distractedly. Then he patted little Edward, who was standing beside him, on the shoulder and walked around the table to gaze down at the kneeling men from Brycgstow. 'Look at me, then, Diuma,' he said. 'Look at me, and let me judge your truthfulness.'

Their eyes locked and the hall fell completely silent; even the crackling fire seemed to still for those few moments as the two men stared at one another.

'Have you been sent here as an agent of Guthrum?' Alfred asked softly. 'Do you intend me, and my people here in Athelney, harm?'

'No, lord,' Diuma replied, and his tone was strong and his gaze did not waver from the king's.

'Swear it,' Alfred said.

'As God is my witness,' Diuma intoned, voice echoing powerfully around the compact hall. 'I am loyal to you, King Alfred of Wessex, and always have been. My life is yours, lord.'

Alfred searched his eyes a long time for some sign of duplicity and then, at last, said, 'I once gifted you a seax – a token of my gratitude for your loyalty and service. You gave it back to me that night when we came to the gates of Brycgstow.'

Diuma's expression was utterly miserable as he replied hoarsely, 'Yes, lord.'

'I have been carrying this seax,' said Alfred, reaching down to his belt and drawing out the blade there, 'in hopes that one day I could kill you with it.'

Tatberht stiffened in alarm, wondering if he should make a move to protect his lord.

'Instead,' Alfred said, spinning the weapon and holding it out to the kneeling thane, handle first. 'I return it to you, with all the honour and friendship it was originally given. You are forgiven.'

Diuma's eyes filled with tears as he took the gift and allowed Alfred to help him up to his feet. They embraced, and Ealhswith was suddenly there, holding out her hand for Diuma to kiss. He did so fervently, murmuring apologies to her and her children, and swearing to help Alfred retake his throne, or die trying.

The atmosphere had completely changed within the hall, as most of the hearth-warriors accepted Alfred's decision to allow Diuma back into the fold. Both the thane and his young captain were given drinks and seats at one of the benches, there to answer the myriad questions the Athelney folk had, and to fill them in on what was happening in Brycgstow and further afield.

Wulfric had grasped wrists with Diuma, but, typically of the bluff ealdorman, showed little inclination to have the previous cordial relationship with the thane restored. Even Alfred could not tell what Wulfric truly felt about this turn of events, but now was not the time to discuss such things, for the king wanted to gather as much intelligence as possible from Diuma before deciding on their next course of action. If Guthrum was mustering an army Alfred would need to do something about it, or face losing his grip on Wessex forever.

Some of the folk in the hall were disappointed that Diuma hadn't been dealt with more harshly for his previous actions, not quite believing his side of events, but, with no further entertainment to be had, the inhabitants of the little fortress soon went back about their usual business, leaving Alfred, Wulfric, Oswald, and Ealhswith to talk more with the pair from Brycgstow.

'Have you heard from Ealdorman Wulfhere?' the king asked Diuma as they supped ale near the open door, where a cool breeze came through.

'No,' Diuma said, shaking his head. 'My father was sending messengers back and forth to him, but stopped telling me what was being said when I started making more of a fuss about cutting ties with the Danes.'

'Then we must assume Wulfhere still sides with Guthrum,' Wulfric said.

'But he might choose to support us,' Ealhswith put in. 'Once he knows Diuma's fyrd is with us.'

Alfred was nodding at his wife's assertion. 'True. Well, then… I think I have indeed received the sign from God that I had been praying for earlier, eh, Oswald?'

The priest was smiling, overjoyed by the happy reconciliation. 'I agree, lord.'

'What next then?' asked Ealhswith. 'Now that our army has grown by a fyrd, while Guthrum's has shrunk.'

'Next?' Alfred asked, grinning. 'Next we send out messengers to all of those loyal to me, and command them to muster their fyrds at my grandfather, Egbert's, stone. You know it, Wulfric?'

The ealdorman nodded.

'Then send word, if you would,' Alfred said. 'And you, Diuma, return to Brycgstow and prepare your men to march.' He stood up and once again embraced the thane warmly. 'This is the day we've been praying for,' he murmured, walking out through the door and looking up at the sky, face glowing in the sunshine. 'We march to war, my friends!' he cried, smiling at the guards on the wall and the others cleaning their gear and butchering the animals that had been hunted recently.

They all cheered, every one of them, overjoyed to be finally, after months of hiding away, ready to strike at their despised oppressors. 'To war!' they roared, powerful voices carrying out across the steaming marshes.

'To war!'

CHAPTER SEVENTEEN

'You want me to go to war?'

'That's what I said, isn't it?'

The Dane glowered at Wulfhere, and the Ealdorman of Wiltunshire wished he could strike the bastard down.

How dare this man come striding into his hall here in Wilton as if he owned the place? Wulfhere was one of the wealthiest and most powerful noblemen in the kingdom! Still, this Dane was an emissary from Guthrum who, to all intents and purposes, was ruler of Wessex now that Alfred had been forced into exile. It would not do to anger such an emissary – Wulfhere was already walking a tightrope, since many of his fellow West Saxons despised him for turning against Alfred and giving his support to the Danes. He did not want to anger Guthrum too.

So he held his temper and waited until servants had provided the visitor and his companions with food and drink. There was a dozen of them, and their war-gear marked them as important members of Guthrum's army. Fine mail-shirts, shining helmets, arm rings, rune-carved swords, and fine seaxes adorned every one of them, and they'd ridden into Wilton on magnificent horses. Their leader was called Leif Ormsson, and he was tall – of course! – with a bristling grey beard and pale blue eyes that seemed to bore straight through Wulfhere every time the Dane looked at him. It was quite unsettling to feel so impotent within one's own hall. Of only average height and wiry build himself, with long grey hair and neat beard, Wulfhere knew he did not cut as imposing a figure as any of these burly Danes.

'When am I supposed to take my fyrd to join with Guthrum?' the ealdorman asked once his guests had eaten and drunk their fill.

'*King* Guthrum,' Leif snapped, lip curling. It was quite clear he did not care for Saxons, even wealthy ones. 'You are to summon your warriors immediately, and come with us.'

Wulfhere nodded but the gesture masked his feeling of shock. Summon his army immediately? Then join the sea-wolves and fight other Saxons in order to strengthen Guthrum's stranglehold on Wessex? Such a scenario had never crossed his mind when he chose to allow the Danes to pass through his lands without attacking them. He'd been happy to receive payment from Guthrum for that, and it had suited Wulfhere to have Alfred deposed, but to actively fight alongside these hard men who'd come to these lands purely to rape and pillage... It was inconceivable!

And yet, as he felt Leif Ormsson's iron gaze upon him, Wulfhere knew he had no choice. He could not stand against the Danes alone. Drawing in a deep breath, he tried to steady himself, gather his thoughts. What a mess Wessex was in, and much of it was down to him. He should have supported Alfred as he had sworn to do, but the king had not shown himself to be as strong a ruler as many of the ealdorman wished, and it had brought them to this point. Or so Wulfhere told himself.

'Should you not be sending your messengers out with orders to gather the fyrd, Saxon?' Leif grated, tearing a piece of roast beef into shreds with his teeth. 'The day is passing, and King Guthrum wants your men with him as soon as possible.'

The arrogance of these men! Lounging around at Wulfhere's benches, filling their bellies with his meat and ale, all while staring at the ealdorman as if he was nothing more than a thrall.

'Yes, I'll have my captain begin preparations immediately,' he heard himself say meekly, and he despised himself for it. For a man who supposedly wielded great power, Wulfhere felt at that moment like a child being bullied by older, bigger, stronger boys. In his mind's eye he imagined drawing his sword and hacking Leif Ormsson and his comrades to pieces, but his face betrayed none of his inner turmoil. Instead, he beckoned to one of his own guards.

'Yes, lord?'

'Take word to my thanes,' Wulfhere said, feeling like even more of a traitor than he had in the days following Alfred's flight from Cippanhamme. 'I want the fyrd mustered.'

The guard hurried off and Leif grinned, his mocking gaze still not moving away from Wulfhere.

'I thought Alfred was hiding in Athelney,' said the ealdorman, trying to ignore the Dane's unsettling countenance. 'How is *King* Guthrum planning on finding him, never mind fighting him?'

'Who said we were fighting Alfred?' Leif drawled, lifting his ale mug and sipping without once taking his eyes from the Saxon.

Wulfhere was taken aback. 'Well, if not Alfred, who are we fighting?'

'Everyone who hasn't pledged allegiance to us,' the Dane replied. 'If Alfred dares to crawl out of his hiding place to help them, so much the better.'

Taking this in, Wulfhere quickly understood the implications. 'You mean people here, in Wessex? You would have me raise my army to attack the towns and settlements bordering my own lands?' This was even worse than he had initially believed!

'Only if they refuse to abase themselves to Guthrum. All they have to do is bend the knee to him, pay a suitable tribute, and all will be well. You see, Guthrum has decided he wants to play at being a real king here in these lands. He likes how green they are, and wants to settle down.' Leif snorted. 'He's younger than me, but he's decided it's time he gave up raiding.'

Wulfhere returned his icy gaze, appraising the Dane. His skin was weather-beaten and heavily lined, and his beard was turning white in places, yet he moved with the grace of a young man.

It was hard to tell just how old Leif Ormsson might be. 'And you have not decided to give up raiding?' he asked.

The Dane shook his head, baring his teeth in a wolfish grin. 'I will never give up raiding, I am a *vikingr* and always will be.'

His men cheered at that and thumped their mugs on the benches.

'What will you do when Guthrum settles down and no longer needs you?' Wulfhere demanded, his hatred of the arrogant invaders finally making him bold. 'Will you forego your oath to him, and move on to pastures new, to rape and kill and destroy lives as you've spent your whole existence doing?'

Leif glanced at his men. Some of them smirked, but others, including Leif himself, were not amused.

'I have sworn no oath to Guthrum,' the Dane replied. 'I serve him because he is useful. When he is no longer useful, I will sail away with my men and find another warlord to follow. Unlike you, Saxon, I would not renounce an oath.'

Wulfhere felt his face flush scarlet and rage did threaten to overpower him at the slight on his honour. He made to stand up, teeth bared, but reason quickly overcame his anger – attacking Leif Ormsson would lead to a bloodbath within the hall, and Wulfhere would likely be killed before he could even land a blow on his so-called allies.

'That's right,' drawled the Dane, smiling grimly as the ealdorman slowly eased himself back down on his seat. 'Sit there and do as you are told, fool. What are you so angry about anyway? Did you *not* betray Alfred?'

Wulfhere stared at him, feeling sick to his stomach. The fact Leif was right only made it worse. He was not about to give the Dane the satisfaction of an answer, however.

'I have a fyrd to muster,' he growled, getting to his feet properly this time. 'Finish your meal, sea-wolf, and get the hell out of my lands. Your presence offends me.'

Leif popped another piece of meat in his mouth and masticated it slowly, eyeing Wulfhere disdainfully, but his eyes glittered with amusement as he replied, 'I am not leaving your lands, Saxon, not yet. We will remain here until you and your army march to join Guthrum, and then we will travel with you.'

Wulfhere could feel his own guards' eyes on him and the shame and fury within him burned white hot, but he somehow held it in check and stalked out of the hall. He did not turn back, even when the mocking laughter of the Northmen followed him out into the early afternoon sunshine.

Alfred stood on the fortress wall, gazing out at the marsh that had been his home for weeks, now. It was a fine, sunny day and the sound of insects buzzing filled the air as they pollinated the colourful spring flowers dotted around the land. His hearth-warriors had stripped the stronghold of any valuables and supplies that morning, carrying what they could in packs, and loading it all into the punts that had been their lifeline to Sumorsaete. Men and women's voices could be heard, chattering loudly, happily, as they worked to vacate their temporary home.

Temporary. Somehow it did not feel like Alfred was about to leave a place that could be described in such a fleeting term. Athelney had – incredibly, given the circumstances – found a place deep within the king's heart. Part of him did not want to leave.

Especially since they did not truly know what they would be marching towards once they left the hastily constructed yet sturdy walls of the fortress. Had Guthrum managed to enlist yet more Danes from lands across the sea, as he'd done before? Had he swelled his ranks by bribing more West Saxon noblemen to join him? Would Diuma hold true to his word?

'Are you ready to go, lord?'

Alfred turned and saw Oswald climbing the steps towards him. His tonsure had been freshly trimmed and he was beaming. The king might be feeling strangely sad to be leaving the marshes behind, but the priest was overjoyed and looking forward to being amongst the people of Wessex, doing God's work again.

'Just about,' Alfred replied, turning back to gaze upon the marshes and breathe deeply of the warm air.

'You don't sound very sure,' Oswald noted, peering intently at the king's expressionless face.

Alfred smiled. The priest had always been able to gauge his mood – that was one reason why he was such a valuable advisor. That, and his honesty.

'We're about to leave this poor excuse for a royal palace,' smiled Oswald. 'You are about to crush the heathen horde and take back your throne! Yet you seem unhappy. Why, my lord?'

Alfred swallowed. He felt like there was a lump of phlegm in the back of his throat and he coughed to try and shift it, but it would not move. Fear suddenly filled him and, in the space of those few moments, he felt a terrible pain flare in his belly. Gasping, he bent over, reaching out for the palisade wall to steady himself. Sweat was already beading his forehead and he coughed again, and again, yet still it felt like there was something in his throat.

'My lord,' Oswald yelped, reaching out to grasp his arm and muttering a Pater Noster faster than Alfred had ever heard it said before.

More footsteps came up the wooden steps then and a surge of relief filled Alfred as he saw Ealhswith.

'Can you walk?' she asked, staring at him fearfully.

'I... Yes,' he managed through gritted teeth.

'Come then, Oswald. Help me get him down to the hall before the men see him.'

The pain was excruciating. Alfred cursed, sobbing as he realised this was the first time he'd suffered these pains in months; since before they'd come to Athelney, he believed. He'd even stupidly allowed himself to think he might have been cured!

Ealhswith and Oswald were not particularly strong, physically, and Alfred was a big, muscular man, so he forced himself to walk as best he could down the steps which seemed horribly shaky, and he was glad when they reached the bottom. Two of his soldiers were in the yard removing sacks of dried fish, and they paused to gape at the trio stumbling towards the hall. One opened his mouth to offer aid but Ealhswith's look was enough to send them on their way without a word. Alfred hoped it would also be enough to keep them from telling the rest of the men, for these episodes always greatly embarrassed him. The less people who knew about it the better, although he could hardly blame folk for talking about this debilitating weakness of his.

He sucked in a long breath, trying to calm his whirling thoughts. He knew from past experience that dwelling on the sensations he was feeling, and the worries the situation brought him, did not help in any way. It usually made his sense of panic worse, if anything.

They came to the door and Ealhswith kicked it – luckily it was not latched and swung open easily, allowing them to head inside. It was mercifully cool within the shadowy hall for the firepit had been extinguished earlier that morning and the warm sweat on Alfred's brow felt cold as it dried. Ealhswith and Oswald led him to the first bench they came to and eased him down. He lifted his feet with some difficulty for he felt as weak as a newborn babe, placing them on the bench so he could lie on his side, arm acting as a pillow as he stared at the wall and tried to slow his breathing. The pain was beginning to subside – thank Christ! – and another laboured cough finally cleared the phlegm in his throat.

There was no one else in the hall, and the quiet helped calm the king further until, after a while, he thanked the priest and asked him to go and help with the work outside. 'You must have prayer books and holy relics to load onto the punts,' Alfred murmured as Oswald stood to leave.

'Oh aye, lord,' the priest replied with a sympathetic smile. 'All this time on Athelney I've been hiding the entire True Cross beneath the little altar we had built!'

Alfred chuckled and Oswald went out into the morning, closing the door behind him. As the latch fell into place, Alfred's smile disappeared and he sobbed again, hiding his face in the crook of his arm so Ealhswith couldn't see his twisted features.

'You're frightened,' his wife said softly, her clear, melodious voice barely echoing in the empty hall.

'Terrified,' he admitted. 'I hate it when this happens.'

'No,' Ealhswith said, placing a hand on his arm. 'I mean you're frightened about facing the Danes in battle. We've been safe here in Athelney for so long it seems, and now we must leave the protection of this hall, and the walls that saved us from being overrun.'

Alfred looked at her, his discomfort momentarily forgotten as he thought about her words.

'It's natural to be anxious, my love,' she said, smiling. 'You care about the lives of your people. Of the hearth-warriors and friends who followed you here, and of the levies who will make up the bulk of your army. I can only imagine how scared you are to be leading them to what might be their deaths.'

He breathed deeply, knowing his wife was right, as she usually was.

'The pains you feel are not going to kill you – they never have, in all these years, have they? And they will fade over time.'

He nodded. 'They'll be completely gone by the time the battle starts.'

'There you go then. Come on. Take a few more deep breaths, and then we'll get back to work. Would you like a drink of something?'

'No, thank you,' he replied, and he was smiling too. He felt much better.

'I know you feel ashamed – weak – whenever these pains come on. But it just shows how much you care, and you're always strong enough to move past them. You should be proud of yourself. I'm certainly proud of you.'

His laugh was almost a sob, but this was one of sheer happiness and they embraced one another, holding tightly for a long time, not speaking, just enjoying one another's strength and love.

'And I'm the luckiest man in Wessex to have you,' he said at last, composing himself and leading Ealhswith by the hand towards the door. 'Come on, it's time we showed Guthrum what he's got himself into.'

'Agreed,' the queen consort grinned, following him out into the sunshine. 'Time to kick Guthrum's hairy Norse arse, and take back your kingdom!'

The men had finished moving all the goods from the island over to the mainland by now, and they looked at Alfred with somewhat surprised expressions as he and Ealhswith came out of the fort and down the slope towards the water, hand-in-hand and laughing like happy children.

CHAPTER EIGHTEEN

AD 878, Sumorsaete

May

Egbert's Stone was exactly what its name implied. There was nothing greatly impressive about it – it was simply a useful local landmark, and a well-known meeting place. Everyone of standing in Wessex knew of it, and where it was, roughly at least. It was the ideal place to bring all the individual fyrds together, and combine them into one army loyal to the rightful king.

'It feels good to be on horseback again, eh?'

Alfred grinned at Wulfric who was riding beside him. 'Aye,' he agreed. 'I've missed this.' He breathed in the warm air, watching as jackdaws flapped noisily past overhead. 'It's good to be out in the open again! To know that I could just kick my heels in and ride over there,' he jerked his head at the rolling landscape to the east, 'for miles, without stopping. Without having to hunt for a safe way across the ground, or to get into a rickety little boat and paddle across haunted marshes!' He laughed at the memory of the day when Aethelflaed had mocked Wulfric for fearing the dead faces in the waters, and heard his daughter joining in behind him.

The commanders and hearth-warriors rode in the front row, while the infantry marched behind, with the king's family mounted in the centre. It was still completely unknown what they were riding towards at Egbert's Stone. Would Diuma hold true to his word and bring the Brycgstow fyrd to join them?

Would any of the other thanes and ealdormen that Alfred's messengers had summoned come, or would they forsake him, as Wulfhere and Wealdmar had done at Christmastime?

If they did, Alfred's party – which numbered around one hundred and fifty at this point, as two of the nearest settlements had already sent men to join him – would be wide open to an attack by Guthrum's forces. Alfred knew the Danes were around, and they would exploit any weakness or chance to kill him.

'How many do you think will join us at the stone?' Oswald asked. His tone was optimistic, and the priest's calming presence helped set Alfred's mind a little at ease.

'A couple of thousand,' Dunstan guessed.

'Three,' Wulfric murmured, eyes continually scanning the horizon for signs of danger. 'At least. Ealdorman Aethelnoth will certainly join us – he's as loyal as they come, as he's shown all through our time in his lands.'

Alfred nodded. 'I pray you're right,' he said. 'Two thousand would not be enough to defeat the sea-wolves, I fear. Three thousand though? That might do it.'

'God will provide what we need,' Ealhswith commented from behind them, her high, melodious voice contrasting sweetly with the hard tones of the men. 'It's not long after Easter, almost Whitsuntide, and, for once, we Christians are the ones taking the initiative instead of preparing to feast.'

The king cringed inwardly a little at that. She was right, it was unusual for the West Saxons to mount a military campaign around the time of an important religious festival, and it pained Alfred to do so – they *should* be celebrating at this time. What was the point in following God, if you could not praise Him properly?

Still, the old ways had broken down, and a new way must be found if Alfred was to retake Wessex. The Danes had ruthlessly exploited the Christian customs – attacking Readingum and later Cippanhamme at Christmas, Eoforwic on All Saints Day, and so on, and only a fool would continue down a path that resulted in so many defeats and losses of territory and life. So, as much as it rankled, Alfred had decided to muster the fyrds at this time, for Guthrum would never expect it.

It might not give the West Saxons a huge advantage, for the movement of so many men around Wessex would be noticed eventually, but even any small gain could prove decisive in war. Given they had no idea how big their army would be, or how many enemies they would face, Alfred wanted to exploit every single tactical opportunity he could find.

The journey passed pleasurably enough, thanks mainly to the camaraderie and the good weather. Somehow the sun and birdsong made Alfred's heart light and it seemed easier to foresee a victory in such conditions. He could not shake the terrifying thought that only a few hundred men would answer his summons and the plans for ousting Guthrum would need to be abandoned, but he refused to dwell on it. God was all around them that day, filling every breath Alfred took with His hope and glory, and promises of a bright future.

The hardships of Athelney were coming to an end, and Alfred had survived to emerge even stronger. How could the Danes possibly prevail?

A few more men joined them as they passed little settlements on the way to Egbert's Stone although not as many as the king would have liked. Oswald did not comment on the small numbers, but Wulfric could not keep the disappointment from his face, and Dunstan grumbled openly, wondering where the hell everyone else was.

It was hard to completely ignore the possibility that 'everyone else' was purposely ignoring Alfred's summons or, worse, had joined Guthrum.

Their course had been set, however, and there was nothing to do but journey on, and pray. Indeed, that was what Oswald was doing. He moved back to ride with Ealhswith and the children, and his pleasant, trained voice rose above the rest of the chatter as he asked for God's blessing on the coming endeavours. Some of the party joined in quietly, though most were content merely to listen and enjoy being part of something they hoped would be momentous.

That whole day had the potential to be one of the greatest of Alfred's life.

Or the worst.

'People ahead,' called Aedan. He was riding a little way in front of the main group, scouting, and he came back towards them now, red hair and beard practically ablaze in the sunshine.

'Friend or foe?' Wulfric demanded.

Aedan shook his head. 'Can't tell from this distance. They're armed, though. At least thirty or forty, maybe more.'

Alfred shared a look with Wulfric. 'How far are we from the muster point?' he asked.

'Not far at all,' the ealdorman replied.

'Then those could be our men, waiting to join us.' They had not stopped moving but he turned in his saddle and shouted back to the rest of their compact warband. 'Be ready for a fight, lads. Just in case.'

Shields and spears were readied, and the party moved on, carrying with them a rather different atmosphere to the one of mere moments before. The threat of death and violence hung about them now, like a great dark cloud. Alfred hoped that, if the soldiers ahead belonged to Guthrum, they would retreat at the sight of the men of Wessex, for he had no desire to lose any of his little army this early in what might be a long campaign. Now was not the time to fight. That would come all too soon.

As they neared the gathered men it became clear there were a lot more than just thirty of them and Alfred's heart practically leapt into his mouth at the sight. If they were hostile, this was about to be the end of his war, and probably his life.

Now the king's party had been spotted and both sides stared at one another, trying to work out who they might be and whether their weapons would be needed.

'My lord?'

Alfred turned to Dunstan and saw him nodding downwards.

'Shall I raise it?' the thane asked, indicating the red banner of Wessex with its golden dragon boldly emblazoned upon it.

The king thought about it for just a heartbeat, and then nodded grimly. 'Aye, might as well. If they're enemies, it's too late to turn back anyway. Let's show them who they face.'

Dunstan smiled, excitement and anticipation mingling on his face as his muscular arms took the strain, and the spear he held with the banner attached was slowly raised up into the air above them.

It fluttered in the gentle breeze and, on a day as clear as that, could be seen from a good distance away thanks to the contrast of its bright, vibrant colours against the mostly green and blue that formed the land and sky around them.

Alfred, and everyone with him, held their breath, waiting to see what the reaction would be from the soldiers they were riding towards.

And then a great cheer erupted from those ahead, and relief washed over Alfred. Shouts of joy rose from those beside him, and he looked at Wulfric. The ealdorman was smiling, Alfred was practically screaming with sheer joy, and Ealhswith and Oswald were singing praises to God. It was an incredible moment.

Those soldiers were not Danes. They were men of Wessex, and they were there to fight for Alfred.

—

The commanders of the individual fyrds did their best to keep their men back but, as Alfred and his party made their way through the burgeoning army it was slow going. The men wanted to clap one another on the back, shouting 'Hail!' and 'Well met!', while others bowed deeply upon seeing Lady Ealhswith and the curious, amused children staring back at them apparently none the worse for wear after months living in a damp marsh. Alfred made eye contact with all he could – smiling, waving, shaking his fist, and nodding in gratitude to those ealdormen or thanes he was able to see and recognise.

Those would be the men he would bestow great gifts upon if this war went the right way. Weapons, armour, silver, horses, lands, and, of course, rings of precious metals. The king would be generous when all this was over, he vowed, for this kind of loyalty deserved rich rewards.

Alfred truly hoped he was worthy of their support.

He spotted Stithulf, a dark-skinned, very tall thane, amongst the throng and their eyes met. The king knew the man, recognising him as hailing from Strood, a town in the south-west. He was a hardy fighter, and exactly the kind of fyrd commander the West Saxons needed.

'How many are here, my lord?' Alfred shouted to the thane who was even taller than Wulfric, towering head and shoulders above most around him.

'It's hard to say, Lord King!' Stithulf called back. 'I've not been here long myself. I'd say about three thousand or so. Enough to give Guthrum a bloody nose, I reckon.'

Alfred grinned although inwardly he felt disappointment. Three thousand was a goodly number, but not enough to guarantee victory. Not by quite some distance. Still, he did not let those gloomy thoughts show on his face and shouted back, 'Find me in my tent later, Stithulf. I'll pour you a mug of ale myself for your loyalty.'

They continued on, slowly pushing through the crowd. Wulfric tried his best to remain close to the king and looked back at Ealhswith and the children constantly, reassuring himself they were all safe. Alfred did not upbraid his captain for his excessive caution – a Dane, or some traitorous Saxon loyal to Guthrum, *could* be amongst the people here, and, by killing Alfred, end the war before it could be rekindled. It would mean a painful, and very quick, death sentence for the perpetrator, but men had died for less lofty causes, so the king merely smiled at Wulfric's anxiety and thanked God again for placing the ealdorman on his side, rather than that of their enemies.

Egbert's Stone was at the top of a low hill and Alfred went up towards it with his hearth-warriors and his family. He knew Ealhswith and the children would be safe now that they were with their own loyal supporters, but he did not want to be parted from them just yet. Besides, he wanted to address his army with his wife by his side. She deserved to be part of that joyous moment as much as anyone, after all. He would have never survived to see this day without Ealhswith's strength to help him on his way.

Many tents had been set up about the hill by the leaders of the fyrds, but space had been left for the returning king, and his small group of riders were shepherded there now. There was a lump in Alfred's throat as he prepared himself to address the levies who'd come to answer his call. It almost felt as if he was about to go into battle and he dismounted carefully, fearful of stumbling in front of so many watchers.

'Ready?' Wulfric asked, and his towering, composed presence helped Alfred gather himself.

'Yes,' the king said, lips curling in the beginnings of a smile.

Although none of this had been planned or rehearsed, it all seemed to happen with such precision and timing that it might have been part of some great play. Alfred grasped Ealhswith's hand, grinned reassuringly at his children, then strode forward to take up a place directly in front of the massive grey boulder named after his grandfather.

For a moment, all he could do was look out at the faces gazing back at him, trying to take everything in. And then he frowned and glanced over his shoulder towards Wulfric.

'What's wrong?' the captain asked, a hint of alarm in his tone.

Alfred's mouth opened. He looked again at the warriors gathered for him, then he murmured to Wulfric, 'There's so many of them!'

For days – weeks even – since he'd first decided to go ahead with this course of action and summon his army to him, he'd had no idea how many would support him. Now his fears were completely obliterated for, filling the land around them, stood a great host of at least four thousand men. Directly in front of him was Aethelnoth, the portly, red-bearded ealdorman who'd supported the king during his exile in Sumorsaete, and a little way along the line, Alfred's old friend, the "prodigal son", Diuma.

Tears filled Alfred's eyes and he felt such gratitude and love for the people of Wessex that he could not help laughing. It was, perhaps, not the response anyone expected, but it was such a genuine display of joy that soon everyone there was also laughing and cheering, and the May countryside was filled with such a cacophony of sound as had never been heard there before.

The king was hugging his wife, and both were crying openly, without shame. Alfred looked back at Wulfric through his tears and saw the ealdorman smiling. Were even Wulfric's eyes sparkling? Surely not!

'Speak to them, my love,' Ealhswith urged. 'Now, while everyone is so happy. Go on, climb up on top of the stone.'

Nodding, Alfred released her and scrambled up the lichen-encrusted rock which was almost as tall as he was. Making sure his feet were firmly planted, he drew himself up to his full height, one hand resting on his sword's pommel, eyes scanning from left to right, and on, all the way around the hillside he looked, turning as he did, smiling the whole time.

'My people!' he finally shouted, lifting his arms and holding them out, as if drawing those loyal men of Wessex into his embrace. 'My people! It is time to crush the Danes once and for all!'

Again, the land was filled with the deafening sound of thousands of voices ready to reclaim their kingdom.

King Alfred had not forsaken them, and now he had returned.

It was time to go to work.

CHAPTER NINETEEN

'That was quite the speech, my lord,' Diuma said, bowing respectfully as he was ushered into Alfred's tent. 'Powerful stuff.'

The king stood up and practically ran to the thane, drawing him into a rough embrace and laughing loudly. The excitement and joy of the day still pounded within his veins and it was only enhanced by the sight of his friend, once more back at his side where he belonged.

'In truth,' he admitted, 'I can barely remember what I said. I was so overcome…'

'We all were,' Diuma agreed with a hint of sadness. He plainly still felt the shame of forsaking Alfred, despite his father's orders.

'You came when I called,' the king said to him, meeting the younger man's gaze. 'All else is past.'

'Thank you, lord,' replied Diuma. 'Tomorrow is a new day, indeed.'

'Speaking of tomorrow,' Alfred said, re-taking a seat on the folding camp chair that had been placed inside his tent. 'We'll not tarry here – on the morrow, we march.'

'Where to?' asked the thane, following Alfred's gesture and dropping gratefully down onto a second camp chair.

Alfred smiled and tapped his nose secretively. 'You'll find out when we get there.'

Diuma's face fell. 'You still don't trust me,' he said.

'Oh, it's not that at all,' the king replied truthfully. 'I just don't want to give that arsehole Guthrum *any* clues about what we're up to, or where we might march to. Don't be offended, Diuma, I've not told any of my commanders where we're going.'

'Any?'

Alfred couldn't help notice the jealousy evident in his friend's simple question, but Diuma had, after all, been let off lightly after his betrayal, so the king did not seek to assuage the thane's bruised feelings. As it happened, Wulfric came into the tent then.

'You know where we're going tomorrow, no doubt,' Diuma said to him.

Wulfric eyed him in silence for a time, and then simply smiled before addressing the king. 'I've spoken with all the fyrd leaders, my lord. They know we'll be moving at first light, and will have their men ready.'

'Good. Where are they now?'

'Outside, lord. Still gathered, just chatting to one another.'

'Perfect,' Alfred said, beaming. 'Then I'll go out and share bread and ale with them. Thank them for coming. Four thousand warriors, eh, lads? That might just be enough... Diuma, go on ahead and have the ceorls prepare things, eh? And ask Oswald to say Mass for us – if ever God deserved praise, it's today.'

The thane stood up and bowed again then, with a final smile that told of his relief to be back in the fold, headed out through the low tent flaps.

'Where are we going tomorrow anyway?' Wulfric asked as Alfred stood and readied himself to meet the noblemen who would form the spine of his army for the forthcoming, hopefully final battle.

'Isley Oak,' said Alfred.

Wulfric nodded, picturing the surrounding geography in his mind.

'And then, old friend,' said the king, placing his hand on Wulfric's arm. 'We'll attack Guthrum in the same place he attacked us. Cippanhamme.'

'Hail to Óðinn, the All-Father!'

'One-eyed!'

'Bring us victory against the weak Saxons!'

Ealdorman Wulfhere sat in his tent, listening to the Danes who were enjoying horns of mead after the day's journey from Wilton. Enjoying it far more than seemed necessary to Wulfhere. And their bellowing and shouted cries to their heathen gods was even more of an affront to good taste than the ealdorman could stomach.

'I'll go for a walk,' he said irritably to his captain, Eada. 'I can't sit here listening to Leif Ormsson and his pagan rabble any longer.'

He left his tent and heard the Danes calling on him to join them. Their words were filled with mockery however, and he ignored them, pretending he hadn't heard. They soon lost interest in taunting the West Saxon nobleman and returned to singing about their gods; Þórr and Loki were the focus now, and Wulfhere gritted his teeth at the crude, sexually-charged song that filled the air over his camp.

His Christian camp.

'Are you all right, lord?'

Wulfhere shook his head at Eada's question. 'No, I'm not all right,' he spat, literally, specks of saliva spraying the grass before him as he strove to put distance between himself and the interlopers accompanying his army to Cippanhamme. 'Listen to those bastards! Wessex is a Christian land, yet I'm forced to bend the knee to Guthrum's men and their one-eyed, idiot gods!' He kicked petulantly at a stone, watching it skitter away across the ground and wishing it was Leif Ormsson's head.

His captain – a bald man who'd lost one of his ears in battle – peered back at the carousing Danes then said, in a low voice, 'It's not too late to change our course, lord. We don't need to fight beside those men.'

Wulfhere sighed, his rage dissipating, and replaced by a deep melancholy. He had always done what he thought right for his people, and, of course for himself. He was not ashamed of that – every man looked after himself, it was the way God had made them. Self-preservation was built into everyone, especially great ealdormen like Wulfhere. He had not sided with Guthrum because he was evil, but because Alfred had proven himself unable to defeat the Danes, losing much of Wulfhere's wealth in the process.

He'd fully expected Alfred to be killed during the raid on Cippanhamme at Christmas and, when the king had somehow managed to escape, Wulfhere thought he would flee to Rome or Francia, never to be seen again, as Burgred had done when the Danes became too much for him to take any more.

Yet Alfred had not run away. Had not forsaken the people of Wessex, which would have been the easy option. Instead, the young king had fought back from a position of weakness. Wulfhere could not help but admire his tenacity and courage. Maybe Alfred was a man worth following after all.

They came to a stream and its clear, burbling waters immediately worked upon the ealdorman's soul, soothing him and washing away the annoyance he felt at hearing Leif Ormsson's bawdy, heathen songs all morning.

'It's too late for us to renounce Guthrum,' he said, lifting a stick and breaking it absent-mindedly into little pieces, dropping them into the water and watching them float away. 'Like those twigs in the water, we can't reverse our course and paddle back upstream. Time doesn't work like that. We'll be carried along with the rest of the detritus, washed ever forwards until we come to the churning sea, and our doom.'

Eada grunted, forcing a smile he clearly did not feel. 'Bit gloomy, my lord.'

Wulfhere shrugged. 'I fear we're doomed no matter what. When Guthrum has Wessex completely underfoot even the likes of us, who supported him, will not be treated kindly. God help us.'

A sudden shout from behind caught their attention. It was the jarl, Leif, and he was standing with his men, watching Wulfhere gaze into the stream.

'What are you doing there, Saxon?'

'He's talking to the water!' another Dane laughed. 'The thought of going into battle has made him lose his mind!'

They all laughed, and Leif called, 'Come and have a drink with us, man. It will help you get over your terror of the shieldwall. We can drink, and talk of victory over the people of Wessex, and how we will enslave them all!'

Eada laid a hand on Wulfhere's arm, 'Don't rise to it, lord.'

Wulfhere snarled at the Danes but held his peace with great difficulty. To be branded a coward in front of his own fyrd, many of whom were standing listening open-mouthed to the exchange… It was the worst possible insult for a proud nobleman like Wulfhere.

'Why are they goading you?' Eada asked as Leif led his men away to find more drink and their mocking laughter faded. 'We're supposed to be allies.'

Wulfhere winced as he shook his head and felt a band of pain around his skull. The stress was becoming unbearable. 'Some of the Danes are honourable, good people,' he muttered. 'Others, like Leif Ormsson and his rabble, are scum. I suspect he's furious at Guthrum's decision to cease raiding and settle for good here in Wessex. He's taking out his rage on me, which is why I truly fear for the future of our lands and our people once Alfred's finally defeated and Guthrum is crowned king.'

'Then let us leave here,' said Eada vehemently. He was completely loyal to Wulfhere, and hated the way the ealdorman was being made a fool of by their so-called allies. 'Let's tell Leif Ormsson to go fuck himself, then march back to Wilton and bar the gates. Guthrum will have a hard time getting through them, and our fyrd is already mustered, ready to defend our lands if need be.'

Wulfhere watched him as he spoke, and felt a momentary twinge of excitement. They *could* do that. Why not? And then he remembered why not: Guthrum's Danes were much too strong. Even if they did not come for Wilton now, they would subjugate all the other lands surrounding Wulfhere's holdings until, at last, Wiltunshire would stand alone. An island surrounded by enemies.

Much like the marshes of Athelney that Alfred had been forced to hide in, Wulfhere thought ruefully. The Danes had made fools of them both, setting Saxon against Saxon and driving a wedge down the middle of Wessex.

Óðinn take them all!

'My lord.' Eada's curious tone made Wulfhere turn and look to the west, where his captain was staring, brow furrowed as he tried to make out what he was seeing on the rippling horizon.

'Who the hell is that?'

'No idea, lord.' The captain shook his head. 'Looks like thirty or so men.'

'A fyrd,' Wulfhere murmured, mind whirling. Where were they going? Were they too being summoned by Guthrum? And who were they? Then another thought struck him, and he felt a sudden surge of excitement. Turning, he made sure Leif and his band of drunks were not in sight, then gestured to a nearby scout.

'You! Bring me your horse. Hurry!'

The man immediately jumped to do as he was commanded and led his horse, a tall, chestnut mare, over to the ealdorman who took it and jumped into the saddle with practised ease.

'What are you doing?' Eada demanded, amazed. 'You have no idea who those men are. They might be hostile!'

'Let's hope this horse can outrun them if that's the case, then,' Wulfhere replied and, without another word, kicked his heels into his new mount's sides and galloped across the open countryside towards the group of marching strangers.

What the hell was he doing? He wasn't sure himself, but the sight of the fyrd on the horizon had set Wulfhere's thoughts whirling with possibilities. Aye, like his twigs in the stream, he could not simply reverse course and swim backwards, undoing the things he'd done before.

But perhaps there was another route to the sea…

His horse proved to be swift and as eager as he was to feel the wind course past them as they thundered across the ground and, soon enough, his quarry noticed his approach. They formed into a ragged line, showing Wulfhere they were armed and prepared for a fight, but not very well trained, and probably not commanded by anyone with much experience or skill.

He decided the best way to deal with them was to act naturally.

'You men!' he barked as he reined his horse in close to the soldiers but out of range of their spears. 'Where are you from, and where are you going?'

A small, plump man in the middle of the ragged formation puffed out his chest and raised his chin in the air. He was the leader, and he wanted Wulfhere to know it. 'We're going to join our king,' he replied respectfully, but somewhat haughtily too, as if he was annoyed to have been waylaid while on such important business. 'Who are you, my lord?' He squinted at the much larger body of men in the distance behind Wulfhere. 'And who are they?'

The man was no longer quite so confident. He'd been put at ease by Wulfhere's strong, local accent and dialect, but one never knew who was abroad in Wessex these days, and everyone had heard that certain Saxons had thrown their lot in with the enemy raiders.

Saxons like Wulfhere.

'Those,' he said, glancing back, 'are my men. I am Ealdorman Wulfhere of Wiltunshire.'

That brought a rush of indrawn breaths and outward gasps, and the haughty plump fellow flushed red as he bowed deferentially. 'I'm sorry, lord, forgive, er, us. We didn't recognise you. You know how it is. We—'

Wulfhere held up a hand to stop the anxious babbling, smiling to put the man at ease again. 'It's fine,' he said. 'You say you're going to join your king?'

'Aye,' the man replied, and his fear returned. Everyone in Wessex knew Wulfhere had refused to help Alfred when the Danes drove him out of Cippanhamme. Still, a defiant look came onto the fyrd commander's face, and he said, 'I am Godric, Thane of Witcerce. We've remained loyal to the rightful king, and he's returned now from exile to lead us again.' He looked directly into Wulfhere's eyes, surprising the ealdorman. 'We march to drive the Danes from our lands, my lord. As every good Saxon should be doing.'

'Where are *you* going?' someone in the shieldwall asked in a none too friendly tone, and Wulfhere's hand dropped to the pommel of his sword.

For a time, the ealdorman merely looked at them, pondering the soldier's question, and gauging their potential worth on the battlefield. They were not very well armed, or armoured, and their shieldwall was ragged and loosely packed, yet they had courage and belief. Enough to stand up to him, which was actually quite impressive, given who he was and how many men were amassed behind him in the middle-distance.

'Where *am* I going?' he repeated thoughtfully, thoughts churning even faster than before. This was it – a crossroads. The men from Witcerce had been sent as a sign from God, Wulfhere knew, and he could not ignore it. 'Come with me,' he commanded in a tone that left no room for argument. Without waiting for their response, he turned his horse and started back towards his army. When he looked back, Godric and his fyrd were just staring at him in surprise. 'Did you not hear me?' Wulfhere asked, smiling again. 'Come. You shall march with us. Safety in numbers.'

'You still haven't told us where you're going,' the portly thane replied uncertainly. All his life he, and his levies, had followed the orders of their betters, and Ealdorman Wulfhere was most certainly classed as one of their 'betters'.

'To war,' the nobleman replied with a broad smile. 'Join me, my friends, and we'll share in the spoils.'

Godric swallowed, obviously unsure what to do, but the choice was made for him. His men – ceorls, farmers, labourers, fishermen – had the desire to follow the ealdorman's orders ingrained so deeply into them that they started to walk after Wulfhere. Instinctively, they obeyed him, and Godric could do nothing but follow suit.

Wulfhere led the way back to his fyrd, smiling at his new troops every now and again to reassure them all was well, and they were not walking into a trap. By the time they'd noticed Leif Ormsson and his Danes it was too late for the men of Witcerce to retreat, and they glared murderously at Wulfhere, wondering what his intentions were towards them.

'You've brought more men to join Guthrum's army!' Leif bellowed, laughing tipsily. 'Excellent. But we have tarried here too long, Saxon. Time we were moving again. There is much killing to be done.'

Wulfhere nodded, staring down at the jarl from his saddle. 'Indeed.' He gestured to his captain. 'Eada. Have our men ready their weapons.'

'You heard him!' the captain bellowed, anticipating where his commander's thoughts had turned. 'Spears at the ready! Shields up!'

The fyrd immediately responded, their reaction to the order drilled firmly into them over recent months and years.

Leif's smug, drunken confidence wavered as he took in the spears levelled against him and his fellows. 'Do not play games with me, Saxon,' he growled. 'I will not hesitate to kill you, and Guthrum will slaughter—'

'Attack!' Wulfhere screamed, bringing down his arm and pointing at the Danes who hastily drew out their own swords and axes, having left their spears with their horses a short distance away.

Like starved dogs finally let out of their cages, Wulfhere's Saxon warriors closed in on Leif's group, whose weapons were no match for the much longer spears. The fight, if it could even be called that, lasted for mere moments. Wulfhere watched every bloody thrust as it tore through the flesh of the arrogant Danes, beaming savagely, and laughing with sheer glee as Leif Ormsson gave one final, desperate cry, then fell silent in a shredded, gory heap.

Considering there had only been a handful of the enemy against a fyrd of hundreds, it was hardly the greatest victory Wessex had ever seen, yet Wulfhere and his people celebrated as if they'd just destroyed Guthrum's entire heathen army. The release of tension was incredible and near-hysterical laughter filled the field they were in, providing a strange backdrop to the blood-spattered scene.

'I told you we were going to war,' the ealdorman said, turning back to the shocked men from Witcerce. Their thane, Godric, simply nodded, dumbfounded. 'Are you ready now, my friends?' Wulfhere roared from atop his horse, pulling free his sword and brandishing it overhead. 'Shall we join King Alfred and show the rest of the Danes who these lands belong to?'

The cheers that came in reply to his short speech were the loudest Wulfhere had ever heard.

CHAPTER TWENTY

Wulfric's face was as dark as the thunderheads that the men of Alfred's fyrd had awoken to that morning. In contrast, a grinning Alfred gazed out at his massed forces and felt like singing a hymn to God's glory.

'Oh, cheer up, man!' the king chuckled at his captain's stony demeanour. 'Wulfhere might be a snake, but what else could I do but forgive him?'

'You could have taken his head, and assumed command of his lands, and his fyrd!'

'That would not be Christian,' Alfred replied, knowing fine well it would only bring another explosive oath from Wulfric, which it did. 'Fear not, old friend,' he chuckled, 'there'll be consequences for his earlier betrayal, once all this is done. For now, though, his presence is another gift from God. Our army has swelled beyond what we ever hoped, Wulfric! We have a real chance of defeating Guthrum.'

'We always had a chance of that,' Wulfric retorted. 'Or we wouldn't have come here in the first place. We didn't need that traitorous fool to take back your throne, lord.'

Alfred shook his head. He didn't want to argue any more. 'Well, Wulfhere is with us now, when he might have been with the Danes. God be praised, we won't be forced to kill our own people. Now, let's get marching, I'm eager to reach Cippanhamme!'

They had travelled from Egbert's Stone to a place called Iglea Wood, where Wulfhere's outriders had come across them and the two armies had merged. It was perfect timing, and, after making a show of magnanimously forgiving the ealdorman, Alfred had been interested to hear Wulfhere's account of how he'd come to be there. It made for a most enjoyable evening's entertainment, with much drinking and celebrating of the slaughter of Leif Ormsson's sea-wolves.

Now, though, it was time to journey on, to face an army composed of more than just a handful of men.

'Guthrum must know by now that we're in the field,' Diuma said once they were mounted and leading the great host of West Saxons north. 'Keeping our movements as secret as possible is all well and good, but it's impossible to hide this much movement forever.'

'I doubt it'll make much difference,' said Aethelnoth, flicking a crumb from his red beard. 'The Danes will not meet us in open battle, it's never been their style. Not unless they know they have greater numbers, and I seriously doubt that'll be the case here.'

Wulfric muttered agreement. 'It's more likely they'll stay safely within the walls of Cippanhamme and wait us out. We can't besiege the place for long, and they'll undoubtedly have plenty of supplies stockpiled.'

Alfred looked thoughtfully ahead but did not say anything.

'You agree, lord?' Diuma asked.

The king glanced at him, then away, lips pursed, shaking his head slightly. 'I'm not so sure. Wulfhere said Guthrum was planning on striking the towns around here, to consolidate his position. He wants to be seen as the legitimate king of Wessex.'

'So?' Wulfric asked.

'So, if Guthrum wants the people of these lands to see him as their king, he must act as if I'm a usurper.'

'That's ridiculous,' Diuma said, laughing in astonishment. 'You're the rightful king!'

'I was,' Alfred said. 'But Guthrum "defeated" me, and seized my lands. He will see Wessex as his, by right of conquest.'

'Yes,' Wulfhere said. He too had been allowed to ride with the leaders of the army, for Alfred needed him to command his own men once the fighting started. 'Guthrum does think he's the rightful ruler here. And his own warriors grow weary of sitting on their arses – they are urging him to fight, to raid, to bring them plunder once again. But still… It would be out of character for him to face us without some obvious advantage.'

A horse was streaking towards them across the field ahead and Alfred raised a hand to shield his eyes from the pale, morning sunshine. 'That's one of our scouts,' he said.

'Aye, and in a hurry too,' added Wulfric, loosening his sword in its sheath.

'What's ahead?' Alfred asked Wulfhere, whose lands these were.

'Ahead?' the ealdorman replied, thinking quickly. 'We're nearly at Ethandun. Just before that are the ancient walls of Bratton Hillfort, my lord.'

'Bratton Hillfort,' Alfred murmured grimly. He knew the place, and knew it was the ideal spot for an army to muster, and defend, even against a bigger enemy force. 'Well, there we are then. That's the obvious advantage Guthrum needed, Wulfhere. Ready our warriors, gentlemen. It seems we're about to meet the Danes in a battle for the throne, and the future, of Wessex.'

—

It was hard going, marching along the ridge of chalk hills towards Bratton for, although the hills were not particularly high, there were steep slopes which men in war-gear struggled to traverse. The clouds had parted by now as well, and the warm sun brought grumbles and curses from sliding, skittering men. Of course, there was also much levity, as the sight of one's companion rolling down a hill, limbs flailing, could never pass without much good-natured mockery and mirth.

Alfred's scouts informed him that the enemy army had taken up a position within the ancient fort right enough, and showed no signs of leaving the ruined fortifications so, when the West

Saxons grew close enough to see their foes, the king called a halt.

Oswald said Mass, begging God for victory over the pagan invaders, and Alfred was so moved by the service that, when it ended, he embraced his old friend, heart filled with joy and purpose.

'God has given us this opportunity,' the king said, turning from Oswald to address his commanders and any others who could hear him. 'During those first, freezing days in Athelney when it seemed like winter would finish the job of killing me, I could not foresee this day.' He raised his hands, much like the priest had done in his sermon, and smiled at his men. 'I did not forsake Wessex, the people of Wessex did not forsake me, and God did not forsake any of us – he has brought us here today with an army so strong that the Danes cannot, *cannot*, stand against us. Are you with me?'

'Yes!' The reply was immediate and unequivocal. Whatever happened that day, Alfred had the unquestioning support of those warriors. Even Wulfhere, who might have been standing alongside Guthrum had circumstances been just a little different, was cheering Alfred lustily.

'Now, let's show these bastards what we do to raiders in Wessex!'

The war cries and shouts of 'Godemite!' and 'Out! Out!' filled the warm air and Alfred looked at Wulfric. 'Ready, my loyal captain?'

The ealdorman nodded and they gripped forearms, knowing this might well be the last time they saw one another alive. No words were needed, however, for it had all been said on the journey from Athelney, and during their weeks together there. All those hearth-warriors who'd lived in the marshes with Alfred would be remembered, having written their own names into the history of Wessex, no matter how this battle near the town of Edington went.

'Forward, then!'

The king's command rang out, repeated all along the line, and the army moved ahead once more, marching at a steady pace, taking care as the wind had picked up, buffeting them from side to side. Soon Bratton came into view, and Alfred could see the ancient ditches had been freshly deepened, with the Danes using the removed earth to build up a low wall all around them. It was not the most impressive fortress the West Saxons had ever seen, but it would slow them enough to make taking the position much more treacherous than on flat, open ground. Guthrum's shieldwall was lined up, many ranks deep behind those ditches, a silent, brooding presence that emanated menace. Somehow the Danes had managed to amass thousands of men. It was hard to say just how many, exactly, but Alfred's count told him both sides were quite evenly matched, in terms of numbers.

That was concerning, but the king kept his anxiety from his face, staring coldly ahead as each step took them closer to the invaders who'd stolen his throne from him.

When they were just outside throwing spear range, Guthrum himself walked forward. He was of average height but had immense shoulders and a fiery beard and was easily marked for he wore a rich, red cloak over his byrnie and, incredibly, a circlet of gold upon his head.

'Bastard really does want us to believe he's the rightful king,' Wulfric laughed sardonically.

When the Dane addressed them, his words proved Wulfric was right.

'What do you think you're doing here?' Guthrum demanded, staring across the ridge at Alfred. 'These are my lands now, by right of conquest. You abandoned them when you ran away like a frightened girl to live the life of a hermit in the marshes. Wessex is mine, and you have no claim to it anymore.' He pulled out a long-handled axe from his belt and pointed the iron blade at the Saxon army. 'Those are my subjects, and they will return to their homes now. I do not want to kill them all, for who would work my farms then?'

'You are not the king here,' Alfred spat, face twisted in rage. The sight of his enemy had kindled a white-hot fire within him, and it was further fuelled by Guthrum's arrogance. 'These are my lands, and today we will cleanse them of your heathen taint forever, so none even remember your names!'

Guthrum laughed at that, and then he shouted, '*Deyr fé, deyja frændur, deyr sjálfur ið sama. En orðstír deyr aldregi hveim er sér góðan getur.* You know what that means, Alfred?'

The Saxon king furrowed his brow, realising Guthrum had recited a verse from the old collection of Norse wisdom known as the *Havamal*. In his head, he pictured that verse, and its translation into Alfred's own tongue. 'Cattle die, kindred die, we even die ourselves. But the fair fame never dies, of a man who has earned it.' He muttered the words to himself, shaking his head in disgust as he finished. 'Enough talking,' he roared, turning to the ranks massed behind him. 'Step forward, men, and loose spears!'

Guthrum had opened his mouth to say more, the hint of a mocking smile on his lips, but he spun now and ran as fast as he could back to the safety of Bratton Camp, holding the golden crown onto his head as he went. It was a comical sight, but no one laughed for they were all too busy following Alfred's directive.

Twenty paces the entire army strode forward, and then those in the front ranks drew back their arms and, as one, threw their spears. A black mass of iron and wood filled the sky and then came down almost majestically on Bratton Camp. Thuds and screams rang out over the hilltop, and then the Danes had their turn to let their missiles fly.

'Shields up!' Alfred cried, hiding behind his own heavy linden boards. He cringed as the enemy spears thundered into his troops, and reeled in shock as a spear punched clean through the shield of a man behind him, drawing a scream as the iron point made a bloody, gaping ruin of the man's forearm.

'Loose!' It was Wulfric, calm and composed despite the horrors all around them. The big ealdorman threw his own spear, the second of three, and another black cloud of death rained down upon Guthrum's position.

Again, there were cries of agony and terror, and then Alfred was cowering behind his shield as the enemy reciprocated. The man with the mangled arm had thankfully stopped screaming now, as his body went into shock, but more men were crying out all around the king. Crying out for aid, for a priest, for their wives, for their mothers…

'Loose!' Alfred roared, forcing himself to forego the protection of his shield long enough to throw his own second spear, then, without waiting, he threw his third and crouched down behind the shield, praying desperately to God that he would not lose an arm like that other poor bastard.

The Danes' third and, hopefully, final volley passed and Alfred looked around at his men. He could still hear the sobs and cries of the injured and dying but, to the king, his army seemed mostly intact. 'Forward!' he commanded. 'Shields up, let's kill these whoresons!'

Like a wave moving inexorably over a beach, the Wessex fyrd marched across the ridge. In the ancient, ruined fort, the Danes, mostly silent until now, began hammering the shafts of their spears against the rims of their shields while shouting insults and crying out to their pagan gods. Many of them were drunk, or perhaps under the influence of poisonous mushrooms, their faces twisted in rage or fear, eyes bulging as they readied themselves for the slaughter to come.

'Careful!' Wulfric shouted as they reached the newly deepened ditches and the ealdorman lost his footing, slipping on the loose earth before righting himself and clambering out on the other side. Alfred and the rest of the Wessex shieldwall followed Wulfric's lead, but another barrage of spears rained down upon them, killing or disfiguring many.

At last, the ditches were passed and Alfred, although feeling the muscles in his legs burning from the effort, could see their enemies almost within touching distance.

'This is it, lads!' he called. 'For God, and Wessex! Forward!'

He did not wait to see if anyone was following him, for he'd noticed Guthrum directly ahead and wanted to be the first to reach the hated Norse warrior.

The two shieldwalls came together in a clatter of wood and metal and now the real work of the battle began. Alfred thrust his spear time and again, instinctively using his shield to protect himself and, as time passed, it seemed like nothing could harm him. His spear was slick with the blood of slaughtered sea-wolves, yet he did not have a scratch on him. He could not see Guthrum now, but it hardly mattered for there were still many Danes in front of him, just waiting for him to kill them. He was happy to oblige.

Eventually, fatigue set in, and his arms started to ache. At that point the bloodlust faded and his feeling of invincibility departed along with the souls of the slain. He forced the point of his spear into one more Dane and then stepped backwards, allowing the men behind him to move forward and take his place in the line.

When he was able to lean down and catch his breath, he was amazed to see a long, deep gash in his arm, another on his calf, and a bruise on his knee that was so painful he could hardly walk properly. Mere moments before he'd thought he was miraculously unharmed, so it was quite a shock to realise that was far from the truth. Still, at least he was alive.

And so was Wulfric.

They grinned at one another.

'How do we fare?' Alfred asked, wincing as he rubbed his rapidly swelling knee.

'We're winning,' his captain replied confidently. 'I can feel it. The Danes don't have the same desire to protect these lands as we do. Their ties are to their longships, not Wessex's green fields. If we can continue to hammer away at them, I think they'll break and run.'

Alfred straightened and tried to get some idea of how the opposing sides were doing, but all he could see were the backs of his own men, and there was nothing to stand on to get a better view. He wished he could have used some clever tactic, some ruse, to win the fight sooner and with less loss of life amongst his own ranks, but today was not the day for that. The terrain did not lend itself to pincer movements, or flanking manoeuvres, or anything of that sort. Like so many of history's great battles, today's victors would win by simply standing and hacking away until their enemies were all dead or running away. It was brutal, and it was a terrible waste of men's lives, but it was the only way to win back the kingdom.

For the rest of the morning, and on into the afternoon, the battle raged. The wind had passed but rain started to fall, making the grass slippery which contributed to the deaths of many warriors on both sides. Alfred found himself in the front rank again, rain running down his cheeks and making it hard to raise his arms for his sleeves were soaked through. His shield had been torn to splinters hours ago, but he'd easily managed to find a replacement from one of his dead troops. He held it tight against his body for his left arm was aching terribly, but his right arm continued to thrust his spear, forward and backward, forward, backward, forward, backward, until it became lodged in the chest of a Dane and was torn from his wet hands.

Drawing his sword, he used it almost like a hammer, smashing it down time and again onto the heads and bodies of those standing against him.

The battle had changed as the day progressed. There seemed to be less noise – pained cries and shouted threats were replaced by harsh, tired breathing, and grunts or whimpers of exertion. On top of that, Alfred believed he could see more fear and uncertainty in the eyes of the men he faced, where they had been colder and harder when battle commenced. That was reflected in the ferocity with which his foes returned his attacks. The enemy warriors were tired, but they were also beginning to lose heart.

Guthrum might want to be king of Wessex, to settle there, and make those lands his home, but the vast majority of his warriors did not feel the same. They fought for glory and plunder, and it was becoming increasingly clear they'd find neither in Bratton Camp.

'You want these lands, Guthrum?' Alfred shouted, though he had no idea if the enemy warlord even remained alive. 'Come and take them, then!' He smashed his sword down into the collarbone of a Dane and, although the man's mail byrnie stopped the blade from cutting deep into the flesh, Alfred could feel the bone shatter and the resultant, agonized screeching made the king laugh. 'Come and take them, you bastard!' he roared, feeling the strength flowing back into his limbs as some of the opposing Danes turned and shoved their way through their own ranks.

They would not be back, Alfred knew, for they'd dropped their shields and spears that they might move faster.

It was as if some signal had been passed all along the enemy line, then – as many of them followed their comrades in dropping weapons and charging in the opposite direction.

'Hold the line!' Alfred commanded, knowing they were safer while in the shieldwall, should this be some ruse of Guthrum's. His order was repeated by Wulfric and Diuma and Aethelnoth and all the other West Saxon commanders. They continued to fight with any of the enemy soldiers who hadn't retreated yet, but it wasn't long before the whole line of Danes had broken, leaving the men of Wessex to catch their breath and cheer at their opponents' cowardice.

'Keep formation!' the king shouted. 'But move forward, after them.'

They marched after the fleeing sea-wolves but without the weight of their shields the enemy warriors were able to run much faster than the encumbered Saxon fyrd.

'Lord!' Wulfric shouted across to the king. 'I really think we should go after them properly. End this now, forever.'

Alfred turned to try and gauge how many troops were still his to command and smiled grimly for there remained many hundreds behind him. By contrast, countless dead enemies packed the old iron age hillfort, filling the defensive ditches or lying in heaps underfoot. The rest were sprinting to the north, towards Ethandun, without looking back. There would be no organised resistance from them any time soon, Alfred could see.

'Charge!' he called, as loudly as his dry, cracked throat would allow. 'Hunt them down and kill 'em all!'

Like starving hounds being let off their leashes the warriors of Wessex dropped their own shields and hurtled across the hilltop after their routing enemy.

'Well done, my lord!' Wulfric gasped, running alongside Alfred. He was breathless but his eyes glittered with joy. 'You've beaten them!'

'Aye,' the king agreed, moving freely, his swollen knee forgotten for now. 'We have. A great victory, Wulfric. But the day isn't done, and the war is not over, until Guthrum lies dead at my feet.'

They ran until exhaustion overtook them, and then they walked. Any Danes who were unfortunate enough to be caught were executed without hesitation. As night fell, the victorious host of Wessex did not stop, hunting their terrified quarry through fen and forest, eager for blood, and the plunder a slaughtered Dane's lifeless body offered.

'They're heading for Cippanhamme,' Diuma said when at last a halt was called and the exhausted soldiers were allowed a couple of hours to rest and eat something.

Alfred nodded. He'd expected Guthrum to head to the town that had been a base for the Danes ever since winter. 'Good,' he replied. 'I'll retake my throne in the very place it was torn from me. Get some sleep, my brave companions – tomorrow is going to be a momentous day.'

CHAPTER TWENTY-ONE

Cippanhamme was a sizeable town, but Alfred's army was still large enough to surround it, cutting off every possible escape route for Guthrum. The Dane was certainly there, too, for he'd been spotted on the walkway above the gates, peering gloomily out at the besieging West Saxons who'd chased them all through the night.

'There'll be enough food in there to support them for a while,' Wulfric cautioned, his tone suggesting he feared they were in for a long, tedious siege.

'And no shortage of water, either,' Diuma agreed.

'We're not going to sit here and hope Guthrum gets bored before we do,' Alfred said matter-of-factly. 'We're taking Cippanhamme as soon as possible. Wulfric, have a couple of large trees felled. I want battering rams built by the time the sun is at its highest point.'

The Danes – penned like cattle within the town that had been their home for months – looked on as Alfred's men worked tirelessly throughout the morning. Saws and other tools were sourced from nearby farms, and sturdy rams fashioned from suitable trees. The sound of logs being cut filled the air, like the buzzing of enormous wasps, and equally as threatening for the besieged sea-wolves. The crashing, thumping, hammering, and shouting of men did not go on for long, however, before the workers brought their hasty constructions into position around the town.

The rams were simple, large logs with a sharpened tip, that could be carried by a dozen or so men. The farms that provided the saws were also stripped of any useful walls or roofs – a barn in one case, and a stable in another. Similarly, some wagons had been divested of their wheels. These had been all been carried to Cippanhamme where they were rebuilt to form crude shelters over the rams. The resultant constructions were inelegant and unlikely to survive much punishment, but they would offer at least some protection for the men chosen to operate them and, Alfred hoped, destroy the town gates within just one or two strikes.

'The Danes have not repaired the fortifications properly,' Wulfric said, eyeing the walls and gates of Cippanhamme critically. 'When they stormed the place at Christmastime they did some damage, but they haven't bothered doing anything about it.'

'They never do,' Alfred said sourly. 'They smash and destroy everything they touch, but never build or rebuild. Not in our lands, at least. Maybe their own lands are filled with wondrous mead halls and marvellous shrines dedicated to their crazed gods, but here?' He jerked his chin in the direction of Cippanhamme's gates. 'The best they can do is hammer a few planks of timber across them.'

'They never expected to be attacked,' Wulfric noted. 'Guthrum thought you were gone for good, and the rest of our people, like a longship without a rudder, would forge on aimlessly, never coming together in numbers large enough to be a danger to him.'

'All the better for us,' Alfred said, appreciating his captain's unusually imaginative analogy as he looked across at the battering rams. 'Since I doubt those ramshackle constructions would have been able to destroy the gates if Guthrum had repaired them properly!'

Diuma walked across to join them, eyeing the rams even more critically than the king had done. 'I wouldn't want to be one of the men pushing that along,' he said. 'The Danes have seen them now and must surely be doing what they can to bolster the gates. If they don't break after the first couple of hits, and Guthrum's men have rocks, spears, boiling oil and so on all ready to drop on the rams…'

Alfred winced at the thought. 'That's what the shelters are for,' he muttered.

'The shelters won't withstand much punishment,' Diuma said.

'No, perhaps not,' Wulfric agreed. 'But the Danes know they have no way out, so with any luck they'll decide to surrender when they see we're committed to taking back the town one way or another. The sight of our rams might just be the push they need to give it up.'

Alfred stared at Cippanhamme's gates, eyes taking in every knot and furl in the wood even at this distance. He did not like what he saw. Yes, they were in poor repair, but the gates were not the only thing stopping his soldiers from entering the town. The Danes had been defeated in battle, but they were not dead yet, and a sudden, terrible image filled Alfred's mind then, of Wessex's proud warriors manning the battering rams, beset with missiles of all kind, their screams of agony so loud that the king felt he could almost hear them in real life.

A deep depression washed over him, and he sucked in a heavy breath that was almost a sob.

'Are you well, lord?' Wulfric demanded with a frown, reaching out to steady Alfred's arm.

'Yes,' the king replied, making his voice tight in an attempt to mask his melancholy. The last thing Diuma and Wulfric needed was to see him falling into despair. 'I need a drink,' he said, forcing his lips to curl upwards in an approximation of a smile. 'And maybe a nap. It's been a long few days, eh, lads?'

His friends grunted noncommittally, as if they weren't fully convinced by his words, but he waved off-handedly to them and wandered towards his tent. It didn't take him long to get there and, as he passed the two guards, straight-backed and steely-eyed, he said, 'Fetch Oswald,' and went inside.

The flaps of the tent may not have been as thick as the timber walls of his royal residences but they were enough to separate him for a while from the realities of war that lay waiting outside. He gazed at the far wall, shrouded in gloom, and took a long, calming breath, in through the nose and out through the mouth. Then, feeling a little less panicked, he poured a cup of ale and took a long swallow before sitting on his folding chair and doing what he could to clear his mind of all thoughts.

By the time Oswald arrived the oppressive melancholy that had settled around Alfred was lifting somewhat and he called out for the priest to enter.

'Ale?'

'Yes, lord, thank you.'

Alfred had already filled the cup and handed it over, gesturing for Oswald to take the seat across from him. They sipped their drinks, enjoying the warmth as it suffused their bellies and slowly began to work its way through the rest of their bodies. The clatter and clangour that accompanied an army on campaign filled the air outside, but the tent somehow insulated those inside, allowing them to relax for a while.

Oswald had been summoned by the king, but he did not ask why, simply nursed his drink and waited until Alfred decided to speak. It took quite a while, and Alfred had refilled both their cups before he opened up to the priest.

'I feel lost here,' he murmured, eyes fixed on the closed tent-flaps as if in a daydream.

'Lost?' Oswald asked.

Alfred nodded slowly and finally turned his gaze to his friend. 'Aye, lost. It feels like…' He trailed off, grasping for the words to properly explain what he meant. 'It feels like I'm on board a ship in the midst of a raging storm,' he said at last. 'Thrown hither and thither by the waves, and not a thing I can do about it. One moment I'm up here.' He held up his hand so that it was level with his forehead. 'Like the moment we routed Guthrum's army. When those bastards broke and ran and I knew we'd finally beaten them… That was a moment of fierce joy, Oswald.'

The priest smiled and nodded but remained silent, allowing the king to continue.

'But then it's as if the sea suddenly draws back and I'm plunged down into the deepest, darkest trough imaginable, with the crushing waves all around me, threatening to dash me to pieces or smash me into rocks.' His eyes glazed over, a combination of ale, exhaustion, and the images his memory – or febrile imagination – played out before his mind's eye. 'Like today, and the realisation that I'm going to have to order healthy young men to take battering rams and try to smash open the gates of Cippanhamme with nothing but a sliver of wood overhead to protect them. Can you imagine it, Oswald?'

The priest pursed his lips but shrugged. 'I can, lord,' he said. 'But this is what happens in times of war. Soldiers die as a result of their commanders' orders.'

'I know that,' Alfred retorted somewhat testily. 'But we've already won the battle! It should be over now! The bastard Danes can have no hope of ever escaping the town when we're camped outside, and I swear, Oswald, by God and all his saints, that we will not depart from this place until Cippanhamme is in my hands again.'

'Then it's just a matter of time, Alfred,' soothed the priest, smiling and touching the cross that hung around his neck. 'Be patient, and try to put thoughts of doom from your mind.'

'How can I?' the king demanded. 'How would you like to be pushing the ram towards the gates? The Danes will have boulders to crush our men's skulls and limbs. Maiming them for life if they are somehow able to survive. Boiling water or even pitch to melt the very flesh from their bones. Arrows and spears to pierce their bodies. And I will expect them to stand firm and hold their position without running away until the ram somehow does its job, which might not even be possible.' He shook his head, a sickly expression on his bearded face.

'I don't know why, Oswald, but I just keep seeing my own son, Edward, pushing that rickety ram. Imagining him forging onwards, terrified, and completely at the mercy of the Danes.' He sighed and stretched upwards, rolling his head back and wincing as his tired neck muscles ground painfully together. 'Is this what God wants, Oswald? Truly? Why? What can His purpose be for all this death and misery?'

Oswald blinked and opened his mouth but must have realised he would need more than simple platitudes to answer Alfred's questions. He stroked his cross absent-mindedly, looking at Alfred almost sadly, but, at last, shrugged.

'God works in mysterious ways, my lord,' he said, holding up a hand to forestall Alfred's irritated response. 'I know, that is not what you want to hear, but it's the truth. How can we, mere men, ever hope to fully comprehend God's purpose? His reasoning? We cannot, and part of being a Christian is accepting that fact. That's what it means to have faith in Him; accepting events as they happen, without questioning them too deeply.'

Alfred huffed, but he had not kept Oswald by his side for so many years for nothing. He hoped the priest would have more to say — and so he did.

'Alfred, do you enjoy being a father?'

Taken aback by this odd question, the king nodded. 'Of course I do.'

Oswald chewed his lip, taking a moment to frame his next question. 'Yet you and Ealhswith have lost more than one child, and suffered a great deal with each of those terrible losses, did you not?'

Alfred felt a lump in his throat and swallowed, too afraid to reply with anything other than a curt nod.

'Together, though, you continued to have children, because the joy Aethelflaed, Edward, and your other surviving children brought and continue to bring was worth even the agony of losing a child.'

'Yes,' Alfred breathed, thinking back to the nights he had held Ealhswith, both of them sobbing over the little ones they had lost.

'That is what it is to be a father,' Oswald went on, and he too had damp eyes for he had shared in the pain of those departed infants. 'To be human.' He looked away and brushed a sleeve across his face, composing himself, and Alfred wondered for the first time if Oswald sometimes doubted his own, seemingly unshakeable, faith in God.

'Life is a series of highs and lows,' the king muttered.

Oswald turned back to him, smiling. 'It is! Exactly, lord. If life was easy, and only good things ever happened, one would quickly grow bored – immune to beauty and joy and happiness. To live is to suffer, Alfred. The measure of a man is how he deals with that suffering.'

'Then I should not question the futility of sending a half-arsed battering ram to destroy a gate defended by savages?'

'Question it, of course,' Oswald replied. 'And perhaps try to find a better way. But, in the end, if you, as King of Wessex, believe that taking Cippanhamme is necessary and using those rams is the only way to do it, well... You must simply come to terms with it.' He drew a long, deep breath and let it out with a rueful shake of his tonsured head. 'I do not mean to sound callous, lord, but men die in war. Be they kings, aethelings, thanes, or the lowliest ceorl. It is simply the way of things, and becoming overcome by gloom at the thought of it will help nothing.'

'You almost sound like Wulfric,' Alfred said with a raised eyebrow.

Oswald tilted his head then smiled. 'I suppose so. But where Wulfric would suggest simply killing more enemies to make oneself feel better, I would counsel prayer and meditation upon the Bible.'

'I could do both,' Alfred replied, starting to feel happier as the priest's stoic presence suffused his soul.

'You should do both,' Oswald agreed without a hint of amusement. 'The Danes must be beaten, but you must also take care of yourself. Would you like to pray with me now?'

'I would,' said Alfred. 'Very much.'

'Then let us start with the Pater Noster, and go from there. As we pray, try to let the light of Christ's teachings push away the darkness that threatened to overwhelm you. Allow the Holy Spirit to take the place of your fears and, by the time we're done, you should be ready to face the hours and days to come.'

Alfred stared at his old friend, already feeling a lightness in his heart. 'I honestly don't know what I'd do without you, Oswald,' he said. 'Wulfric is my strong right arm, and Ealhswith my heart, but you are the rock, the foundation that my strength – Wessex's strength – is built upon.'

The priest smiled, clearly pleased by the praise, but he waved a hand dismissively. 'I am merely God's agent here on Earth. Whatever succour I provide comes from Him, and, although you may not always realise it, from within yourself.'

With that, he began to recite the Lord's Prayer and Alfred joined in with gusto, closing his eyes and allowing himself to fall into his earlier pattern of breathing, in through the nose, out through the mouth. Soon, any hint of gloom had been chased from his soul, replaced by a feeling of power and elation. When they were finished with their prayers Alfred almost felt like a new man, ready to take whatever Guthrum and the Danes could throw at him.

—

The siege was not over as quickly as Alfred had hoped. Despite the hasty building of the battering rams, after two weeks the king had decided not to use them, yet. He'd quickly realised that, although Guthrum had not properly repaired the town's fortifications, he would have undoubtedly piled whatever rubbish and rubble he could find behind the gates. A battering ram could pound against them all day without tearing a way through and, as Diuma had noted, the men holding the ram would suffer all sorts of attacks.

The rams might be needed at some point, but the siege was holding for now, and Alfred was trying to remain patient. His men had shown terrific loyalty, joining him in his return from Athelney – he did not want to throw away a single one of their lives when other possibilities to end the war were still open to him.

Attempts to negotiate with Guthrum had not gone well. The Dane still seemed to think he was in a position to dictate terms, but Alfred was done dealing fairly with the heathen warlord. The war would end in such a way that everyone in the world would know who the victor was. Guthrum would be left in no doubt that he'd been soundly beaten and never come back again to cause trouble for Wessex.

'Damn it, Wulfric,' the king said to his captain once two weeks had come and gone without any change in the opposing sides' positions. 'I'm done with this. Our supplies are dwindling, and the men need to go home to tend to their families and fields. We attack the town today.'

Wulfric frowned but that was the extent of his protestations. Even he must have been fed-up with the situation. 'As you wish, lord,' he replied and, soon enough, the army was up and armed and ready to fight, while the pair of rams had been setup at opposite ends of Cippanhamme; one at the main gates, the other at a smaller, side gate.

Alfred took in the sight of his gathered forces and felt another surge of pride. He was often beset by self-doubt, by fears that he was not up to the task of ruling Wessex, yet these warriors had flocked to his banner. He must have something about him to inspire such faith in men.

And now he was about to sacrifice many of them by throwing them at the gates and walls of Cippanhamme. He sighed and prayed silently to God for forgiveness; men died in war, it was the way of things, as Alfred knew only too well having lost his own beloved brother Aethelred to a festering arrow wound earlier in the conflict with the Danes.

'We're ready, my lord,' said Wulfric striding across to stand by the king's side. 'The rams will hopefully do their job.'

'Our men will cover them by throwing spears and shooting arrows at the defenders on the walls?'

'Yes, lord.'

Alfred grunted. 'As you say, then, let's hope those rams can make holes big enough for us to push into the town. Once we manage that it should be over quickly. Cippanhamme's winter stores must be just about depleted by now.'

'Indeed,' Wulfric said. 'We outnumber the bastards by quite some way, and they'll be weak with lack of food too. I just fear the losses we'll suffer before we break through the gate.'

'As do I,' Alfred snapped. 'But we've tarried here long enough. Begin the attack.'

Wulfric bowed and walked to the front of the army, waiting until the excited, anxious chattering fell silent and he had the men's full attention. He was a tall, imposing man with an unmistakable aura of competency and command about him, not to mention a reputation as a savage fighter who no enemy had ever got the better of – his presence reassured the soldiers, just as much as Alfred's inspired them.

Perhaps Wulfric also frightened Guthrum for, just then, the enemy king appeared atop the gates of Cippanhamme. He stared out at the massed fyrds of Wessex, bristling with sword and spear, the banner of red and gold fluttering in the spring breeze overhead and the righteous faith in their God giving them strength for the carnage that was about to commence.

'Alfred,' Guthrum shouted, and his voice was loud yet strangely subdued.

The West Saxon king walked forward to stand beside Wulfric, taking his time, making Guthrum wait but also trying to gather his thoughts. What did the sea-wolf want? Alfred would have suspected the Dane of trying to divert his attention to the main gates while the rest of the raiders escaped from some other direction. But the army of Wessex had surrounded the town and there was no way through without being noticed.

'What is it, Dane? Are you ready to surrender?'

The enemy king rolled his eyes. 'You know I am Norse,' he shouted back. 'But yes, I am willing now to give up the town. All I ask in return is that you let us leave your lands in peace. No more fighting. No more of our people must die.'

'Norse... Dane... It makes no difference,' Alfred replied dismissively. 'You're all heathen scum.'

His men laughed and cheered, thoroughly enjoying their lord's supremacy. The tables had well and truly turned now.

'Why should I let you leave, Guthrum?' Alfred demanded, not sharing his warriors' mirth. 'You are utterly beaten and at my mercy, should I be inclined to show any.'

'You may have more men,' Guthrum replied. 'But you would lose many of them if we were to fight again. If you let us leave your lands you still win, and no more of your warriors must die. I know you need them to work your fields and farms, Alfred. And your God does preach "mercy", no matter what you say.'

Alfred snorted.

'You can take as many hostages as you please,' Guthrum continued, and his tone was more obviously pleading now, telling Alfred all he needed to know. The Danes were starving within Cippanhamme, and knew they could not fight their way out. Guthrum's jarls and hersirs must be demanding he find a way to get them away from Wessex alive.

Well, that was exactly what Alfred wanted too.

'Fine,' he called. 'Have your men throw their weapons over the walls, and then open the gates. We'll talk more once the town is safely returned to me.'

'Swear that you will not harm me,' Guthrum shouted, adding almost as an afterthought, 'Or my men. Swear it on your holy book!'

Alfred turned and found Oswald was already standing nearby. The priest had been at the rear of the army when preparations for battle were underway but must have run to the front when the king and sea-wolf started conversing. He carried a prayer book with him at all times, and he held it out to Alfred now, who placed a hand on it.

'I swear I will not harm you, or your men, Guthrum, as long as you throw down your weapons and surrender completely to my mercy. You agree to do as I ask?'

Guthrum nodded vigorously. Many of his men were beside him on the walls and they looked thoroughly miserable; not a single one protested their king's capitulation to the Saxons, however. They were clearly fed-up with the siege and wanted to escape, undoubtedly to continue their life of plundering and violence elsewhere.

'Then get on with it,' Alfred commanded, taking his hand from the book of prayers and gesturing impatiently at the Danes. 'Weapons, over the walls. You have one hour to do it, and open the gates to me. I suggest you hurry.'

He needn't have added that last instruction for the enemy soldiers were practically starving and had spent the last week salivating over the walls as Alfred's warriors roasted beef and pork, sending maddeningly delicious smelling smoke wafting across Cippanhamme. The Danes must have hoped they would be able to share at least a little of that succulent meat once they gave up the town.

Long before the allotted hour was up, hundreds of spears, swords, axes, seaxes, and war-hammers had been dropped in great piles around the walls of Cippanhamme. Saxon ceorls gathered them all up to be distributed later by Alfred.

And then the town gates were dragged open, the ballast and refuse that had been piled against them to nullify any possible battering ram strikes cleared away. Guthrum himself led the surviving Danes – downcast, defeated, and drained – out of Cippanhamme. Weaponless, and surely fearing Alfred would renege on his sworn oath as their own leaders would surely have done, it was a strange sight to see so many hard men cowed, their eyes pleading for mercy.

Would the Christians really follow their holy book's teachings?

'Take Guthrum and his commanders prisoner,' Alfred ordered Wulfric and his hearth-warriors. 'Bind their hands and put them in my tent under heavy guard. The rest of the sea-wolves are to be searched for weapons or valuables then sent on their way with an oath never to return.'

'Where will they go?' Guthrum asked.

'They can head north,' Alfred replied. 'And wait for you on the border of Wessex and Mercia.'

'You will let me go?' the Dane asked, voice filled with desperate hope.

'I swore I would, didn't I? First, though, you will do as I command.'

Guthrum nodded readily enough. 'What would you have me do, lord?'

'You, and your highest-ranking jarls shall be baptised,' Alfred told him coolly. 'You, Guthrum, are going to become a Christian.'

CHAPTER TWENTY-TWO

The enemy leaders were taken to Alfred's tent and left there under guard while their army was stripped of their valuables. Any who tried to resist were savagely beaten – Alfred's warriors had been primed for a fight, after all, and any excuse to vent their aggression was to be grasped with both fists. Eventually, Cippanhamme was emptied of Danes, their weapons and goods shared out amongst the West Saxon victors, and the losers escorted northwards, to the border with Mercia. Some might wait for Guthrum and their jarls to join them at some point in the future, while others would probably cut all ties and simply find some other warlord to raid with.

Either way, Alfred had completely neutered the threat to his lands. It would be a long, long time before Wessex would be threatened by this particular heathen army. He was full of joy and plans for the future by the time he returned to his tent with its complement of sullen prisoners.

'A Christian?' Guthrum asked the moment Alfred pushed his broad shoulders through the tent flaps.

'Indeed,' the restored King of Wessex replied with a wicked smile. 'And not just that, Guthrum, but my own godson.'

'Son?' one of the enemy jarls said, confusion on his gaunt face. The past two weeks really had been hard for the Danes, Alfred realised, as he took in their condition and their slumped shoulders.

'Godson,' he replied standing over them. They were all seated on camp chairs, and the remains of a meagre meal was on the table in front of them. At least they weren't starving any more, although most of the spare food had been given to the liberated Saxon inhabitants of Cippanhamme. 'You had parents at birth, Guthrum. Now, in baptism you will have a second birth, and a new, spiritual parent: me.'

'You seek to humiliate me,' Guthrum said. He did not sound angry or upset, merely resigned, as if he accepted his fate as the beaten king.

'No,' Alfred replied, nodding his thanks to a ceorl who brought food and drink for him and the advisors who'd come to join him. Diuma, Oswald, Aethelnoth, and, naturally, Wulfric were all there and helped themselves to bread and cheese, washing it down with mugs of ale. It felt like a wonderful feast to Alfred, given the circumstances. 'I do not want you to feel humiliated, my lord,' he told Guthrum. 'Becoming a Christian is a wonderful thing. Something to be celebrated. By naming you as my godson I'm inviting you into my own family.'

Guthrum eyed him sceptically, but said nothing. Everyone there knew Alfred was asserting his precedence over the Dane, but, considering he might have simply executed the enemy king, allowing a priest to pour some water on his head and call him a Christian must have seemed like something of a let-off.

'And then, once we are all touched by your White Christ's love and kindness,' one of the jarl's asked sourly. 'What then?'

'We shall see,' Alfred retorted, angered by the man's tone. 'In the meantime, Oswald, I would like you to instruct the Danes in their preparations for baptism.'

The priest smiled, nodding serenely at the sullen sea-wolves who looked like they'd gladly sacrifice Oswald to one-eyed Óðinn if the All-Father would only transport them somewhere far away from Cippanhamme and place their weapons back in their hands.

'Good. This is a new beginning,' Alfred said, standing up so he could go amongst his victorious warriors and thank them for their loyal service. 'A new beginning for Wessex, and for you too, Guthrum. You should embrace it, because it's happening whether you wish it or not. You *will* accept Christ, and there *will* be peace in my lands!'

'Here?' Guthrum peered at the ramshackle little church in the village of Alre with surprise, but Alfred simply nodded.

During his exile in Athelney this place, and its elderly priest, Osgar, had been a great comfort to King Alfred, allowing him to worship God in peace. Aye, it was far from the great stone church he'd built at his estate in Ceodre, or the majesty of the one in the royal city of Wintanceaster, but this place was significant to Alfred. Symbolic of his own 'death' and 'rebirth'. It deserved the distinction of bringing Guthrum and his jarls into the loving embrace of Christ.

So they had made their way southeast from Cippanhamme, back towards the marshes that had hidden Alfred after Christmas, until, on the third day, they reached the River Parred and followed it to Alre. Alfred, and the Danes – thirty of them, all dressed in white woollen robes – walked, for the king felt it important to make the pilgrimage on foot. Wulfric, Diuma, and fifty of the *hearthweru* accompanied them on foot or mounted on horses, a heavily armed guard just in case the prisoners/would-be penitents tried to escape before renouncing their heathen gods. Ealhswith had also travelled with them, for Alfred wished her by his side when this momentous ceremony took place. The children remained in Cippanhamme for now, safely guarded by Alfred's hearth-warriors Dunstan and Aedan – the youngsters had travelled enough, and their parents were looking forward to getting them back into a normal, settled routine after the harsh life as fugitives in Athelney.

For now, though, Alfred was fully focused on the coming ceremony, hoping and praying that it would bring Guthrum and his jarls into the light of Christ. He glanced at Wulfric whose face was set in a stony frown.

'You think this is madness, don't you?' the king asked him jovially.

Wulfric side-eyed him and gave a snort of humourless laughter. 'Of course,' he said. 'You know as well as I do that many Danes have "converted" to Christianity after a defeat in battle, only to go back to their old ways when it suited them.'

'True,' Alfred conceded. 'I'm not completely simple. But some heathens have taken their conversion seriously and become pious Christians. Guthrum will recognise this as an opportunity to live alongside the people of these lands in relative peace. An alliance with Wessex will benefit him more than constantly being at war with us.'

'You're assuming he really does want to settle after all his years of raiding,' Wulfric pointed out.

'I am. You've seen him. You've spoken to him. Do you doubt that's what he wants?'

Wulfric's mouth curled downwards but he shrugged. 'Maybe.'

'Then take heart from the fact that Harald Klak – a pagan king of the Danes – was baptised and pronounced godson of King of the Franks, Louis the Pious. Harald embraced our faith and fought against his old heathen allies in support of Louis. So,' Alfred leaned across on his horse, grinning at Wulfric, 'sometimes it does work.'

The ealdorman simply grunted and stared at the church as they approached.

It was modest in size, and in its timber construction; a typical village church in the countryside really although, like the fortress on Athelney, it was built on an island in the marshes. The priest standing at the door fitted perfectly for he had a rustic, weather-beaten look about him, with an old – if spotlessly clean and patched – cassock that reached his feet, to go with his newly-trimmed brown tonsure. He was beaming, like a proud father watching his children coming along the road to visit.

Which, in a way, was true, Alfred thought, returning Osgar's smile.

'It's good to see you again, King Alfred,' the priest said, stepping onto the causeway to welcome them with open arms. 'And with new, prospective members of our flock!' He beamed at the Danes, who remained silent save for a noncommittal grunt or two. Guthrum at least appeared genuinely interested in what the Christians had in store for him, and he followed Alfred into the little church with much less trepidation than his fellows.

Osgar stood at the door, blowing in the faces of each Dane as he passed, symbolically exorcising the evil spirits that had, until now, inhabited them, while Oswald waited inside to begin. Some had suggested a bishop, or perhaps Archbishop Ethelred of Cantwareburh, would be more suited to such a momentous, symbolic occasion, but Alfred had stood firm. Oswald was his friend and the clergyman he relied on most, and it was fitting that he should be the one to perform the ceremony.

It was an incredible sight, thought Alfred, as he stood at one side of the shadowy building and watched the ceremony unfold, the thirty grizzled warriors clad in spotless white rather than the usual blood-splattered mail and leather the men of Wessex usually saw them wearing. Candles flickered in alcoves, their scent mingling with incense to create a powerful, heady atmosphere.

Oswald met Alfred's gaze and they shared satisfied smiles, proud to have reached this point together after so many years and months of uncertainty and turmoil. This, surely, was the culmination of that time, and of all the battles that had been fought between heathen and Christian in Wessex.

After thanking God for His many gifts, Oswald addressed the thirty penitents lined up in three rows of ten near the front of the church.

'Do you forsake the devil?'

'I forsake the devil,' came the response, murmured hesitatingly by the Danes.

'And all idolatry?'

Guthrum and his men had been coached beforehand in the correct responses. Even so, the majority of them looked completely bemused as they replied, 'I forsake all idolatry.'

'And all the devil's works?'

This would be the most telling moment of the entire day, Alfred knew, and a sudden anxiety clutched at his heart as he stared at Guthrum, wondering if the defeated enemy king would actually speak the correct response, and, if he did so, would it be genuine?

'I forsake all the devil's works and promises,' came the reply from the white clad penitents, and Guthrum led them as they went on. 'I forsake Þórr and Óðinn and all those devils who are their followers.'

Alfred released the breath he hadn't even realised he'd been holding in, and he was beaming, for he truly believed Guthrum meant the words he'd just spoken.

'Do you trust in God the Almighty Father?' Oswald continued, and he too was searching each supplicant's face for signs of duplicity.

'I trust in God the Almighty Father.'

Nodding, the priest said, 'Do you trust in Christ, God's son?'

'I trust in Christ, God's son,' came the reply, less hesitatingly now as the shorter responses were easier for the Danes to remember.

'Do you trust in the Holy Ghost?'

'I trust in the Holy Ghost.'

That final line was said louder than the others, for the Danes knew it was the last in this section of the ritual and the lines they'd had to memorise were over. Still, the concept of the Holy Ghost clearly confused or outright baffled Guthrum and his jarls as their expressions showed. It did not really matter, Alfred thought, smiling at his counterpart.

They had said everything required of them, and in apparent good faith.

Oswald and Osgar went from Dane to Dane, making the sign of the cross over various parts of the white-robed men's bodies.

Then the priests placed a little pinch of salt in each candidate's mouth which was supposed to impart wisdom.

Now, it was time to move onto the next part of the ceremony.

The baptismal font was essentially a large, wooden tub filled with water. It was a warm day, outside yet, even so, Alfred guessed it would be quite a shock to the system when the Danes were immersed in the water by the two priests.

Guthrum was brought forward first, and his robe was taken from him by a young ceorl. Naked but for a linen cloth to cover his manhood, he stepped into the font, wincing at the cold but remaining silent, perhaps touched by the solemnity of the service.

Oswald had a small bowl in his hand which contained chrism oil. He dipped two fingers of his right hand into it, and used the sweet-smelling oil to draw a cross on Guthrum's chest. Then the Dane crouched down in the water as Osgar filled a jug with some of the water in the font, raised it up, and tipped it over Guthrum's head. There was a gasp from the man then, and Oswald made the sign of the cross three times above his soaking head.

Alfred was positioned beside the font, and he reached out now, touching Guthrum's arm and helping the man rise back up to a standing position as the cleansing water ran in rivulets down his face and hair. By being assisted in this manner, Guthrum was marked as Alfred's godson.

Oswald anointed the Dane on the crown of the head and intoned, 'You came into this House of God as Guthrum, a heathen warrior. Now, you have become a Christian, filled with the glory of the one, true God. As befits a man reborn, I bestow on you a new name: Athelstan. Go in peace, Athelstan, and be guided in your new faith by your godfather, King Alfred of Wessex.'

The two men smiled at one another then, relief mingling with joy for both, Alfred thought, and the spot on the Dane's head that had been anointed was bound with a white linen cloth before he was helped out of the font, drying himself with a towel handed to him by the ceorl. And then he put the white robe back on and stood at the side in contemplative silence as the next candidate was baptised by Oswald and Osgar.

It was a slow process with so many men, but it went past quickly for Alfred who stood in a pleasant, almost numb haze, the scent of chrism, candles, and incense combining to make him quite light-headed.

When the ceremony was complete, and Oswald had blessed them all, they filed outside, no longer two distinct groups of Christians and pagans, but one unified collective. As Alfred stood in the afternoon sunshine and looked at the Danes, he felt optimistic that most of them, at least, would embrace their new faith rather than falling back into their heathen ways. Their white robes and white linen head-coverings made them appear far more like pious pilgrims than bloodthirsty warriors.

In that joyous moment, it was easy to believe anything, and Alfred allowed himself to simply bask in it, and trust in God.

Some villagers were there, watching curiously if somewhat nervously. They were not used to seeing noblemen and women gathered in their church, and, since Alfred had sent word ahead to let the people know what would be happening, they knew the newly baptised men were actually powerful Danes. It was a strange atmosphere all round, and the king was glad when his wife took control.

'This is a great day, friends,' Ealhswith said, walking towards the villagers with a broad, infectious smile, Aethelnoth and two hearth-warriors following her protectively. 'God has welcomed thirty new sheep to his flock. Come, and I will help you prepare things.'

The people smiled, put at ease by the queen consort's open, friendly manner, and, once she reached them across the walkway that was raised above the marshes, they fell in behind her and headed towards the village which was only a short distance away.

Alfred, heart full to almost bursting with love for his wife and his fellow man, turned to Guthrum-Athelstan who also seemed genuinely pleased.

'What now?' the Dane asked.

'Now?' replied Alfred, spreading his hands wide and raising his voice so the rest of their party could hear. 'Now we get drunk, my friends. It's time to celebrate!'

CHAPTER TWENTY-THREE

From the joyous, yet fairly modest feast in the village of Alre, Guthrum and his jarls travelled with Alfred's retinue to the nearby royal vill of Wethmor. There, they spent eight days feasting on a grand scale, as Alfred wished to show the Danes just how glorious it was to be a Christian nobleman, and the benefits of being a friend rather than an enemy of Wessex.

The headbands that had been wrapped around the anointed heads of the thirty men were removed in another ceremony laden with symbolism and so began more days of feasting to fully welcome the converts into their new faith.

The king's hall in Wethmor was a far cry from the hastily erected one Alfred had grown used to in the marshes of Athelney. The one in this royal vill was much bigger, constructed from sturdier timbers, and draped with the finest wall-hangings as well as old, ceremonial weapons. To both Alfred and Guthrum this place seemed like something straight out of *Beowulf*, a tale which both Dane and Saxon alike enjoyed and heard recounted during the days and nights of feasting.

Although Guthrum professed to be awed and even humbled by the grandness of the religious rituals that welcomed him into his life as the Christian, Athelstan, it was the feasting in the king's hall that truly brought the Danes to life. Eating, drinking, gaming, flyting, singing, story-telling, and gift-giving were all traditions that warriors knew and loved no matter their faith.

Alfred made a great impression upon their guests, giving them valuable seaxes, helmets, swords, and, especially, rings. It had long been a king's duty to reward his most loyal warriors with gifts of rings, and Alfred handed out ones made from gold, silver, and bronze, many of them inlaid with exquisite gemstones.

'You have been good to my people here,' Guthrum-Athelstan told his new godfather on the twelfth, and final, night of celebrations. They were seated at the high table, with Alfred in the centre, Guthrum-Athelstan on his left, and Ealhswith on the right. Wulfric and some of the other high-ranking West Saxons were spaced out around the hall amongst the Danes in hopes of them all forming lasting bonds of friendship or at least respect.

'As Christians,' Alfred said, smiling as he looked at the happy revellers surrounding him, 'it is our duty to be merciful, even to our enemies. You, Athelstan, are no longer our enemy – you are a friend, and, I hope, will remain so for the rest of our lives. My gifts are given not as a conqueror, but as a lord to his loyal hearth-warriors.'

Guthrum-Athelstan looked at him, face a blank mask. 'You see me as one of your *hearthweru*?'

'I do,' Alfred replied, meeting his gaze. 'In time, perhaps you will see the benefits of being a loyal friend to Wessex and, at that point we may possibly be equals.' His voice lost its playfulness then, and his features grew hard. 'Make no mistake, *Athelstan*, the war between us is over and I am the victor. I chose to be magnanimous and accept you as my godson – as a friend – but don't mistake that for weakness. My days of simply letting you be on your way with a wagon full of my ealdormen's silver, only for you to raid these lands again a short time later, are over. You are a Christian now.'

Guthrum-Athelstan frowned. 'I believe you are in earnest,' he said, nodding as his fingers idly played with the intricate carvings on the horn of mead before him. 'I must admit, though, I am a little surprised that you put such faith in me. Especially after I broke my oath to Óðinn, and killed the hostages we'd taken from you at Werham.'

Alfred's face grew dark at that horrific memory. It had been quite a shock for him to find so many of his own warriors – noblemen, and the sons of noblemen – with their throats cut, and left where they fell on the streets of Werham while the Danes simply marched off to plunder another town. 'That's all true,' he admitted. 'But your army is no longer as strong as it once was, and your very public conversion to Christianity will undoubtedly deter more sea-wolves from joining you. Especially since so many of your hersirs were also baptized. Like it or not, Athelstan, you will be viewed as a Christian, no matter what you do henceforth.' Alfred shrugged and skewered a piece of pork with his knife, popping it into his mouth and chewing contentedly as he went on. 'You will see that having me as an ally will be worth more than having me as an enemy.'

'What exactly do you foresee for me and my men?' Guthrum-Athelstan asked, appearing genuinely curious in the flickering glow from the low flames smouldering in the fire-pit.

Alfred finished chewing the meat and used a fingernail to dislodge a piece trapped between his front teeth. 'Foresee?' he laughed. 'I am no seer, Athelstan, like one of your strange *volur*. But my advice to you would be to take the remnants of your army north, to Mercia, or perhaps to East Anglia, and settle there. If you were to become king in one of those lands it would benefit you to have me as a strong ally, as we could look out for one another's borders.'

The Dane listened, taking time to absorb Alfred's words as the revelry continued around them, and then he pursed his lips and gave a slight bow of his head. 'You once asked me if I was ready to settle down and give up my life as a *vikingr*. Then, I was not.'

'And now?'

'Now, I believe I am ready.' He offered a broad smile. 'Some of my men may not be, but they will go their own ways. I think many of them will remain loyal to me though. I have been impressed by your vision, and by the way you do things here in

Wessex, my lord, and I would like something similar for myself.' He nodded, staring unseeingly at the men and women laughing and drinking at the benches before them, perhaps imagining the possibilities an alliance with Alfred could bring. 'I will travel to the nearby lands, and do my best to settle down there, Óðinn, I mean Christ, willing.'

Alfred beamed, feeling like Oswald must do when one of his flock promised to live a life free of sin. 'Then we shall remain firm friends, Athelstan,' he said. 'I shall protect your border with Wessex, and you shall do the same for me.'

'Agreed!'

'Enough talk, then,' cried Alfred, once more filled with happiness as he saw, finally, an end to the constant years of raiding, rebuilding, and more raiding, and the dawn of a future filled with peace and prosperity. Guthrum had been something of a bloodthirsty, unfeeling maniac when they had first crossed paths seven years or so before, but Alfred could see a real change in the man recently, even before his conversion to Christianity.

Athelstan was not the man Guthrum had been, and it gave the king of Wessex real hope.

CHAPTER TWENTY-FOUR

Alfred did not immediately evict Guthrum-Athelstan and his army from Cippanhamme. They had been quite effectively gelded for now, so no longer offered a real threat to Wessex – even if they intended to go back on their vows of friendship. However, that did not seem at all likely to Alfred or his closest advisors. Even Wulfric had been impressed by the apparent sincerity of the beaten Danes who'd allowed themselves to be baptised. Any previous doubts the big ealdorman might have had about Guthrum-Athelstan's conversion to Christianity were almost completely dispelled during the days of feasting at Wethmor.

So, Alfred gave the Danes permission to remain in Cippanhamme until October of that year. He retained the hostages he'd taken from them after the town had been surrendered, but agreed to let Guthrum-Athelstan and the other Christian converts have their own swords and other weaponry back, while their men were allowed to craft new shields and spears to replace the ones now in the possession of victorious Saxon warriors.

'I still think you should have kicked them out of Cippanhamme earlier,' Diuma grumbled when Guthrum-Athelstan and his nobles had departed Wethmor to return to their army. 'Why give them time to rebuild their strength? They may seem friendly now, but once they're armed again they might not feel so well-disposed to us, my lord.'

Alfred sat atop his horse and watched the Danes ride northwards. There had been a solar eclipse just a few days before which had caused much excitement and consternation in

Wessex. Some of the nobles saw the sun's daytime disappearance as a terrible omen, but Alfred had taken it as a sign from God that being merciful to Guthrum was the right thing to do. 'If we kick the Danes out of Cippanhamme now they'll be a target,' he replied to Diuma as the departing horsemen grew smaller and smaller until they could no longer be seen. 'Any thane or ealdorman in Mercia might attack them.'

'So what?' Diuma asked. 'That's not our problem. The Mercians would be doing us a favour!'

'You think so?' Alfred asked with an enigmatic smile.

Diuma looked at him and his eyes narrowed. 'You have some reason for not wanting them dead, lord?'

'Apart from the fact the king of the Danes, and his most powerful jarls and hersirs are now Christians?' He turned his horse and started the ride back to Wethmor with Diuma, Aethelnoth, and a handful of others cantering after him. Wulfric had gone off with Guthrum-Athelstan, taking fifty warriors of Wessex with him to make sure the Danes made it safely to Cippanhamme without incident. Already, Alfred missed his captain's brooding, yet reassuring, presence. He was glad Ealhswith and Oswald were still in Wethmor to support him.

'Christians or not,' Diuma said as they approached the royal vill once more. 'I don't think it would be any great loss if Guthrum, or Athelstan if you prefer, was to be killed, either by Mercians or someone else. He's proved a formidable foe over the years.'

'Exactly!' Alfred replied forcefully. 'But Athelstan is tied to me now, my godson as well as an ally, and who better to have on our side? As you say, he's proved himself a capable leader. He'll find someplace to settle and become king, and he'll act as a deterrent to any other heathen armies.'

Diuma did not look at all convinced by that. 'You believe those warriors you've not only spared, but lavished rings and other gifts upon, will actually fight their own countrymen? Guthrum will attack sea-wolves who come to his lands, rather than letting them join him, growing his army as before and using those numbers to strike once more at everyone within marching or sailing distance, including us?'

Spoken thus, it did seem a mad thing to believe, and Alfred knew Diuma and many of his other nobles thought him too trusting and too pious – not ruthless enough – to ever truly be rid of the threat of the Northmen. But Alfred had seen his new godson in the days after his conversion, and spoken at length with him during the feasts and games. Aye, Alfred did believe Guthrum-Athelstan would remain loyal to him. If he was wrong, and his judgement was so severely flawed, well, he didn't deserve to be King of Wessex and any fresh raids by those particular Danes would surely see Alfred deposed once and for all.

God's blood, he would give up the throne himself in that case, and sail for Rome like his departed brother-in-law, Burgred!

'Have faith,' he said to Diuma, a phrase Alfred had found himself repeating both out loud and internally many times over the past few weeks.

Have faith. God will see us through this. So far, He had.

They rode through the gates of Wethmor and Aethelnoth, hand resting on his portly belly, said, 'I too looked into the eyes of those Danes and saw no duplicity there. If things don't take a turn for the worse, I believe you're right, my lord, and they'll be steadfast allies to Wessex. Perhaps not all of them, for it's not unusual to find one or two rotten apples within a batch, but that could be said even for our own people.'

Diuma winced at that. 'True,' he conceded. 'My father was not as loyal to King Alfred as he should have been. But it's for that very reason that I would advise caution when it comes to the Danes.'

'You're right,' Alfred granted, reining in his mount and jumping lightly down onto the ground as stablehands ran over to take care of the valuable animals. He led the way to the great hall, the guards there throwing open the doors as the king and his entourage approached, allowing them into the cool interior. 'Although I have every faith that Athelstan and his army will no longer pose any danger to us, that hardly guarantees our safety. There's plenty more sea-wolf longships coursing along the whale road, searching for rich towns to plunder. As long as our people are prosperous, they'll be a target for raiders. So, as of today, we must do what we can to make sure Wessex is prepared for them.' He took a seat at one of the benches and his men followed suit, taking positions respective to their status and favour with the king. Wulfric's place on his right was filled for now by Ealdorman Aethelnoth while Ealhswith came into the hall through the door at the side, the queen consort helping to serve drinks to Alfred's advisors before taking her seat on the king's left.

He smiled and grasped her hand beneath the table, squeezing it lovingly. When they were first married, he'd not wanted her to serve the men, believing that was the job of the servants, but Ealhswith had disagreed. She was in charge of the upkeep of Alfred's household, no matter where it was geographically, be it in the marshes of Athelney or here in the royal vill of Wethmor, and the running of the hall was a huge part of that. As hostess, she saw it as her duty to serve the thanes and ealdormen their first drink, and to make sure they were comfortable before they conducted any business.

Some of the older, stuffier nobles were not greatly impressed by the queen consort's behaviour, but most of Alfred's advisors were gratified by Ealhswith's attentiveness. For his part, Alfred was content to let his wife do whatever made her happy, and damn the opinions of a handful of inflexible old men. The times were changing, and Alfred and Ealhswith would be the ones at the very forefront of those changes.

The main doors opened then, unexpectedly, and the outline of a broad-shouldered man filled the entrance. Alfred stared at him, not recognising him at first but then remembering the red-face and moustache, although the thinning brown hair the king remembered the newcomer once sporting was completely gone now.

'Sicgred,' Alfred said in surprise, unsure how he felt about the man's arrival. Ealdorman Sicgred had been his brother Aethelred's captain, and this was the first time Alfred had seen him in some years. Still, the king, like his wife, had a part to play as host, and so he beckoned the ealdorman forward, bidding him take a seat and enjoy an ale with them.

His greeting faded, however, as a second person walked into the hall behind the ealdorman. Again, it took Alfred a moment to recognise this smaller, younger figure, but, when he did, his breath caught in his throat and he quickly stood up, mind whirling.

It was Aethelhelm, eldest son of Alfred's dead brother.

'Nephew!' the king said, beckoning the youngster forwards and taking a better look at him when he was illuminated by the firelight.

The lad must have seen about thirteen summers by now and his resemblance to his father was obvious, not only in his facial features but in his gait and the haughty expression he wore as he faced his uncle.

'Why did you not send word you were coming, Sicgred?' Ealhswith demanded and, despite her desire to always play the courteous host, the irritation was plain in her voice. 'We would have prepared for your arrival. Had a place ready for you and the aetheling.'

Sicgred was already supping an ale and merely shrugged as Aethelhelm said, 'It's all right, Lady Ealhswith. We need no special treatment – Sicgred and I are content to sit here, rather than at your high table.'

His words were polite and delivered coolly, but Alfred detected a hint of anger in the set of the young prince's jaw. Sicgred's somewhat belligerent body language was also troubling, and Alfred wondered exactly what had brought them here after keeping to themselves in Aethelhelm's estate in Eashing for so long. True, they did provide men for the fyrd when called upon, but Aethelhelm, and his little brother, Aethelwold, were too young to play any part in the running of the country. In truth, Alfred had mostly put them out of his mind in recent years, having more to worry about than the aethelings. He felt guilty about that now, especially with Aethelhelm looking so much like his father – Alfred and Aethelred had been very close after all.

Ealhswith refilled Sicgred's ale cup and poured one for the aetheling, smiling and making a fuss of the lad. He did not look impressed by her ministrations, but Ealhswith showed no annoyance and retook her seat next to Alfred.

'What brings you here, my lords?' she asked sweetly. 'You are, of course, most welcome. It's good to see you, nephew – and you, Sicgred, old friend – after all this time. Why the unexpected visit, though?'

'I am almost a man now, my lady,' Aethelhelm replied with icy dignity. 'And the son of a king. I felt it was time I took my rightful place within Wessex. Sicgred agreed with me. I've hidden away in Eashing for too long.'

There was nothing openly hostile within his words, but his haughty tone, and the surly expression on Sicgred's face, made Alfred uneasy.

'Well,' Ealhswith said with a smile that lit up the room even more than the firepit. 'It's wonderful to see you both again. Eat, drink, and be welcome!'

She was a strong woman, and Alfred knew he would need to be a strong king now for what he was about to propose would not be popular amongst the men gathered in his great hall. Nothing was ever popular if it cost money, and Alfred's plans were going to cost money. A *lot* of money. He put Aethelhelm and Sicgred's sudden arrival out of his mind and pushed on with the meeting.

'I've discussed this with Ealdormen Wulfric,' he said once the men's thirsts were sated, and trenchers of bread, cheese, and smoked trout had been placed around the bench by serving girls who quickly disappeared into the shadows as the assembly began in earnest. 'Years ago, not long after my brother, God rest his soul, died and I took the throne, I decided to make a series of improvements to the kingdom.' He glanced at Aethelhelm, but the boy's face remained stern as Alfred forged on, wishing he knew what was going on behind the aetheling's bright eyes. 'For one reason or another, I never quite got around to doing much about those improvements I'd planned.'

'You built the ships,' Ealhswith noted, and the king nodded.

'Yes, that's the kind of thing I'm talking about. That first fleet came in handy when it helped us see off a raid, proving that spending money on defensive improvements of that sort was worthwhile.' He squeezed Ealhswith's hand again, pleased by her shrewd input.

'Spending money?' a yellow-haired, grey-bearded thane asked suspiciously. He clearly did not like where this was going, and the low murmurs from some of the other noblemen told Alfred that he was not alone.

'We lost a lot of our wealth thanks to the Northmen's raids,' the king said. 'Either paying the bastards to leave, or being forced to rebuild our towns and villages – remaking broken weapons, and planting new crops that had been destroyed or picked clean by the Danes.' He shook his head grimly. 'Livestock was stolen or eaten. Bridges damaged. Warriors killed. Men, women and children carted off as slaves. It all weakened us, and not just in silver.' He gazed around at his advisors, forcing them to meet his eyes and truly take in what he was saying. 'You all lost people close to you during this war with Halfdan and Ubba and then, latterly, Guthrum. I did too. My brother dying was worse than any amount of silver being taken from my coffers.' He did not look at Aethelhelm but felt the youngster's gaze boring into him. The rest of the men nodded grudgingly at his words though.

'I would like to ensure that Wessex can no longer be attacked as easily as it has been in the past.'

'This is where the money comes in,' Diuma said, and he was smiling, perhaps touched by Alfred's short speech or, more likely, just happy to be part of the Witan again.

'Aye,' the king admitted. 'I would like to build a series of settlements – burhs – all within twenty or thirty miles of one another. Each will boast high, sturdy walls and thick gates, and will be manned by enough warriors to properly defend them.' He stood up, taking his cup of ale with him. His eyes were glittering in the sunshine that came through the main doors, left unsealed by the guards to allow light and fresh air into the gloomy interior. 'If one is attacked by raiders, the fortifications will be enough to withstand the assault, while messengers ride out to the other nearby burhs for reinforcements. No longer will it take weeks to muster a fyrd strong enough to help a besieged town – the close proximity of these burhs will mean that a sizeable relief army can be engaging the enemy raiders within a short space of time.'

Aethelnoth slapped his leg. He'd spoken with Alfred about some of this during a clandestine meeting in Athelney, although not in very much detail. What he was hearing clearly inspired him for his round face bore a wide grin and he said, 'This is brilliant, my lord. Any Danes foolish enough to raid our lands would soon find themselves surrounded. No longer would the likes of Halfdan or Guthrum be able to sneak into Wessex and plunder at will before making off like wraiths before we could engage them in battle.'

'Would Easing be one of these burhs?' Aethelhelm asked, his voice not yet broken but confident enough despite his youth and unfamiliarity with the noblemen around him.

'Of course,' Alfred nodded. 'Sicgred is exactly the type of man we need to oversee building works like these and, when you are of age, nephew, he'll help you run Easing as he helped your father run the kingdom.'

He'd hoped his encouraging words would please the youth, but neither Aethelhelm nor Sicgred seemed impressed by the compliments.

'We would need defences along our rivers too,' said Diuma, mercifully moving the conversation along. 'Or the Danes will just escape in their longships.'

'Quite right!' Alfred agreed enthusiastically. He gestured at the thane with his ale cup, the contents spilling over the rim unnoticed. 'We will build more ships of our own, and… chains – yes chains – like the ones used by the kings of Francia that can be raised across the rivers, blocking the enemy from sailing past! Fortified bridges too, where needed.'

'This is going to be expensive, my lord,' Ealdorman Wulfhere said quietly, almost sheepishly. He had still not faced any punishment for betraying Alfred the previous winter and it plainly weighed on his mind, as if he knew the hammer could fall at any time. Still, the fear was not enough to make him stay silent over this threat to his silver reserves. 'Forgive me,' he said. 'I simply wonder if we can afford all this, having only just ended the war with Guthrum. Perhaps we should let things settle a bit before throwing money at a problem that doesn't exist yet, and possibly never will, now that the Danes have left for Mercia.'

Alfred sipped what was left of his ale, eyes hard over the rim of the cup. Part of him wished to make a terrible example of Wulfhere for his betrayal, but the ealdorman *had* come back on the right side in the end and, besides, as Oswald continually reminded him, a Christian should forgive his transgressors. Alfred had forgiven Guthrum for his heinous actions, after all, so how could he do any less for one of his own noblemen? So, the king bit back the furious retort that was on the tip of his tongue and swallowed it with the dregs of his ale, making a mental note to deal properly with Wulfhere soon enough. 'You're right,' he said coldly. 'It will be expensive. But it'll be worth it. If anyone truly believes there will never be another raid on these lands, by Danes or some other enemy, they are a fool.'

Silence settled upon the hall and the other noblemen eyed Wulfhere warily, with those seated nearest to him surreptitiously leaning away from him as though he might suddenly explode into flames beneath the heat of Alfred's glare.

Alfred let the wayward ealdorman stew for a moment longer and then tipped his cup into his mouth, swallowed, and continued. 'Existing towns, and royal vills in particular, will have their fortifications greatly improved. New burhs – or at least signal towers – will be built where needed to provide sufficient protection for those settlements located further away.' He used his empty cup along with some others to show, crudely, what he meant exactly as the nobles watched with interest. It might cost money, but the idea of being safer from raids was an attractive one. 'And each of these burhs will be garrisoned with enough warriors to stand atop the walls, shoulder to shoulder, with barely a gap between them. They will be armed with a decent spear and a shield each. Any thane or ealdorman not providing their soldiers with those basic items will be punished.' He looked up at them, running a stony gaze along each of them, including Sicgred. 'Wessex almost fell to the Danes this time, but, praise God, we were just able to hold fast. We're now the last bastion of Anglo-Saxons within Britain and, if I have anything to do with it, we'll remain masters of our own destiny for generations to come, unlike our beaten neighbours!'

There were murmurs of agreement at that, as Alfred expected. 'That will mean money for weapons and building works, and I expect you all to contribute. Ultimately it will benefit every single one of us, and allow us to finally grow our wealth without giving it away to armies of Danes every few years.'

'Yes!' Aethelnoth cheered, thumping the table with his fist, and smiling fiercely at his peers.

Of them all, Aethelnoth probably hated the Danes more than any, so Alfred was gratified that he'd gone along with all his plans up to this point. The ealdorman was as loyal as Wulfric, but not blindly so, and his support showed the king he was on the right track with his ideas for the future.

'Are we in agreement, gentlemen?' Alfred asked, letting his gaze linger for longer on Wulfhere than any of the others. 'Will you spend silver to defend your lands? Or would you prefer to continue as we've been doing, given how unsuccessful those tactics have proved? In short, my friends,' he said, standing up and walking around the table so the nobles had to turn to watch him go. 'Is hoarding wealth more important to you than ensuring Wessex does not go the way of East Anglia, Mercia, and Northumbria?'

How could any of the men gathered at that table refuse his proposal after such a speech? They could not, and they did not, even Wulfhere, who nodded along with the others and joked about tightening his belt in the coming months and years. Sicgred and Aethelhelm remained silent, aloof, as if they were not really part of the discussion.

'Good,' the king said, and the joy in his tone was evident. 'Some of you called my leadership into question before.' He held up a hand to forestall any unnecessary objections. 'Maybe you had a point,' he admitted, surprising them all. 'I should have enacted these reforms years ago and we might not have suffered so much death and destruction. I was not strong enough then to push through such expensive changes, but I am now. Together, we will make Wessex unconquerable by even the greatest of heathen armies, my lords, and truly make it a land of peace and plenty.'

The men – all of them, not just the king's closest supporters – appeared to share Alfred's enthusiasm now, seeing the sense in his proposed system of fortified, properly defended burhs, and so they raised an impromptu and unplanned toast to him now. As the thanes and ealdormen lifted their cups and proclaimed their renewed loyalty and faith to him, Alfred was almost overwhelmed and had to return to his seat.

To be at this point, after so much hardship, and those long, frightening months of uncertainty in Athelney... It felt something like a dream, and that feeling was only heightened as he looked at Ealhswith, being instantly reminded of how much he cared for her. He would never have believed things would turn out so well for them all.

God, truly, was great.

There was one other item he wanted to bring up with the council, but, seeing how well they'd reacted to his first proposal, he decided not to mention the second. It was sure to be controversial, since it offered even less obvious benefits yet would also be expensive. So, he remained silent and simply let his nobles eat, drink, and make merry. There would be plenty of time to discuss his other proposal some other time, or perhaps he would simply enact it without telling them.

If Wessex was to be truly great — as great as Rome itself, perhaps — it had to be strong in ways other than simply militarily; Wessex must become a place of learning, where scholars would come and thrive, and marvellous libraries would flourish, and even the lowliest ceorl would be able to read.

That was Alfred's dream, and as he sat there in the comfortable hall supping fine ale with his wife and most powerful advisors, it was easy to believe it would one day be a reality.

He turned his eyes on Aethelhelm and found his nephew looking back coldly at him. The king held his gaze, staring at him until the youngster looked away, face flushing.

It was possible the aetheling felt he had some claim to the throne, with Sicgred bolstering that belief as Aethelhelm and his younger brother grew up. In truth, as sons of the previous king, Aethelred, the boys would indeed have been next in line for the throne, if Alfred hadn't convinced the Witan to sign a charter confirming Alfred's son, Edward, should one day succeed him as king instead of them.

There was nothing, legally, that his nephews could do about it, and, at just thirteen and nine years of age, Aethelhelm and Aethelwold posed no great threat. Not yet, at least. Perhaps they would one day be a problem but, for now, Alfred had far more pressing matters to deal with.

CHAPTER TWENTY-FIVE

AD 880, Wilton

Summer

Aethelhelm and Sicgred returned to Eashing where they lived quietly enough through the following months, and Guthrum-Athelstan did not attack Wessex again. In fact, he proved to be a decent ally to Alfred, surprising many of the West Saxon ealdormen and thanes, but not the king himself. He believed himself to be a decent judge of character, and much less artless than he'd once been. He'd believed the enemy king ready to give up his life of raiding and plundering and so it proved. Guthrum-Athelstan eventually moved from Mercia to East Anglia which had remained under his control all throughout the war with Wessex, and there the Dane set himself up as king, settling down and apparently remaining true to his new Christian faith.

In Mercia, King Ceolwulf – who'd been little more than a puppet of the Northmen – had died. He was not replaced by a king, but by an ealdorman named Aethelred who was related to Ealhswith's deceased father. Obviously, this was beneficial to Wessex, and doubly so when Aethelred formally acknowledged Alfred as his overlord. This meant western Mercia essentially fell under Alfred's control, while the east remained in Guthrum-Athelstan's hands.

Other independent kings, notably those of Dyfed, Brycheiniog, Gwent, and Glywysing, sought Alfred's protection from their warlike neighbours, greatly extending his influence in the west.

Truly, Alfred's power grew with every passing season.

His strength within Wessex had also grown stronger, for after the triumphant celebrations at Wethmor he'd moved to reorganise his Witan. Men who'd refused to support Alfred during his recent tribulations were demoted or removed, while his supporters were elevated to even higher positions than they held already. Diuma escaped any further punishment for his part in Alfred's exile, officially taking over Brycgstow in his ageing father's place, but Ealdorman Wulfhere was not quite so lucky – not only was he removed from the Witan, but some of his lands were seized and his days as a major power in Wessex were ended.

When Alfred summoned this new, loyal Witan to a council at Langdene and asked them to confirm the line of descent for the throne, he fully expected them to vote in his son, Edward's favour. There had been some murmurings of support for his nephews, Aethelhelm and Aethelwold, and Alfred decided it would be prudent to confirm again, in law, that his own line should succeed to the throne upon his death. By demanding the Witan – who did have the power to deny his claim – support him or take the nephews' side, the matter could be settled for good.

And so it was, as Alfred expected. His loyal ealdormen and thanes were not likely to go against him in such a public setting, even had they wanted to. So, once they professed their support for the king, Alfred had their names added to an official document which they all swore an oath upon, and another possible problem for the future was resolved.

For now, at least. The eldest nephew, Aethelhelm, had been at that Witan and signed the document himself, but Wulfric and Oswald both noted how angry he was at seeing any chance of ever taking the throne of Wessex slipping through his fingers. Alfred knew his nephews might cause trouble over it in future years but, for the present, all was rosy in the king's garden.

This time of relative peace allowed Alfred's builders to begin constructing his proposed system of burhs. Making sure no major settlement in Wessex was more than a day's travel from another was a massive undertaking, requiring many workers and enormous wealth. Ditches needed dug; roads, bridges and earthworks built; existing walls repaired while new ones were erected; and numerous trees felled to provide enough resources for all of this. So many workers, and animals to pull carts and wagons, also required food and drink, so vast quantities of this had to be found.

As a result, progress was not as fast as Alfred and his ealdormen might have liked, but the king was still pleased to have finally started his program of improvements.

'Look at that,' he said to Wulfric one fine July afternoon in Wilton.

His captain turned and nodded, lips pursed approvingly as he took in the stone tower that formed one corner of the new burh. Originally one of Ealdorman Wulfhere's lands, Alfred and the Witan had stripped it from him and given it to the thane, Dunstan, in return for his service to the king in Athelney.

'Stone towers at each corner,' murmured Alfred, looking around at the building works. 'And a strong, timber palisade wall all around, with a deep ditch outside and fighting parapets on the inside.' He grinned somewhat maliciously. 'I'd like to see an army of Northmen try to break in here once the fortifications are all finished and defended by well-armed warriors. It'll be a bloodbath!'

Wulfric nodded agreement. 'True. I doubt the sea-wolves would even try.'

'No, you're right,' Alfred laughed. 'The craven bastards hate a fight that isn't loaded in their favour. They would leave here and march on to the next settlement, only to find that one just as well protected as this.' He laughed again, and Wulfric even joined in. This was no mere fancy of the king's; his burhs genuinely did seem like they'd be worth the exorbitant cost of building them.

With Wilton being so close to Wintanceaster, which had become Alfred's main residence these days, the king wanted it to be both easy to defend and easy to get to. With the latter in mind a new road had already been constructed, part of a system of *herepaths* or "army roads" which would allow his warriors to travel to and from the burh quickly, as well as allowing the local workers to quickly find safety should an enemy force be sighted in the area.

'And look, there,' Alfred smiled, nodding towards the only other stone building within the burh.

'A church,' Wulfric muttered unhappily. 'All that stone would have been far better used for another tower, lord. There's no need for it to be used there – the Danes very rarely destroy churches. They just like to steal everything inside.'

'A house of God is the most important part of any settlement,' Alfred retorted. 'Besides, if an enemy warband does manage to ever get through the walls, the people can take refuge within the church.'

Wulfric grunted but did not argue the point as they continued their leisurely ride around the burh.

There were only a few finished buildings at this point which provided temporary lodgings for the workers, but many more were being constructed: houses, stables, blacksmith's, butcher's, tanner's, workshops, storehouses, and, of course, the burh's great hall, where its lord would reside.

'Impressive,' Wulfric said as they came to that building now and the thane, Dunstan, hurried out to greet them. 'That's quite a hall you're making for yourself, my lord. Almost as big as the king's in Ceodre.'

Dunstan stared at Wulfric, a flicker of anxiety momentarily crossing his features as if he feared the king would think him having ideas above his station, but then he grinned toothily and shoved the big ealdorman. 'Oh, shut up, Wulfric,' he laughed. 'I almost thought you were serious for a moment there!'

'I am,' protested the ealdorman. 'It *is* an impressive hall.'

'Indeed,' Alfred agreed. 'And no bigger or smaller than it should be. You'll have plenty of hearth-warriors to look after, Dunstan, and this hall will be perfect for the job.'

'Thank you, my lord – it's all thanks to your generosity,' the thane replied, bowing deeply before turning to shake his head ruefully at Wulfric once more and then leading them into the hall as stableboys came to take their mounts. They went inside, Dunstan practically preening with pride at the finely made firepit, benches, and chairs that furnished the room. Thus far the walls were almost bare – no tapestries had been hung to add much-needed colour yet – but there were some shields and polearms placed decoratively, adding at least a little interest and breaking up the otherwise bare timbers.

Alfred got straight to business once the three were seated and a ceorl had furnished them with ale and a platter of bread, butter, hens' eggs, and cheese.

'You mentioned my generosity,' said the king, chewing a piece of the fresh, aromatic bread with obvious pleasure. 'But you've earned your place here in Wilton. I needed strong, loyal thanes in Athelney, and you proved to be exactly that.'

'Agreed,' said Wulfric, washing down some of the crumbling cheese with his ale. 'You were a fine man to have beside me on the raids we conducted, and a rock in the shieldwall.'

Dunstan's face flushed. To be praised so highly by the king *and* his captain was not an everyday occurrence. 'You know how much I hate the Danes,' he replied somewhat hoarsely. 'It was a pleasure to kill the bastards in your name, my lord. You deserve the loyalty of every man in Wessex!'

Alfred nodded thoughtfully and finished eating, fixing Dunstan with a serious look. 'I'm glad you feel that way,' he said. 'For many of my ealdormen and thanes are unhappy about my decision to build so many of these new burhs.' He held out his hands and looked up at the hall's rafters, soaring high and already becoming blackened with smoke from the cooking fires.

Dunstan had come to know Alfred and Wulfric well during their time in exile. He knew he could speak freely, indeed was required to speak his mind. He did so now. 'I suppose I can understand their displeasure, lord,' he said. 'I had nothing to lose for my old village was destroyed by the Northmen. I have no wealth to lose in these great building works – on the contrary, I've *gained* these lands, and for that, you have my everlasting gratitude.' He shrugged. 'But for someone like, say, Ealdorman Odda, who's already seen his fyrd depleted, and his wealth torn from him during the years of fighting... I can see why he wouldn't want to throw away what he has left. The main thing is that the dissidents grumble and complain all they like, but still do as you've asked. I trust that *is* the case?'

Alfred gave a nod in reply to Dunstan's cocked eyebrow. 'So far. But I'm going to anger them even further, by demanding they grant half their warriors to a new, standing army that I can call on whenever it's needed.'

The thane merely looked from Alfred to Wulfric, and then, when no further explanation was forthcoming, he asked, 'What d'you mean, lord?'

The king laughed gently and took a long drink before wiping his upper lip and placing the cup back on the table. 'I mean, Dunstan,' he said, 'that from now on, we will have strong burhs dotted all across Wessex, but we'll also have enough men to man their walls at all times. Half,' he held out his left palm, 'will work the fields and go about their usual business, keeping the kingdom supplied with the food and resources needed for everyday life. The other half,' right palm extended, 'will patrol the burhs and the lands around them, manning the walls and marching to help their neighbours if attacked by raiders. A standing army, Dunstan, always ready to react to enemy threats.'

'With the added benefit of not buggering off in the middle of a siege because they need to go home and bring in the harvest,' Wulfric put in sourly. As ridiculous as it sounded, such a thing had happened more than once in the recent past.

'The two halves of our populace will rotate,' Alfred said. 'Each group will perform their duties as workers or warriors, and then they will switch places, meaning every man will play their full part in the running of Wessex.'

Dunstan took all this in, absorbing it for quite some time for it was a novel and new idea for him to get his head around. 'I can see why you fear the reaction of the Witan,' he said at last, nodding slowly. 'With half the workers on active military duty, that will mean half the work being done. Half the wealth being brought in.'

Alfred mirrored his nod. 'And the soldiers will need fed, putting even more of a burden on the burhs to continue producing at a high level.'

Dunstan blew out a long breath, frowning deeply. 'Can it be done?' he wondered.

'Perhaps not at first,' Wulfric said, and it was clear he was not quite as blindly optimistic as Alfred when it came to forcing through these reforms. 'Maybe we'll need to take things slowly.'

'Maybe,' the king said coolly. 'But it *will* happen. I will see it done, Wulfric. Now is the time to force these things through, when we've just defeated Guthrum and the people are happy with my leadership. If we don't force the Witan to do these things now, they'll never be done. I'll never be able to wield as much goodwill and, well, power, frankly, as I can at this moment.'

'True enough,' said Dunstan with a wry smile. 'It would take a brave ealdorman to go against you just now. We saw that at the Witan when they all swore their oaths upon your charters and made sure your nephews had no further claim to your estates.'

'You'll support me then, my lord?'

Dunstan looked amazed at the king's question. 'Of course! I owe my lands to you, Alfred. Whatever you ask of me, it'll be yours.' He stood up and walked to the hall doors, looking out on his burgeoning new burh with obvious pride. 'Once those walls are finished, and the gates are closed, no Danes will ever be able to walk in here unless we let them. Three ditches we're going to dig, my lords, outside the walls. It'll be a very brave or stupid raider who tries to storm Wilton once it's all finished! And then,' he turned and walked back to the bench, raising his cup in salute to the king. 'And then, if you require half my men, they're yours. I'll find a way to make it work, and the other thanes and ealdormen will have to do the same.'

Alfred and Wulfric shared a happy look. It was nice – inspiring, even – to see Dunstan so enthused by their plans, and it boded well for talks with the other noblemen.

'Have you had enough to drink? Eat?' the thane asked, revelling in his role as host. 'Good! Come then, my lords, and let me show you around Wilton. Have you seen the space we've laid out for the market yet? Or the signal towers? No?'

They went out into the burh, Dunstan still talking about his settlement and the great plans he had for it.

Alfred did not have the heart to break into his friend's excited monologue, not even to reveal to him his one, final plan to make Wessex the greatest kingdom in all of Britain or, perhaps, one day, even the whole world.

Education!

That could wait for another day. For now, it was enough to know Dunstan would support him in whatever reforms he saw fit to enact. He just hoped the rest of the Witan would be so accommodating.

CHAPTER TWENTY-SIX

The winter of 880 was a hard one, with snow and ice striking mercilessly at Wessex and, indeed, all of Europe. Merchants brought tidings of famine and hardship throughout Francia and Flanders, with the Rhine River even freezing over in Germany. Alfred thanked God repeatedly throughout those months, relieved that the Danes had been pacified for a time, allowing the farmers of Wessex to gather enough food to see the people didn't starve the way many were in other lands.

Alfred also had another blessing to thank God for, as his fifth child, and second son, Aethelweard, was born in December.

'A playmate for Edward,' said Ealhswith as she cradled the tiny baby in her arms and smiled in exhaustion at her husband.

'He already has playmates,' Alfred noted, but Ealhswith laughed.

'Aethelflaed, you mean? She's too old for him. Too much of a leader herself. Edward needs a younger boy to order about.'

The king smiled, realising his wife was right. Edward was six now, and looking to assert himself as Alfred's heir even at that young age, but his big sister Aethelflaed, at ten summers, was bigger than Edward, and as ferocious in a playfight as any boy. 'I suppose so,' Alfred said, nodding as he stared at the wrinkled newborn in his wife's arms. 'Edward will be able to order this one about without fear of having his arm twisted up his back.'

'Do you think that's our family complete, now?' Ealhswith asked, stroking her new child's downy, dark hair.

Alfred shrugged. He knew it was hard for his wife, or any woman, to give birth, so he wanted to be careful with his words.

He loved his children and would be happy to have many more, but that was easy for him to say, when he was not the one having to carry their weight around for months, and then go through the pain of the actual birth. 'I'll be happy whether God blesses us with more or not,' he said tactfully. 'Five is enough, and more than most parents are granted, especially in these hard times.'

'Five, yes,' Ealhswith said softly and there was a distinct note of sadness in her tone. She had actually been pregnant nine times over the years, losing two babies before they reached full term, another stillborn, and another living for just a few hours before being gathered into God's arms.

Alfred took her hand in his and grasped it tightly, feeling tears in his own eyes. It was the way of the world for babies to die, though, and most parents suffered such losses. He knew they were lucky to have the five children they did, and silently thanked God for them all as he pressed his head against Ealhswith's.

He was content with what he had, that was true, but he still found himself weeping when he was alone at times as he remembered, particularly, their little girl who'd been stillborn, and the boy who'd only breathed for a short time before departing this Earth. What kind of world was it when even a king could not protect his children against such cruel deaths?

'What are we going to call him?' Ealhswith asked, her voice cracking so Alfred knew she was sharing the same dark thoughts as him but doing her best to move on and celebrate the latest addition to their family. He owed it to them both to do the same. It was always hard at these times, however, for the birth of a beloved child brought back the memories of those they'd lost, and the pain never truly went away. Alfred did not think it ever would, even if he lived to be a hundred years old.

'I thought we'd agreed on Aethelweard if it was a boy?' he said.

'"Noble protector",' murmured Ealhswith. 'I don't know.' She ran her fingers along the little infant's pudgy fist. 'He's so small. I'm not sure I like the idea of him being a "protector".'

'He won't always be small!' Alfred laughed, and he too reached out and touched the sleeping baby's hand, amazed as he always was by how smooth a newborn's skin was. 'One day he'll be bigger than me, and stronger. More handsome too, probably. He has both our bloods, remember.'

She looked up at him and, despite her exhaustion, she looked beautiful to Alfred and his heart, already filled with love, swelled even more. They shared a brief kiss and it seemed at that moment like everything in the world was right, as if it could never be better.

'Mother!'

The door to the birthing chamber was thrown open, making both Alfred and Ealhswith jump – although the tiny bundle in her arms was so tired from his ordeal that he barely stirred as Aethelflaed, Edward, Aethelgifu and Aelfthryth burst in, wide-eyed and laughing.

'We heard you'd had the baby,' Aethelflaed said, standing next to the queen consort and holding out her arms. 'Let me hold it.'

'Not an "it",' Ealhswith retorted with mock outrage. '*He* is named Aethelweard, and *he* is your baby brother. Now calm down, all of you, or you'll wake him.'

Chastened, the children settled, all staring at the baby in their mother's arms. Aethelflaed and Edward had seen their siblings at similarly young ages so were not quite so awed by the new addition, but Aethelgifu with just five summers, and Aelfthryth with only three, gaped in wonder.

Alfred looked at them all with pride. Of all the things he'd done as king, he felt quite sure that the greatest was helping to bring these incredible little people into the world. He prayed to God that, before his time was up, he would complete his reforms and make Wessex not only a safe place for the children to live, but also an inspiring and culturally significant one.

The baby stirred in Ealhswith's arms then, his eyes slowly opening as everyone looked on. Well, apart from little Aelfthryth who was too small to see, but Aethelflaed had already noted as much and lifted her sibling up now, that they all might enjoy the sight.

Aethelweard gazed at them, eyes moving slowly and deliberately from one to the other, and then he promptly vomited a small stream of milk down his chin and onto Ealhswith's hand.

'Gah, that's disgusting,' Edward cried, shrinking back from the bed as Aethelgifu and Aelfthryth hooted in delight.

'That's enough, Edward,' Ealhswith said, brow drawn into a frown. 'You did the exact same thing a hundred times, so stop being silly and fetch the nursemaid.'

'It's alright, mother,' Aethelflaed said matter-of-factly, placing Aelfthryth on the ground and fetching a fresh rag from the pile the midwives had left in the chamber. She threw Edward a disdainful look as she reached out and wiped the baby's chin herself then cleaned her mother's arm too. 'There, all fine again.'

Edward stuck his tongue out at her, and Alfred stood up, gesturing towards the door. 'Right, you lot, that's enough. Back to your lessons. You'll see your new brother later when we have the feast to celebrate his arrival.'

Grumbling at being put out of the room the children moved slowly, reluctantly, with Edward leading the way and Aelfthryth tottering at the back. Alfred placed a hand on Aethelflaed's shoulder, smiling in gratitude at her for cleaning away the sick.

'Do I have to go to my lessons?' she asked. 'I could help you and mother take care of the baby.'

He grinned. 'We'll be fine here ourselves,' he said, giving her a quick hug as they reached the door before he ushered her out. 'You look after yourself, by learning as much as you can.'

'Can I ask to do some work on battle tactics then?' she asked, standing her ground as he tried to push the door shut. 'I'm tired of reading old poems. It's boring.'

For a moment Alfred hesitated – he loved those poems she was complaining about – but he relented in the end.

'All right, tell your tutor I said you could do that for the rest of the afternoon. But it's back to the poetry tomorrow, and no arguments!'

She grinned, threw her arms around him, and hurried away, exhorting the other children to get moving almost as if she was their tutor.

Alfred watched them until they'd disappeared out of the hall, smiling the whole time. He wondered if he was doing the right thing with Aethelflaed – she'd always been more interested in learning about fighting and battles than the usual lessons a royal girl would receive, such as how to run the household, how to sew, how to brew ale and so on. It had been Ealhswith who'd suggested they let the girl share some lessons with Edward, whose tutors would teach him how to be king one day. Alfred had disagreed at first, simply because it was not the custom – but then he remembered their years of war with the rampaging Danes and realised it would not be a bad thing for Aethelflaed to share some of her brother's lessons.

The likes of Ivar and Ubba did not care whether they faced a man or a woman on the battlefield, they'd happily slaughter everyone before them.

Besides, even at ten, Aethelflaed was wise beyond her years and her arguments could be very persuasive, especially to a father as easily swayed as Alfred.

Shaking his head at his own leniency as a parent, he closed the door and walked back to Ealhswith.

'I'm tired,' she said. 'And Aethelweard needs fed. Could you bring the nursemaid?'

The king nodded. 'Of course. Would you like me to stay here with you while the baby's being fed? I could read to you?'

'No, thank you. I just want to sleep.'

He leaned down and kissed her on the forehead. 'Thank you for giving me this little boy,' he said. 'You've been the best wife I could have ever wished for, and the best mother.' He was going to kiss baby Aethelweard too, but the baby's face was already twisted and a cry burst from his mouth, amazingly loud, given how tiny his little lungs were. 'I'll fetch the nursemaid,' Alfred said, and practically ran from the room.

He did not have to look long for the woman he sought – the baby's cry had brought the nursemaid to the chamber in an instant, as if she'd been sitting outside just waiting to be called upon. Which she probably had, the king thought, moving aside to let her into the chamber and closing the door behind him after one last, happy glance at Ealhswith.

He stood there then, in the main hall, wondering what he should do for the rest of the day. One of his clerks appeared at the main doors, sweating despite the winter cold. He spotted the king and came hurrying towards him, carrying a parchment. Alfred could not be bothered dealing with the man – whatever was written in that parchment could wait until the morrow.

'My lord,' the clerk said, smiling as he moved around the benches, coming for the king like a dog spotting a morsel dropped amongst the rushes. 'I have something that needs your attention—'

'It'll have to wait,' Alfred replied, holding up hand and shaking his head with an apologetic smile. 'I have other, even more pressing matters to attend to. Sorry.'

The man gaped stupidly at him, mouth working silently as the king passed him and went out the main entrance, in the same direction his children had gone. So he'd told the clerk a lie – taking Aethelflaed out of her lessons to go horse riding was hardly a "pressing matter", but the girl's education could wait a few hours and, besides, she'd not be ten for long. Soon – too soon – she'd need to be married to some suitably noble husband, and Alfred wanted to make the most of his time with her before that day came.

Aethelflaed was overjoyed to miss her lessons, even if it was studying a subject she enjoyed. Riding was one of her favourite things in the world. Alfred felt guilty for not taking Edward along, but the boy was too small yet to keep up with them on his little pony. Well, they had the rest of the winter ahead of them and, God willing, no more attacks by the Northmen to worry about. He would take Edward out tomorrow, fishing or riding or sparring or whatever the lad wanted to do.

For today, though, when their horses were saddled and ready to move, Alfred led Aethelflaed out of the town and onto the fields, kicking his heels in and galloping towards the afternoon sun with a whoop of sheer delight.

CHAPTER TWENTY-SEVEN

AD 882, Wintanceaster

June

There followed a time of relative peace in Wessex, as it seemed pagan Guthrum's defeat and very public conversion to Christian Athelstan had combined to deter further raids by ambitious Danes. The economy slowly but surely began to stabilise and, eventually, after a couple of years, even showed signs of growth. The extra wealth being produced allowed the burh building plans to move forward with more rapidity than even Alfred had expected, although not all of the thanes and ealdormen in charge of those works took their task as seriously as the king demanded.

'This list of towns,' Alfred said, staring at a piece of parchment which Oswald had handed him first thing that morning. 'It's concerning.'

The priest nodded, and said, 'Yes, lord.'

They were seated together beside the River Icene which flowed through Wintanceaster, clad in short sleeved tunics and breeches that stopped above the knee, fishing poles resting on frames next to them. The sun was high overhead, birds were singing, and bees buzzed from bright flower to golden dandelion, busily harvesting pollen. Peace in the kingdom meant Alfred had more time to spend with his friends and today seemed the perfect opportunity to do a bit of fishing with Oswald. They hadn't caught anything yet, but it hardly mattered when the afternoon was so fine and hot.

The only thing spoiling Alfred's good humour was the parchment he was holding, and periodically shaking his head at or even cursing.

It was a list of towns and, more importantly burhs, and the men in charge of them, which were not improving their fortifications as rapidly as expected. Some, perhaps, had valid excuses – perhaps they didn't have enough labourers or skilled craftsmen, or their harvest had been poor the previous year, so they didn't have the excess wealth available to afford the building materials needed for palisade walls and gates. Others, however, Alfred knew were simply not putting enough effort into their duties, or even, in some cases, siphoning off their town's excess wealth into their own coffers instead of strengthening their fortifications as Alfred, and the Witan, had commanded.

Such mismanagement would have gone unnoticed had the Danes continued to harry Wessex's borders but now, with peace across the land, Alfred's clerks and auditors were able to spot it easily enough.

'This one,' the king grunted, pointing at the parchment. 'Cenwalh, thane of Burnham. He's only half finished the walls there, despite construction starting two years ago. Send a messenger, Oswald, and tell him they'd better be finished by midwinter, or I'll strip him of his lands and give Burnham to someone else.'

The priest nodded, staring hopefully at his fishing line as it tugged momentarily. Whatever had been showing an interest in the bait must have changed its mind though, for the line remained steady and unmoving.

'And here,' Alfred went on, oblivious to either fishing pole. This was the first time he'd properly looked at the list since Oswald had handed it to him, and he was not pleased by what he was reading. 'Aelfstan, ealdorman of Wellow. He's completed the walls but still has the old, flimsy gates in place! That's just… laziness! Why isn't he finishing the job? Too busy frittering away his wealth in whoring and drinking, that's why. I mean, we all like a bit of that, but not at the expense of our duties! Send a messenger to him too, Oswald. I want those gates finished by the end of the month.'

'Yes, lord,' the priest replied, jumping forward as a fish did now appear to have become caught on his hook.

Alfred's attention was drawn away from the parchment at last, and he grinned as the priest, tonsured head glistening with sweat from the summer heat, expertly pulled in his catch. It was a grayling, and a fairly small one, but it was the only thing they'd managed to catch between them so far and, as such, was hailed with glee as Oswald placed it on the grass between them and quickly ended its thrashing.

'That'll make a fine meal for you tonight,' the king said, frown returning as his eyes once more began to scan the list of errant noblemen and underperforming settlements. His expression grew even darker as he came at last to the final entry and he glanced up at Oswald. The priest was looking back at him, as if he'd been expecting the name there to draw the king's ire even more than the others.

'My nephews?' Alfred growled. 'In Eashing. A town chosen to become one of the burhs. Yet they are, according to my auditors, not doing enough to complete the defences.'

Oswald nodded. His expression was blank, playing his usual role of impartial advisor.

Alfred read the reasons for Eashing's lack of progress. Or their excuses, Alfred thought grimly as he took in the auditor's writing and then turned to Oswald again. 'Apparently they lack funds, for my taxes have been too high the past year.' He kept his voice steady, but rage was bubbling within him, and the simple pleasure of a sunny day's fishing was as dead as the gaping grayling on the grass beside them.

Oswald nodded, lips pursed. 'I read it, lord.'

'And?' Alfred demanded. 'What do you make of it?'

'Eashing is only one land their father left to them in his will,' the priest replied levelly. 'They have a good income and are not poor by any means. No poorer than many of the other ealdormen or thanes anyway. They could – should – be further along with the building works.'

The king was nodding. 'Agreed. The fact that they are not, and are claiming poverty, is their way of sending a message. To me, *and* the Witan.' He stroked his bearded chin thoughtfully. 'Just as they did when Aethelhelm and Sicgred turned up unexpectedly at Wethmor. That was to remind us they were still a power in Wessex, or at least would be soon, and this is the same.'

Oswald's eyebrows lifted and he offered an almost imperceptible nod of agreement.

'Aethelhelm and Aethelwold are young, and perhaps think it amusing to defy me in this manner,' Alfred murmured. 'But Sicgred is no immature fool, he's an old warrior and knows as well as any man in Wessex how these things work. He was an advisor to kings, after all, including my brother.'

'You think this is his doing?' Oswald asked.

Alfred's eyes returned to the river, watching as the sunshine glittered on the rippling water. 'Whether it was his idea or not, I don't know. But Sicgred should have advised my nephews against taking this course – the fact that he has not tells us a lot.'

'Maybe he did, and the brothers ignored him.'

Alfred shook his head. 'Sicgred isn't a man to be ignored. He's been my nephews' advisor since they were small children, something I should perhaps have foreseen would cause problems once they reached manhood. Sicgred was always fiercely loyal to my brother, and may see his sons as the rightful heirs to Wessex's throne. If he's spent years telling them that, well, I could see why they would feel rebellious.'

'You think they will rebel?' Oswald leaned back, shocked. 'Just as peace has finally come to the kingdom?'

'No,' Alfred said reassuringly. 'Sicgred is a dangerous man, but they aren't strong enough, unless they've somehow managed to gather support without me knowing, and I doubt that for I've been slowly expanding my network of informants.

I want no repeat of Cippanhamme, when I was oblivious to the conspiracy amongst some of my own nobles.' He shook his head emphatically. 'No, my nephews are too weak, politically, and I'm too strong for them to pose a threat. However...' He trailed off and let out a long, deep sigh, pondering the future and seeing more battles and wars in the years to come. 'They may stake their claim when I die and Edward becomes king.'

Oswald relaxed somewhat at that. 'Then we're in no immediate danger, and your nephews are, as yet, still too young to do much. We have time to prepare for whatever they may have in mind, although,' he smiled, 'I'm sure you have many years left in you, lord.'

Alfred snorted, but his earlier good humour had returned as they talked through this thorny issue, and he came to a decision.

Oswald, as perceptive as a man who'd spent so many years in the king's company could be, said, 'You have an idea.'

'I do,' Alfred replied. 'The biggest threat to peace in Wessex has, so far, been foreign raiders. We've begun to address that threat with our burhs. Now, I will nullify any possibly of danger from within our own ranks.' He stood up, the enthusiasm that often filled him when he knew a problem must be dealt with removing any further notions of lounging about on the riverbank that day. 'Come, old friend,' he said, gesturing to the grayling which, despite being dead still appeared quite beautiful to Alfred, its scales glittering in the afternoon sun. 'Take your supper and let's head back to the hall. I have documents to prepare before my nephews fully come of age.'

'But that won't be for months,' Oswald protested. 'Years, in Aethelwold's case! Must we leave so soon? With just this sad grayling to show for our trip?'

'It's better than nothing,' Alfred grinned, patting the priest beatifically on the back as if he were a bishop as well as king. 'But I'm filled with the Holy Spirit right now and feel the need to get to work immediately!'

Oswald could never resist talk of divine inspiration as Alfred knew and soon the pair were striding across the lush grass, heading for the path that would lead them back to Wintanceaster's hall. The Witan might not be meeting any time soon, but Alfred would be ready when they did.

Peace would reign in Wessex, he vowed. Even when he himself was dead and gone.

'Oh, and by the way, Oswald,' he said. 'Before I forget – have a messenger ride to Eashing and tell Aethelhelm he'd better get his burh in order, or I'll make an example of him. Even aethelings must do as their king commands…'

CHAPTER TWENTY-EIGHT

Alfred's burhs, including Eashing, did grow in both strength and size that summer; slowly but surely. The king – making the most of his current popularity – also started to erect sturdy bridges across many of the rivers which the Danes had previously used to sail their feared longships up and down. This was a simple, but effective way of stopping free movement along the waterways which Alfred had borrowed from the previous King of Francia, Charles the Bald.

To provide further protection against the waterborne threat from the Northmen, Alfred's fleet also expanded, as his shipbuilders used techniques learned from the Danes themselves to craft better, stronger vessels.

The king's chance to discover just how good his new ships were came that August, when word reached him that four enemy vessels had been operating around his borders, raiding settlements and brutalising the locals. Wulfric, of course, accompanied him as he rode to Hamwic and met the captains of four of his brand-new ships.

'You know we have more than just these four ready to fight for you, my lord?'

Alfred nodded, eyeing the craft with some satisfaction. He was no expert in sailing, much less shipbuilding, but what he saw before him looked impressive enough. Four large vessels, similar in style to the Danes' longships, built with thick, sturdy timbers and crewed by hard-looking sailors. All four sails, unfurled as yet, were made from wool with the golden dragon of Wessex proudly emblazoned upon them, while the prows were not adorned with mythical animal heads like the heathen ones, but with the Christian cross.

Even Wulfric was impressed by what he saw.

'I know there's more than four ships here,' Alfred said in reply to the captain who'd addressed him – a middle-aged, stocky fellow with arms as thick as the king's thighs. 'But I want to send a message to these raiders. I want to meet them on equal terms, and show them our ships are more than a match for theirs.' He turned from the harbour with its glistening waters and fixed the captain with a searching glance. 'These ships of yours *are* strong enough to defeat them, aren't they?'

The captain thought about it for a moment and then nodded. 'I believe so,' he replied simply.

'And the crews are ready to sail?'

'Aye, lord. Everything is prepared.'

Alfred nodded, smiling in anticipation. 'Then what are we waiting for? Let's go!' He walked towards the nearest ship and Wulfric hurried after him.

'You're going with them?' he demanded.

'Of course,' said Alfred. 'I commissioned these ships. I want to see if they were worth the silver they cost. You can wait here if you like, Wulfric, I know you don't enjoy sailing much. I'll see you when we come back. Victorious!'

Wulfric did not return Alfred's grin; his face remained as neutral as ever. He did, though, follow the king as he climbed into the ship and took up a place at an empty oar, muttering as he did so.

Alfred made no comment, as much as he wanted to. He simply smiled knowingly at his friend as the ship's captain commanded the craft be cast off and it slowly made its way out into the deep water, followed by the other three.

The rowers were guided by the captain who expertly navigated the lapping, shining sea, first one bank of oars pulling and then being joined by the other, with both Alfred and Wulfric doing their part, muscles straining, powering the vessel away from dry land with each stroke. There was no place on these ships for passengers, or cargo; these were designed for war.

It was a calm, pleasant day, despite Wulfric's complaints about how choppy the sea was, and Alfred found himself enjoying the journey once the oars had been brought in and the sail raised. The four ships moved through the water with all the speed and grace of any Danish vessel the king had ever seen, and it was impossible not to feel both pleasure and pride as he looked around at the coastline of Wessex, bright in the late morning sunshine, and his small fleet with its competent crews. The creak of timber, the murmured conversation of the other men, and the cries of gulls overhead made it almost feel like a pleasure trip rather than a hunt for a dangerous enemy.

'No doubt you'll be wanting to take part in any fighting,' Wulfric grumbled. His chin rested on his hand as he too gazed out on the sea but with much less pleasure than his lord.

'Of course,' Alfred replied. 'No king can send his warriors into battle facing a terrible death, if he's not prepared to stand in the front ranks and share in the danger.'

Wulfric made a face. 'That's fine on dry land, but you've never fought on board a ship. You're inexperienced, as am I.'

'We all are,' said the ship's captain with a glint in his eye. 'Best way to learn,' he suggested, 'is to do.'

Alfred laughed at this wisdom and slapped Wulfric on the bicep. 'See? We will "do" as the rest of the crew do, old friend, whether that be rowing or fighting. Even if we never take part in another seaborne battle, seeing how they're conducted will stand us in good stead. It'll help us with tactical decisions in future, and give us a valuable insight into how these mighty vessels actually work.' He nodded and turned back to stare out at the rippling horizon. 'We will fight, Wulfric.'

They sat in silence for a time, with even the bluff ealdorman seeming to relax a little as he became more used to the rocking of the ship. At length, however, he turned a slightly worried frown on the vessel's captain and asked, 'You've never fought a battle on board your ship either?'

'No,' the man replied. 'But I've spoken with men who have. Don't worry, all four of these ships and their crews are well drilled. We know our business as well as it can be learned without taking part in an actual fight.'

'That doesn't fill me with much confidence,' Wulfric muttered gloomily.

'Oh, cheer up,' Alfred smiled. 'Put it this way: the Danes have no more experience in this kind of warfare than we do. Any battle we get into on the waves will be as equal as it can be.'

'Depending on how many ships and warriors they have, my lord,' the ship's captain noted.

Alfred waved a hand. 'Yes, of course, but our intelligence suggests there's four of the bastards, so it should be an evenly matched fight.'

Wulfric cleared his throat, spitting over the side. 'So, it'll come down to two things,' he said. 'Who wants the victory the most, and who has the more skilled warriors.'

'Just like any battle on land,' nodded Alfred. 'But a third factor will come into play, which you've forgotten about as usual.'

Wulfric gave a rueful smile. 'We better get praying then.'

The ship's captain suddenly started, shading his eyes with a hand as he squinted towards the east. 'Aye,' he said just a little hoarsely. 'Praying would be a good idea. There's a sail on the horizon.'

All on board turned to look at the distant vessel. Its sail was soon joined by another, then another, and finally a fourth hove into sight as they came along the glittering sea towards the West Saxon fleet.

'That has to be the Danes,' said Alfred and he felt happy to have found their enemy so quickly. Eager to test his new ships and their crews and, of course, his own military mettle in this unfamiliar setting. His initial pleasure soon faded, replaced by trepidation and the usual, expected fear that tightened one's guts before every battle. He could die today, or perhaps Wulfric would. Certainly, many of these good men he'd shared the task of rowing with would be dead by the time the sun set. Unbidden, images of men falling into the sea and being pulled down by the weight of their armour filled the king's mind, along with memories of past brutal encounters when he'd witnessed skulls destroyed by hammers, bellies torn asunder by spears, and limbs completely severed by sword or axe blades.

The gorge rose in Alfred's throat and he coughed, desperately trying to clear his airway as the two sets of ships drew closer. By the time he could make out a huge, bearded warrior in the Danes' lead craft the rising terror had faded within the king, replaced by a pleasant numbness that spread throughout his body. It felt much like the sensation where one would swallow a strong beverage too fast and drunkenness would come quickly.

'Are we ready, lads?' he shouted, voice strong and filled with iron.

'Yes, lord!' came the reply and Alfred could see the same anticipation in his warriors' eyes as he felt himself. Some had not shaken off their fear and gripped their weapons fiercely, thin-lipped and silent. One or two even had damp patches on their breeches, but the king did not judge them harshly – sometimes the most frightened men were the ones who fought best once battle was joined.

There was no shame in being terrified, only in running away. And there was no chance of that happening here Alfred thought with dark humour.

The enemy ships continued to close in and the confused expressions on most of their crew boded well. They did not suspect what was about to happen, giving the Saxons an immediate advantage, although one that would not last for long.

The captains of Alfred's four vessels skilfully guided them into position, lowering their sails, and now the Danes did begin to anticipate what was coming, running to lift their shields from where they were displayed on the sides of their ships.

'Spears!' Alfred called, reaching down and lifting one of his own short missiles. 'Loose! Loose before they can defend!' As he gave the order, he drew back his right arm and threw the weapon as hard as he could. The captain had brought their ship close to the foremost enemy craft and, with nowhere to run or hide, the vicious iron tip of Alfred's thrown spear hammered into the side of a Dane.

That initial scream of agony was joined by more, as the rest of the king's crewmen let fly and their missiles also struck targets. The volley created chaos amongst the enemy sailors, and it was only exacerbated when the Saxon captain commanded his men to use their grappling irons. These were duly thrown across, the hooked heads finding purchase in the Danes' sturdy oak hull and the attached ropes were pulled by Alfred's men until the ships bumped together.

'Board them!' Alfred yelled, leading the way with reckless abandon, blood thundering in his veins as he hefted his sword and shield and landed with a thump on the enemy longship. He was attacked immediately but managed to parry the blow, and then he was hacking down and feeling the terrible, savage joy of blade tearing through flesh and shattering bone. His opponent fell, screeching horribly, until a second strike from Alfred's blade silenced him forever.

The king, teeth bared, sword-arm splattered with warm blood, looked for another sea-wolf to slaughter but, to his amazement, the fighting was over already.

'God's bones,' he muttered, slowly feeling the battle fury draining from him as he took in the sight on the longship. The Danes were dead – all of them. Many had been struck down by the early missile attacks, but those who'd survived those volleys were ruthlessly and mercilessly cut down by Alfred's companions as they followed him onto the enemy ship and fought their way between the rower's benches and oars. 'God's bones,' Alfred repeated, awed by the success of their attack.

And then he remembered there were other ships locked in battle and he gazed across at them, praying that God would grant the rest of his Saxon comrades as comprehensive a victory as Alfred had enjoyed.

'Cast us off!' the king shouted, running to dislodge one of the grappling hooks. 'Hurry!'

He was quickly joined by more of his men and soon the tethered ships were freed. A couple of his warriors remained on the captured enemy craft while the rest returned to their own ship and the captain commanded them to take up oars and row as he guided them towards the nearest fighting pair. Again, the hooks were deployed, and again Alfred led the way onto the enemy vessel. This fight was also over quickly, as the West Saxon reinforcements quickly tore through the Danes, leaving not even one alive.

'Two down,' Alfred said with grim satisfaction. 'Two to go.' He turned to see Wulfric holding his head and slumping down onto one of the rowers' benches. 'Are you all right?' the king demanded, immediately hurrying to his friend's side and trying to inspect the wound on Wulfric's forehead. 'Was it a spear? An axe? I see no blood!'

Without warning the ealdorman suddenly vomited, mostly water spilling from his mouth onto the deck as he retched and groaned. In a moment his nausea passed, and he looked sheepishly to Alfred, who could see now a lump that had quickly swollen to the size of a hen's egg on Wulfric's forehead.

Fear filled the king as he imagined a life without his most loyal companion by his side.

'No sword, or axe,' the ealdorman gasped, wincing as he forced an embarrassed smile. 'I tripped when we were boarding this ship and hit my head against the bench.'

'God Almighty!' Alfred shouted, standing up and stepping back a pace while shaking his head angrily. 'I thought you were dying, you big fool!'

'What a way to go,' Wulfric replied, closing his eyes as if he might vomit again. 'A fine, glorious death for King Alfred's right-hand man – tripping and hitting his head on a bench. What a story that would make for the scops, eh?'

Alfred was still shaking his head, but his anxiety had dissipated. He reached out now to help the ealdorman up, relief making him smile as he did so. He reversed his motion, however, upon seeing that Wulfric was still unsteady. 'Just sit there awhile,' he commanded. 'The fighting's over on this ship anyway.'

Moving to the stand in the prow, the king tried to make out what was happening on the other vessels. His head ached from squinting into the sun which was reflected so brightly by the water now that it was difficult to make anything out. As before, he ordered a couple of men to take control of the captured enemy ship with the still nauseous Wulfric, while Alfred led the rest of his sailors back onto their original ship and then cast off the grappling hooks and headed towards the remaining enemy craft.

'Why haven't our men attacked them?' he demanded, noting the lack of movement on the decks of the four ships they were approaching.

'Looks like the Danes have setup shieldwalls and are hiding behind them,' the ship's captain replied thoughtfully. 'Our lads must be waiting for us to join them so you can decide how to proceed.'

Alfred saw the banks of shields the sea-wolves were hiding behind and guessed the captain was correct. There was no point in throwing men at such a defensive wall, not until Alfred's reinforcements arrived at least.

'Lord king!' called the captain of the nearest Saxon vessel once they were close enough to converse without the breeze whipping away their voices. 'We have them tethered. What would you have us do now?'

'I'll bring this ship around on their other side,' Alfred shouted, pointing to the starboard side of the Danes' craft. 'And attack them from that side.'

'Wait!' A thickly accented cry came from the trapped enemy longship and a man with a shock of orange hair and similarly unkempt beard raised his head above the blue and white shield he was cowering behind. 'Wait! Are you led by Alfred of Wessex?'

'That's me,' the king shouted back.

'I have heard you are an honourable man,' the Dane called.

'I like to think so,' Alfred agreed. 'What of it? You are not honourable men, attacking my settlements, killing the people there and making off with their wealth. So – what would you ask of me, dog?'

The man bristled at the insult but kept his temper in check as he replied, 'No more need die here this day. You have already taken two of our ships, and their crews. Let us call a truce, and we shall sail away from your lands, swearing an oath never to return. What say you, Alfred, King?'

'What say I?' Laughing, Alfred turned to his men who shared in his merriment. 'Why should I let you sail away? You, and your other ship, are completely at our mercy.'

'Not completely,' the Dane retorted. 'You will lose more of your men if you try to board us. We have our shieldwall in place, unlike the other ships you took, whose crews were not properly prepared for you.' He shrugged his broad shoulders and leaned down behind his shield. When he straightened, his orange hair was hidden beneath a gleaming helmet of fine quality. 'We will be more of a test for you, Alfred, for the sea is our domain. Everyone knows my people are master sailors.'

Alfred laughed acerbically. 'That makes sense,' he called. 'For the sea is a place for animals and beasts, that's why it's given names like 'whale road', 'gannet's bath', 'swan's way', and 'seal's track'. You are not men, and you are no threat to us.'

The Dane bristled but replied levelly enough. 'You know that is not true, Saxon. Let us call a truce, and have no more death here.'

The king turned to his ship's captain and conversed with him in low tones for a few moments, gesturing at the captured ships and punching his fist into his hand. What the captain told him pleased him and he addressed the enemy leader once more.

'What's your name?' he shouted, tilting his head up curiously.

'Jarl Kveldulf,' the man called back proudly.

'Well, Kveldulf,' Alfred shouted, loud enough so that the crews of both remaining enemy longships could hear him. 'I do not think any more of my men need die.'

'Agreed!'

Alfred laughed, shaking his head. 'You misunderstand me,' he said. 'What if I was to use my captured ships to ram yours? Do you think you would sink?'

Jarl Kveldulf appeared visibly shaken by the threat, but he shook his head. 'That would damage both ships.'

'So?' Alfred retorted. 'I would gladly lose two captured ships to watch you and your sea-wolves drown, Kveldulf!'

'My ship is built from strong oak,' the jarl called, still shaking his head, almost as if trying to convince himself of his words more than anyone else. 'It will not break apart so easily.'

'Let's find out, shall we?'

'We'll tie ourselves to the benches so we aren't thrown overboard!'

'Go ahead,' Alfred suggested, waving his hand at the open deck of the enemy ship. 'As soon as you leave the protection of your shields my men will fill your bellies with their throwing spears. Same goes for any of you who seek to cut away our grappling hooks.'

Kveldulf's face was deathly white against his fiery hair and he looked utterly terrified now.

Alfred understood why.

'What happens to men who drown?' the king asked conversationally, stepping across to stand upon a bench so he could see the enemy jarl more clearly. 'Do they go to Valhöll? Do they play dice with Óðinn? Drink and feast with their comrades?'

The Dane did not reply, merely chewed his lower lip.

'Or do drowned men find themselves caught up in the goddess Rán's net and taken to live in her husband, Aegir's, watery hall beneath the waves, until Ragnarök?'

'What would you know of our gods and goddesses?' Kveldulf demanded furiously. 'You are a follower of the white Christ. A weakling! A nailed god who preaches weakness!'

'Never mind "nailed god", I know of Naglfar,' Alfred grinned. '"Nail-ship". The biggest longship ever seen, made entirely from the fingernails of everyone who has ever died.'

'Silence!' Kveldulf roared, but his shout was addressed to his own warriors who were muttering and grumbling amongst themselves as they listened to the West Saxon king's terrible words. Drowning was always a danger for a sailor, but none of the Danes there had suspected it might be their fate when the sun came up that morning and another day of raiding had beckoned to them like a beautiful maiden at the door of a brothel.

'Who will be the crew for Naglfar?' Alfred asked. 'Will you not answer, Jarl Kveldulf? No matter, for I already know.' He turned his head as if talking to his own men now, telling them what the Danes believed of the end of the world: Ragnarök. 'The crew for the ship made of human fingernails will be the drowned. It will be captained by the giant, Hyrm, and Loki will be at its helm as it's drawn towards the final battle where the giants will fight the gods. While the true heroes of Valhöll will fight for the gods, those who died by drowning will be forced to fight on the side of the giants. Against mighty Óðinn, on the side of chaos and evil!' He straightened his back and gazed at the men cowering behind their shields on the enemy ship. 'That will be your fate. No heroes' afterlife for you dogs; instead you will be caught in Rán's terrible net and dragged to your doom!'

'We surrender!' A new voice shouted out now, at the left side of the Danes' shieldwall, and a huge warrior who wore his beard in a braid stood up, towering over his shield.

'Silence,' Kveldulf screamed again.

'Oh, shut up yourself,' the second Dane retorted. 'I do not want to drown, Kveldulf. I will face Ragnarök beside Óðinn –

not on the side of the trickster, Loki, and the frost giants.' He looked at Alfred and nodded. 'I surrender, lord.'

'And the rest of you?' the king demanded.

His question was met with murmurs of assent, and even Kveldulf could see it was finished.

'Swear on your Christ that you will not kill us,' the jarl demanded. 'That you will treat us as well as you treated King Halfdan's men when you defeated them.'

'Surrender now,' Alfred said. 'And I swear to let you live, and treat you fairly and honourably.'

Kveldulf sighed, looked sourly at the huge Dane with the braided beard, and then dropped his shield and spear and stood up, as if inviting the West Saxons to break their king's oath and tear him apart with their missile weapons.

'Bend your knee to me,' Alfred commanded, and the crews of both the remaining longships did as they were told, dropping shields with thumps and falling to their knees, heads bent, perhaps begging their gods to protect them now that they were completely at the mercy of the warriors of Wessex.

'Take their weapons,' Alfred shouted. 'And bind their hands so they can cause no mischief on the way back to land.'

The Danes offered no resistance, accepting their fate now that it was sealed. Once they were disarmed, and securely tied up, the captains of Alfred's ships allocated sailors of their own to take control of the enemy vessels and, releasing the grappling hooks and unfurling the sails, the entire fleet of eight ships – all belonging to Wessex now – made their way back to Hamwic.

Alfred remained standing in the prow of his ship, the wind whipping his long, brown hair about his face. *What a day*, he thought. *What a victory!* He laughed with sheer joy at their accomplishment, a first naval victory for his burgeoning fleet, and looked across at the craft that was keeping pace beside his. Wulfric still sat on the rower's bench, but the colour had returned to his face and even the ealdorman looked happy.

'Feeling better?' the king shouted, voice disappearing into the wind.

Wulfric heard him though, and grinned in reply.

This was just the beginning, thought Alfred, staring at the coastline of Wessex. His Wessex. Today had proved his ships were more than a match for those of the Northmen. What would the future bring, now that his naval fleet was growing along with his burhs?

With the West Saxon lands finally being closed to violent raiders, Alfred knew it was time to invite friendlier visitors to his kingdom.

It was time to make Wessex the greatest kingdom in Britain.

PART THREE

CHAPTER TWENTY-NINE

AD 885

August

Despite his recent successes in other matters, Alfred was finding it depressingly difficult to locate the men he needed to bring Wessex back to its former glory. There were enough warriors – seasoned veterans now, thanks to the wars of recent years – but the king didn't just want his people to be strong and safe. He wanted the West Saxons to be renowned as men and women of great learning and culture.

Unfortunately, education had been neglected for so long that even many of those who should have been able to read and write – such as monks and ealdormen – were almost as illiterate now as the lowest ceorl.

'It probably shouldn't surprise me,' Alfred said to Oswald and Ealhswith as they sat in his hall in Wintanceaster one wet and windy summer evening. 'My father was not too interested in education – I didn't even learn to read myself until I was twelve. So it should be no great shock that I'm struggling to find tutors who can come to my court and instruct us here.'

Oswald nodded sympathetically. He could read well enough, but he did not have the temperament to be a teacher. Reading bible verses and poetry to the king and his wife were the limit of his skills as a tutor. 'Surely there are one or two learned men – bishops perhaps – who will answer your summons eventually? Maybe they just haven't heard your request yet.'

Alfred snorted. 'You know how well I've promised to reward any who can act as a tutor here in my court. If any bishop was able to do it, I'm quite sure they'd have heard about it and come by now. *Everyone* of any standing has heard my summons.'

A gust of wind rattled the wall and even made the little fire blaze higher, sending shadows dancing around them as a servant brought them a trencher piled with cuts of cold pork and various cheeses. These were two of Alfred's favourite foods to nibble of an evening, but he barely touched them, so deep was his gloom. Even the three cups of ale he'd downed hadn't lifted his mood much.

'There's only one solution,' said Ealhswith, helping herself to small pieces of both pork and cheese and popping them in her mouth, chewing daintily but with clear relish.

'Oh?' Even Alfred's response was half-hearted.

'Look outside Wessex. What about that bishop from Mercia? Wærferth?'

Alfred pursed his lips and stroked his bearded chin thoughtfully, trying to remember the man she spoke of. 'Wærferth of Wirceaster,' he said at last, an image of a middle-aged bishop coming to him. 'Yes, a very shrewd fellow. I recall discussing Gregory's *Dialogues* with him. He would be exactly the type of tutor we'd need, Ealhswith, interesting idea! Oswald, send word to Bishop Wærferth, would you? Tell him what we desire, and what we'll pay him in return.'

The priest smiled. 'Of course, my lord. I'll dispatch a messenger to Wirceaster on the morrow.'

Alfred shared his smile. He knew Oswald had been terrified he'd end up having to act as court tutor, so this new development gave the priest hope.

'I don't see why this is such a pressing matter,' Wulfric suddenly interjected. He was seated on Alfred's right as usual, although he'd not been paying much attention, for he was scarcely interested in learning or culture. Not when Wessex might still be attacked by marauding Danes any day. 'I'd counsel spending whatever silver you're planning to bestow on this Bishop Wærferth on the burhs we're building. Or the new bridges we need. Or better weaponry for the levies. Or...' He trailed off, waving his hand vaguely in the air as if spending silver on pretty much anything would make more sense than handing it to some clergyman.

Alfred sighed heavily, as if Wulfric was an idiot. It was an old ritual, and the ealdorman took no offence at it, but the king couldn't help feeling just a little irritation at his friend's inability to grasp the intricacies of Wessex's situation.

'Wulfric,' he said, as if he were a tutor imparting words of great wisdom to a five-year-old. 'The Danes have been a scourge on these lands for years now. Do you know why? I'll tell you. Again.' He paused to take a long sip of ale, glad to see he had his captain's full attention. 'Our people, and I include myself in that, have failed God. We have not been pious enough, and we've become like savages, forgetting how to read. Forsaking learning and culture for baser pursuits such as hunting and fornicating.'

Wulfric raised an eyebrow at that, and his mouth even dropped open a little, but he wisely did not make mention of Alfred's well-known love of both those pursuits.

'I did say I included myself in this!' the king snapped, pointedly making sure he didn't meet Ealhswith's stern gaze. 'We – all of us – have fallen into ignorance and strayed from God, and the Danes have been His way of punishing us. It's all very well building mighty walls and gathering a great army, but such weapons are not enough to defeat our enemies and regain Almighty God's favour. We must cultivate wisdom as well as warriors, Wulfric.'

Wulfric was still listening, but he did not reply. His eyes followed the pieces on a nearby table, where two of Alfred's hearth-warriors enjoyed a game of tafl.

'Before everything was burned and ransacked, Wessex, indeed all the surrounding kingdoms, were places of learning, as Bede recounted in his *Historia ecclesiastica gentis Anglorum*. It can be no coincidence that the raids of the Danes began around the same time as our people lost that love of learning.'

Wulfric nodded. He agreed with that, at least. 'Of course,' he said. 'With those bastards attacking, the people had little time for reading books.'

'Well now that we've pacified Guthrum-Athelstan, God has granted us peace. Our burhs will ensure that peace continues, and we will use the respite from war to rekindle the West Saxon desire for knowledge. Starting with us!'

A frown pulled Wulfric's eyebrows together. 'Us?' he asked.

'All of us,' Alfred confirmed, spreading his hands wide to encompass everyone in the hall. 'We will become a new type of army,' he said, and his boyish grin made the words seem far less pompous than they might have. 'An army of scholars, Wulfric, as well as warriors.'

'All of us?'

'Yes, Wulfric,' the king said, nodding fiercely. 'I know you can read a little. Well, it's time you learned properly. Oswald will help you.'

Ealdorman and priest shared horrified looks, but Alfred simply laughed. 'What? My two friends, my closest advisors, working together. It'll be fun.'

'I'm not so sure it would,' Wulfric protested, as Oswald vigorously shook his head beside him.

'Well perhaps Bishop Wærferth could teach you then,' Ealhswith broke in, smiling sweetly at Wulfric. Alfred knew she loved the ealdorman, saw him almost as an older brother, but his dismayed expression invited some gentle teasing.

'Aye,' Alfred agreed. 'But we'll need more than Wærferth. Who else might we invite, my lady? Any other suggestions? Oswald? What about you?' He paused, sipping his ale as he tried to think of any learned men from the nearby kingdoms. 'I remember hearing of a hermit named Plegmund – well, a former hermit. He's a monk now, I believe. From Cair Legion. Invite him too, Oswald, if we can locate him.'

The priest nodded. 'There's a couple more priests from Mercia we might approach,' he said. 'I know them personally, from meetings years ago. I'll send messages to them both. Clever men, ideally suited for your needs, my lord.'

'Excellent!' Alfred laughed. 'God's knuckles, I feel so much better now. I was thinking we'd never find anyone to teach our people, but that's four names we have, and more will come surely. We can look even further afield, too – to Francia perhaps. No reason why not.' He reached out and hugged Ealhswith tightly as she laughed at the public show of affection.

'I hate to spoil your good humour,' Wulfric said somewhat irritably, clearly still rattled by the news that he'd be expected to embrace learning and knowledge as much as anyone else in Alfred's court. 'But how do you expect to persuade the rest of the ealdormen and thanes to suddenly become scholars? You can't just order them to do it, as you've done with me, my lord.'

'Oh, don't be so sour, Wulfric,' the king laughed, refusing to let his captain's black mood ruin his own good humour. 'I've already thought of that. My noblemen are supposed to be the wisest of all our people, yet they've not lived up to that lofty status. They *will* do so now, or I'll strip them of their ranks and titles.'

Wulfric blanched at that. 'You're going to upset a lot of people, Alfred,' he said. 'We already suspect Sicgred has been stirring up the nobles, complaining about your leadership in hopes of gaining support for your nephews. Something like this might just tip a few more over the edge.'

'Perhaps,' Alfred admitted, face darkening for a moment as he thought of Sicgred and the rumours, unsubstantiated thus far, that Wulfric alluded to. 'But as with the burhs, and the money we required from the ealdormen to build them, now is the time to make such demands. I don't expect people to learn to read overnight, it'll be a slow process, just like the burhs, but it'll be worth it in time. Everyone in Wessex will benefit from it, Wulfric. Everyone. Even my nephews.' He halted and turned to Oswald with a thoughtful frown, using his nail to work free a piece of pork from between his teeth. 'I've just thought of another man who'd make an ideal tutor for my court. Do you remember we met with the King of Dyfed, when he sought my protection from his neighbours?'

The priest nodded.

'He brought a monk with him that day. I was very impressed with that monk — we must summon him here as well. Tell him there will be great rewards for his service. I feel he could be the very foundation for us to build our army of scholars upon.'

'Yes, lord,' Oswald said. 'I believe that monk was a kinsman of the former Bishop of St Davids, but I forget his name. Do you remember it?'

'I do indeed,' said Alfred. 'His name is Asser.'

—

'Think it'll rain again tomorrow, my lord?' The guard shuffled his feet on the walkway, tired after his long shift. 'I'm sick of it. It's supposed to be summer!'

Aedan, newly promoted to thane of Hrofescester as a reward for his loyal service to King Alfred, grimaced and shook his head, drops of rain flying from his helmet. 'Me too,' he agreed. His accent betrayed his Irish roots, but he was a clear speaker and easy to understand. He was enjoying taking charge of Hrofescester after being one of the king's loyal hearth-warriors. It was good to have his own command, especially here, so close to the sea, which Aedan had always loved. He squinted into the rain which was at least showing some signs of lessening. 'It's impossible to see in this,' he grumbled. 'But keep your eyes open anyway, lad. And your ears.' He smiled at the guard who was so young he had only the beginnings of a wispy blond beard on his smooth face.

The boy nodded and snapped out, 'Yes, lord,' as he'd been trained, and Aedan moved away, continuing his circuit of the walkway. It was highly unlikely any of the guards would be dozing in this weather, but Aedan had made it a habit of his to periodically show himself on the wall. It kept the men on their toes if they knew the thane might appear at any moment. He'd caught a pair playing dice once, when he'd first come to Hrofescester, and made an example of them by fining them – it had been a useful lesson for the rest of the garrison, and such examples of slackness were few and far between now.

Hrofescester was not officially one of Alfred's burhs, but Aedan had been granted money to complete improvements to its defences – a task which had begun seven years before, in 878. The walls had been heightened and strengthened with new timbers and the walkway repaired where needed, while the town gates were replaced, and the defensive ditches all made deeper. Hrofescester was an important port town, a centre for trade, which was why Alfred had sent one of his best hearth-warriors to oversee its running. Any town so close to the sea or even a river would always be a potential target for enemy raiders in their feared longships. As Hrofescester was within just a few miles of the sea, and also sat beside the River Meduwey, it made sense to upgrade its fortifications.

Aedan looked up as the thunderheads finally sailed westwards and the sun peeped through a small gap in the grey. He removed his helmet and ran a hand through his hair, feeling the rain on his forehead mingle with the sweat from the leather liner. He hated wearing a helm, finding them warm and uncomfortable especially in summer, but he knew it was important to set a good example to the soldiers guarding the walls. When on duty, one should be properly armed and armoured, ready for battle even if it seemed entirely unlikely to happen.

'My lord!'

Aedan spun at the shout, seeing the young man he'd been speaking with gesturing to him. Even at this distance he could see the guard's eyes wide with fear and the thane ran along the walkway, past the other guards who watched him go with varying degrees of trepidation.

As he reached the northern gate and joined the youthful guard it was easy to see what had caused the alarm to be raised. Dozens of men, women, and children were hurrying through the rain towards the town, often looking back over their shoulders as if the devil himself were coming after them. The gates were open, as they always were during the day, but Aedan shouted at the guards to get ready to bar them once the folk were safely inside.

'What's happening, lord?' the guard asked, and it was obvious he suspected the same as Aedan.

'They're running from something,' the thane replied grimly. 'Whatever it is, it can't be good news. Are you ready to do your duty, man?'

The young guard swallowed but gripped his spear fiercely and nodded. He did not reply though, probably worried that his voice would crack from fear.

'Good.' Aedan smiled reassuringly. 'Don't fret, it would take a huge army to break through these walls. Hrofescester has nothing to fear from enemies once those new gates we installed are closed and barred. Just stand here and look imposing, all right?' He patted the lad on the arm, grinned, and jumped down from the walkway, heading towards the gate which already had people streaming through it.

He pulled aside a middle-aged woman who looked more composed than most of the others. 'What's happening?' he asked her.

Taking in his good quality clothing, the fine sword at his waist, and his obvious air of command, she bowed her head. 'Danes, my lord,' she replied, sending a shiver down Aedan's spine.

'How many?' he asked, eyes straying towards the open gates, fearing he would see the enemy warriors already charging towards the town. He did not, but the downpour wouldn't delay them for long, he knew.

The woman thought about it, shaking her head the whole time, before shrugging and saying, 'There were a lot of sails, lord. I'd say at least twenty, with more behind them.'

'God's blood,' Aedan cursed. At least five hundred enemy warriors, and possibly as many as a thousand. He could not muster anything like as many soldiers as that. 'Thank you,' he said to the woman. 'Find somewhere to shelter before we bar the gates.'

'Yes, lord,' she said. 'I'll make myself useful. I know a bit about binding wounds and the like.'

Aedan heaved out a deep, heavy breath and nodded. 'Aye, that's a skill we're going to need before long, I fear,' he muttered, and hurried towards the stables which were located on the southern edge of the town walls. He found two riders already getting their horses ready to move, anticipating his orders, and commanded them to take word to the two nearest burhs – Eorpeburnan to the south, and Suthriganaweorc in the west.

'Don't spare your animals!' he shouted as the riders made their way towards the gates. 'We need reinforcements as soon as possible!'

The day went on as the people from the surrounding settlements and fields made their way to the safety of the town and, at last, as the rain lessened, the fleet of enemy ships filled the Meduwey with their sinister bulk and Aedan commanded the gates be shut. He watched, a knot in his stomach, as his orders were carried out, the great oak beams that would hopefully be strong enough to withstand the enemy attack being dropped into position with heavy thumps.

The place was filled to bursting with refugees and his warriors did their best to marshal the women and children into shelter while the men were given weapons and armour if any was available and sent up onto the walls. The puddles that filled the streets earlier had been churned into mud, making it harder to move people and animals, but, now that the gates were shut, Aeden felt much more secure. He left the task of dealing with the non-combatants to the town council members, and headed up to the walls to try and gauge what the Danes next move might be.

Of course, he had a good idea what the sea-wolves plans would be, and he was not surprised when they had finally secured their longships and mustered their men into a terribly impressive army not far from Hrofecester's northern wall.

'How many ships?' he asked his captain, a brutish-looking local fellow named Cuthwulf.

In a surprisingly soft voice the big soldier replied, 'Forty, lord. Possibly more behind them, back along the Meduwey. The bridge stopped them coming any further, though.'

Aedan nodded. The bridge dated back to the time of the Roman legions, whose engineers had built the original structure. That had been built upon by successive generations and recently strengthened thanks to King Alfred's reforms. 'You think the bastards will seek to destroy the bridge and move on?' he asked his man-at-arms.

'No,' Cuthwulf replied, jerking his head upwards in the direction of the sea-wolves, who were gathering outside Hrofescester like scavengers around the carcass of a dead animal. 'I think they plan to attack us, kill the warriors, enslave who they can, and steal whatever wealth they find.'

Aedan grunted agreement. 'Aye, and *then* they'll destroy the bridge and sail on to the next settlement.' He shook his head in angry disbelief. 'The bastards never seem to tire of raiding, do they?'

'Maybe they'll get bored of it today,' Cuthwulf replied, his smile completely altering his rough features.

Aedan laughed. He liked the man, who fought as fiercely as his appearance suggested, but also had a keen intelligence and a skill for organisation. As a second-in-command, the thane knew he could do a lot worse. And that thought reassured him, for the Danes had begun the short march towards the town now and it would not be long before every warrior there was pushed to their limits. The healers too.

It was going to be a long day, he thought, hoping desperately that his messengers would bring aid in time to save the town, and everyone trapped within.

CHAPTER THIRTY

Aedan spat an oath and ducked down beneath the palisade wall as a short-shafted spear tore through the air where his face had just been. Immediately, he rose again and, taking the merest of moments to aim his hunting bow, released an arrow, thanking God that the two fingers he'd lost in an earlier battle were on his left hand, rather than his right. The bowstring snapped and the length of ash with its grey goose feathers flew downwards. With so many tightly packed targets surrounding Hrofescester's northern gates it was a simple matter to hit one. Aedan snarled with savage glee as his arrow hammered into the unprotected neck of a Dane, sending blood spraying in the air as the man reeled back in shock, the crimson spattering across his comrades as he died.

That had all happened in the space of a few heartbeats, and Aedan had experienced it all as if in a cocoon of silence. Sound rushed back now, as the screaming of men struck by spears, arrows, and stones mingled with battle cries and shouted commands. The thane had been impressed so far by the noblemen and leaders of Hrofescester's fyrd – most were holding their nerve and organising their groups of defenders with skill and good sense. It seemed the people of the town were as dependable as the recently fortified gates and walls.

So far, at least.

The Danes had come towards the town at a run. Full of confidence and shouted prayers for their heathen gods and goddesses of war – Óðinn, Þórr, and Freyja – to grant them a quick, glorious victory. They clearly expected the defences to offer little impediment to their progress, and it was little wonder, for that was what usually happened when an army of Northmen attacked one of the towns of Wessex. Usually, the gates and walls would not withstand much punishment and soon enough the raiders would be swarming within the town like honeybees searching for a new hive.

That had not happened today, and it seemed to have shocked the leaders of the attacking force. For longer than was sensible, the Danes continued to use their axes and warhammers to batter the gates, but the sturdy wood and massive retaining bars held firm. At the same time, some of the enemy warriors carried ropes with simple iron grappling hooks attached. These were used to climb the walls, but if the Northmen made it to the top, they were brutally dispatched. Those who got into the town and onto the fighting platforms found themselves massively outnumbered and were quickly torn apart by the defenders' spears.

'How are the other gates?' Aedan asked Cuthwulf. His captain had been dispatched on horseback to check how the battle was going at the other three main entrance points, for Aedan feared more groups of Danes might be encircling them, seeking to strike at more than one place in hopes of spreading the defenders thin.

'The west and south gates haven't been touched,' Cuthwulf reported, slightly out of breath from his run up the stairs to the walkway. 'The east gate is beset but holding fast. I don't think there's any danger there, the raiders are taking heavy casualties. How's it going here, lord?'

Aedan chanced another look over the top of the wall and snorted with grim humour. 'I think they've finally realised they're not getting into the town this way.' He gestured with his bow and Cuthwulf came to stand next to him, peering gingerly over the wall.

There was no need for his caution, as the Danes were no longer loosing missiles of their own. Instead, they'd thrown their shields over their heads and were slowly making their way backwards, away from the gates. Arrows, spears, and stones clattered against the upturned shields with the occasional missile making its way between the gaps and injuring or killing whoever was unlucky enough to be struck.

'Ha! Odin's single eye wasn't looking out for that poor bastard,' Cuthwulf said happily, nodding at an enemy soldier who'd been knocked down by a rock to the back of his skull and then had his right arm pinned to the ground by a thrown spear. The Dane was screaming for help as his comrades marched inexorably away, leaving him too weak to free himself, but alert enough to understand exactly what was happening. He wasn't the only enemy warrior who'd fallen and was now lying injured outside the town, but he was the most noticeable, his situation proving to be the source of much bleak fascination from the defenders on this section of the wall.

'Someone put him out of his misery,' Aedan shouted, looking along at his men on the wall. The Danes' main warband was out of range now, and the thane's request was answered by at least a dozen archers, their bowstrings snapping in quick succession. The men of Hrofescester, like those in Alfred's official burhs, had been training for war these past few months, and, as a result, the injured Dane was quickly dispatched, as almost all the arrows loosed in his direction struck home. There were cheers and whoops of delight, and Aedan and Cuthwulf both joined in, the sea-wolf's death marking the end, for now, of the battle.

'Victory!' Cuthwulf shouted in that high, melodious voice, raising his bow and shaking it fiercely over his head. 'We've won, my friends! Well done!'

His cry brought further cheers and whoops of delight, and Aedan shared in their joy as he gazed along the wall, noting the very few casualties on the fighting platforms. It looked like they'd lost hardly any defenders, while making the Danes pay a heavy price for their folly. Still, he knew how the Northmen operated, and they would not simply sail away after this first, initial setback.

They would return soon enough, and next time they'd not act so rashly. They'd also be furious, and hellbent on making the Saxons pay a terrible price.

Aeden met the gaze of two of the town's nobles who'd commanded nearby detachments of defenders. Their eyes told him all he needed to know – they were no fools. They understood as well as he did that the enemy would be back. With that in mind, Aedan allowed the people to celebrate their victory. They'd earned it, and it would boost morale which, God knew, would be needed in the coming days, for, even if his messengers rode as hard as possible, aid would not come for some time.

Hrofescester was on its own, and the Northmen had not retreated far at all. Rather than getting back on board their longships and moving on, the raiders had found a patch of land they must have thought looked defensible, and there they were already digging a ditch.

'Cuthwulf,' he said to his second-in-command. 'Let the men rest – only those who were due to be on guard duty will remain on the walls. Everyone else can celebrate with an ale or two. Let them enjoy the victory, for now.'

Cuthwulf nodded. He too had seen the enemy digging themselves in beside the Meduwey. The earth from the ditch they were digging would be used to make a wall; it would be a crude representation of Hrofescester's own defences, but it would be enough to protect the Danes should the townsfolk seek to mount an attack of their own.

'They're going to besiege us,' Aedan said, gazing out at the distant activity. 'Look at them, working away like hairy little ants.'

'What are we going to do, lord?' Cuthwulf asked without a trace of fear, although he must have understood the dire peril they were in. The Danes still greatly outnumbered them and, with no way to leave the town for food or other supplies the good folk of Hrofescester would soon begin to starve.

'Do?' Aedan replied with forced levity which he knew his captain saw right through. 'We're going to celebrate our victory, man! And we'll see to our injured, make any repairs to the walls and gates that are needed, and continue to repulse any more of those whoreson's assaults.' He reached out and grasped Cuthwulf's forearm in the age-old warrior's grasp, smiling genuinely now. 'Our warriors fought well today, and they'll continue to do so until reinforcements can come to relieve us.'

Cuthwulf nodded but did not appear convinced. 'You think help will come in time?' he asked in a low voice that only the thane could hear.

Aedan did not reply immediately – he did not want to lie to his friend. Cuthwulf deserved to know the truth, as the thane saw it. So, he thought long and hard about the question, weighing everything up in his mind, until, at last, he nodded firmly. 'I do,' he said. 'I have faith in Alfred and everything he's done in Wessex since returning in triumph from Athelney seven years ago. We do our part, and defend this town with our lives, and God will see us right.'

Cuthwulf accepted his commander's words and smiled. 'All right then, lord. I'll go and make sure the men are rested and refreshed. Ale earned as a reward for victory on the battlefield is always the tastiest! What will you do?'

Aedan turned away and stared out at the shadow-wreathed land to the north, where the Danes continued to work away, their earthworks strengthening their position with every passing moment. 'I'll speak with the town council,' he said. 'Make sure our food and drink is provisioned as well as possible. And then,' he finished with a laugh, 'I'll come and have some of that ale you mentioned. I think I've earned a cup or three!'

–

The Danes maintained the siege over the next few days, sometimes leaving the safety of their hastily constructed earthwork fortifications to forage. They also attempted to take Hrofescester again a number of times, attacking the different gates and searching for weak points along the ditches and walls that might grant them ingress to the town. Each time they were beaten back, the recently strengthened walls holding firm, as did the troops manning them. Every failed attack left dozens of Northmen dead, while the Saxons suffered hardly any casualties.

Still, the town could not hold out forever. With so many refugees added to the population the food stores were already starting to run out. Aedan had conferred with the town council on how they would proceed if no aid reached them before supplies were completely exhausted.

'The Danes are only here for plunder,' one wealthy trader had argued. 'So why don't we just pay them to leave? That's what the king's done, and it usually works.'

Aedan felt a surge of anger at the man's cowardice. Hadn't the walls stood firm? Hadn't the townsfolk held their nerve and repelled everything the Danes had thrown at them? Yet this trader would gladly throw away the town's wealth rather than put himself in any more danger.

Still, if the food ran out, there would only be two choices: Fight, or pay the raiders to leave. Aedan would not let such weak thoughts enter the council members' heads though – or at least, he wouldn't allow those thoughts to take root and flourish more than necessary.

'We'll not be paying those bastards a single silver coin,' the thane growled, left hand idly fingering the handle of his sword. 'I wouldn't even give them the steam off my shit if they asked for it! We'll continue to pick them off if they want to throw themselves at our gates, and we'll continue to give out half rations – a third from tomorrow – to give our reinforcements time to arrive. Alfred didn't put me in charge of Hrofescester just to surrender the place at the first sign of trouble.'

'Trouble!' The trader, an older man with a bald, freckled head and rheumy eyes was not about to give up his position easily. 'You call this 'trouble', my lord?' He waved an arm towards the wall, in the direction of the Danes' earthen ramparts. 'There are hundreds of heathen raiders out there! Even if help does come from Suthriganaweorc or Eorpeburnan, they're not going to send their whole garrisons, are they? We'll *still* be outnumbered!'

'You don't know that,' Cuthwulf argued, his clear voice bringing an element of calm to the meeting.

'No, you don't,' Aedan agreed, glaring at the watery-eyed trader. 'King Alfred has put much effort and planning into his system of burhs, and the army that's to be used to guard them. This will be its first real test — have you no faith in the king's leadership?'

The trader blinked furiously, mouth hanging open but not moving now, for how could he answer such a question without appearing treasonous?

'Well?' Aedan demanded.

Every eye was on the trader and, although some of his fellow council members had murmured agreement with him when he originally suggested paying the Danes off, they did not speak up on his behalf now. At length, the trader shrugged with bad grace and muttered, 'You're in charge, my lord. We should do as you command.'

Aedan held him fixed with his stare for a time and then nodded. 'Good. Then we'll do as we've been doing, with no talk of surrender. Go among the people and keep their morale up with smiles and encouragement, as I expect men of high rank such as yourselves to do at a time like this. We're safe within the town. So let's just give our comrades time to march to our aid, eh?'

The councilmen knew Aedan had been given command of their town as a reward for his service to the king. It was common knowledge that the Irish warrior had fought with distinction and savagery on Alfred's behalf. It was also very plain to see that he would not stand for dissent, and none of

Hrofescester's noblemen wanted to get on the wrong side of so formidable a soldier. So they left Aedan's hall and went about their business without further argument, leaving the thane alone with Cuthwulf.

'You know it might well come to paying the Danes to leave,' the captain muttered.

Aedan sighed. 'Of course. That's a last resort though. I hate those bloody sea-wolves. They've brought so much death and suffering to these lands, and I'll not reward them for it unless there's no other choice.'

'Do you truly believe help will come in time?' Cuthwulf asked in a low voice, looking at the hall doors just in case the trader or one of the other council members came back and heard his uncertain tone.

Aedan shrugged. 'I hope so. We'll just have to pray to God that Alfred's reforms haven't been for nothing.'

'Not all of the ealdormen or thanes have been as supportive of those reforms as you, lord,' Cuthwulf noted.

'That's true,' Aedan admitted. 'But we'll have to hope those living nearest to Hrofescester have done their part, as Alfred commanded. We should know in a few more days, I'd imagine.' He stood up and walked towards the doors, going through them and out into the early afternoon. It was another drab day, with only a hint of blue showing through the white and grey clouds, and the town was filled with noise. Those who could – butchers, bakers, blacksmiths, tanners, builders and so on – were carrying on their usual work, while the tightly packed refugees had little else to do other than chatter. It made for a stifling, unnatural atmosphere that Aedan, like everyone in the town, was unused to.

No wonder the council members were growing increasingly edgy.

Aedan and Cuthwulf made their way onto the fighting platform that ran the length of the nearest wall, which happened to be the western one. The soldiers there immediately stiffened to attention at the appearance of their commanders, but there seemed to be little danger outside the town just then. Perhaps the Danes had learned their lesson and finally understood it was a waste of time and men trying to storm Hrofescester. Aedan was not sure if that was a good thing or not – a bored soldier, cooped up within a town under siege, could be a dangerous thing. At least the Northmen's occasional attacks gave the Saxon troops an outlet for the anxiety, fear, and rage that was building up within them.

The thane could already see it in some of the men's eyes – or at least, he thought he could. The madness that came on certain people when placed in situations of great stress. Aedan had seen such men before – men who'd been badly injured in previous battles, or had seen comrades horrifically killed, or family members perhaps, and carried those terrible memories deep within them for years only to find them erupting, manifesting in terrible violence or even self-harm at times like this when hope seemed in short supply.

Aedan did not fear battle, but he suddenly found himself terrified of the responsibility that had been given to him here. These men looked to him to keep them alive, as did the many civilians gathered in the town, and the thane was simply not sure he would prove equal to the task.

'Perhaps paying the Danes to go away isn't such a bad idea after all,' he murmured as he met the anxious gazes of his soldiers.

'My lord?'

Drawing in a calming breath and letting it out slowly, Aedan turned to Cuthwulf. 'Nothing,' he said, forcing a smile. 'I was merely thinking out loud.'

'No, my lord, look,' his captain said, and Aedan noticed a new, and unexpected expression on Cuthwulf's face. Not fear – excitement. The captain pointed, and Aedan turned to look southwards.

'Riders!' someone shouted.

'Hundreds of them!' one of the other young guardsmen added.

'Who are they? More Danes?'

Aedan squinted, trying to make out some details, some clue as to who the horsemen might be. The ground shook as they thundered closer until, at last, the thane whooped with sheer joy and grabbed Cuthwulf's arm. 'Look,' he cried. 'Look at the banner!'

'I can hardly make it out. Is that a... dragon?'

'Aye, it's a golden dragon, by God!' Aedan laughed, looking around at his gaping warriors. 'The king!' he shouted. 'The king himself has come! We're saved!'

God had answered their prayers, and the people no longer had to fear the sea-wolves.

By the time the great force of armoured riders were within shouting distance, it seemed like the whole of Hrofescester was chanting the name of their lord and saviour – the sound echoing out across the land so that even the enemy raiders must have known who was to be their doom.

'Alfred! Alfred! Alfred!'

CHAPTER THIRTY-ONE

It was not hard to imagine what the jarls were thinking within the Danes' earthwork fortification. The fact that the entire force began to run towards their ships once the size of Alfred's army became clear told its own story.

The Northmen were now outnumbered, and undoubtedly shocked that reinforcements had come to help the Saxons besieged within Hrofescester so soon. This was the first real evidence that Alfred's reforms had been worth the expense and the unrest amongst the nobles of his kingdom.

Had the Danes besieged the town on the Meduwey like this even a couple of years before, there would have been a very different outcome. Either there wouldn't have been enough men to defend the walls and they would have been overrun, resulting in a bloodbath; or the town's food stocks would have run out and Aedan would have been forced to pay the enemy jarls to leave them alone. Which probably would have still resulted in a bloodbath as the Danes often killed people anyway, regardless of any payment.

Now, however, Alfred's riders galloped past the town to cheers of relief and delight from those watching on the walls, including Aedan. He quickly came to his senses, commanding the garrison to march out and add their numbers to the king's relief force.

'I don't think we're going to get a fight this day,' Cuthwulf said as they jogged through the gates and headed towards the river. 'The craven bastards are sailing for their lives!'

Aedan wasn't sure whether he should feel relief or disappointment – he wanted nothing more than to slaughter the sea-wolves who'd kept his people imprisoned behind their walls for days. It was always good when a fight could be avoided, though, for it meant there would be no Saxon casualties, and God had to be thanked for that, even if many of the warriors racing towards the riverbank were desperate to let their spear-points taste enemy blood. Aedan was responsible for more than just himself now, after all.

The king's riders were much too fast for all the raiders to outrun, and Aedan watched as they closed the gap on the fleeing, terrified enemy. He guessed Alfred had allowed his horses to walk for the last couple of miles of their journey, giving them enough of a rest that their charge here would be more effective. And it was certainly proving to be so, as those in the king's vanguard caught up with the slowest Danes, hacking down at them with swords or simply plunging spears into unprotected backs.

'They're escaping!' Cuthwulf shouted as the first of the sea-wolves' ships could be seen moving downriver, the current of the Meduwey combining with the strength of panicked rowers to power it away from Alfred's vengeful warriors with great speed.

Aedan and his men ran faster, sensing this as an opportunity to do real damage to this particular pagan army. So shocked were the raiders by Alfred's sudden appearance that they still had not formed any kind of defence. Their sole intention appeared to be making it to their ships and escaping, and Cuthwulf gave an unintelligible cry of frustration as another longship moved out into the river, and then another, and another.

The king had split his riders into three sections now, with Alfred remaining in the middle as they harried and cut down any they caught up with. The other two sections thundered past the Danes on either flank, and then, when they were in front of the bulk of the enemy army, dismounted and formed a shieldwall blocking the way to the river.

Split up as they were, the shieldwall was not as formidable as it might have been, but it was enough to slow the Danes as they sought the courage to try and break through. Their comrades who were already past this point did not even contemplate returning to aid them – instead, they continued sprinting until they were on their longships and then they sailed off.

Aedan and Cuthwulf led the Hrofescester fyrd onwards, covering the ground quickly in their eagerness for battle and they were soon mingling with the king's group of dismounted riders. Alfred had waited, allowing Aedan to catch up so their numbers would be overwhelming for the Danes who were now caught between hammer and anvil, with two shieldwalls penning them in.

'My lord!' Aedan laughed as they met and embraced as if they were long lost brothers. 'You came.'

'Of course I came,' the king replied with a frown. 'Did you doubt me?'

'Not for a moment, but I wasn't sure you'd reach us in time. A town like Hrofescester only holds so much food in reserve, and we took in a lot of refugees from the surrounding farms and settlements when the Danes arrived.'

Alfred nodded grimly. 'In truth, it was good fortune, or God's will, that I wasn't too far away with the army, or you'd have had less men here to help you. As it happened, I was in Thunderfield, so when word came, I was able to ride here quickly. We met the fyrds of Eorpeburnan and Suthriganaweorc on the way.' He smiled. 'The Danes have had quite the surprise, eh, seeing so many Saxon riders coming for them? The bastards didn't even think of hiding behind that rampart they'd built, they just ran!'

'Aye, lord,' Aedan agreed. 'Many of them have managed to escape, but now we have a chance to deal with those who didn't reach their ships. It seems we'll fight Danes side by side once again, Lord King.'

They faced the trapped Northmen who had not yet attempted to break through the line of shields that barred their way to the river.

'Ready, lads,' Alfred roared, and his voice carried easily for the opposing warriors were strangely quiet, considering the carnage that was about to happen. 'Shields up, spears at the ready! Leave none of these whoresons alive, all right?'

That brought deafening cheers, unsurprisingly, with the loudest coming from the men of Hrofescester who looked forward to repaying the Danes for the trouble they'd caused to the town and surrounding farms and smallholdings.

It was enough to completely break the spirit of the enemy raiders, who seemed to have decided life as *vikingar* was maybe not for them after all. Throwing down their weapons, those in charge came forward, begging Alfred for mercy.

'No mercy,' Cuthwulf shouted, as did most of the other West Saxon warriors. This would be a massacre now, with the enemy having completely lost their discipline and heart for the fight.

Aedan looked along the line of bloodthirsty men and gripped his spear tightly. If there was one thing that really made a warrior want a battle, it was the knowledge that his foes would not offer much resistance.

Unfortunately, the jarl in overall command of the Danes had heard all about King Alfred of Wessex, and tried one last ploy to save his skin, and that of his remaining men.

'Alfred, my lord!' the Dane called out in a wheedling voice that was quite at odds with his looks. Slim, and even taller than the sea-wolves who stood beside him, the jarl had a poorly healed scar which ran the full length of his face, splitting his moustache and braided beard and giving him a strange, yet somehow even fiercer appearance. 'My lord,' he shouted again, staring directly at the Saxon king. 'Are you the same Alfred who defeated the mighty warlord Bagsecg in battle?'

'What do you want, dog?' Alfred demanded, ignoring the man's question as many of his West Saxon troops howled and suggested there should be no more talking; it was time to kill these raiders who'd come to ravage the countryside and wreck Hrofescester.

'Lord, my name is Hjalmarr, jarl, and many of my men are Christians,' the Dane replied, his begging tone still there but his voice powerful enough to be heard over the baying Saxon mob. 'I ask you, as a fellow Christian, to grant us mercy. That's what Christ taught, was it not?'

Aedan could not see Wulfric. He suspected the ealdorman was in command of the shieldwall blocking the Northmen's passage to the Meduwey. He could just imagine what Alfred's captain would be saying right now, though. Indeed, Aedan felt the same disgust and anger as Wulfric must surely be feeling, for the jarl was clearly using this tactic as a ploy to avoid being slaughtered.

Surely Alfred would not fall for it? And yet, as Aedan thought that, he knew all too well that the king could fall for such a transparent trick. He looked at Alfred and felt his heart sink at the expression on the king's face. Then, features framed by his helmet and the long brown hair that spilled out beneath it, Alfred stared up at the sky and Aedan guessed he was silently begging God for guidance.

Wulfric's voice suddenly piped up and Aedan spotted him then, standing on the other side of the king. 'You know God – in the Old Testament – was a wrathful, violent deity,' the ealdorman pointed out loudly. 'Remember, Alfred, he commanded the Israelites to exterminate everyone within Jericho. Everyone! Look to God for guidance, my lord. Be ruthless.'

Alfred preferred to seek counsel from the later, New Testament Gospels, though, particularly those passages which taught forgiveness and mercy, so it was not a shock to Aedan when a serene smile tugged at the corners of the king's mouth, grim frown fading.

The thane just managed to restrain a groan of disappointment as the king shouted to Hjalmarr, 'Since you have

Christians amongst your ranks, I shall grant you the mercy you plead for. Throw down your weapons and prostrate yourselves before me. You'll not be harmed.' He stepped ahead of his shieldwall and looked along it, glaring at every man there, particularly his ealdormen, thanes and other section commanders. 'You hear that?' he roared. 'The Danes are not to be harmed! Strip them of their weapons and valuables, then let them go. You!' Turning back to the raiders he pointed to the huge jarl. 'Come to me, Hjalmarr. I would talk with you.'

Aedan watched as the jarl strode confidently, arrogantly, towards the line of Saxon soldiers, casting baleful glances at them before he stopped and bowed to Alfred while Wulfric took away his weapons. When the Dane straightened, and began answering Alfred's questions, Aedan examined his face.

The jarl's features were gaunt, almost to the point that he appeared ill. His pale skin stretched tightly over hooked nose and high cheekbones, and his unsettling, staring eyes were sunken deep within the narrow skull. And yet, he was as tall as Wulfric, his shoulders were broad, and his forearms rippled with muscle when he crossed them over his chest. The man suddenly glanced at Aedan, who felt as if the Dane was reading his thoughts – a sensation only strengthened when Hjalmarr's mouth turned upwards in a mocking half-smile. Aedan was glad when that piercing glare moved on from him and, instinctively, he made the sign of the cross.

If Alfred felt the same fear as Aedan, he did not show it. He barked questions at Hjalmarr, making it very clear who was in charge, meeting the Dane's disconcerting gaze with a stony, unblinking resolve. He demanded oaths and promises from the jarl, who seemed impressed by the Saxon king and readily agreed to the demands while offering compliments with repeated deep bows of his head.

And so, the battle for Hrofescester was over before it had really begun. Aedan and the rest of the warriors of Wessex did as their king commanded and, by late afternoon the enemy soldiers, had, like their jarl, seen their spears and swords taken from them but were then allowed to sail away to safety without a scratch. Alfred even let Hjalmarr go, but insisted on taking twenty of the Northman's hersirs as hostages.

By nightfall the bodies of the Danes who'd been hacked down as they fled towards the river were removed and there was a celebratory atmosphere as Alfred's army set up camp outside Hrofescester.

'This was a mistake,' Aedan murmured to Wulfric once the gruff ealdorman had joined the victorious Saxon leaders and casks of ale – taken from the enemy longships, along with any food, silver, slaves, and the many horses that had been stowed on board – were broached.

'Mistake?'

'Aye,' the thane affirmed. 'Letting so many of the scum just leave like that. We should have killed them, and set an example. Especially that big jarl. Did you see the smug look on his face as he sailed away? We've not seen the last of him I fear.'

Wulfric nodded slowly. 'On one hand, you're right,' he said. 'Alfred already has a reputation for being weak in situations like this. Too ready to forgive, as Christ would do. I've often counselled him to be more ruthless.' He took a long drink of ale and, as it went down, let out a sigh which Aedan wasn't sure indicated exasperation or contentment.

'And on the other hand?' prodded the thane.

'Well,' Wulfric smiled. 'Letting them go without a fight means none of our men had to die. That's always a good way to end the day.' He raised his cup in salute, eyes reflecting the light of the many cooking fires that had been lit around the camp.

Alfred, Aedan, Wulfric and the rest of the noblemen in the army might have retired to more comfortable quarters within the town's hall, but the king had refused to leave his men, believing they would respect him more if he suffered the same hardships as they did.

Not that this was much of a hardship, Aedan thought, picturing Hrofescester which was practically overflowing with people at that moment. He breathed deeply, letting the aromas of roasting meat and freshly poured ale wash away the stresses of the last few days. Still, despite their victory and this well-earned night of revelry, Aedan could not help but feel a sense of foreboding.

'You're right,' he said. 'It's always desirable to finish the day with a full complement of men, rather than digging graves or building pyres for our fallen. And yet...'

'And yet,' Wulfric interjected with a knowing look. 'Those Danes we let go may return to cause more mischief one day. Especially Hjalmarr, who had the look of one who lives for blood, fire, and death.'

'Exactly,' Aedan growled, eyes scanning the dark horizon, fearing enemy longships might appear there at any moment.

'Well, they might return,' Wulfric said. 'But it won't be this night, my friend. I suggest you enjoy yourself, and celebrate your successful defence of Hrofescester. You did well here, so drink up. There'll be ample time to worry about Jarl Hjalmarr and his Danes tomorrow. For now, we'll enjoy the meat and ale we plundered from their boats!'

He tore off a chunk of pork, glistening with warm juices which ran down his chin, and Aedan laughed and joined in with the victory song that had slowly spread all around the camp and even to the guards on the walls of the nearby town.

Wulfric was right. Today was a time to praise God for their good fortune. Ultimately, the sea-wolves had not proved a great threat here thanks to Alfred's recent military reforms, and perhaps they never would again, now that the raiders knew they wouldn't have things all their own way anymore.

Still, the memory of Hjalmarr's unhinged stare as Aedan had momentarily locked eyes with him took many hours and many mugs of ale before it faded and was forgotten by the Saxon thane.

CHAPTER THIRTY-TWO

As was so often the way, Aedan's tentative optimism was misplaced. Within days, word came to Alfred, who was still in the field near Hrofescester, that the beaten Danes had not all sailed far away along the whale road. Some had, with perhaps half of the survivors heading for Francia, but the rest simply followed the coast until they arrived in East Anglia and there, re-armed by some unknown allies, plundered and pillaged Alfred's lands with such brutality that even the king was shocked.

'Someone in East Anglia is working with them,' Wulfric said, leaving the sentence hanging in the air, heavy with portent and accusation.

Alfred stared at him, eyes hooded. 'Athelstan? Is that what you're suggesting?'

Wulfric shrugged innocently. 'Well, Guthrum-Athelstan is king of East Anglia. It wouldn't be that much a surprise to find out he's returned to his old, heathen ways, would it?'

The king thought about it, a deep frown furrowing his brow. 'Yes,' he said at length. 'It *would* be a surprise to me. He seems to have remained true to his new faith and been a good ally to us, don't you think?'

Wulfric merely cocked his head on one side and grunted.

Alfred rolled his eyes at the ealdorman. 'You're always so cynical, Wulfric,' he muttered. 'But I don't agree. Athelstan is not to blame for this. East Anglia is full of Danes, and not all of them are friendly towards us, or even to Guthrum-Athelstan.'

'Again, no surprise,' Wulfric said, and Diuma, who'd arrived with a detachment of his own riders agreed.

'Most of them remain pagan,' the younger man noted. 'They bear no great love for Athelstan, ever since he changed his name from Guthrum and became a Christian.'

'It's all so bloody confusing,' Wulfric grumbled. 'Guthrum, Athelstan, Christian, heathen. The question is, Alfred, what are we going to do about it? As usual, the Danes we captured at Hrofescester swore sacred oaths to leave our lands in peace, yet they've broken those vows. That goat's turd, Hjalmarr, had no intention of ever doing as he promised, you can be sure of that.'

'Aye,' Alfred said irritably. 'And no doubt you all think I'm an idiot for showing him mercy.'

No one replied to that, and the silence was pointed, angering the king even further.

'What about you?' he demanded, turning to the priest, Oswald, who had become rather gaunt in recent months although no one knew why and he claimed to feel as fit as ever. 'Do you think me a fool too?'

Oswald shook his head. 'No, my lord. God is merciful, and we should always strive to be more like Him.'

'Speak up then, Diuma,' Alfred demanded, rounding on the thane. 'Your face tells its own story. And you, Aedan! What say you? What would your counsel be, my lords? What should I do now?'

'Kill the hostages we took,' Diuma said without hesitation. 'They're just more mouths to feed. An expense and hassle we don't need, and their deaths will be on their jarl's head, not ours.'

Alfred stared at him. Diuma had always been somewhat bloodthirsty, but perhaps the king needed to listen to such advice more often.

'And then hunt down Hjalmarr and the Danes attacking our lands – make sure we don't let them off so easily this time.'

'Kill the lot of them,' Wulfric nodded.

'Agreed,' Aedan murmured.

Alfred looked at Oswald, expecting the priest to protest, at least about the fate of the enemy prisoners. The man remained silent, however, touching his tonsure absent-mindedly and gazing back blankly at the king.

'Fine,' Alfred said at last. 'We'll show the sea-wolves the full might of Wessex. Get the army ready to move, Wulfric. Aedan, Oswald, send messengers out to the captains of our new ships. I want them ready to take our army along the coast, hunting for *vikingar*.'

'And me?' asked Diuma.

'You suggested killing the prisoners,' replied the king sourly. 'See to it.'

-

The combined fyrds of much of Cent, an army numbering almost seven hundred, took to the water as soon as Alfred's fleet made it to the Meduwey. It was not a simple undertaking for so many vessels, so many men, and so many supplies to be carried northwards, but the captains knew their business well enough and, eventually, more than twenty ships bearing the golden dragon of Wessex on their sails were on the open sea, patrolling along the East Anglian coastline.

'God, that didn't take long!'

Alfred turned at Diuma's shout, peering into the smirr that had accompanied them during the whole journey. He felt the familiar, and now even welcome, thrill of excitement and fear as he saw enemy longships heading directly for them. They'd only been sailing for a single day, not moving particularly fast as they searched for their prey, and now, at the mouth of the River Sture, their prey had come to meet them.

'They want a fight,' the king said, loosening his sword in its sheath and standing in the prow to see better what they were up against.

'Looks like twelve longboats,' Wulfric said, squinting.

'More,' Diuma suggested. He counted them with a finger and pronounced with certainty, 'Sixteen of the bastards.' This was confirmed by others aboard their ship, which was the lead vessel, and Diuma smiled wolfishly as he spun to look at the king, confidently crowing, 'We outnumber them again!'

'We do,' Alfred nodded, sharing in the thane's confidence although not quite ready to show it to his men. The Danes were expert seamen after all, while the West Saxons were far less experienced on the waves. Still, neither side had fought from the decks of their ships very much, so that levelled things somewhat and, as Diuma noted, Alfred's forces outnumbered the enemy by quite some margin. He counted in his head, assuming thirty sailors to each longship. 'If they have five hundred warriors, we have nearly two hundred more.'

His figures might well have been correct, but it didn't seem to dissuade the Danes, who were approaching the Saxon fleet at a fair rate of knots, and their hulls were filled with armed men screaming threats, insults, and imprecations to their sea gods. Alfred wondered if Jarl Hjalmarr was with the enemy sailors, but he could not see the gaunt warrior.

'You think they want to get revenge for how easily we beat them at Hrofescester?' Wulfric asked with a smile that showed little trace of anxiety for the battle that was about to begin.

'Undoubtedly,' replied the king whose own fear had begun to give way to the strange calm that always overtook him when death was so close at hand. 'But they're not going to get it today.' He looked to his right where the ship's captain stood awaiting orders. 'You know what you're doing much better than I do,' he told the man. 'Pick your target, and let's get those oath-breaking sheep-humpers slaughtered!'

The captain, a grizzled veteran who appeared almost as calm as Wulfric, bowed before turning to bellow orders to his men. The sailors went about their business while those who usually spent their time on dry land waited with varying degrees of patience until, after what seemed a very short space of time, grappling hooks were flying through the air and Alfred's ship was entangled with one of the Danes'.

'Board them!' screamed the king. 'And be careful you don't fall over this time, Wulfric!'

His laugh, and the ealdorman's crude retort, were lost in the tumult as the crews of both vessels sought to take control of the other.

Wulfric did not fall over this time. Instead, he landed on the enemy ship with a resounding thump just in front of Alfred and the king looked on as his captain's blade snaked out, piercing a Dane right through the neck. Blood gouted as the dying man tried without success to scream, and then the king was in a fight for his own life, barely managing to bat aside the tip of a Northman's sword.

For a long while the crews of the many vessels battled as Oswald prayed loudly for Saxon success. Both sides took casualties, either struck down by a weapon or, perhaps more terrifyingly, by falling into the sea and drowning. Two of the enemy longships tried to escape, cutting away the ropes that held them to Saxon craft and then desperately rowing for safety. The nearest of them was not successful, as two of Alfred's ships quickly came alongside it, his men seizing control from the Danes in terrible, bloody fashion. The second fleeing longship was fast, however, and not so easily caught.

'That's Hjalmarr!' Diuma suddenly shouted, pointing at the receding enemy vessel. 'I'm sure of it.'

'They're faster than us,' their ship's captain said sadly. 'Even if we manned the oars and rowed as if Satan himself were after us, they've got a head-start and…' He shrugged and spread his arms, looking at Alfred apologetically.

'Let the bastard go, then,' Alfred growled in frustration as they watched their despised enemy disappear into the smirr. 'Hjalmarr can carry word of yet another defeat to the rest of the sea-wolves. Perhaps it'll put them off mounting further raids.'

When the screams and war cries finally died down and the creaking of hulls and ropes could be heard once more, the King of Wessex examined what remained of the thirty-nine vessels that had begun the battle, and the many hundreds of men that had taken part in the savage fighting.

Ignoring the screeching of the gulls that wheeled overhead hoping to feast on the carrion that battles usually left, Alfred, Wulfric, and Diuma went amongst the boats, asking their captains and crew how they'd fared. The fallen enemy warriors were already being stripped of their weapons and valuables before being unceremoniously tossed overboard to sink into the foaming waters, much to the fury of the hungry gulls.

'It seems we've won yet another famous victory here,' Diuma said happily once the three noblemen were together once more on board the ship they'd started that day's adventure upon. 'The Danes thought their greater experience would make us easy targets, despite our numbers. They were wrong!'

'They were,' Alfred agreed, and he too was greatly pleased, although his smile was not as wide as Diuma's, for a fair number of Wessex's sailors had fallen or been sorely injured. Still, they *had* won, and the Danes had much plunder on their longships which now belonged to the West Saxons. God could not really have granted them much greater fortune that day.

'We should head for shore and begin repairs, my lord,' the ship's captain said respectfully to Alfred. 'We may have won, but some of the craft are in a bad way, especially those we've captured from the sea-wolves.'

Wulfric grunted. 'Good idea. I've had enough of ships for a while. Now that the battle's over and the Danes have had their arses kicked, we could take horses and ride back to Wintanceaster.' His tone was hopeful, but Diuma was also nodding, and Alfred understood their reluctance to remain out on the sea.

'Fine,' the king said. 'I've started to quite enjoy being a sailor – you know I've always loved taking little boats out on the rivers near my estates, Wulfric – but it'll be good to feel hard ground beneath my feet again.'

The ship's captain shook his head in wry amusement. 'We've only been sailing for a day or so!'

'That's long enough,' Wulfric retorted.

The great fleet of Saxon and captured enemy ships was brought into the mouth of the River Sture and repairs begun. While the sailors worked, the booty taken from the enemy warriors and longships was gathered together, and Alfred – with Diuma's help – oversaw its dispersal among the men. Even the lowest ranked warrior was given something for his part in the victory yet, by the time it was all given out, the king's portion was quite sizeable. Being so heavy, Alfred ordered it to be taken on board some of the ships, which would carry it to royal vills along the Tamyse for safekeeping.

Alfred's hearth-warriors would ride with him from the mouth of the Sture the following day, and head back to Lady Ealhswith in Wintanceaster where Oswald would celebrate a special Mass in thanks for their victories over the Danes.

'There'll be feasting, too, my lord?' Diuma asked hopefully. 'I think we've earned it.'

Even Wulfric laughed, and Alfred promised there would indeed be feasting. 'A good king knows how important it is to reward his warriors after a battle,' he said. 'And besides, I enjoy a good feast as much as the next man!'

It turned out there was not a great deal of damage to the ships after all. One of the captured enemy craft had a terrific crack in its hull which was simply not worth the time to repair, so it was left for the people of the nearest settlement, Douorcortae, to either mend or use its timbers for other things. The rest of the vessels were all deemed seaworthy and so, by the time night fell, work had ended. Whatever supplies of ale that could be sourced from the army's own supplies or from little Douorcortae were being quaffed, while songs of battle and fallen comrades filled the sea air.

Oswald and Alfred prayed together, with a few of the most pious of the army's and fleet's commanders, but afterwards they too enjoyed the camaraderie of their soldiers.

'It's the best place in the world,' Diuma said, raising his ale mug to his lips yet again. His eyes sparkled, and not just from the cooking fires that had been lit. 'An army camp after a good win, I mean. Eh, Wulfric?'

The ealdorman shrugged as if he cared little for the celebrations, but Alfred, and even Diuma, knew the taciturn warrior was as pleased as any of them to have vanquished the Danes not once, but twice in recent days.

'I still say the hall is the best place to be,' the king opined. 'On a midwinter night, with the firepit blazing, full mugs of ale, a pig roasting, and you, my friends and hearth-warriors, to keep me company.'

That was met with cheers, and they were heartfelt for the men of Alfred's company knew he meant what he said.

'Soon, lads,' he went on once quiet fell again. 'Soon enough we'll all be back in my hall, enjoying God's bounty.' With that he raised his cup in the air, downed his ale, and then headed to his tent for some well-earned sleep. Tomorrow would be the start of a long ride back to Wintanceaster, and the king intended to be fresh for it, travelling as fast as possible.

Wulfric walked with him, a familiar, protective shadow even within the safety of their own encampment. 'Retiring already, lord?' asked the ealdorman. 'I thought you'd be enjoying more ale with us. The singing will start in earnest soon!'

'Aye, old friend,' Alfred replied, raising his hand in salute to the happy warriors they passed on their way to his quarters. Wulfric loved a good sing-song, even if he was tone deaf. 'Tomorrow will be the start of a gruelling but welcome ride back to Wintanceaster. I want to be ready for it, and travel as quickly as we can.' He slowed, lowering his voice as if he didn't want anyone to overhear them, and said, 'The older I get, the more I miss Ealhswith. Is that strange?'

Wulfric shrugged. 'No,' he replied with some conviction. 'The more we age, the more death and suffering we see, the more we realise it could strike us or our loved ones at any time. It's only natural to miss your wife's company while off facing Danes in battle. I miss my wife to this day, as you know...'

Alfred stopped as they came to his tent, which was not a grand affair, only big enough for two people at most to sleep in. Guards were already there, making sure all remained well throughout the night. The king reached out and grasped his captain's forearm and they looked at one another. No more words were spoken, yet Alfred felt like much passed between them at that moment – emotions, feelings, and an understanding of one another's place in the world and the struggles they'd faced in it together. It was a bond Alfred shared with very few people, and he treasured it.

'Go,' he said to the ealdorman, squeezing his arm one last time and nodding back towards Diuma and the others. 'Enjoy your night, Wulfric. You, of all my *hearthweru*, have earned it the most.'

'Yes, lord,' came the reply, and Wulfric turned, walking straight-backed as ever to return to the revelry. 'Have no fears, though,' he said, looking over his shoulder as he went, shadows from the firelight making his craggy features appear even harder than usual. 'I'll be up at dawn, ready to ride as hard as anyone for home.'

Alfred didn't reply to that, he simply nodded and smiled, then went into his tent and was snoring softly within moments, undisturbed even when a multitude of drunken voices filled the starlit night with a bawdy victory hymn.

CHAPTER THIRTY-THREE

Alfred shook his head, affecting a stern expression that did not truly reflect his good humour as he watched his men either ready the ships to sail south, or break camp to ride west with him. They were regretting the previous night's drinking and wishing they'd slept for longer, rather than staying up, wearing out their vocal cords with triumphal songs.

The king eyed Diuma smugly as the young thane rubbed his head, groaning as he went about the business of stowing away his tent. Wulfric stood beside Alfred, just as fresh as the king and even sterner of countenance.

'Don't,' Diuma muttered, rolling his eyes at his two commanders.

'Never said a thing,' Alfred replied sweetly.

Wulfric snorted so eloquently that no words were needed to convey his disdain for Diuma's hangover.

'Are we ready?' the king asked, sharing a smile with Wulfric whose mouth twitched and even turned into a grin when he saw Diuma glaring at him.

'Aye, lord,' the ealdorman replied. 'Despite their headaches the men are ready to depart.' He nodded towards the nearby ships, their hulls filled with sailors, plunder, and the vast bulk of Alfred's fyrd who would be travelling by sea rather than on land with the king.

'And here's the horses,' Diuma said, wincing as his eyes took in more of the morning sunshine than he wanted.

Alfred glanced around to see a number of animals being brought towards them. They'd been sourced from nearby farms and villages and, being only small places, the horses they were able to supply were not of the finest stock.

'By God's toenails,' Diuma grated as the beasts came closer, revealing their rather malnourished and even elderly appearance. 'That one looks like it's seen a hundred winters! It can barely walk, never mind gallop.'

'That one's yours,' Wulfric said jovially, taking the reins from the ceorl who was leading the elderly horse and handing them to Diuma. The thane opened his mouth to object, but, in truth, none of the animals were particularly fine, even the one Alfred chose, and Wulfric's hard stare was enough to deter anyone from arguing, especially when they were suffering from a stinking hangover.

Alfred took it all in with a light heart, still basking in the glory of their sea victory the day before. 'Mount up,' he called to the men that would be riding with him. 'We can find better animals on the road, and more for those who'll need to do without for now. I'd feel bad pushing these poor fellows too hard anyway, they look like they've done enough in their lives.' He patted his horse's neck affectionately and spoke directly to it. 'You're fit enough for one more job though, eh, old man? You can carry me to the next decent sized town, I'm sure.'

They'd only been able to obtain nine horses so Alfred, Wulfric, Diuma, and six of the next highest-ranked men would ride while the rest of the hearth-warriors would march until more animals could be found, which, Alfred prayed wouldn't be too long. Wintanceaster was calling to him and each moment on the road away from Ealhswith would be a hardship.

'Farewell, Lord King!'

Alfred's eyes travelled to the River Sture, where the captain he'd sailed with during yesterday's fight was saluting him.

'Farewell, friend,' the king bellowed. 'Safe journey!'

'And to you, lord,' the captain returned in a voice that carried easily on the sea breeze, and then he gave the order to his men to take the ship out into the open river. They moved with practiced ease, quickly travelling from the shallow waters out into the deeper part of the river, followed by the rest of the Saxon fleet, including the captured longships.

'An impressive sight,' Diuma noted, saluting to a friend on board the last vessel.

Wulfric grunted agreement, and Alfred could almost feel his chest swelling with pride. It *was* an impressive sight, and proved the money he'd spent on his fleet had been worth it. Indeed, much of those costs had been recouped with the plunder they'd taken from the beaten Danes.

'When will we reach the next town?' the king asked, not aiming his question at anyone in particular – just anyone who might have enough local knowledge to give him an answer.

'Who's that?' one of the other riders demanded, ignoring the king's question, and Alfred spun in his saddle at the note of alarm he heard in the warrior's voice.

'Is that one of ours?' Diuma asked, pointing out to sea where a ship could be seen heading their way from the south.

'Maybe?' Alfred replied. 'Could be a fishing vessel.' He could see the approaching ship was not the type used by fishermen though, so instead suggested, 'Or one of our scouts?'

'Oh, shit,' Diuma gasped then, as more sails appeared through the morning mist, and it became horrifyingly obvious that they could not possibly belong to Wessex.

'Danes!'

The oncoming longships had been spotted by Alfred's fleet now, and their crews could be heard and seen working quickly to prepare for whatever was to come. By now the king and his hearth-warriors could see that the enemy vastly outnumbered the West Saxon fleet, and Alfred's heart sank as he realised what had happened.

'Hjalmarr must have carried word of our victory to the rest of the Danes in East Anglia and beyond,' he said.

'And they couldn't let us have that victory,' Wulfric agreed, staring in grim fascination at the rapidly approaching enemy longships. 'The sea, the "whale road", has belonged to them for generations. They've sailed here as fast as possible, through the night even, to show us, and everyone else, what happens to any who challenge their mastery of the waves.'

His voice trailed off then and his eyes narrowed as he tried to focus on the tall figure in the enemy's foremost longship. Everyone on the beach followed his gaze, and those with younger, or better eyes than the middle-aged ealdorman swore, with some even throwing Alfred accusatory glances.

The man in the prow of that lead ship was unmistakably Hjalmarr.

The Dane noticed Alfred's men standing impotently beside the water and he raised his arm in the air, calling something unintelligible but clearly triumphant that was whipped away with the sea-spray as his rejuvenated fleet coursed through the roiling waves.

'What's he shouting?' Aedan demanded, making the sign of the cross.

'Who knows?' Alfred muttered bleakly. 'Does it matter? God take the oath-breaking bastard!'

The king's curse was punctuated by the opening of battle, as grappling hooks were thrown out, ships locked together on the churning waters, and another brutal fight erupted.

Shouting support was all Alfred and the others on the beach could do, watching helplessly as their friends and compatriots were given a harsh lesson in sea-borne violence. When it became clear how things were going, their shouts faded away and they looked on in horrified, sickened silence. Even Oswald, who'd been murmuring hopeful prayers, grew quiet.

It was a massacre. Things the men of Wessex had laughed and cheered about during the preceding night's celebrations – enemy sailors hurled overboard, for example, or a vessel being captured once all its crew were cut to pieces – were not so amusing when it was one's own people on the receiving end. The clash of weapons, and terrified, pleading cries of those who were not yet dead when they were tossed into the roiling surf carried all too clearly to Alfred and the others on the shore.

'I can't watch this anymore,' murmured the king, turning to Wulfric with tears in his eyes. 'Let us ride for home. There's nothing we can do here.'

'What about survivors,' Diuma asked, surprised by the king's words. 'Any who make it to land will need—'

'None will make it to the shore!' Wulfric snapped. His eyes were dry, but his tone left Alfred and the others in no doubt he was suffering too. 'Not alive, at least. Look,' he spat, gesturing angrily towards the clash of fleets. 'The Danes are slaughtering everyone. They're like demons. D'you think any of our comrades could survive such brutality?' He shook his head. 'The king is right. Watching this will do us no good, it'll merely give our nightmares fodder.' He trailed off and turned from the water, staring at the land behind them, as if that might hide the horror of what was happening on the waves.

'All that plunder...' a man said sadly, causing Wulfric to round on him.

'Plunder? Fuck the plunder!' shouted the ealdorman. 'Those men—'

Alfred went to the ealdorman and laid a hand on his arm. 'Leave it, my friend,' he said softly. 'This is a disaster. Our comrades, our companions, are dying out there. But he,' the king waved a hand towards the warrior who'd bemoaned the loss of their freshly-gained wealth, 'is right. That plunder would have helped us build more ships, buy more weapons, build higher walls. Its loss is...' He trailed off, sighing heavily. 'It's depressing, and you were correct when you said staying here will do us no good. Mount up, lads, and let's get the hell away from here.'

Those with horses climbed back into their saddles, leaving Alfred to gaze out one final time at the battle which was almost over already. He mouthed a soft prayer, begging God to take care of Wessex's fallen, crossed himself, and then went to his aged palfrey whose sad eyes seemed a reflection of his own.

How could this have happened? He drew in a long, tortured breath and hauled himself onto the horse. Christ preached mercy, yet, when Alfred tried to live by those blessed teachings, and showed compassion to evil men such as Hjalmarr, this was the result.

When would he ever learn?

The journey back to Wintanceaster was a sombre affair, with the king's thoughts taken up almost entirely by what they'd witnessed on the beach: The dead Saxons, hacked apart or drowned; the wealth that he'd planned to use wisely and in ways that would strengthen his kingdom; the loss of his entire fleet; and the despised, lean features of Hjalmarr, revelling in blood and pain.

Depressing, Alfred had called it, and the ride back to his capital was certainly that.

CHAPTER THIRTY-FOUR

AD 886, Wintanceaster

February

The weeks after the fleet was destroyed were hard for Alfred, who blamed himself completely, since it had been his misplaced mercy that had allowed Jarl Hjalmarr to live. His hearth-warriors must have thought him a fool, and he had to admit they were right. The king had despatched a messenger to Guthrum-Athelstan in East Anglia, demanding the Dane take Hjalmarr into custody if the jarl turned up in his lands. Some of the West Saxon nobles still suspected Guthrum-Athelstan might have been helping Hjalmarr himself but the reply, when it came at last, was clear: 'Jarl Hjalmarr acted without Guthrum's knowledge or support,' the messenger reported. 'And Guthrum says the jarl has sailed off to see out the rest of the winter in the south, perhaps in Londinium or thereabouts.'

The screams of his terrified men being thrown into the sea haunted Alfred's dreams for a long time, and his stomach troubles flared up painfully once more. He sought solace in the church, as he always did, going there to pray every morning before the sun had come up. Even that didn't give him the comfort he needed, however, for he found himself there alone each day, without the reassuring presence of his loyal priest to cheer him.

'How have your guts been? I've not noticed you having pain so much recently.'

Oswald grimaced and ran a hand across his shaved crown before it came to rest in what was left of his thinning hair, and he rubbed at it absent-mindedly. 'It comes and goes,' he replied, and it was obvious he was attempting to be stoic, but the fear was plainly written on his face. He'd taken to spending almost all of his time in bed, barely eating and becoming terribly gaunt as a result.

Alfred watched the priest sympathetically, struck really for the first time by how aged Oswald had become. It was something of a shock to think the priest must have seen more than sixty winters, and that made Alfred realise just how old he was himself at thirty-seven. He'd taken to visiting Oswald every day after his trip to the church, and every day his friend looked thinner and less like the man who'd been his spiritual advisor for so long.

'We're not youngsters anymore,' the king said with a bark of forced laughter. 'Aches and pains are part of ageing. I wouldn't worry about it too much. Look at me – those pains in my belly have plagued me for practically my whole life now, but they've never killed me yet! You learn to deal with it.'

Oswald nodded but did not smile. 'What's this rumour I've heard,' he asked through clenched teeth.

'Rumour?'

'About Sicgred sending bribes to someone on behalf of your nephews.'

Alfred raised his eyebrows, wondering how the bed-ridden priest had managed to hear about this latest piece of worrying news. Alfred himself had only heard about it the previous night when a messenger arrived from Eashing.

'I'm not sure what the story is there,' the king admitted. 'A chest full of silver was found by my auditors making its way out of Eashing. When they questioned Sicgred about it he claimed it was heading to Burpham, to pay for materials used for building works.'

'Sounds feasible,' Oswald grunted, but Alfred was shaking his head.

'It's not true. I sent riders to Burpham, but no one there knew anything about payments from Eashing, and the chest of silver never arrived there. That's what the messenger was reporting to me last night.' He stroked his beard pensively. 'It's a worry. Who is Sicgred paying, and why? Is he buying the support of my thanes, bribing them, in advance of a rebellion designed to put Aethelhelm on the throne? Like Guthrum did before, paying off the powerful nobles who don't fully support me? It seems far-fetched, but Sicgred is a dangerous man when you get on the wrong side of him and, as you know, some of my recent reforms have not been popular, and losing our entire fleet to that whoreson Hjalmarr didn't help.'

Oswald grimaced but did not reply. His lips were pinched tightly shut and, as Alfred watched, the priest let out a muffled gasp and his hand went from his tonsure to his stomach, pressing it convulsively, much as Alfred did at times.

'Has the surgeon been able to help—'

'Not at all,' Oswald interrupted breathlessly, a clear indication of how bad he was feeling. 'Other than suggesting I drink wine to mask the pain.'

Alfred felt utterly impotent and desperately wished he could do something to help this man who'd been such a selfless and invaluable servant to him over the years. Oswald had been suffering these pains for the past couple of months and only grown worse after they travelled to besieged Hrofescester and thence to the naval battle at the River Sture. As Alfred knew all too well, pains in the guts were debilitating, terrifying, and, unfortunately, seemingly incurable even with the power of prayer. If God chose not to cure a man so good as Oswald, so pious and dedicated to His service, what chance did anyone else have?

'At least the wine we've been importing from Francia recently has been good,' the king offered in a desperate attempt to lighten the mood. 'We might have lost most of our fleet in that disaster, but until then it was doing a good job of keeping the *vikingar* from attacking the trading vessels.'

Oswald did manage a genuine smile at that. 'Thank God for small mercies,' he said. 'I do enjoy a nice cup of wine. How has trade been lately? In general, I mean, lord.'

'Very good,' Alfred nodded enthusiastically. 'The old docks at Lundenwic are seeing ships from all over now, and more arrive every day bringing honey, tin, wool, leather, fur, spices, wine, pottery, and more. It's all either coming in or out, and turning a profit too.'

'Lundenwic,' Oswald said thoughtfully. 'Is that our town now? Or does it still belong to Mercia?'

'Good question,' Alfred replied, leaning back on the stool that he'd pulled up beside Oswald's bed. 'I couldn't give you an answer to it, either! As you say, it's always been Mercian, but Guthrum-Athelstan thinks he has some claim to it, as much of Mercia's land was granted to him.'

The priest grunted. 'I thought it was ours. I don't know why.'

'Well,' murmured Alfred with a shrug. 'It *is*, really. Unofficially. Mercia is ruled now by Ealdorman Aethelred, and he is sworn to me so…' He trailed off but the implication was obvious.

What belongs to Mercia belongs to Wessex, no matter what the Norse king of East Anglia thinks.

'You should really make it official,' Oswald suggested. 'Remember, you did send a letter and alms to Pope Marinus a couple of years ago, asking him to pray for your success in evicting the Danes from Lundenwic. One can only assume that his holiness did so. He sent us a piece of the true cross after all.'

Alfred eyed him suspiciously. It almost felt as if the priest had steered the conversation to this point. Well, perhaps he had. Oswald knew the king coveted Lundenwic, not only for its trading power, but also its strategic importance. The old Roman ruins in the adjacent town of Londinium were often infested with raiding Danes too, and Alfred had long wanted to clear them out once and for all. The possibility that Jarl

Hjalmarr might be found there was also tempting to Alfred, whose desire for vengeance against the duplicitous Dane had only grown in recent weeks. He smiled. 'Maybe you're right. Although it might be more prudent to give the town, officially, to Aethelred, and let it be ruled by him, for me. Guthrum-Athelstan could not complain too much about that.'

'A fine idea, my lord,' Oswald grunted, holding a hand to his side as another spasm flared in his guts.

'Aye, it is!' The king was smiling widely now, thoroughly taken by this plan to bring Lundenwic under Wessex's full control, and hopefully killing Hjalmarr in the process. 'It can be a wedding gift, of sorts.'

Oswald looked at him in surprise. 'Wedding gift?'

'Indeed,' said Alfred. 'That was the main reason I came to see you this afternoon. My daughter, Aethelflaed will be sixteen soon. She should be married. I've discussed it with Ealhswith, and we would have her wed Ealdorman Aethelred of Mercia.'

'I see,' murmured the priest in a tone that suggested his approval. It would certainly cement the alliance between Mercia and Wessex. 'And what part do I have to play in this, that you came to visit me in my bedchamber?'

'Well,' the king grinned, rising from the stool and peering down almost imperiously at his friend. 'A wedding needs a priest. So, you had better pray for God to cure your mystery ailment, since we want you to wed Aethelflaed and Aethelred.'

'But—'

'No buts, Oswald. Preparations are already underway, so you make sure you're ready. As your king, I command it!'

—

'You're taking this very calmly, I have to say.' Ealhswith was smiling but there appeared to be an undercurrent of anxiety in her expression. And no wonder – telling their daughter that she was to marry a man of their choosing was something both Alfred and Ealhswith had been dreading. Not just because they both loved the young woman deeply and had no great desire for her to leave their side, but also in part because they knew Aethelflaed's headstrong nature all too well. If she did not see the ealdorman of Mercia as a suitable husband, she wouldn't be slow in voicing her displeasure.

'I'm not a fool,' Aethelflaed replied though, and there was no hint of anger or even surprise. 'I was brought up in a royal court. I was there when we were forced to ride for our lives from Cippanhamme, and I was there on Athelney – I've seen and heard things, lofty things, most children never hear. And I've always known that, as a king's eldest daughter, I'd likely be married off to some noble to cement an alliance.'

'I trust our choice of husband is acceptable to you then?' Alfred asked, leaning forward earnestly. His mind was made up that this marriage should go ahead whether the girl liked it or not for, politically, it was the best thing for Wessex and Mercia, but he genuinely wanted his daughter to be happy. 'Ealdorman Aethelred is a good man. I'm sure he'll treat you well.'

'He's quite handsome, too,' Ealhswith added with a little smile which widened at Alfred's look of mock-disapproval.

'Handsome enough, considering he's about twenty years older than me,' Aethelred replied archly. 'And he'd better treat me well, or he'll be sorry.'

Alfred laughed. There was the familiar haughty streak he'd been expecting to see. 'I'm sure he will. But you must treat him well too, my girl. That's how a marriage stays strong and happy. Like us.' He reached out and grasped his wife's hand, squeezing it gently, feeling a great sense of happiness at how things were playing out. He'd half expected his daughter to angrily refuse the marriage to Aethelred, and make everything much more difficult and stressful than it had to be.

'You'll be following in our footsteps,' Ealhswith said with a similar contented smile to Alfred's on her face. 'A Mercian marrying a West Saxon. Hopefully God will bless your union as he has ours.'

They were in the mead hall in Wintanceaster and it was a gusty, late winter morning. Guards were positioned outside as usual, but, inside, the place was empty save for the three of them and a trusted, elderly serving woman who sat sewing in the corner ready to be called on for refreshments when required. The fire was small but crackling merrily, slowly roasting a boar which the servant rotated every so often, filling the air with the mouth-watering, meaty smell. The flames gave off just enough heat to make the royal family members cosy as they sat at the bench together, discussing this momentous matter. And it truly was momentous, for all three of them, and for the country.

'We already have a good relationship with Mercia,' Alfred said to his daughter.

She nodded and replied perceptively, 'And this marriage will make it even stronger. I understand. It'll also mean you have a spy in the very heart of Ealdorman Aethelred's household, eh?'

'Now, Aethelflaed, that's not what this is about,' Ealhswith tutted.

'No,' Alfred agreed. 'But it is true. I would hope you'd protect the interests of Wessex, Aethelflaed, and do your best to see Ealdorman Aethelred acts with those same interests in mind where possible...'

'He always has so far, hasn't he?' Aethelflaed asked with genuine curiosity. 'Why should he not in future?'

'When men are given power, it sometimes makes them want more and more. It can make them forget their allies – that's one reason why we bring powerful families together with marriages.'

'Aethelred doesn't strike me as the type to betray you,' Aethelflaed said. 'I've met him often enough to think him as honourable and trustworthy as any man could be.'

Ealhswith smirked at her daughter's little jibe, but Alfred merely rolled his eyes. Aethelflaed had always enjoyed poking fun at him, and he loved her for it, although he seldom rose to her bait.

'I completely agree with you,' he said, dragging his chair a little closer to the fire as a gust of wind blew outside, whistling through gaps in the walls and making some of the finely embroidered wall hangings twitch and sway. 'Aethelred seems a decent man, or I wouldn't be letting him marry you. But he has ruled Mercia for the past six years as an ealdorman, not as a king. I'd like him to remain content with his lot, and that's where you come in.'

'This all sounds very cynical, father.'

Alfred looked at Ealhswith and they couldn't help laughing.

'Aye, I suppose it is. But that's how the world works, Aethelflaed, as you well know.'

'I do,' she admitted primly, lifting the wine cup the serving woman had filled for her earlier and taking a sip. 'Fine,' she announced, placing the cup back down and wiping her mouth daintily. 'I'll do it. I'll marry him.'

She spoke as if it had all been her idea and Alfred began to wonder if she had, somehow, planned this all along. Perhaps wanted to marry Ealdorman Aethelred for some time, and subtly manoeuvred Alfred and Ealhswith to set up the union. On the surface, it seemed absurd, but the cool smile on his daughter's face, and his understanding of her clever, cunning nature, did make him wonder if he'd been manipulated. It was an unsettling thought, but then he remembered these were the exact qualities that would make Aethelflaed such a valuable presence in the Mercian ruling household. They could have chosen a much worse husband for her after all.

The king smiled. 'Good. Thank you, daughter. You'll make a superb wife, of that I'm absolutely certain.'

'And an even better spy,' Aethelflaed murmured, winking conspiratorially at him.

'You'll not be a spy,' he retorted irritably, then broke off, shaking his head, smile returning. He had a sudden memory of the girl, much smaller, running past his library with her friends, she rather younger than the others yet clearly their leader. A lump came to his throat and for a frightening moment he feared he might weep in front of his wife and daughter. Quickly, he reminded himself that Aethelflaed was not dying, he was not losing her the way he'd lost his siblings, his mother, his father, and all the friends who'd been killed fighting the Danes over the years. She was merely going to live a few hours' ride along the northern road, and he would still see her. He averted his face from the light of the fire and drew in a deep, calming breath. Ealhswith, as always, sensed his mood for he felt her squeeze his hand and when he looked, he saw her eyes were moist too. She did not mind crying happy tears in front of their children.

Laughing, he drew his wife into a long embrace. Long enough for his own tears to dry.

And then he turned to Aethelflaed, beckoning her over, and she left her chair to put her arms around them and the three of them held onto one another as if they never wanted to let go.

CHAPTER THIRTY-FIVE

Lundenwic was in a strange position. It was ostensibly part of Mercia, and brought in much wealth for Ealdorman Aethelred – and Alfred, too – as their ships sailed to and from the town. Every so often, however, an army of Danes would appear and decide to spend their time there, not halting trade for long, but stealing whatever silver and goods they took a fancy to, killing any who stood in their way. It was never exactly a siege, for Lundenwic had no proper walls to defend it, and had not enjoyed any real defences since the distant days when it had been a mighty Roman town. When raiders turned up now, they simply walked into the place and took control by sheer force of numbers and ferocity.

'We've begun building our burhs throughout Wessex,' Alfred told his commanders as they rode towards the town in early March. 'But the Danes still move with impunity around our borders, causing a great deal of mischief in places like Lundenwic. It's costing Wessex money, my lords, and it's time we put a stop to it.'

'We will take Lundenwic from the occupying Northmen,' Wulfric went on at a nod from the king. 'And be back in our homes in plenty of time to enjoy the Midsummer feast.'

'Indeed,' said Alfred. 'Back home and ready to celebrate the Nativity of John the Baptist.'

'Good,' a grey-haired thane from near Readingum called out somewhat testily. 'It seems like I spend half my life riding about the place fighting raiders these days. It does not agree with my ageing bones.'

'It doesn't agree with any of us, I don't think,' Alfred replied levelly. 'But we go where and when we must to deal with the Danes. Or would you prefer we go back to the old ways, when our towns fell with barely a whimper of resistance, and your silver was given away to the bastards in hopes they'd leave our lands?'

'Of course not,' the thane blustered, face flushing bright red against his grey fringe. 'I did not mean that, Lord King. I'm merely getting a little too old for riding abroad so much.' He held up a hand, swollen with arthritis, as evidence of his discomfort.

Alfred smiled and nodded. 'I understand, my friend, and I sympathise. I often wish I was as young as I was when I rode to fight Ivar in Snotengaham at my brother's side.' He looked around at the other noblemen riding in the fyrd's vanguard with him, still smiling, hoping to inspire confidence and morale within them. 'Soon the day will come when there'll be no need for journeys like this. No need to defend our lands and our borders, either in summer sun or when the snow makes a blanket on the road and wind whips the very flesh from our bones. We're almost at that day already, my lords, and taking Lundenwic will do much for our cause, trust me.'

His cheery words seemed premature, as drops of rain began to fall on the riders and the infantry who marched behind them.

'That's all we need,' Wulfric murmured darkly, peering up at the lumpen grey clouds that had rolled in quickly and let hardly a glimmer of sunlight through despite it being near midday.

'At least it's not windy,' Diuma said with a grim laugh.

'Yet.'

'Oh, stop being so gloomy, Wulfric!' Alfred laughed. It was strange, he thought; the older he got the more relaxed he seemed to become. His issues with his guts had never gone away completely but they were usually less severe, and, even riding to yet another battle that he might not survive, his mood was light. Perhaps it was because his grasp of Wessex's throne was more secure than it had ever been, and his men followed him without too much dissent. 'We've journeyed in worse weather than this. We had to live in nothing more than tents during the winter in Athelney, by God! A few drops of spring rain in your hair should be easy by comparison.'

'I'm not bothered about my own discomfort,' Wulfric grumbled. 'I just don't want us getting slowed down by muddy roads.'

'Not bothered by your own discomfort,' Diuma repeated in mock amazement, eyes wide. 'Mighty Wulfric, untouched by even the fiercest of thunderstorms, who only cares for the welfare of his charges! Truly an angel sent to us from Heaven, Lord King – don't you agree?'

'You ever been punched in the face by an angel, Diuma?' Wulfric demanded, balling up his meaty fist and glaring at the younger man.

'Will the pair of you shut up?' Alfred cackled in exasperation. 'It's like riding to war with my youngest children! Actually, I think little Aelfthryth and six-year-old Aethelweard have more sense than you two.'

Wulfric smiled. 'Makes the journey more interesting though, eh, lord?'

'I despair,' Alfred muttered. 'You used to be a sensible, dour fellow, Wulfric.'

'What's to stop another load of Danes from taking control of Lundenwic once we've left?' the grey-haired thane asked, oblivious to the childish banter going on between the king and his two companions. 'Without a wall and an army to defend it, the town will remain wide open to future attacks.'

Alfred pulled the collar of his heavy cloak around his neck, bunching up his shoulders to try and stop the damp air blowing down his back. 'Of course,' he agreed happily. 'That's why we're going to slaughter them all, and then rebuild the Roman walls around Lundenwic and extend them to enclose old Londinium as well.'

The old thane's face twisted as if he'd just bitten into a handful of sour buckthorn berries. 'That sounds expensive.'

'It'll be worth it!' Alfred cried. 'The trade a secure, enlarged Lundenwic should bring in will soon recoup any building costs we incur, and then – pure profit, my lord.'

The thane shook his head, but he was chuckling at the king's enthusiasm for it was hard not to be moved by it. Indeed, there were no other arguments or dissenting voices for the rest of the way to the town, which they reached early on the fourth day after departing Wintanceaster. The men were fresh, even those on foot, for Alfred had not pushed them hard on the third day and allowed them to get a good night's rest before they made their way to Lundenwic around mid-morning.

The town militia, what there was of it, turned out to meet them with spears at the ready. The commander, a tough-looking middle-aged warrior with a beard that reached down to his ale-swollen belly, stood proudly, barring their way and demanding to know their business. That conversation did not last for very long, and soon enough the militia had been assimilated into Alfred's fyrd and the entire force was moving through Lundenwic.

Although most of the nobles in the army had visited busy port towns before, many of the lower ranking soldiers had never seen such an eclectic mingling of cultures. The different languages, manner of dress, skin colour, and exotic smells mixed freely with the usual barking dogs, rumbling wagons, and Saxon merchants loudly hawking their wares. One group of people were conspicuously absent, however.

'Where are all the Danes?' Alfred asked the militia commander as they travelled.

'Word of your coming reached us a while ago, lord,' shrugged the man. 'Some of them buggered off in their long-ships. Others headed for the old Roman ruins a mile or so east – there's a lot of them there, they've got a big camp.'

'Londinium,' Alfred nodded.

'Aye, so the Romans called it, my lord,' the man agreed, patting his round belly as if it was a habit of his.

'How many sea-wolves are there?' Diuma asked.

'In the ruins? One hundred? Two? Maybe three? I'm not sure, we never go there. Place is haunted.'

'Haunted? Why don't the ghosts bother the Danes then?'

The commander frowned at Diuma as if he was stupid. 'They follow the heathen gods, don't they?' he replied at last, as if that explained everything.

'Three hundred Danes,' Alfred interjected as they moved northwards through the town, towards the bridge that spanned the River Fleot. 'Could there be more?'

'Could be,' the militia commander said unhelpfully. 'Not many more though. This army you've brought with you will be plenty, my lord.'

When they came to the bridge that would grant them passage over the Fleot, Alfred eyed it with some trepidation, for it was narrow and not particularly sturdy.

'It'll take some time to get all our men over here,' Wulfric noted, as if reading the king's mind.

'It will,' said Alfred. 'And the Danes could come charging at us while half of us are still crossing, rendering much of our army useless. Trapped on the bridge, or here, on this side of the river.'

'There's another bridge,' the militia man told them. 'Not too far upriver.'

Alfred gave Diuma command of one hundred riders and they galloped off, hooves churning the sodden road, to make the crossing. A short time later, the king led Wulfric and the warriors who'd remained with them across the narrow wooden bridge towards the crumbling Roman walls which were still impressive despite their dilapidation.

Their presence had been noted by the men within Londinium but, rather than charging the Saxons as they made the ponderous bridge crossing, or even running for their longships, the Danes simply took up positions behind the ruined fortifications.

'Either they're confident they have the numbers to beat us,' Wulfric said, eyes scanning the spears and helmeted sea-wolves that stood on and around the Roman defences. 'Or they're hoping their pagan gods will protect them, because those old walls certainly won't.'

'Surely no jarl would believe himself that blessed by the gods,' Alfred snorted. But the smile faded from his face as he rode closer to the derelict town and caught sight of a familiar figure standing on what must have been a platform behind the wall facing them.

'By God's great knackers,' Wulfric breathed, turning to Alfred with a widening grin. 'Look who's up there, waiting for us. Guthrum was right!'

'God be praised,' the king replied grimly, eyes fixed on the man his captain had pointed out. 'Jarl Hjalmarr. No wonder they haven't run – that bastard really must think himself protected by his gods after he fooled me into letting him go at Hrofescester. Oh, this is going to be a good day, Wulfric. Not only are we going to take this old city and rebuild it as one of our own burhs, but we're going to get our revenge on Hjalmarr too!'

As they spoke their men continued to jog across the bridge, its planks and timber supports creaking and groaning beneath the great weight of pounding feet. And then it seemed that Jarl Hjalmarr recognised the proud figure on horseback at the head of the Saxon army. The Dane disappeared and soon enough came out from behind the wall with a dozen or so heavily armed bodyguards.

'Hjalmarr!' Alfred roared as soon as most of his men were across the river and standing in an impenetrable line behind him. 'You swore an oath to leave these lands, but, like so many of you honourless sea-dogs do, you broke that oath. Your gods have sent me to punish you for it.'

'My lord!' the jarl stepped forward a pace, in front of his warriors, smiling ingratiatingly although the expression did not reach his cold eyes. 'I broke no oath. We simply came here to repair our ships – once that's done, we'll leave as I swore we would.'

'You attacked my fleet on the River Sture, you heathen sack of dog shit!' Alfred bellowed, removing his helmet and shaking it towards the jarl. 'You murdered defenceless men, throwing them into the sea to drown. You shouldn't even have been in those waters – you had sworn an oath to sail back to Francia or your own homeland!'

'No, my lord, not me,' Hjalmarr objected, dark eyes boring into Alfred, the hint of a mocking smile tugging at the corners of his mouth. 'You are mistaken.'

'Am I really?' the king asked, cocking his head on one side, as if the Dane's words had made him question his narrative.

'*Ja*,' the jarl replied, still with that infuriating smirk playing around his lips. 'I would not attack you. By Þórr, we have no quarrel with you, my lord.'

Alfred smiled as if in relief. 'Well, this is good news then, eh Wulfric?' He glanced at the ealdorman who frowned, apparently fearing his king was about to let the Danes simply sail off once more.

'Good news, yes, Lord King,' Hjalmarr called. 'Come, let there be peace between us. We have food and drink even a nobleman of Wessex will enjoy.' He gestured for Alfred to join him within the crumbling town walls. 'Your men can rest. They are safe from us, as you are.'

'If you did not break your oath,' Alfred shouted back, still mounted on his horse. 'Then, as you say, I have no quarrel with you after all. However, I want you out of my lands. As before, Hjalmarr, I would ask you to command your men to throw down their weapons. If they do that, you can all sail away in peace, without any unnecessary killing or… unpleasantness.'

'What are you doing?' Wulfric hissed out the side of his mouth. 'You can't let them get away again, for goodness' sake.

That bastard has already shown he can't be trusted, and he *was* part of the fleet that destroyed all our ships – you saw him there yourself. He must pay. You risk losing the support of all your nobles if you let him go again!'

'I'd rather we drew them all out from behind those walls if possible,' Alfred murmured. 'So let Hjalmarr continue to think me a weak, guileless fool, eager to be merciful in the name of Christ. Besides, the longer we keep him distracted, the more time Diuma has to get behind him.'

Alfred's smile never wavered as he spoke softly to his captain, but Hjalmarr's did. The Northman was frowning thoughtfully, perhaps wondering whether he had enough men to defeat the fyrd of Wessex if he chose to try. Did the jarl know about Diuma and his contingent of riders who must, God willing, be in position by now?

'I don't think my men will give up their weapons as you ask,' Hjalmarr replied at last. 'I do not have enough power over them.' He shrugged as if to say, *Bloody Danes, what are they like?* before going on in a loud voice. 'But you have my word, Alfred: we will sail from here at first light tomorrow. Now come and share my mead. It is good and strong, and will warm your blood like a whore at yule!' He waved for Alfred to come forward again, but again, the king remained where he was.

'Either throw down your weapons and surrender to me,' the king called in a clear, firm tone. 'Or we will attack, and this time I won't be as merciful as when we last met at Hrofescester, Hjalmarr.'

The Dane looked genuinely pained, but not as much as Alfred thought he would if he was aware of Diuma's warriors converging upon them. The jarl's frown was grim, but not that of a man who knew he was outnumbered two to one and facing an attack on two fronts.

Good. Alfred still had the element of surprise on his side. He did not want to lose it.

'Throw down your weapons,' he barked. 'I won't ask you again.' He hefted his spear and pointed it along the enemy line, staring into the eyes of the men who faced him. 'Surrender, or die.'

The Danes had not enjoyed so much success as raiders over the decades by being afraid of battle, though.

'If it is my time to die,' Hjalmarr replied grimly. 'Then so be it.' He looked at his bodyguards, tall and proud, and well-armed and ready for battle, then he strode towards Alfred. He carried a long-handled axe and a round shield painted red, and there was a determined glint to his eye as he stopped halfway between his own men and the West Saxon line. Alfred glanced at Wulfric, who shrugged, and then the king allowed his horse to carry him to within three or four spear-lengths of the enemy jarl.

'You have more to say?'

'I do,' Hjalmarr nodded, casting another glance back at his men. It was clear he did not want them to hear him. Alfred thought this a good sign, believing the jarl was about to surrender to him. He was wrong.

'I am ashamed of how I behaved at Hrofescester,' said the Dane, staring up at Alfred with that black, piercing stare that might turn lesser men's bowels to water. 'Never before have I run from a fight like that. Never before have I sworn an oath to a Christian warlord.' He spat on the ground in front of the king's horse. 'But my gods know such an oath is meaningless, and I have proved myself a worthy warrior by helping to destroy your entire fleet of ships on the river you people call the Sture.' He held Alfred's gaze unflinchingly, narrow jaw set firm. 'We will fight, Saxon, and the gods will grant victory to those most deserving. You do not outnumber us as you did at Hrofescester, for I've been recruiting more warriors, ready to attack your lands once more come the summer.' He smiled slyly. 'A chest full of Saxon silver can pay for a lot of men.'

With that, he made an obscene gesture and walked backwards, shield still held ready in case Alfred decided to attack, and was soon assimilated into the wall of enemy shields.

'What was that all about?' Wulfric asked when the king had returned to his own starting position before the army of Wessex.

'He believes they can beat us,' Alfred replied, mind whirling as he thought about that last, throwaway comment Hjalmarr had made. Had this been where Sicgred had had sent the missing chest of silver? He swallowed, pushing aside his suspicions and focusing again on the task at hand. 'D'you think Diuma is in position yet, Wulfric?'

'He should be,' the ealdorman said. 'And, since we've not heard any fighting or an alarm being raised within the ruined walls there, I'd say they've not been discovered.'

'Good.' Alfred raised his right arm, holding his spear up. 'Ready men? These pagan bastards think they can kill us all!' There were angry jeers and the king continued. 'They have a hoard of treasure, stolen from our kinsmen, hidden within those old ruins. Are you ready to slaughter the whoresons, and make yourselves rich? For I promise you this – whatever we find in Londinium this day will be shared out *equally* amongst you all!'

The earlier jeers were replaced now by eager roars. Lowly infantry soldiers did not usually come out of a battle as rich men for the wealth was generally distributed first among the nobles, with only scraps filtering down to those at the bottom of the social scale. By promising to give every soldier an equal cut he was offering them a huge incentive to win.

Wulfric frowned. 'You sure about this?' he muttered.

Alfred nodded. 'I won't be making it a habit, but I want that twisted dog Hjalmarr dead, and this fight over with as quickly as possible. Come on.' He dismounted, as did Wulfric, and their horses were led away by a couple of young ceorls. Then the king raised his spear once more and bellowed, 'Spears ready! Shields together! Forward!'

CHAPTER THIRTY-SIX

Diuma's men had left their horses a quarter mile or so from the old Roman town, walking the rest of the way, alert for any sign of attack. Strangely, there seemed to be no guards or lookouts posted along the route.

'Arrogance?' he murmured to his young captain, Tatberht who wore a helmet older than he was himself and dressed, like Diuma, in a mail shirt covered by a green cloak. 'They think themselves too strong for anyone to sneak up and cause them trouble?'

'Maybe,' Tatberht replied, eyes moving from left to right and back again, constantly searching for hidden enemy warriors as they grew closer to the dilapidated stone walls. 'Or the whole lot of them have gone to face King Alfred's fyrd. Should I scout ahead, lord? Get the lie of the land?'

Diuma agreed. They were already at the northern wall of the town and he had his men form up and wait in silence as Tatberht went on ahead. It wasn't long before the young captain returned, grim faced but excited.

'There's women in there,' he said, pointing to the centre of the town. 'In amongst all the ruins. Cooking and washing clothes and stuff. Look, you can see the smoke. Smell it too,' he muttered, sniffing the air appreciatively.

'The Northmen's wives,' Diuma growled. 'Or captured slaves more likely. The whoresons really have made Londinium their home, eh?'

'Looks like it,' Tatberht agreed. 'But we should be ready to move. The king's fyrd will be across the bridge and lined up ready for battle.'

Diuma nodded thoughtfully. The fact that there were no enemy guards here did seem to suggest that they'd all been ordered to the western side of town, to face Alfred's fyrd.

'Shit, it's started!' Tatberht cursed. 'Listen.'

The sounds of fighting were intimately known to every man hiding beside the wrecked walls, and Diuma knew he only had one choice.

'Let's move!'

They passed through the gaps in the fortifications, filtering quickly into the town.

'It's too quiet,' a grey-haired veteran said as they walked through the streets. 'I don't like it.'

'Quiet?' Tatberht asked in disbelief. 'Have your ears failed you in your dotage? Do you not hear men screaming and dying on the other side of town?'

The older soldier shook his head, the grey mane that spilled out beneath his helmet shaking from side to side. 'I hear it,' he replied gruffly. 'But there's something not right.' He broke off then, as an arrow appeared from a sky that had been clear just a moment before. The missile's wicked iron head thundered into his chest, the mail shirt he wore doing little to rob it of its terrible power, and he stumbled backwards, mouth agape.

'Shit,' Tatberht gasped, turning to see the grizzled warrior draw his last breath before the light went from his eyes and he collapsed on his back.

'Shields up!' Diuma commanded, voice reverberating off the ruined walls and buildings around them. 'Sheilds up! It's a trap!'

The veteran warrior's concerns had proved correct, even if they'd done nothing to save him. Danes were pouring out of the ramshackle buildings both in front of, and behind Diuma's warband, many of them holding bows which they'd already used to loose the volley of arrows that had killed the grey-haired veteran and were now raining down on the rest of the Saxons. Shields were hastily held aloft, the timber boards thumping and thudding as the arrows struck home, barbed points punching right through the wood in some cases, adding unbearable weight to the already heavy shields.

'Keep them up!' Diuma bellowed, kicking the man next to him who was lowering his shield to try and pull out the missile embedded in it. 'Keep them up and hold formation until the bastards are done!'

The Danes were, in fact, done already, either having no more arrows to continue the long-range attack, or simply preferring to use their swords, spears and axes to dispatch their enemies face-to-face.

'Here they come,' Tatberht called in a surprisingly steady voice. 'Half you men turn backwards with me, form a shield-wall. The rest turn with Ealdorman Diuma and prepare to meet the sea-wolves coming from the front!'

There had been casualties in that single missile attack, although Diuma had no way of knowing how many. He could hear screams of anguish but there was no time to help those who'd fallen, they would have to look after themselves as best they could for now.

'Brace!' he roared just before the mass of charging Danes smashed into the shieldwall.

The Saxons were thrown back on both sides but, having their own comrades packed behind them meant they did not lose any ground. The first enemy attack was blunted, their thrusting spears and wildly swinging axes doing less damage than Diuma had feared. Teeth gritted so hard he worried they might crack, the thane used his shield to deflect the Northmen's weapons and then, as the momentum faded from their charge, Diuma ordered his men to strike back.

His spear quickly found an enemy, sharpened tip tearing a great chunk of flesh from the man's neck. Without hesitating, Diuma pulled back then thrust out again, and again. He barely noticed a Northman's axe clattering against his shield, breaking one plank of the linden wood. That attacker was killed by someone else, and Diuma became lost in the battle trance, sounds becoming a low rumble, sensations numbed, things almost seeming to move in slow motion as instinct kicked in and carried him forwards.

At the back of his mind was the realisation that Alfred was also fighting a battle at that moment, and expected Diuma to help him. Everything was going wrong, the thane screamed in his mind. Their simple plan had seemed foolproof but, somehow, whoever was commanding the sea-wolves had managed to ruin it. The thought sent rage coursing through his veins and he screamed, '*Godemite!*' as he fought with renewed savagery.

His surge of energy inspired his men, who took up his cry to God Almighty and very quickly the Danes realised they were losing. Dozens of the enemy were strewn about the ground, limbs hacked from torsos, skulls crushed, guts torn open, blood pumping from myriad wounds, and all accompanied by soul-wrenching cries. The sights and sounds only drove Diuma and his Saxons on, fighting with, although it seemed impossible, even more vicious wrath.

Soon, the line of attackers facing them thinned out as Danes fell or decided they wanted no further part in the battle and ran away, leaving their comrades to the mercy of the Saxon blades.

'Shall we go after them, lord?' Tatberht shouted, breathing heavily, blood streaming down his face from beneath his old helmet. 'There's not many left, and their spirit is broken.'

'No!' Diuma called back, then realised there was no need to shout as the cessation of fighting had left the air around them strangely calm, broken only by the abject cries and whimpers of the dying. 'Two of you help our wounded if you can,' he ordered, pointing at a group of men. 'The rest of you, follow me to the western wall. We have to help Alfred before he's overrun!'

Diuma led them as fast as he could, given how tired he was from the battle. Through the Roman streets which were still in astonishingly good condition given their great age they hurried. More screams and war cries quickly came closer and then Diuma actually laughed as they made their way through and around the gaps in the ruined western wall, for the whole enemy shieldwall was before them, backs turned, facing Alfred and his men and completely oblivious to Diuma's reinforcements.

No command was necessary. The thane stopped running and let fly the first of his throwing spears – unused thus far thanks to the speed of the earlier enemy ambush. His men followed suit, and then Diuma threw his second and third.

The missiles caused absolute carnage as they came down like the fist of God, hammering into the unsuspecting Danes. Even those who wore helmets and armour were not safe from the wicked, iron points which shattered bone and ripped through flesh as easily as if it were freshly churned butter.

'Charge!' Diuma screamed, and so they did, stepping over the bodies of those they'd just killed and leaning down to thrust their long spears into the whimpering injured, putting them out of their misery and sending them on their way to Valhöll, or Hell, or whatever fate their heathen exploits had earned for them in the afterlife.

The enemy had finally realised they were beset on two sides though, and now Diuma's warriors found themselves having to defend themselves from ferocious, desperate spear thrusts and pounding axe heads.

A shield boss struck Diuma directly in the face and he reeled back, stars exploding in his vision at the same time as his mouth filled with warm blood which made him retch, trying to spit it out. Tatberht was at his side, thank God, and managed to stab the attacking Dane through the chest with his spear. Diuma was utterly dazed, however, and felt himself collapsing onto his backside, unable to make his legs support him. A thrill of fear rushed through him to be so defenceless, and he gasped as he began to hallucinate, for Alfred was standing in front of him.

'You alright?'

Diuma gaped, wondering if he'd actually been killed by the blow to the face, but then he realised the fighting had stopped, and Wulfric was also there, glaring down and shaking his head in disgust at him.

'Taking a rest, are you?' the ealdorman demanded. 'Typical.'

'We won?' Diuma gasped, closing his eyes to try and regain his bearings.

'Of course we won,' Alfred laughed, reaching out and helping Diuma to stand. The king held onto him, making sure he was steady before stepping back and looking around at the bodies strewn across the ground. 'Have the men clear out the entire town,' he said to Tatberht. 'I want Londinium purged completely of enemy warriors by the time the sun sets.'

Tatberht hurried off and Diuma sniffed blood up his nose, hawked, and spat it out. He did not mean to hit a dead Dane with it, but there was no clear space on the ground. 'That's a lot of bodies we'll have to get rid of,' he murmured, breathing heavily.

'Aye,' Alfred agreed sourly. 'The stink of their pyres will be an affront to God. Maybe we can fill their ships with them and send them off, burning, to the sea.'

'Now?'

'No, Diuma,' the king laughed. 'Now, you find somewhere to sit until your nose stops bleeding and you don't look like you're about to fall over again. And then? Well, you know how it goes after we win a battle. I hope you're well enough in a few hours to join in the feasting!' He slapped Diuma on the shoulder, almost sending the thane reeling again. 'Londinium belongs to Wessex, my friend, and as soon as we're done celebrating, we're going to make it one of the most powerful trading centres in all Christendom. A burh. Lundenburh!'

He looked down at one of the enemy bodies, face down on the ground. Using his foot, the king pushed the warrior over and growled in satisfaction. It was Hjalmarr.

'Did you know he was here?' Diuma asked.

'I knew some of the raiders who'd sunk our fleet were wintering here,' Alfred replied, still staring at the still features of the enemy jarl. 'I hoped he would be with them, but I wasn't sure of it until I saw his ugly face on the old wall. Here.' He handed his spear to Diuma who took it gratefully, using it as a crutch to support himself for he was still shaky.

'Help me...'

Diuma frowned, and shook his head, believing his head injury was affecting his mind, for he could have sworn the dead man on the ground had just spoken.

'Please help me, Alfred.'

'By God, he's still alive!' the king exclaimed as the enemy jarl reached out a hand to him.

'Alive, aye,' Wulfric cried. 'But look, there's not a mark on him. Get back, lord!'

CHAPTER THIRTY-SEVEN

Wulfric's shout came just in time – warning Alfred of the danger as the sword hidden beneath Hjalmarr's body suddenly whipped out, slicing through the space which had just been occupied by the king's legs.

Hjalmarr moved with a grace and speed Alfred had not expected, jumping to his feet as Alfred stumbled backwards in surprise. Wulfric was just as quick as the Dane, however, and the ealdorman threw himself into Hjalmarr. Down they went, the jarl's sword flying from his grasp as the two men struggled amongst the corpses of the fallen for supremacy. Hjalmarr might have been tall, but he was not as heavy as Wulfric, who was quickly gaining control of the fight before three of Alfred's hearth-warriors came across to help subdue the enemy warlord.

Alfred stared at Hjalmarr as he was dragged up to his feet, drawn swords and spears aimed at his back and chest. Wulfric was right, Hjalmarr had not suffered any visible injures – his brynja was intact, and the only blood on him was from the Saxons he'd cut down. He'd been playing dead in hopes of somehow escaping notice in the aftermath of the battle and his ploy might have succeeded if Alfred's probing foot hadn't turned him over.

Emotions swamped the king as he stared at Hjalmarr. Many enemies had stood against Alfred in his life, yet, for some reason this gaunt jarl with the unsettling gaze filled him with a hatred he found hard to contain. It wasn't simply the good men that had died as a result of Hjalmarr's commands, for other Danes, including Alfred's ally and godson Guthrum, had caused more deaths. No, this was a deeply personal hatred, born of the shame Alfred felt at being fooled by a heathen yet again.

Wulfric had counselled him to show no mercy to Hjalmarr, to be ruthless and to treat the Dane with the brutality the jarl would surely have shown to Alfred had their roles been reversed after the battle at Hrofescester. Alfred's deep Christian faith was the bedrock of his kingdom, yet it had also proved to be its greatest weakness on more than one occasion. It was galling.

'Let me go, lord,' Hjalmarr was saying, interrupting Alfred's reverie. 'Show your wisdom once more. Your fabled mercy.'

Alfred looked from the Dane to Wulfric and saw uncertainty and doubt on the ealdorman's craggy face and that struck right to the king's heart. Even his loyal captain thought him a weak fool, and expected Alfred to allow Hjalmarr to walk away from this.

'Your Christ would want it, Alfred,' Hjalmarr went on, the familiar mocking smile tugging at the scarred mouth.

The fact that the Saxon warriors that had now gathered around them remained silent rather than commanding the Dane to shut up said much to Alfred. Like Wulfric, they too wondered what the king would do, and their eyes were hard, clearly dreading Hjalmarr being pardoned again.

'What would you know of Christ?' Alfred demanded, rage making his voice shake as he took a step towards his enemy. 'Of his suffering? Of my suffering as I watched your sea-wolves pitch screaming men into the sea?'

Hjalmarr winced, taken aback by the venom in Alfred's voice. He had wanted to live, to play on this king's well-known weakness – a weakness Hjalmarr and his fellows had undoubtedly often laughed about together. Aye, Hjalmarr had hoped to escape that battlefield unscathed, but Alfred saw that hope fading now, replaced by scorn.

'What do I know of Christ?' the jarl demanded. 'I know he allowed himself to be nailed to a cross. I know he preached that his enemies be forgiven. I know that he taught his followers to "turn the other cheek" when an enemy struck them.' He spat at Alfred, face twisting in disgust. 'I know that your god, your Christ, is a weakling, too frightened to fight like a man, seeking any opportunity to avoid battle. As you do, Alfred. As you did at Hrofescester when any true king would have slain me and my men. You are a coward, just like your nailed god!'

The Saxon warriors cried out in anger at this blasphemous tirade, infuriated by the disrespect Hjalmarr showed to both their earthly and heavenly rulers.

Alfred knew he was being goaded. Knew very well that Hjalmarr was manipulating him again. The jarl feared a painful, slow execution at the hands of Wulfric and the rest of the soldiers baying for blood – instead, Hjalmarr wanted to die a warrior's death, with a weapon in his hand, on the field of battle.

'You think me a coward?' Alfred asked lightly, drawing his sword and using the point to gesture his men away from the enemy jarl.

'Ja, you are like a frightened woman,' Hjalmarr retorted with a laugh. 'Hiding behind your holy books and your priests. Even your own thanes do not support you.'

'What are you doing, lord?' Wulfric asked in a worried tone as the surprised Saxon soldiers did as they were commanded and stepped back, leaving Hjalmarr standing on his own, just a few paces away from the advancing Alfred.

'I am going to show this sea-wolf, and his gods, who rules here in Wessex,' the king said. 'Give him back his sword.'

'Oh, by the blood of Christ,' Wulfric cried, throwing a hand in the air in exasperation. 'Must you do this, lord? Really? Can't I simply run him through and let that be an end to it?'

Hjalmarr snorted in grim amusement as he accepted his sword from one of Alfred's men and said to Wulfric. 'You can try, Saxon scum, once I've slaughtered your king like the squalling pig he is.' He spun his sword in his hand, twirling it expertly as he settled into a defensive stance and focussed his attention on the oncoming king of Wessex. 'If I win, I go free?' he asked, grinning.

'No. If you win, Wulfric will cut you down, you heathen filth,' Alfred retorted, and thrust the tip of his sword at Hjalmarr's guts. 'Either way, you will not leave here alive.'

The jarl parried the attack easily enough, but Alfred had expected that and continued his forward motion, slamming his head into his opponent's. It was not a clean strike, but it did catch Hjalmarr on the side of his left eye and he fell back, blinking and cursing.

Alfred did not allow him a moment's respite though, slashing his blade through the air, first to the left, then to the right, rolling his arm as each attack was desperately parried. He had just taken part in a pitched battle, yet somehow he felt fresh and full of energy, and he lashed out again and again.

Suddenly he realised he was lying on his back, the air blasted from him, and Hjalmarr's sword glinted as it slashed down towards his helmeted head.

Crying out, Alfred threw himself to the side, kicking out as he did so and feeling his ankle striking home. It was Hjalmarr's turn to fall now, but Alfred coughed, trying desperately to suck in a breath, feeling like he was slowly suffocating and wondering if striking the ground so hard had done him some terrible internal damage.

He did not have time to dwell on it, which was probably for the best as Hjalmarr sprang back to his feet and swung his sword as if it was an axe and he was attempting to fell a young sapling. Alfred was forced to knock the blade aside, and then they were trading blows once more, swords hammering against one another with fearful power.

They were evenly matched in speed and skill it seemed, and a tiny ember of doubt kindled within Alfred's mind. This had not been a good idea he realised. He'd allowed himself to be manipulated – used! – yet again, and there was every chance the crazed Dane would kill him.

Hjalmarr must have sensed his own ascendancy, for his dead stare grew even more intense as they traded blows and he spat some insult or curse at Alfred before kicking out and catching the Saxon king in the calf.

It was not a painful blow, but enough to knock Alfred's foot sideways and upset his balance. Hjalmarr grinned and stepped forward, but Alfred lashed out in desperation, his blade slicing cleanly into the Dane's unprotected thigh.

Hjalmarr looked down, seeing crimson spilling from the wound and forgetting his attack, instead dropping his left hand to try and stanch the bleeding. It was plainly hopeless though, and all who stood in that place knew it. Such an injury would soon lead to death, unless it was tightly bandaged.

Alfred had regained his equilibrium by now and grasped the advantage, bringing his sword around in a shallow arc. The king channelled all his remaining strength into the blade and, when Hjalmarr desperately parried, his weapon was knocked out of his hand. As he stood there, blood already soaking his breeches and completely defenceless, Alfred threw an uppercut that clattered the heathen warrior's teeth together and sent him sprawling onto the grass.

'Please, Alfred,' Hjalmarr begged, red spittle flecking his lips as he gaped at the man who would be his doom. 'Spare me. Your Christ would want you to show mercy.' He'd made a similar statement before their fight, but the mocking smile that had accompanied the words then were replaced now by naked fear.

'Tell me who sent you a chest of silver,' the king hissed, marking his enemy's change of tone. 'And I will make your death as quick and painless as I can.'

Hjalmarr's jaw tightened, and his face grew even more hateful – if that was possible. 'Ask your nailed god,' he said, and spat a gobbet of bloody phlegm at the king.

Alfred stared at him, as if unsure what to do, and the watching men of Wessex held their breath. Then, at last, Alfred raised his sword high in the air, its sleek, bloodied blade glinting in the cool afternoon sunshine, and with a great shout of fury, slashed it down.

Hjalmarr threw up his arm and screamed as flesh and tendons were torn through and his bones splintered and shattered. Then Alfred hacked down again, this time into the Dane's neck, and the screaming finally stopped. The king's sword was as sharp as any in Wessex for he maintained his gear with a care bordering on obsession, yet, even so, it took a few goes, Alfred grunting bestially with his gruesome exertions, before Hjalmarr's head was finally detached from his body.

'Christ might have wanted mercy,' the king shrieked, rising and sucking in deep lungfuls of air. 'But the good Saxon souls you threw screaming into the Sture demanded vengeance.'

It was as if Alfred's men had each been holding their breath until this moment and, as one, they let it out now in massive, joyous cheer. Even Wulfric was laughing and joining in as comrades and kinsmen hugged one another in relief. Apparently, Alfred hadn't been the only one who feared Hjalmarr was winning the fight.

The king wiped the gore from his sword on the jarl's cloak, thrust it into its sheath, and then, taking the spear back from Diuma, thrust its iron point into the bottom of Hjalmarr's decapitated head.

'You!' Alfred called to a warrior who was stripping fallen enemies of their valuables. He handed the man the spear with its gruesome trophy and the soldier took it gingerly. 'Take this to the docks and stick it in the ground somewhere. Let any heathen who sails along the Tamyse see what happens if they attack Christian warriors.'

The soldier took the spear, holding it in both hands so it wouldn't overbalance for it was surprisingly heavy, and hurried away, calling to his comrades as he passed so they could all look and laugh at the fate of the jarl who'd thought to stand against Alfred of Wessex.

'Ready, Wulfric? Diuma?'

'Yes, lord,' said the thane, stretching up and finally looking like himself again, despite the dry blood caking his mouth and chin. 'Ready for what?'

'Ready to go and talk to those women the Danes have left behind. I don't know what they're cooking, but it smells delicious, and there's bound to be ale too!'

Diuma laughed. 'Food, ale, and women. What more could a man ask for?'

'Fighting works up an almighty appetite, don't you agree?' Alfred replied, his laugh fuelled by battle fury and the triumph of victory, and his warriors joined in with fierce delight. 'Lundenwic is ours, lads!'

It was theirs, and soon he would make it the trading centre it had the potential to be, with a new harbour, new walls, and men to defend it all.

And then he would give it to Aethelred of Mercia along with his beloved daughter, and Alfred would move a step closer to bringing all the Anglo-Saxon people together in one kingdom, under one red banner bearing a golden dragon.

The banner of Wessex.

Alfred's banner and, one day, his son, Edward's too.

That thought suddenly reminded him of the document he'd been drafting for the past four years, constantly tweaking and adding to as the political landscape shifted within Wessex. The document he'd started work on when he and Oswald's fishing trip to the River Icene was cut short on that distant summer's day. The document that would make sure Edward's path to the throne was never challenged by Alfred's nephews, Aethelhelm and Aethelwold. The document that would, he prayed, neuter Sicgred for good, and ensure a lasting peace for his son and all within Wessex: Alfred's will.

CHAPTER THIRTY-EIGHT

The rest of the year was busy for Alfred, as he sent resources to his new, expanding town now to be known as Lundenburh – overseeing the rebuilding of the old fortifications and even constructing a new harbour, which was big enough to truly make the place a centre of trade and commerce. Alfred's men had found no trace of any chest of silver within the old ruins, and, without any evidence, he had not been able to tie his nephews or Sicgred definitively to Hjalmarr's efforts to undermine Alfred.

So, in Wessex, peace reigned, and the reformation of the education system continued to gather pace, with Alfred pushing his thanes and ealdormen to learn how to read and write despite their continued protestations. In his own court at Wintanceaster, the king tried to set an example to his subjects by also studying hard and bringing more and more scholars there.

One learned man – Alfred's favourite – was not faring so well, however. As winter drew in, Oswald's gut pains grew worse, and he remained confined to his bed.

'Is that the priest again?' Wulfric asked as the November gales blew through the hall and mingled with another, similarly high-pitched although even less pleasing sound. 'Is there nothing anyone can do for him?'

'No,' Alfred replied, face pale, lips bloodless as he too listened to Oswald's sudden wailing. 'And I feel guilty, as I fear for myself almost as much as I do for his sake.'

'Yourself?'

'Will my own guts one day be in a similar state to Oswald's?' Alfred muttered, looking at the door that seemed to do little to separate them from the priest. 'The thought of such suffering... Aye, it terrifies me, Wulfric.'

They sat in silence, the charters they'd been drawing up to cement Alfred's successor – Edward, of course – forgotten for now. Although it had already been agreed that his eldest son would take the throne when Alfred died, the thorny issue of his nephews had been increasingly on the king's mind in recent months. Aethelhelm and Aethelwold were almost men now, and it had become clear their advisors, particularly Sicgred, thought they had as good a claim to Wessex as Edward. The last thing Alfred wanted was for a civil war to break out upon his death, undoing much of the work he'd overseen in recent years.

For the past few weeks then, Alfred and Wulfric – with the help of those scholars who knew much about law, and about precedents set by previous rulers of Wessex – had been drafting charters and documents to make absolutely certain the nobles of the kingdom knew exactly how things should go when Alfred finally made his way to Heaven.

'I can't work on this when he's like that,' the king said, leaning back in his chair and shaking his head.

'We could do it somewhere else,' Wulfric suggested. 'Or have the priest moved.'

'This is his home,' Alfred snapped. 'My God, man, you've known Oswald as long as I have. Do you feel no compassion?'

The ealdorman blinked in confusion. 'What difference does it make if he's in pain here, or somewhere else? I doubt he feels it less because he's here. What about the church? It's comfortable enough there, and his brother priests could take good care of him.'

Alfred let out a small gasp of laughter. There was no point being angry with Wulfric – he was a soldier, the finest Wessex had known for a generation or more, and he thought like one.

Pragmatic and calculating, rather than emotional or sentimental like Alfred. Perhaps Wulfric was right – Oswald's loud cries were beginning to grate on everyone's nerves after all, not just the ealdorman's. Had it been anyone else, Alfred likely would have had them shifted elsewhere already.

'That's enough for today then,' the king said, standing and swallowing the small amount of ale that was left in his cup. 'Take this charter to Werwulf and ask him to check it over. I'm fed up drafting these, only for him or one of the other scholars to find some error or wording that my nephews might exploit. If this isn't good enough, tell Werwulf to write it up properly.'

'Yes, lord,' Wulfric said, stretching out his neck and rolling his head. He too had been forced to learn to read and, although he took to it quickly, Alfred knew he would much rather have an enemy soldier in front of him than a dry legal document.

When the ealdorman had gone, Alfred shut his eyes and pressed a hand against his stomach. The pains still came, although not as often, or as bad as they'd once been. Unless he overindulged in carnal pleasures, of course, and then God would punish him as he deserved. There had to be a price paid after all, for drinking far too much ale, eating too much roast pork, and humping too many serving women. Such wickedness deserved painful repercussions but even after so many years of indulging, Alfred still hadn't been able to fully put aside his vices. He thought he never would, and then he heard Oswald crying out again and feared he would end up suffering like the priest.

He drew in a long, steadying breath and walked towards the door Oswald rested behind. When he reached it, he stood with his hand on the latch, steeling himself for what he would find inside. He winced when he realised the priest was not simply moaning unintelligibly, he was trying to sing a hymn. The melody was familiar, but the words were little more than grunts and squeals. Fighting down the anger and dismay that was rising in him, that God could treat his faithful servant so horribly,

Alfred pushed down the latch and went into the gloomy room, softly singing the hymn that Oswald was mangling.

The chamber smelled terribly – sweat, urine, and stale wine vied with one another to overpower Alfred's senses, even stinging his eyes so strong were the vapours emanating from the sickbed.

'We should have you moved to a room with a window,' the king said, trying his best not to gag. 'This stuffy air can't be good for you.'

'I prefer the warmth, lord,' Oswald replied through gritted teeth. 'Could you ask a servant to come and pour me more wine?'

'I can do that,' Alfred protested. 'I'm not above serving you, my old friend.' He took the jug that sat beside the bed, surprised by how strong it smelled. It was unwatered, and clearly would keep the priest in a permanently intoxicated state. Yet still the pain assailed the man, whose tonsure was now ragged and unkempt, fresh hair growing on his previously shaved pate and making him look untidy. Alfred felt a lump forming in his throat as he handed the cup to Oswald, seeing new, deep lines on the priest's face, etched by his suffering over the past few weeks and months.

'How is Wessex doing, my lord,' Oswald asked, taking a deep pull of the wine although much of it ran down his chin as his hand was shaking. 'Does Guthrum-Athelstan remain a good ally and godson?'

Alfred nodded, glad to have something to talk about and take his mind off the state of his friend. 'So far, yes,' he said, trying to sound cheerful. 'He doesn't seem to have fallen back into heathen ways.'

'Good,' the priest grunted. 'What of Sicgred and your nephews?'

Alfred's face twisted sourly. 'No doubt they scheme, and plot to enhance their position. But, for now, they are quiet.'

'And your system of burhs is coming along nicely?'

'Indeed,' Alfred replied, enthused somewhat by this favourite topic of his. 'It's slow going, building new fortifications in so many places, but we're getting there. Same with the army – the men have been training well and we have them mostly well-equipped now.' He nodded. 'Any Danes thinking we'll be a soft touch will get a nasty surprise, and we'll only grow stronger over time. God be praised, I wish we could have done all this years ago but...' He trailed off.

'Don't allow those regrets to consume you, Alfred,' the priest advised. 'Things happened as they did for a reason. God has brought you to this point, to a position of great strength. Simply be thankful for that, rather than looking to past mistakes.' He took another trembling gulp of wine and let out a small, high-pitched hiss of pain.

Alfred stared at him but to ask how Oswald was feeling would be an insult to the older man. It was glaringly obvious how he felt.

They sat in silence for a time, only the sounds of the servants in the main hall going about their business and Oswald's laboured breathing breaking the silence.

'We've been through a lot over the years, haven't we?' the king said at last, a sad smile tugging at the edges of his lips. 'You've always been here for me, with wise counsel and sage advice. Not to mention spiritual guidance.'

Oswald reached out and weakly grasped Alfred's hand. The priest's cold skin felt smooth and dry, almost like parchment. As if it might tear apart at any moment.

'You never needed much guidance, my lord. You were always destined to be a great king. Perhaps the greatest Wessex has ever known. I would have liked to be by your side to see the burhs completed, and to enjoy seeing the fulfilment of all your plans and reforms. I fear I will not be around for much longer though.'

Tears filled Alfred's eyes and he struggled to find the words to comfort them both, opting to remain quiet in the end. He knew his voice would crack if he tried to speak anyway.

'It is for the best,' the priest went on. 'The pain is unbearable now. I dread waking from my drunken stupor every day and, no matter how much of this wine I drink, it never completely dulls the agony in my belly. Even the wormwood tea you have the servants brew for me does not have any effect.' He gasped and the cup in his hand spilled the wine all over his sheets. He closed his eyes and pressed the empty vessel against himself, murmuring a soft prayer.

Alfred could not quite make out all the words, but some of them sounded like gibberish to him and he wondered if Oswald was perhaps going mad. The king had tried drinking wormwood tea himself, for it was an old remedy for stomach pains. But he knew it could make a man dizzy, or even see things that weren't there.

A sudden desire to press a cushion down on the old priest's face and end his suffering came over Alfred, but it passed immediately, leaving the king horrified and deeply ashamed. Oswald was a priest, he would accept his fate no matter how painful it was, knowing it was all part of God's plan.

Besides, the old man wasn't dead yet. God might cure him. Alfred had seen people with worse illnesses get over them in time.

'We need to get you eating better food,' he said. 'More meat. Build your strength back up.'

Oswald actually managed a smile and raised his eyebrows as if to say, *Really?* He did not dismiss the suggestion out loud though, and his smile soon faded, to be replaced by his now habitual pained frown.

'We once had a good discussion,' the king said, changing the subject and standing up to open the chamber door and hopefully let some fresher air in from the hall. 'A long time ago, in the church in Dorcaestre. You remember? I had just about given up on ever defeating the Danes. Their raids had worn me down – this was when I was aetheling, mind, not king yet.'

'I remember,' Oswald replied, and the words were slurred.

'I was so low that I even questioned whether the heathen gods were stronger than our own, true God.'

Oswald mumbled woozily.

'But you bolstered me with your unshakable faith, old friend. You reminded me not to give up hope.' Alfred smiled. 'It was a turning point in my life, Oswald. Your words were exactly what I needed at that moment and,' he held out his hands as if to encompass all of Wessex and the great things the two of them had seen and done since that day in Dorcaestre. 'You brought us to where we are now. I couldn't have done it all without you, I mean that. You've been a great friend to me and my family.'

He turned from the open door and looked back at the priest whose eyes were closed and, for the first time since their conversation had begun, Oswald actually looked peaceful.

Alfred stepped lightly across to the sleeping priest, glad that the wine had knocked him out for a time, allowing him at least a few hours of respite. The cup was still resting against Oswald's chest and Alfred took it so it wouldn't clatter on the floor and wake his friend. As he lifted it, he noticed how cold the priest's unresisting fingers were, and how utterly still his breathing.

The king felt an icy chill run through him, and drew in a sharp breath, staring at Oswald, desperately praying that he'd see the priest's lips moving or his chest rising and falling.

There was nothing.

God had called his servant to Him at last, and, for the first time in his adult life, Alfred of Wessex was without his spiritual advisor.

'Don't go, old friend,' the king mumbled, voice cracking as he grasped Oswald's cold hand to his chest and felt tears roll freely down his cheeks, salty and warm as he tried, and failed, to find the right words for the pain he was feeling. 'Please, Oswald, don't go.'

He remained like that for a long, long time before, at last he lifted his head and stared at the dead priest, unable to let him go, and unwilling to leave the room in case the servants in the hall saw how upset he was.

Images of the things they'd done over the years came to mind – images of a much younger Oswald, never a warrior but strong and vital, nonetheless. From those early skirmishes with the Danes, the priest had been by Alfred's side. For the births of his children, and the death of his brother, Oswald was there to offer guidance and support and friendship. His final task should have been to preside over Aethelflaed's wedding this summer, and that Mass would surely have been the most poignant and beautiful Alfred would ever see, more so because he knew Oswald did not have much time left in this world.

Now, though, that time was up. The priest's candle, after burning so brightly in Alfred's world for years, had guttered and given out at last, leaving behind a terrible darkness.

Bowing his head, the king did his best to say a prayer commending Oswald's soul to God through the shuddering sobs that wracked his body and left him on his knees, utterly heartbroken, by his departed friend's bedside.

CHAPTER THIRTY-NINE

Alfred sent messengers out that autumn to call the Witan to Wintanceaster. After defeating Jarl Hjalmarr and once again proving his military dominance over the Danes the king knew he would rarely, if ever, be able to wield as much influence over his nobles. Now was the perfect time to deal with his nephews before they became an issue.

Had they really supported Hjalmarr, and perhaps even plotted in other ways against Alfred? Almost certainly, but he had no real proof of it. Still, the thought of once again meeting Aethelhelm, the eldest of his nephews, had been a source of some anxiety for Alfred. If the young man was anything like his father, he'd be a shrewd thinker and a formidable warrior — exactly the kind of charismatic leader who could draw men to him and cause real trouble should he feel he was missing out on his birthright.

'You think this is a good idea?' Wulfric asked as they made their way towards Wintanceaster's great hall, icy November rain rolling in from the west and quickly soaking into their cloaks. 'Your nephews might not take it well.'

'What can they do?' Diuma asked, pulling his hood further over his head. The three men had been praying in the nearby church, asking for God's blessing on what Alfred knew could be a momentous day and, as usual, Brycgstow's thane was willing to be more aggressively pro-active than the king's loyal captain.

'Maybe not much now,' Wulfric conceded. 'But in the future? Aethelhelm's a man now, and he'll seek to gather support for his cause wherever he can. Indeed, he already has, if we can believe the whispers that have reached us from all across Wessex.'

'That's exactly what we're here to sort out,' Alfred said as they reached the great hall and the guards bowed, opening the doors for them to step inside. 'The future. This should make sure Edward meets no resistance from within Wessex when it comes time for him to take the throne. Aethelhelm might have notions of grandeur, but legally he'll not have a leg to stand on after this Witan. You're right though, Wulfric – my nephews could prove dangerous, so Edward won't be attending the Witan. He's too young at twelve summers, anyway.'

It had long been tradition to hold Witans outside, on the hilltop known as Swinbeorg. Such councils were often in the winter and ended up cold, uncomfortable and unpleasant affairs in which the nobles complained constantly and drank themselves into a stupor – mainly to stave off the freezing conditions. As a result, Alfred had made the decision to break with tradition and have the Witan meet at his own court there in Wintanceaster. It would be warm and more comfortable for the noblemen to spend their days and nights inside a proper timber building, rather than in tents, huddled about campfires and praying it didn't rain or snow.

Of course, there would be someone who'd complain, loudly proclaiming they'd rather be on a hilltop in the pissing rain rather than there, with a blazing fire and the sturdy timber walls to shield them from the storm that seemed to be building outside. Alfred smiled wryly – he was as much a believer in tradition as the next man, but, as a serving boy handed him a mug of ale and he took his place at the bench closest to the fire he was glad they weren't at Swinbeorg.

The members of the Witan were already gathered within, apart from one or two who hadn't made it yet for whatever reason. Perhaps the roads in their lands were blocked or they'd taken ill. Alfred looked about the hall, seeing Aedan, Aethelnoth, Odda, Dunstan, and others he considered personal friends as well as mere council members. Good. At least he could count on their support, no matter how things went. His eyes roved around the room, taking in Archbishop Ethelred of Cantwareburh, who had finally seemed to warm to Alfred now that the Danes were subdued, and settling at last on Sicgred. The craggy ealdorman might have aged since he was captain to Alfred's brother, Aethelred, but he was still an imposing figure. Beside him sat Alfred's nephews and he nodded a silent greeting to them which they returned with blank, unreadable expressions.

Sicgred had trained them well.

Aethelhelm was more of a man now than when Alfred saw him at Wethmor. He sported a wispy beard which he stroked often, as if he was proud of it. He was not much broader than he'd been four years ago, however and, now that the king examined him in more detail, he wondered if the lad was ill, for his cheeks were gaunt and, while every other man there had a trencher filled with food, Aethelhelm's only contained a small piece of cheese which he merely picked at.

Alfred felt relief flow through him as he examined Aethelhelm. Such a physically weak individual was unlikely to inspire a rebellion, and the anxiety that had built up within the king evaporated, leaving him with a sensation of guilt. The boy was his kin after all. Still, Alfred's throne appeared safe from Aethelhelm, and Edward should face little trouble from him in years to come.

The king's relief faded quickly, however as his gaze moved on to his other nephew. Aethelwold, in stark contrast with his brother, was broad shouldered and robust, despite being four years younger than his sibling at only seventeen. He had no beard, but he did have a great pile of roast beef, chicken, cabbage, and carrots in front of him, and he was devouring it with gusto, eyes darting about the hall as he took in everything that was happening. He did not look ill – on the contrary, Aethelwold was practically bursting with life. He nudged Sicgred often, nodding towards the other thanes and ealdormen, asking questions which the old warrior answered shortly but readily enough.

The sight of the lad eating reminded Alfred of his own packed trencher, and he lifted a piece of meat and popped it into his mouth. It was soft, and quite delicious, having been slowly roasted throughout the day by Alfred's expert cooks. The king savoured it just as he savoured the company of his *hearthweru* and advisors on that bitter November evening and his spirits rose again. Neither Aethelwold nor Aethelhelm would be a threat after this Witan, Alfred thought, chewing the pork happily.

He noticed Wulfric eyeing him with a frown.

'What?'

'Are you alright, lord?'

Alfred laughed. 'Never better, my stern captain. Don't I always say there's no better place to be than in a hall with good company, good food, and good ale?'

'Aye, you do,' Wulfric agreed, still frowning. 'But we have important business to deal with. Let's hope you're still in such fine humour by the time we're done.'

'Never change, Wulfric,' the king said, shaking his head ruefully, smile never wavering. 'You're right, though. Ealhswith? Are you finished your rounds?'

The queen consort had just taken her seat beside him, and she nodded. 'Yes.' Her lips were tight, as if she was troubled, but her darting glances at Sicgred told Alfred all he needed to know. His wife knew exactly what was in his will – she'd been instrumental in its writing after all, along with Oswald and Wulfric – so it was no surprise she should feel some trepidation as the king got to his feet and called the Witan to order.

As expected, even before the meeting got under way, as Alfred was completing the welcomes and other, traditional niceties, someone questioned their location.

'The Witan should be held at Swinbeorg,' a white-bearded thane called out loudly. 'As it always is. Your father held them there, as did your grandfather. Your brother too.' At that, the thane glanced at Aethelhelm and Aethelwold and the young aethelings nodded in enthusiastic agreement.

'You'd rather be outside in the pissing rain?' Wulfric demanded. 'Wind blowing through what's left of your hair?' Some laughed at that although Wulfric did not look as if he was making a jest. 'We can have the guards open the door, my lord, and you can sit outside in the storm, listening to what we're saying in here.'

Again, there was laughter and the thane's face turned as pale as his beard. 'I'll go outside,' he retorted furiously. 'Why don't you come with me, you big squirrel's turd, and I'll teach you some manners!' He made to stand up but those seated nearest to him hauled him back onto his bench and he did not fight them off with much vigour. He had no chance of besting Wulfric in a fight, and everyone knew it. But his suggestion had at least allowed him to regain a little of his dignity.

'Tradition?' another older nobleman shouted, shaking his head in amusement. 'Back in King Aethelwulf's day you two would have gone outside and had a proper fight. That's what we did back then. Real men, no quarter asked, and none given! There's your tradition.'

'Some traditions are better off in the past,' Ealhswith said irritably. She did not need to shout to be heard, her melodious voice easily cutting through the deeper tones of the chattering men. 'So let's just be glad no one is getting their noses broken, and we have this fine hall to shelter us from the winter cold.'

Almost to a man, the Witan took her words to heart and the childish banter ceased, allowing Alfred to get on with business.

He dealt with the usual matters first. Run-of-the-mill, everyday items such as taxes, food distribution, the amount of silver in the coins being produced by the mints in the kingdom, military reports, and other, relatively minor, things were addressed as the men feasted and jabbered backwards and forwards over contentious points. It was practically the same Witan that Alfred had been present at many times in his thirty-seven winters – the faces might be different, but the words and the complaints coming from them remained the same. It would be mind-numbingly boring, he thought, if not for the food and drink to keep his spirits up, and the occasional wry quip from one of the wittier council members.

Even those could not stem the rising discomfort Alfred felt stirring in his guts. Sicgred cast lingering glances his way often, as if the wily old ealdorman suspected something was coming once the usual business was completed. In truth, the king was questioning himself, wondering if he was doing the right thing. He had loved his brother deeply, after all, and, when his nephews were infants, he and Ealhswith had loved them too.

Aethelred was dead, though, and the years had passed them all by, changing them as much as they had changed Wessex itself.

He was doing the right thing, Alfred told himself, for the good of his son, Edward, and for the good of the kingdom. There was no other option.

Ealhswith sensed his discomfort even before he pressed a hand against his abdomen, gripping his fingers in hers and nodding reassuringly at him. He returned her nod and swallowed a small sip of ale, making sure there was nothing in his throat that might force its way back up if he faltered...

He heaved a deep, angry sigh and silently told himself to act like the king he was supposed to be. God's blood, he was a warrior who'd fought in shieldwalls! There was nothing to be anxious about, not with Ealhswith and Wulfric flanking him. With those two beside him he'd taken on the might of even the greatest Norse warlord and his *vikingar* and defeated them all. Although Oswald had been with him then too...

He angrily pushed that thought aside and breathed deeply, slowly, the scent of woodsmoke, sweat, roast meat, and spilled ale making him momentarily light-headed, and then he let out the breath through his mouth and stood up.

The time had come.

He stretched up to his full height, smiling now as he felt the same sense of calm that always came over him before battle. A gust of wind whistled through the gaps in the walls, making the fire spit and crackle and shadows dance about the hall. Strangely, the bad weather made Alfred feel somehow more secure.

'My lords,' he said in a loud, commanding voice before softening his tone. 'And lady.'

The gathered nobles fell silent, all red-faced and cheery looking. A belly full of ale had lifted the spirits of everyone there, including the king's nephews. Aethelhelm looked healthier than he had earlier, his hollow cheeks ruddy, eyes sparkling merrily.

'I called this Witan to deal with the business we've already discussed.' He lifted his ale cup and hoisted it high in the air, grinning. 'And, of course, to enjoy the great pleasure of your esteemed company. *Waes hael!*'

The bishops, thanes and ealdormen eagerly lifted their own cups, eagerly giving the traditional reply of, '*Drink hael!*'

Alfred allowed the men to settle again before he continued, saying, 'I gathered you here for another reason too, though.' He did not give them time to murmur amongst themselves, forging onwards in clear tones that rang through the hall. 'I have drafted a new will.'

His pronouncement was met with thoughtful silence as the nobles absorbed it, and the implications filled their ale-muddled minds. Many of them, the minor thanes, could expect nothing in the event of the king's death, but those of higher status might hope to be granted lands and gifts. Men like Wulfric, Aethelnoth, Diuma... and Alfred's kinsmen, Aethelhelm and Aethelwold.

'The will has been completed, and witnessed,' Alfred said, his gaze travelling around the hall, lingering on his nephews and stern-faced Sicgred. 'It is legally binding, and, as such, shall not be questioned, either now, or when I am... no longer here.' His earlier, jaunty tone was gone, and his countenance was as grim as Sicgred's, whose stare he met unflinchingly.

There were loud rumbles of agreement, from Alfred's most loyal supporters, primed by the king in advance. If anyone wanted to contend the will, they should know they were in the minority.

'Let's hear it, then, uncle,' called Aethelwold, seemingly rather drunk and caring little for the attention his shout drew. In fact, he got unsteadily to his feet then and peered about at the older men who were watching him with keen interest, undoubtedly hoping for some extra entertainment. The young aetheling spread his arms, looking at Alfred again. 'Go on, *my lord*. Let's hear who gets what. Let us all see just how kind and benef— beneficent you are.'

Many of the men were muttering at this behaviour, and even Sicgred was hissing a warning at the lad, but Aethelwold had said his piece and he sat back down now, lip curled sardonically, quite happy with himself judging by the smug look he shared with his older brother.

Alfred smiled tightly and gestured with his hand. Originally, Oswald was supposed to read the will, but, with his sad passing, the task had been given to Werwulf, one of his fellow priests. He was a small fellow with an easy smile, brought from Mercia to act as tutor to the members of Alfred's court. His presence that day only reminded the king of Oswald's death however, and part of him bitterly resented Sicgred and his damned nephews for making this Witan necessary.

Werwulf stood up now, holding in his hand the parchment which would, the king prayed, ensure the safety of Wessex for at least the next generation, notwithstanding further attacks by the Danes.

Without preamble, the little priest started reading from the document in crisp, strident tones, as if he was leading his congregation in prayer.

'I, King Alfred, by the grace of God and on consultation with Archbishop Ethelred and with the witness of all the councillors of the West Saxons, have been inquiring about the needs of my soul and about my inheritance which God and my elders gave to me.' The priest took sips from his water cup every so often as he continued, laying out the justification for Alfred's will, and his right to do so, before eventually describing what each of the beneficiaries would receive upon the king's death. Edward, his eldest son, was granted 500 pounds and many important estates from Cornwalas in the west to Cent in the east; Aethelweard, as youngest son, would also inherit 500 pounds and a number of estates, mostly in the south; Ealhswith and their daughters were granted lands and 100 pounds each; his infant kinsman Osferth, who was related to Alfred's mother, was granted estates in the southeast; loyal Wulfric and the other ealdormen, bishops, and archbishop were to be given 100 gold coins, with Aethelred of Mercia receiving a sword of similar value; other noblemen and institutions were granted sums of money; and then Werwulf came to the two sections which dealt with the aethelings.

Alfred watched his nephews as this section was read out, taking in the expressions on their faces as they heard what would be theirs, and pictured that inheritance in their minds.

'To my brother's son, Aethelhelm,' read Werwulf in his clear, neutral tone, 'the estate at Aldingbourne, at Compton, at Crondall, at Beeding, at Beddingham, at Burnham, at Thunderfield, and at Eashing. And to my brother's son Aethelwold, the estate at Godalming, at Guildford, and at Steyning.'

As the king expected, neither young man was content with their lot.

Aethelhelm appeared to shrink within himself as he listened to the meagre list of lands he would be given. He truly did appear sickly to Alfred, the cheekbones almost jutting out through the skin on his face, and the earlier flush of inebriation that had brought colour and vigour to his features had passed, leaving him pale and almost feverish.

'That boy is not long for the world,' Wulfric grunted, leaning in close to the king so no one could overhear him. 'There's something wrong with him.'

Alfred felt a pang, knowing his captain was probably right. Aethelhelm was battling a foe that even Sicgred could not defeat.

Aethelwold was another matter, however. The seventeen-year-old aetheling's face had turned pale as the priest read out the will, listing only three estates which would become his upon Alfred's death. The young man's mouth worked silently as he sought for words to express his feelings which, by the depth of his frown must surely be furious outrage. At last, the words came to him and Aethelwold jumped to his feet again.

'This is a fucking disgrace!' the aetheling bellowed, spittle flecking his lips as his fists clenched and unclenched spasmodically and the members of the Witan gaped at him in wonder.

CHAPTER FORTY

'A disgrace!' Aethelwold repeated, gesturing furiously and silencing Werwulf, who eyed him with open disapproval. 'We are your kinsmen,' the aetheling continued through gritted teeth, visibly shaking and gripping the table in front of him for support. He was not physically weak, like his brother, though, merely enraged. 'Your own brother's children. Yet you think us worth, what? A handful of towns? Lands we have been building up for you over the past few years anyway? Are we not worth more than that? Are we not worth more to you than some brat distantly related to your long-dead mother?'

'Osferth is, like you, my kinsman,' Alfred replied levelly, refusing to show his anger in front of everyone. He had suspected his nephews might react badly, although he'd not really thought they'd call him out in front of the entire Witan like this.

'Osferth is a child, and but a distant relative of yours. We are your nephews!' Aethelhelm barked. It seemed his ire was enough to overcome his illness, at least for a short time. 'Yet you would bequeath more lands to him than us in your will? It is an outrage. You profess to have loved our father, yet treat his sons in this despicable way? This is merely your way of making sure we are never powerful enough to be a threat to your whelp, Edward, isn't it?'

Alfred's own rage was building but he held his peace, for now. He believed it would be worthwhile to let the young men get everything out in the open and deal with it there and then, rather than brushing it aside only to fester in the coming months and years. Get it over with today, and move on.

Aethelwold certainly had every intention of making his feelings known, and he carried on as his brother finished. 'If you hadn't forced our father into changing his own will,' the aetheling shouted, ale and fury making his tongue as loose as it would ever be, 'the throne of Wessex would pass through us, not Edward! When you die, Aethelhelm should become king. That is what would have happened, had you not forced our father to agree to your demands, bypassing us, and making your own line the successors.'

'Forced your father?' Ealhswith had heard enough and stood up, ashen faced. 'No one forced Aethelred to do anything he did not agree to, what happened is all laid out in the will. Your father was no fool. The decision to make Alfred's sons next in line to the throne was a pragmatic one, made to save *you* from danger! Had your father's will not been changed, and Alfred taken over the running of the kingdom upon his death, you boys would have been targets for anyone who foresaw what is happening here right now.'

'Lies!' Aethelwold screeched, his immature features twisted in sheer rage.

'It is true!' Alfred roared, slamming his fist onto the bench. 'You have been listening to Sicgred's poison, it seems. I should never have let him be your steward.'

'Alfred had to become king when your father died, because you were too young,' Ealhswith said, appealing to Aethelhelm who was sitting with a pained look on his face. 'But Aethelred changed his will without anyone forcing him to, it was his own choice.'

'Why would he?' Aethelhelm replied in a low, weak voice. 'You're twisting it, my lady, and I'll hear no more of it.' He stood up, taller than his brother but so much slimmer. As if he might blow away should a strong gust come in through the hole in the roof that let the smoke out. 'Your husband has stolen our birthright from us, and now spits in our faces with this "will" of his.' He looked about at the gathered noblemen, seeing stern, outraged faces, but also amused expressions. 'Are we entertaining you?' he demanded. 'Well, we shall tarry here to be laughed at no longer. Sicgred, we're leaving.'

Even Sicgred was shocked by that. He laid a bear-like hand on his young lord's arm, gently tugging the sleeve. 'A storm is raging outside,' he muttered, trying his best to speak quietly but everyone heard him, so enraptured were they by the whole performance. 'In your condition...' He shook his head with a warning frown. 'We can leave in the morning, but to go now, into that...?'

'Ealdorman Sicgred is right,' Archbishop Ethelred put in, speaking imperiously, clearly angered by the reaction to the will which he himself had been a witness to. 'This is no weather for travelling in.'

The eastern wall of the building shook then as a gust dutifully blew as if on cue, and the sound of rain lashing against the thatched roof high overhead could not be ignored.

'I'm not so sickly that a bit of rain will melt me away to nothing,' Aethelhelm said testily, pulling his arm away from Sicgred and glaring at Ethelred and Alfred. 'We are leaving. Come, Aethelwold.'

His brother was nodding, a smile that was more of a grimace signalling his pleasure at the chosen course of action. 'Agreed, brother,' he said, and his eyes were even more hate-filled than Aethelhelm's as they bored into Alfred. 'We should not remain here another moment. We're clearly not wanted, or valued.'

Alfred was, in truth, tired of the whole bitter scene, and felt nothing but relief at the thought of his nephews leaving, even in such a black mood. Ealhswith was more compassionate.

As the aethelings reached the doors with Sicgred dutifully following at their backs, the guards threw them open and the howling wind blew inside, making the fire dance and tossing super-heated embers up towards the chimney-hole, bright sparks that were quickly snuffed out before they made it into the night. The thanes and ealdormen were talking excitedly, but in low tones, filling the room with a rumble that the gusting wind mingled almost sinisterly with.

Ealhswith hurried after the aethelings, breaking free of Alfred as he tried to stop her.

'Where are you going?' the king called, forced to navigate his way between the benches at an undignified run to catch up with his wife. 'What are you doing? Let them go! They can sleep in the damn stables!'

That raised cheers and laughter from the council members, even the aloof archbishop, but the queen consort went out past the door guards, shaking her head in annoyance. Alfred could only just make out her words as the storm whipped them away: 'We can't let them go like this! They're your kinsmen, and Aethelhelm is clearly unfit to travel.'

'Fuck 'em!' someone cackled crudely in the hall behind them, drawing more cheers and howls of derision for the departed aethelings.

Alfred could only agree with that harsh sentiment, especially as he made it outside and the freezing rain struck him, reminding him that neither he, nor Ealhswith, had their cloaks on.

Wulfric was following him, as were Diuma and a half dozen hearth-warriors and they all cowered into themselves as the downpour drenched them, as if hunching their shoulders would somehow keep them dry.

Night had not quite fallen yet, so there was enough light to make out Aethelhelm, Aethelwold, and Sicgred, the surly ealdorman using his bulk to help the elder of Alfred's nephews to walk through the storm towards the stables. They had not travelled alone, of course, but their guards and retainers were camped outside Wintanceaster's walls, as were the rest of the council members' retinues. Only the three horses were required for the outraged nephews and their captain to be on their way, and Aethelwold was already shouting for the stablehands to be about their business.

'Stop, Aethelhelm,' Ealhswith called. 'Wait!'

Alfred had caught up with her now and the sight of the rain streaming down her face and soaking her good woollen tunic made him even angrier than he already was.

'Let them go,' he said to her, dashing water from his brow to little effect. 'If they want to ride out into that, what should we care? After the way they've behaved this day? Let them drown like the ungrateful rats they are.'

'Rats?' Aethelwold spun to face the king, his fury matching Alfred's.

Wulfric was suddenly there too, a silent, brooding presence, protecting his lord. Sicgred appeared beside them as well, the ealdorman seeming to Alfred like some mirror image of his own loyal captain.

'You made a terrible mistake with that will,' Aethelwold hissed, eyes burning like black coals that even the sheeting rain could not extinguish. 'You may feel like you're untouchable just now, surrounded by your lackeys and old, witless fools too comfortable to rock the boat. But we have support amongst the people, and it grows daily. When word gets around that you've not only stolen the throne from us, but granted us such a pittance in your will, well... Everyone will see what you are.'

He had come right up against Alfred, pressing his face close into the king's, but neither man would back down and it seemed the two captains did not want to get involved for fear of making the situation worse.

'What I am?' Alfred demanded. 'And what would that be, nephew?'

'You are a weak fool,' Aethelwold replied harshly.

'Weak?' the king snorted mirthlessly. 'From the looks of it, the only weak one here is your brother.'

There was a sudden pain in Alfred's face then, and he stumbled back, wondering what was happening. Blood ran from his nose, down his philtrum and into his mouth, carried there by the relentless rain. Utterly amazed, he almost started laughing at the absurdity of it. His nephew had punched him, here, in his own town, surrounded by his friends and hearth-warriors!

The blow had been delivered so quickly, and the reaction to it so delayed, that no one seemed sure how to react. Even Wulfric, for once, did not move.

Alfred's astonishment soon passed, however, quickly replaced by a black rage that was fuelled as much by Aethelwold's attack as by pent-up grief over Oswald's recent passing. Wordlessly, the king's bloodied features twisted, and he threw a punch of his own.

Aethelwold saw it coming, his youthful reflexes allowing him to move to the side so his uncle's blow glanced off his shoulder, and he reacted by lashing out again. Alfred was a seasoned warrior, though, and he expertly parried this attack, knocking Aethelwold's arm to the left and then landing a thundering right hook on the lad's cheek.

The aetheling reeled back, stunned by the power in the king's punch, and momentarily unable to defend himself as Alfred came forward to finish the bout off.

'That's enough!' Ealhswith shouted. 'Wulfric! Sicgred! Split them up, by God. What the hell are you waiting for?' She was standing beside Sicgred, and shoved him on the arm, exhorting him to move.

Aethelhelm had shuffled across to the confrontation and, at the sight of the queen consort apparently lashing out at Sicgred, he assumed she was getting involved in the fight and reached out. Whatever his illness was, the young man was strong enough to grasp Ealhswith by the material of her tunic and, when he dragged her to the side, her feet slipped on the sodden ground.

From the corner of his eye, Alfred saw his wife falling, and heard her wail of surprise. When he saw it was Aethelhelm who'd perpetrated the outrage, the king lost all control of his temper. Stepping forward, he went for his terrified nephew, who threw up his hands to defend himself, but Sicgred, Wulfric and Diuma were in between them now, pinning the combatants' arms and hauling them away from one another. The muddy road made them slip and slide, so some of them stumbled and ended up with dirty stains on their hands and clothes, every one of them shouting for calm, or for blood.

Had Alfred not been in the epicentre of the trouble he might have found the scene amusing, but it mattered little to him that Sicgred's backside was covered in mud, and Diuma had fallen over so his entire right side – from head to foot – was heavily smeared dark brown. All Alfred wanted to do was smash Aethelhelm's teeth out, for daring to touch Ealhswith.

'Calm down,' the queen consort was saying. She'd come into his line of sight, looking up into his eyes, somehow apparently untouched by the mud she'd fallen in. Wulfric and one of the hearth-warriors were holding him back, and it took a moment for his wife's calming words to penetrate the fog of war that had overcome him. 'Calm down,' she repeated. 'This is undignified.'

Seeing her apparently unharmed and in stern mood had the desired effect, and his fury faded, washed away like the blood on his mouth and chin. Breathing heavily, he looked at Ealhswith, feeling sensation returning to his limbs where sheer instinct had been carrying him before. He shrugged his captors off and wiped the dripping rain from his brow again. His clothes were soaked through he realised, as were Ealhswith's.

The absurdity, and, yes, indignity of it, hit him even harder than Aethelwold had done, and he shook his head, sloughing off the wooziness that blow had engendered, and taking control of himself properly once more.

'Come, Ealhswith,' he said, putting out his hand for her to take. 'Let us get back to the hall and change into dry clothes before we catch a chill.' He glared at his nephews, shaking his head at the pair of them. 'I know you sent money to Hjalmarr, hoping the Dane would attack your own people. What kind of monster does such a thing? You're a disgrace to your father's memory, and if either of you cause me any more trouble, it won't be my fists I'll be using to put you down. I swear, I will slit you open with my own sword and drag your stinking guts all around Wintanceaster for the worms and crows to feast upon!'

Even Ealhswith shrank back from the terrible threat, while Sicgred looked utterly mortified by what had happened, as if he realised just how badly the Witan had gone for his two charges and, by extension, himself. Aethelhelm was shivering within his cloak, face hidden by the hood so Alfred couldn't read his expression. Aethelwold, however, stood defiantly, ignoring the water that cascaded from his hair and the sleeves of his cloak.

Alfred met his eyes and saw the hatred within – a black malevolence emanating from his young nephew like a living entity. If Aethelwold had felt resentment for his uncle when the Witan started, the will, and Alfred's violence, had tempered it into sheer hate. It was just as well the lad would have a meagre number of lands and correspondingly little wealth or power, for Alfred knew for certain now that the aetheling would be trouble one day. The less power he could wield, the less bother he could cause, be it for Alfred himself, or for Edward when he eventually took the throne.

'This is not over, you thieving, craven turd,' Aethelwold spat, a fierce grin twisting his mouth as if he was enjoying the altercation and looking forward to continuing it in the future. 'You think to neuter us, Alfred, like a man does to his hunting dogs to make them less aggressive. But we are not dogs, and, by Christ, we will not be put aside so easily. Hjalmarr may be dead, but our strength grows with each passing day, and we'll be back soon enough to take what's rightfully ours.'

Alfred shook his head, tired of the whole affair and feeling the cold that his anger had hitherto kept at bay. 'Get them out of here,' he repeated, looking at Wulfric. 'And if they give you any trouble, kill all three of them.'

Aethelwold made a crude gesture at the king, but Alfred had already turned away and was hurrying with Ealhswith towards the shelter and roaring fire within the hall.

'Get moving,' Alfred heard Wulfric bark at the three wayward nobles, and then the warmth and light from the hall's open door embraced them, welcoming them back inside. They were met by the wide-eyed gazes of thanes and ealdormen, but Ealhswith was too embarrassed to pause or make jokes or anything else. She practically dragged him into their chamber, closing the door behind them.

They undressed in silence, stripping off their sodden tunics and leggings, dropping them onto the floor with wet, slapping sounds, shivering as the damp left their skin. Servants had come at Ealhswith's call and they helped the royal couple to dry and slip into fresh clothing, layers and layers of it to try and get warm again.

As they performed the simple tasks mechanically, without a word passing between them, all Alfred could think of was Aethelwold's twisted features and his words, so heavy with dire portent: *This is not over.*

The Danes had been a thorn in the side of Wessex for decades. Now that Alfred had finally gone some way to pacifying them, and actually formed a strong alliance with Guthrum-Athelstan, had he made another, even more hate-fuelled enemy for his people, for his children, to deal with in the coming years?

The sounds of laughter and revelry filtered through the walls to Alfred and Ealhswith and they looked at one another, smiling at their wet hair and ruddy cheeks. Aethelwold would be gone from Wintanceaster by now, along with his brother and Sicgred. Maybe they would be a problem in the future but, for now, Alfred and Ealhswith were in their warm hall, surrounded by their most loyal friends and supporters and the king simply wanted to rest and drink a mug of ale.

'Come, my lady,' he said, offering his arm to his wife with a bow of his head and a smile she returned readily. 'We have guests to entertain.'

AUTHOR'S NOTE

The first question that had to be answered while writing *Sword of the Saxons* was whether Alfred's family were actually with him on Athelney, or had they been hidden away somewhere safe? Where, though, and who with? It had already been proven in devastating fashion that Alfred could not trust his own nobles so how could he ever believe his family were safe if he allowed some thane to take them into his home? Even assuming such a protector could be found, with Danes seemingly travelling around Wessex at will, there would always be a chance Ealhswith and the children would be found, and I think we all know what would happen to them in that case... So, for me, it seemed natural that Alfred would want to keep his family beside him, for reasons of safety but also from a selfish standpoint. It would be hard enough living in the wintry marshes, and even worse if one had to suffer the loneliness of being separated from their loved ones.

The fact is, people in ancient or early medieval times cared for their families and friends just as strongly as we do today. There were, of course, some differences in outlook and custom, when it came to family so, although Alfred would have loved his immediate family – Ealhswith and their children – it would not be at all unusual for him to have little, or no, contact with his nephews. Especially given the turmoil his kingdom faced at the time, thanks to the Danes. There is often a lot of talk about 'kinfolk' and 'kinsmen' in historical novels or dramas, and it's a fact that such bonds of community were intensely powerful back then – much more so than nowadays. Yet, at the same time, relationship with individual family members may have been fleeting, just as they can be today. Aethelhelm and Aethelwold could have felt entitled to more support from their uncle, but Alfred's reasons for not offering such support are easy to understand. Many kings would simply have offed the troublesome little brats, and Sicgred along with them! Given the chaos that threatens to overtake Wessex in the next book, maybe that's exactly what Alfred should have done. Being merciful did seem to come back and bite him in the arse rather a lot, but in this case, given how much he loved his brother, Aethelred, it's understandable.

Speaking of Aethelred, there were a LOT of them around at the time. It seemed like half the male population of Anglo-Saxon England was named Aethelred when I was researching this novel but, since it's based on actual history and real people, I could hardly change their names, as much as I wanted to. I hope you were able to distinguish between them – I even spelled one of them as Ethelred, just to try and differentiate a little.

Even worse than all those Aethelreds, I had to deal with the fact Guthrum changed his name to Athelstan halfway through the book! Should I have stopped calling him Guthrum and named him Athelstan from then on? That would have been incredibly confusing. So, the simplest solution was to call him Guthrum-Athelstan, as unwieldy as that was to write or read. To be honest, he probably never used the name Athelstan in daily life although we know he issued coins with that baptismal name on them. No wonder so many authors write fantasy – it must be great when you can just make up cool names like 'Druss' or 'Raistlin' as you go along!

The last point I wanted to address in this note was whether Alfred and Ealhswith had more children than the ones that history records. Alfred's biographer, Asser, names the five we already know of in his *Life of King Alfred* but then adds, rather cryptically, 'leaving aside those who were carried off in infancy by an untimely death and numbered...' At that point, the text is corrupt and can't be read, leaving us wondering just how many times the poor parents were forced to grieve for lost little ones. As regular readers of mine will know, my wife and I had to deal with the pain of a stillborn daughter, Lianna, so I felt it important to mention how such an event might have affected Alfred.

The king had to endure much death and suffering in his life; is it any wonder he sometimes drank too much ale and was beset with crippling stomach pains?

Book 3 will bring us to the end of Alfred's reign and I'm looking forward to seeing how it all turns out. I hope you are too. See you there!

Steven A. McKay,
Old Kilpatrick,
23rd January 2024

PLACES

Abbandune – Abingdon, Oxfordshire
Alre – Aller, Somerset
Ascesdune – Ashdown, Oxfordshire
Athelney – Athelney, Somerset
Baseng – Old Basing, near Basingstoke
Bensingtun – Benson, Oxfordshire
Beodericsworth – Bury St Edmunds, Suffolk
Bere – Bere Regis, Dorset
Berrocscire – Berkshire
Botuluesbrige – Battlesbridge, Essex
Bratton hillfort – Bratton Camp, Wiltshire
Brycgstow – Bristol
Bryn – Brean, Somerset
Brugia – Bridgwater, Somerset
Cair Legion – Chester, Cheshire.
Cantwareburh – Canterbury
Ceodre – Cheddar, Somerset
Cent – Kent
Celmeresfort – Chelmsford, Essex
Cippanhamme – Chippenham, Wiltshire
Cirotesige – Chertsey, Surrey
Corf – Corfe Castle, Dorset
Cornwalas – Cornwall
Cynwit – Countisbury Hill, Devon
Defenascir – Devonshire
Dorcaestre – Dorchester on Thames, Oxfordshire
Douorcortae – Dovercourt, Essex

373

Eashing – Eashing, Surrey
Englafeld – Englefield
Eoforwic/Jorvik – York, Yorkshire
Eorpeburnan – Rye
Ethandun – Edington, Wiltshire
Exanceaster – Exeter
Fleot – River Fleet, London
Gegnesburh – Gainsborough, Lincolnshire
Grantebrycge – Cambridge
Hamwic – Southampton
Hægelisdun – Outskirts of Bury St Edmunds
Hrofescester – Rochester, Kent
Icene – River Itchen
Iglea Wood – Southleigh Wood, Warminster
Kennet – River Kennet
Lichet – Lytchett Minster, Dorset
Lintun – Lynton, Devon
Loidis – Leeds, Yorkshire
Lundenwic – London
Medehamstede – Peterborough, Cambridgeshire
Meduwey – River Medway
Meretun – Unknown. Possibly in Winchester or Wiltshire.
Muleforda – Moulsford, Oxfordshire
Nortcory – North Curry, Somerset
Parred – River Parrett, Somerset
Polle – Poole, Dorset
Pydel – River Piddle
Ragheleiam – Rayleigh, Essex
Readingum – Reading, Berkshire
Snotengaham – Nottingham
Severn Sea – Bristol Channel
Sumorsaete – Somerset
South Sea – English Channel
Strath-Clota – Strathclyde
Sture – River Stour

Suthriganaweorc – Southwark, Greater London
Swanawic – Swanage, Dorset
Tamyse – River Thames
Theodford – Thetford, Norfolk
Thunderfield – Horley, Surrey
Tweoxneam – Twynham/ Christchurch, Dorset
Wethmor – Wedmore, Somerset
Werham – Wareham, Dorset
Whistley – Whistley Green, Berkshire
Wichamtun – Witchampton, Dorset
Wilton – Wilton, Wiltshire
Wiltunshire – Wiltshire
Windlesora – Windsor,
Winburnan – Wimborne Minster, Dorset
Wintanceaster – Winchester
Wirceaster – Worcester
Witcerce – Whitchurch, Hampshire
Valhöll – Afterlife of the Danes/Norse, later known as Valhalla.